DAUGHTERS OF THE DAWN

Also by Sarena Nanua & Sasha Nanua

Sisters of the Snake

DAUGHTERS OF THE DAWN

SARENA NANUA &
SASHA NANUA

HARPER TEEN
An Imprint of HarperCollinsPublishers

HarperTeen is an imprint of HarperCollins Publishers.

Library of Congress Control Number: 2022935788
ISBN 978-0-06-298562-0

Typography by Chris Kwon
22 23 24 25 26   PC/LSCH   10 9 8 7 6 5 4 3 2 1
❖
First Edition

To Bademom, for telling us stories and teaching us about our culture and traditions. We love you!

THE MASTERS OF MAGIC

SNAKE MASTER

Magic of serpents and stories
Descendants: snakespeakers
Talisman: scepter

MEMORY MASTER

Magic of mind and visions
Descendants: mindwielders
Talisman: cuffs

EARTH MASTER

Magic of stone and soil
Descendants: stonebringers
Talisman: map

SKY MASTER

Magic of air and wind
Descendants: currentspinners
Talisman: feather

FIRE MASTER

Magic of flames and light
Descendants: flametalkers
Talisman: compass

TIDE MASTER

Magic of water and storms
Descendants: tidesweepers
Talisman: sword

SOUL MASTER

Magic of life and death
Descendants: specterwalkers
Talisman: none

The Masters of Magic were brought into this world as healers
and left as prisoners. They cleansed the world of its poison and
gave life to fire, earth, sky, and water. But as the Masters were
banished one by one and magic drained from the world, hope
did not wither. For an artifact that had done much harm still
existed in our world, begging to be used . . . and to be broken.
—Excerpt from *Saira's Songs*, Chapter 3: "The Night the
Masters Disappeared," by Queen Saira of Retan, published
posthumously by the Retanian Academy Press

The First Descendants forged six magical talismans as
extensions of their Masters' power, capable of housing
magic in all its forms. To possess a talisman, a piece of
a Master, is to possess a piece of the world itself.
—Excerpt from *The Complete History of Magic*
by Suneel Nanda

PART ONE

A Sign
from the North

Prologue
Amara

The man's dead body reeks of sweat and cowardice, bent over like a broken statue with its hands clasped in supplication. If Amara ignored the blood and rancid smell of the afterlife, she could imagine him praying to her. In death, at least, the man could finally see her as who she wanted to be.

A Master.

"Such a pity," she snarls, the man's lifeless eyes beaming up at her. She nudges his head over to the other side with the toe of her boot, examining his worn crow's feet, withered brown skin, wide unblinking gaze. A pity indeed.

A pity that he wasn't of more use to them.

Around her, wind whips through the White Mountains, frigid as ice yet comforting to her skin. After all, her blood runs cold now.

Terror, delicious terror, lingers in the dead man's eyes.

"Death is a necessary precaution," comes a voice next to her.

She turns her gaze over to him—to the man they spent ages searching for, and finally found in the cold winds of the North. His cloaked figure lifts himself from where he had been crouched by the dead man. "We couldn't have villagers realize my cohorts and I are back on the rise."

"*Your foresight will be rewarded, Black Viper,*" the voice hisses within her, using the man's moniker, for he moves lithely and quietly, like a serpent in the grass. "*And now that we've finally found you . . . we must head for the Snake River.*"

Amara obediently rises and heads for the jutting rock on the outskirts of the cave, located next to the winding river. There, she produces a gem from the inside of her cloak. The Bloodstone, dark as crimson, winks even in the dying daylight. The gem that will bring them the wishes they desire most.

The voice within her rumbles with power, echoing off every wall of the cave hidden deep within the icy mountainside.

The first time she'd seen her Master, it had been like a fever dream. She'd thought she was dying, was being swallowed by the Snake Pit, when she heard him. First, just a voice. Then the visions. Visions had never come to her, not with her magicless blood, but she had seen him—seen his eyes—in a still pond of water in a lone Abaian cave. She thought, for a moment, that she was hallucinating.

Then there came the snap of acid, the taste of copper and blood. *Magic.* In a blink, she was in the sky. No longer simply Amara Gupta, a woman who had lost her husband, who had manipulated the raja, who had poisoned her own son.

A woman who had been abused so thoroughly that she refused to find herself a victim again.

Cruelty is no stranger to her. But the cruel would never again be able to threaten her.

It is time for her to tell her own story.

Time for her to hold her own power.

I will become the Soul Master. A being above all others.

She imagines the control she would have over all who cross her. What she could do to the nation that had betrayed her!

She could see Kaama burning to the ground at her will, flames licking the air. She could envision the kingdom cracked in two, its pieces crumbling into dust.

Amara tucks her hands around the golden cuffs on her wrists. The Memory Master's talisman glows like a caught star, and she watches the air fill with blinding gold light.

The Black Viper flicks his knife into the air. Amara extends her bare arm and lets him slice into her skin.

Blood, red as roses, fills the river. The water bubbles into a lingering crimson, as if alive, before settling back into its calming blue churn. She grins.

After weeks of shivering in caves and preying on the lost to gain strength, Amara feels her and her Master's dreams drawing ever closer. Dreams once tasting of dust, now sweet as clouds, ringing true.

"I will inform the others," the cloaked man says in farewell.

Alone, Amara stares at the river. "In one month's time," she says, gazing at her twisted reflection, "you will get what is yours. And I'll get what's mine. We will find all the—"

"*Say no more on the matter,*" the voice within Amara cuts in. Something shifts inside her—her Master, sharpening his focus. "*She's listening.*"

1

Ria

I've got two problems, and one of them is trying to remember how to act like a commoner.

Not even two moons ago, no one gave me a second glance. Now, anytime I step outside the palace walls, it's like I've forgotten how to turn invisible.

A small tavern lies before me, lit by sconces that cast the building in shadows. I slide the silver bangles up my arm so they don't rattle, then pull my cloak tighter around me. The crimson cloak is the perfect disguise, but it's also keeping me warm. It's getting chillier in Abai, and I shiver down to my toes. Where I once complained about the heat, I now wish for an inkling of it. Admittedly, those shivers are mostly from nerves—from who I'm about to meet . . . and the nightmare I had. That hiss of a voice, reaching my ears, throbbing in my temples.

"She's listening."

My second problem. The voice woke me at midnight. I found

myself drenched in sweat, breathing heavily. I cursed inwardly, reaching under my bedside for the journal I've kept there for the past few nights. *Another nightmare*, I recorded in scribbled handwriting. *Amara, again. But this time . . .*

It was more vivid than the others. Like I was there, watching a scene play out instead of dreaming it. I can still see her, Amara, standing next to a cloaked figure. Yet as soon as I awoke, small details from the dream fell away, turning fuzzy instead of sharp.

I had hoped, after Amara disappeared from the Snake Pit, that she could no longer haunt us. That she was gone for good. But then why would I be dreaming about her almost every night?

My gaze refocuses on the tavern and I force myself to drop the thought of Amara. *Just play it cool, Ria.* I've been so used to pretending to be Rani that tonight's charade—and my all-consuming thoughts of that nightmare—has me tangled up in worried knots. I force out a breath and step inside.

Whispers flit through the tavern. I catch some of the hushed tones as I head toward the barkeep. Do the patrons recognize me?

"*Heard the Blood Moon's comin',*" one man says.

"*As if that's even real,*" scoffs another.

I sigh with relief. No one's given me a second glance. But what is this about the Blood Moon? And why—

"Welcome," the barkeep tells me once I'm before her.

Right. Focus on the task at hand.

I keep my head low, raising two fingers. She nods and escorts me to a table at the back of the establishment. Calling this place a tavern would be a bit . . . generous, but I've lived in far worse places when I was on the streets. Who am I to judge?

I settle into my seat and swiftly pull out my small coin purse. It's really Rani's, but she doesn't need to know I've been snooping in her closet today. After all, I might've told her a little white lie about where I was headed—to visit an orphanage friend. She didn't question it, but, stubborn sister that she is, she did make a Chart accompany me.

I wasn't about to let the soldier follow me inside, which means I need to be quick. He'll come looking if I take too long, and the sky is already darkening. Soon, a celebration will be underway. *Long-lost twins, finally found,* our mother said. *Tonight, we'll finally introduce you two to the whole kingdom.*

No pressure.

I tap the coin purse against the table, letting the few coins inside clink. A candle has been set on the tabletop, its flame flickering, hypnotizing. Melting wax pools at the base, the saucer beneath it barely holding the candle aloft.

After a few minutes, a woman approaches with shambling steps. She sits in the seat directly across from mine. Her eyes are a deep, verdant green unlike any I've ever seen.

A newcomer in Abai isn't all that strange, but one with her description *definitely* is. *White hair. Nails like claws. Unearthly eyes.* She's all anyone's been talking about this past week . . . besides Amara. A shudder runs through me at the thought of Saeed's mother. No one knows where she went. Most speculate she's dead. I wish I could believe them.

I first heard about this newcomer from the best gossips

around—children. A few days ago, I visited an orphanage just outside Anari. The king and queen—my *father and mother*, I still remind myself—let me leave with a bundle of food and some spare coin. It's not nearly enough for the orphans, but the smiles on their faces warmed me up like steaming-hot chai.

"*We call her the Winter Witch,*" one child said, because of her silver-white hair. "*I've heard that she can read people's minds. And control them, too—she can make them do whatever she wants!*" Some children cowered at the older kids' overexaggerated descriptions: pupils like a cat's, stringy hair that held a web of spiders.

"Thank you for agreeing to meet me," I tell the woman.

"I seldom get mail from the palace," the Winter Witch intones. Her voice is like a biting wind, and her mouth twists into a sour grin. She lays her hands flat on the table, revealing her nails, long and curved.

Perhaps her appearance was not that exaggerated after all. "You are her, then? The other princess?"

The other *princess. Princess Ria.*

"Yes," I whisper. I glance around, making sure no one heard. I don't want to cause a scene.

"And why, Princess Ria, do you request *my* services?" She croaks a laugh at the end. Like a princess already possesses everything she could ever need. I once thought the same.

"They say you're a witch. A mindwielder. I'd like to know if this is true." If she truly does have this power, then that makes her a descendant of the Memory Master.

Like Saeed.

Just a few moons ago I thought stories of magic were old wives' tales. My sister believed that only the royal family could possess the power of the Masters, and that talk to the contrary was blasphemy. But if there's anything we learned these past few moons, it's that neither of us is as wise about magic as we believed.

Gazing at the Winter Witch, I recall the rumors swirling through the palace about her. Memories unlocked, secrets revealed, runaways found—this witch could warp any mind you'd like, for a price. A man saw a green-eyed woman in the streets of Anari Square. One look, and his mind bent as if he were looking at his lover. All memory of his wife was gone.

"Call it magic or call it intuition." The woman chuckles again, but her tone is grim. "Either way, services require coin."

"I'll pay when I get my answers," I tell her.

She only cackles. "I suppose I'll leave then—"

"No!" I whisper harshly. I didn't come all this way—by horse!—for nothing. I huff and pass over the coin purse. Let her have it. I'm good at taking what I need in the end.

And what I'm asking for is worth any price.

"I need to know something," I tell the woman, leaning in as last night's nightmare comes back to me. "A . . . man I know has been on a journey, searching for a woman named Amara. He's important to me. I need to know where he is. Can you tell me?"

The woman digs through the coin purse and eyes the money. Then she shutters her eyelids. "Hmm. Describe this Amara."

I recount Amara's appearance. It's not one I can ever forget. "Red hair . . . dark eyes . . ." I continue on, picturing Amara exactly as I last saw her, before she fell into the Snake Pit. That manic grin, the gleam in her eyes that made her look almost inhuman.

"And this man who seeks her?"

My stomach flutters. "Curly hair with a white streak. Hazel eyes. He's tall and . . ." *Muscled*, I want to add, but I bite my tongue. I don't want to sound like some foolish, lovesick girl. Even if I am one.

"He's been gone for weeks," I add, my voice more desperate than I want it to be. These dreams remind me constantly how dangerous Amara is. "I just need some information. Is he safe? Is he well?"

I don't realize how far I've leaned over the table until the woman snaps her eyes open, drilling them into mine. The candle continues to melt, dripping hot wax onto the table.

"This man . . . his name is Saeed?"

My body stiffens at the sound of his name. "Yes."

Either an *extremely* lucky guess, or this woman really knows what she's talking about.

"He is well," she reveals. "In fact, he is not far."

"What?" I start. "Where is he?"

"Somewhere dark. He has traveled a long way to find this woman . . . his mother. But he has failed."

A stone fills my throat. Every day I've stared out my window, hoping to see him. Every day I'm disappointed. I've tried to busy myself, scour the palace library, search through nearly every book Rani and I could think of that could tell us more about the Bloodstone. About how Amara might access the lifeblood of the Creator, Amran, within it, and make her wish to become the Soul Master come true.

So far, bust. And now I hear that Saeed has had the same luck.

From the front of the tavern, I see my Chart attendant march in and gaze around. His eyes find mine. I hold up a hand. *Halt.*

It's strange to me now, how I can control a Chart. A soldier that once made me freeze with fear, a title that sent shivers down my back long before I was conscripted for war. But if I'm being honest, I haven't stopped shivering at the bloodred jackets they wear, the caps that shield their eyes.

I'm running out of time, but there's one last thing I need to ask this woman. Something else that's been haunting me.

I think of the strange voice in my dream. *She's listening.* "Have you ever heard of a nightmare coming true for someone who isn't a mindwielder?"

"Depends on what you believe a nightmare to be."

I swallow. "I have no memory magic, but I've been . . . *seeing* things. It's like I've been peering into someone else's life and they know I'm . . . listening." That deep, haunting voice has plagued my memory all day. Maybe this woman knows something.

I know I'm right when she raises a silver brow. "Someone is always listening." She taps her fingers along the edge of the table.

"It's not every day I'm called to a secret meeting by a royal with such odd questions. Is this why you called me here today? Your . . . nightmares?" She gazes deeply into my eyes, and I force myself not to look away.

"Yes and no." I debate. "Mostly yes."

The Winter Witch laughs. "I cannot provide information on something you already know. You do know, don't you? Where these nightmares are coming from?"

I shuffle through my memory. Each nightmare I've had, I've seen Amara in some strange mountains, and there is a voice like one from the skies.

The Winter Witch tuts. "Don't you have a ceremony to attend, Princess Ria?"

I freeze. "I have my reasons for being here."

The woman's lip curls up. "Do you? Or are you avoiding your new life at the palace?"

My blood heats at her accusation. "*I* am the one asking questions. And if you won't answer them, I have no reason to stay longer." I get up and bolt for the door.

"Wait," she says, her voice deep and haunting. I stop in my tracks and turn, watching as her eyes go off into some unknown place. The candle starts shivering; the table quakes. I glance around, but no one else seems to be disturbed.

"*Your time runs short,*" the Winter Witch whispers, voice rough. "*She who holds the stone will cross rivers and scale the White Mountains to find the treasures she seeks.*"

Chills creep up my spine at her words. The White Mountains in the northwestern kingdom, Amratstan, are infamous. And haven't I been dreaming of mountains? *She who holds the stone.* Does this mean Amara is already there?

Still, I've had enough fortunes and prophecies to last a lifetime. It was a skies-damned *prophecy*—about the newborn twin princesses harming each other—that made our parents separate Rani and me in the first place. Which got me into this whole mess. It wasn't until we used Shima's venom to bring back our parents' memories, the ones *Amara* took from them with the Memory Master's talisman, that we set things right.

"The treasures. What are they?" I ask. "What does Amara seek?"

The woman blinks, returning to the present. "May the Masters preserve you, Your Highness." She takes her coins, blows out the candle, and brushes past me without another word.

I clutch my cloak tighter. Smoke curls in the air, and the melted candle wax stares back at me. It's spread across the table and taken the shape of—

A snake. I shiver, thinking of my magic.

"Princess?" the Chart asks, his voice low. I don't realize how close he's come, and I nearly jump at the sound of it. "Are you ready? The queen—"

"I know," I say, a bit too harshly. I hurry back outside, the Chart on my heels. There, in my haste, I collide with a villager and the hood of my cloak flies off.

"Sorry!" I cry, but the man before me makes me pause. He's staring at me intently, with a seedy smile, almost as if he's been waiting for me. As he raises a hand, I spot a strange burn on his palm in the shape of a snake.

The man bows and touches the ground at my feet. "Apologies, Princess! I am honored to have a snakespeaker in my presence!"

I give the man a lukewarm smile and skirt around him. I'm not used to the whole bowing thing, and this guy is creepy. The Chart next to me looks entirely befuddled as he leads me away from the man and toward the royal steed that's waiting. I mount the horse easily, now having become much more practiced at riding, but that doesn't make me any less afraid.

When I glance back, the man is gone.

When I was a thief, I would bump into townspeople, too. Apologize profusely after thieving a little something from their too-full pockets. I pat down my cloak, but nothing appears to be missing.

Forget him, I think. I'm too worried about what the woman said as we gallop back to the palace. Her words roll over in my mind, sticky as syrupy mithai. *Your time runs short.*

I shake off her voice and turn my focus back on the road. It's getting late—and tonight, the entire kingdom will be waiting.

2

Rani

A princess never stumbles were some of Tutor's first words to me.

Now, as I lie face-first in muddy, sodden grass—in my best vestments, no less—I groan. Mother will not be happy. My tailors won't be happy, either, that much is certain. But I've found I don't really care, at least not exceedingly.

"Have I won this round?" my opponent asks, lifting me up and pressing me to his chest, deep-brown eyes alight. For a moment, I forget about the mud. I don't think I'll ever get tired of those eyes, or the way they bloom with hope, like the petals of a lotus.

Amir Bhatt, my lotus. I like the sound of that.

"Amir," I huff, glancing down. "Let go. You're getting your clothes dirty."

And they're going to need more than one washing. Amir is dressed in princely attire, a kurta threaded with gold and billowy ivory pants. But I'm not paying attention to that. I'm distracted by the way he gently clasps my arm, lending me support, heat spreading from his fingertips and warming my skin.

"I don't mind," he whispers, breath feathering my cheeks. The starry sky casts a glow on his head, as if he truly is a prince wearing a crown. We're a ways away from the palace, in the Moga Jungle, our own little hideaway.

"And no, you didn't win. That wasn't fair. You have longer legs. How am I ever supposed to beat you in a race?" Not to mention, the muscles in my legs are absolutely on fire, but I won't tell him that.

Amir smiles. Slowly, a little lopsided. "Ria's rubbing off on you." He winks. "She can be a sore loser, too."

I roll my eyes, grinning despite myself. This boy meant nothing to me when we first met right here, in the Moga Jungle, weeks ago. *A means to an end*, I told myself.

And now . . .

"Wanna go again?" Amir says, about to jog back to the start line, a shady path between two large banyan trees. The sky cloaks us, a blanket of night ready to descend. "Maybe with a little more practice you can beat Ria, at least."

But I don't want to sprint again. Instead, before he can get far, I take him by the hand and spin him toward me. I lift myself up onto my toes and press my lips to his.

I don't think I'll ever get used to that squeak of surprise that escapes his throat whenever I kiss him. Or the way he tugs me closer when I do.

"Well," he murmurs when I pull back. His breath tickles my

cheek. "That's another way to run out of breath."

I punch him in the arm.

"Ouch! Why must you abuse your loyal subject this way, Princess Rani? You know I'm sensitive," he pouts.

"Yes, and knowing you, you probably took a rupee from my cloak pocket while we kissed."

He grins sideways, producing a silver coin between his fingers.

I raise a brow. "You are as fair to behold as a flower, but indeed you are a thorn in my side."

"Guilty." But his grin disappears just as swiftly as he hands me back the coin. "So—what did I do to earn that kiss?"

Before I can answer, we're interrupted by the peal of palace bells, ringing a reminder. A reminder of tonight's grand celebration.

I glance down again at my ruined clothes. It seems we'll be making a late entrance. And Ria . . .

Is off doing Masters-know-what, Shima says for me. She is smart. Too smart for her own good. Ever since Ria performed the Bonding Ceremony, our connection to our snake familiar has grown stronger—to the point where we can exchange words with Shima without ever having to speak aloud.

Has Ria returned? I ask.

She is not here at the palace, but my sense of her grows stronger, the snake answers. *She is on her way. I expect her shortly.*

I gaze into Amir's eyes. "We have to go back."

His grip stays firm. "You haven't answered my question."

I smirk. "A princess needs no occasion. Not if she likes you."

"Oh! You *like* me! I had no idea! Whew. What a relief."

I would normally laugh, but Mother's voice enters my head. *We want to help you, beta. Even if it means . . .*

"No," I mutter to myself. I won't let myself think of that.

"No . . . what?" Amir repeats. I bite my lip. Why did I speak aloud? I used to do it all the time in the palace, before I met Ria. And Amir. And all of our friends.

When I was alone.

"Nothing," I say resolutely. "Race you back to the palace?"

"Winner gets the first pick of dessert?"

"You're on." I smile. "But we both know who'll get to the dessert table first."

"Sanya," Amir laughs, his sister's name bright as sunshine on his tongue.

"I've never known a person with such a sweet tooth. Not even *you*," I tease, poking his chest.

Though Amir and Sanya had been separated for over a year, my hunt for the Bloodstone put them back in each other's path, and resealed their bond. They are happier together, and all I want, I find, is Amir's happiness.

His smile lights up the night sky, highlighting the slim scar that snakes across his face. A reminder of his past life. As for his future . . .

Amir doesn't wait until I give him the signal; he's off like a sandtiger weaving between the trees, and I race to catch up, breathless.

Breathless like our kiss.

Abai's sun, Amir was right. I did kiss him for a reason. Because when I kiss him, I forget my worries. I forget Mother's warning. The secret lingering between her and me.

And I don't know how much longer I can keep it before I burst.

"He's awake, Princess Rani."

I sit before my vanity as my maid, Neela, snaps my hairpin in place. The delicate pearls are mismatched, some larger than others, some ivory white and others a soft pink. It might not match the rest of my outfit, but it's something Amir made for me with a few mismatching jewels he found—or likely stole—a few nights ago.

Amir. A stone fills my throat when I think of him. It's been a mere hour since we returned to the palace and went to our respective rooms to get bathed and dressed for the celebration, which is due to start any minute. Already I miss him. The truth of it is startling. I've never felt so captivated by someone, not even when I thought I had been in love with Saeed, my former betrothed.

"Thank you," I tell Neela. She smiles with genuine enthusiasm and leaves the room. I glance at my reflection one last time in the mirror. My lehenga will match Ria's tonight: a gold-and-black ensemble with painstaking beadwork on the blouse.

The voice repeats itself: "He's awake."

I turn to find Aditi standing at the threshold to my room, hands clasped firmly. Her eyes widen, but not with trepidation. Instead, she looks like many of the other servants in the palace.

Shocked by how closely I resemble Ria. I suppose not everyone is used to twin princesses just yet.

"Who?" I ask.

"The man from Anari Square. The snake venom seller who gave Am—" She stops short, as if the name would scald her tongue.

I recall Ria telling me about the man she and Saeed found in Anari Square, Amara's snake venom supplier, knocked unconscious by Amara's now-dead Chart companion. The man has been in our infirmary for the past two weeks, and had only awoken within the last few days for brief moments and little coherence. It seems he has finally come to in a more stable way.

I gather the folds of my lehenga with tense fingers and face Aditi. "Has he said anything about . . . *her*?" I swallow thickly.

Aditi shakes her head. Her twin braids fly around her. "He seemed afraid, miss."

I spin to my vanity. Fear, I understand. I would be remiss to say I haven't felt the same, every time Amara has been spurred to mind. Which has been far more often than I would like these past two weeks.

If the vendor can give us information, that is an opportunity I cannot let pass.

I slip a few spare jewels and coins from my vanity into a velvet coin pouch. "Take me to him."

The man stirs on his cot when I gently set my pouch on the bedside table, the chime of money singing him awake.

"A-are you . . ." He blinks, sitting up. The infirmary is a small white room, and the walls press in on him until he looks slouched and sloppy like a rag doll. A tuft of graying hair swirls over his head, matching his caterpillar eyebrows. His gaze narrows on the coin pouch. "The princess?"

"One of them," I confirm. The man looks confused, but I press on. "We know you were working with a woman named Amara Gupta."

The man shakes his head. "You—you've got the wrong man." His face flushes, pale with indecision. He shivers.

When I sought the Bloodstone, I disguised myself as Ria—a street thief. My nearly month-long charade taught me the simple tells of a liar, if nothing else.

"I have a reward for you." I shake the pouch. "We just need your cooperation."

Those caterpillar eyebrows furrow. "You'll turn me in to the raja. The Snake Pit—"

"Is closed . . . for the time being," I finish. More like *permanently*, if Ria and I have our way. We don't need more senseless deaths in the Pit. Such punishment is a relic of the time Amara held sway over my father and the court.

Finally, the man gathers his wits, lips pressed in a thin line, and speaks.

"I never knew her name. She was a regular patron. My best, in fact." He groans in pain, one hand plastered to the side of his head. The bump is still slightly visible, although I can see the marks from where the bandages were removed.

"May I ask your name?" I keep my voice light, gentle. There's no need for interrogative methods. Yet.

"Baljeet," the man replies shakily, sliding his hand back down to the cot. A pale flush crosses his face. "I'm a criminal now, aren't I? Or at least an accomplice. Someone came in here the other day saying I nearly caused the death of the future king consort."

The servants have certainly been chatty. I don't blame them. Amara's departure was unexpected, much like her motives. And even with her disappearance, Father has not stopped working to make sure our peace talks with Kaama will go ahead as planned—a radical change from his previous calls for war.

A war that Amara wanted, that she nearly willed into being using the power of her talisman and its influence over my father.

A war to punish the kingdom that sent her husband to battle—never to return.

There will be a peace summit with Kaama in one moon's time, to take place in the Kaaman palace. That much, at least, is reassuring.

And as for the *future king consort*, Saeed will be fine. The doses of snake venom Amara gave him were merely to cloud his mind, make his memory magic dull. She was protecting him, supposedly, from having anyone find out he had magic. In truth, she was preventing him from seeing the future—a future in which Amara would have the Bloodstone, destroy Kaama, and leave thousands dead in her wake.

"You're no criminal." Not entirely, at least. Selling snake venom isn't exactly condoned. While many venoms are nothing but poison, some can be used for healing purposes.

"Just tell us what you know," I say gently, summoning the calm demeanor of Jas Auntie, my tutor's old wife. She has been staying here with Amir's sister, Sanya. They both deserve their rest after the long journey we took to find the Bloodstone.

Baljeet gulps. "It must've started a few moons ago. She would visit Anari Square with a special Chart. I didn't say nothin', because I didn't want to get hurt by the Chart. Just nodded when she asked for what she wanted. Supplies came in every week. I once plucked up the courage to ask her what this was for. How she even found me."

He pauses to take a sip of water from his cot-side table. "She said I came recommended. Honestly, I had no idea what that meant."

"Where did you get your supplies?" I ask.

"From a group of animal healers in the south," the man says. "While they don't have magic, they were well trained. I gave them a pretty coin for whatever venom they had. Most people buy venoms for healing, in very diluted doses," Baljeet explains. "But this woman was a high-profile patron. I could tell from the clothes she wore and the soldier at her side. The damned Chart who hit me over the head." He groans again. "I overheard them talking about something. The woman said when her plan was complete, she'd have someone back again. She'd have . . . *him* back. Whoever that is."

I swallow thickly. "Was there anything special about the venoms she bought?"

He nods. "They were diluted, like a lot of healing medicines are. But the venoms she wanted had special properties, only found in snake species of the southern regions of Kakur."

"The naja cobra?" I ask. Rare indeed. Those cannot even be found in the Snake Pit.

"Yes," the man confirms. His mouth twists to the side. "It's not entirely poisonous—their venom incapacitates, but not physically. It's said that only one bite from such a cobra would cloud your mind, fog your brain."

I ponder this. Indeed, Amara was trying to cloud Saeed's mind—and his magic—using this venom, combined in a potion of sorts. But what worries me most is Amara's knowledge of snake venoms in the first place.

She has been planning her war for a long, long time.

"He needs rest," a nurse says as she enters the room, sliding aside a curtain. She starts when she sees me. "Oh, Princess—"

"It's fine. We've spoken enough. Thank you, Baljeet."

I leave the coin pouch on his lap as he settles back down onto the cot. Aditi, having waited outside, glances at me furtively as we prepare to leave the infirmary.

"Wait," Baljeet calls out, his voice wavering. His brows elongate into one long gray caterpillar.

"Yes?"

"I've learned much from selling snake venom over the years.

Stories included. But I've never had the chance to talk to a snake-speaker before. Is it true what they say about the world being born from a snake's mouth?"

"What is he talking about?" Aditi asks, tugging on my sleeve lightly.

The nurse moves to subdue him under a blanket, as though he is talking nonsense. But I straighten my back and approach him once more.

"It is. Snakespeakers pass on the tale from generation to generation," I say, the words spinning a memory into my mind like a wispy cloud.

Father told me the story when I was just five summers of age:

"Many do not believe in such fables," Father had said, sweeping a hand across his black beard. "Many who once possessed other magics *chose* not to believe this story. But I do. For it is a story passed down for generations, a story of how the world began with a bloody, poisoned moon."

We both sat cross-legged on a paisley-patterned rug in the palace music room. Father's hand brushed over a taus, a stringed instrument shaped like a peacock's body. He plucked one of the strings, causing a wailing croon to soar over us.

"The world first existed as a heavenly plane. Within it lived Amran, the Creator, and his only companion—a snake.

"As time passed, the Creator grew lonely, and the snake, too. So the snake bit its tail, nearly swallowing itself whole."

"A symbol of infinity," I told Father. The snake had been on the first flag of Abai, before it was changed by Raja Suman, who found the idea of a snake eating itself putrid. Even at five, I understood the king's sentiment.

"When the snake bit its tail, forming a circle, a sphere took shape within. The snake gave itself to the world: its emerald-green eyes formed the land, its fangs grew into mountains and trees, its mouth bore oceans, and its heart became the earth's very core."

Father drew a circle in the air, then grabbed it with his fist, as if crushing it. "But this world did not last. The lands grew dry and cracked; the oceans, once clear, became black as night; and the trees burned aflame. Even the moon turned a bloody red."

"The Blood Moon," I whispered. I had heard of it. But I never knew what it meant. "But why, Papa? What made the world so horrible?" Back then, I hadn't yet been scolded into calling him Father. *Papa* wasn't yet too gentle for the raja.

"Because of its heart. You see, this snake's very heart was filled with venom. A poison only this snake could survive. But as soon as its heart became the core of the world . . . the land was poisoned, too. And everything with it."

"So who fixed it?" I asked innocently.

"The Creator, of course. He made four Masters of Magic to control the poison of the new world. A Fire Master to harness the flames. A Tide Master to fix the floods. An Earth Master to heal the land. And a Sky Master to calm the winds."

"So the snake was . . . bad?" I asked Father, confused. After all, we were the descendants of the Snake Master. Father and I both had our own snake familiars.

"Not necessarily," Father explained. "A poisoned heart did not mean a poisoned mind. And in today's world, at least, snakes are nothing to fear. They are our friends, our companions, and our bearers of truth."

"That story," Baljeet says now, snapping me back to the present. "The Blood Moon! When I woke last night, the moon wasn't white. It was beginning to turn red." He shivers after he speaks. "It is a sure sign, is it not, Princess? The Blood Moon is returning. Our world is falling to ruin!"

I laugh. "That depends upon what you believe," I say coolly.

But I have heard whispers all around me. *A poisoned moon*, servants have said. Yes, there was something a bit off about the night sky yesterday, but one could easily chalk that up to the movement of the stars. Hardly any know the truth of the snake being the origin of the world. I give Baljeet a tight smile. "Get some rest," I say gently. I depart from the infirmary and head toward the palace's main quarters with Aditi.

"Do you think he's truly innocent?" the girl asks.

I pause. The cool marbled halls of the palace feel more like a warm embrace. Perhaps it's the buzzing coming from outside—voices. The guests, dignitaries from all over Abai, have arrived from their private suites by Anari Square.

"Yes," I reply. I could have used my snake magic on Baljeet, prodded him to believe me and influenced what he said. Ensure the truth. But I wanted pure honesty, and I believe that was what I got.

Still, my conversation with Baljeet had brought everything I fear back to the surface. About Amara's mysterious disappearance after she fell into the Snake Pit. If she is still alive, she'll try to continue her plans, and the threat is still here.

I unfurl a crinkled sheet of paper from *The Complete History of Magic* that reads *The Myth of the Soul Master.* Ria showed this to me, explaining how she and Saeed found it in Amara's shrine room. They had stepped into a memory of Saeed's father, Kumal, on his final day of battle. But Amara's desire to bring her husband back to life wasn't the only thing she wanted.

Another thing my father told me when I was young—in order to defeat your enemy, you must know them.

3

Ria

As I return the stallion to its stable, a familiar voice sings behind me.

"You're la-ate."

"Am I?" I wonder, turning around. Rani stands ten paces away, dressed in a black-and-gold lehenga with a matching blouse and chunni. Her hair is piled on her head and threaded with a simple pin of mismatching pearls. Strange to think my once-lavish sister isn't going over-the-top with her jewelry tonight. Fine. More jewels for me.

Very late, a voice confirms. Shima slips out from behind Rani, her scales bluish-green in the moonlight.

"Two against one isn't fair," I tell them.

Shima tilts her head, amused.

"Okay, fine. I'm late. But finding a stranger takes some time."

"I thought you were meeting a friend," Rani says, voice laced with curiosity. With hesitation, she steps into the stable, lifting her skirt so no mud drags along the fabric.

"Oh." My cheeks burn. Lying used to be second nature, as easy as stealing a coin from a rich man's pocket. "My friend is . . . a stranger."

"Uh-huh." Rani glances down at Shima, and I swear they both have that same doubtful look on their faces. Shima turns a startling shade of orange. That's new.

"Orange. It means she knows you're uncomfortable," Rani explains. "Ria, what's going on?"

My sister crosses her arms, sounding concerned. It's her new thing—looking out for her little sister. What Rani doesn't know is that I'm still keeping secrets of my own. Just because we're twins doesn't mean we share *everything*. It's been so long since I had anyone, except Amir, to confide in. Having a real *sister* is still a mystery to me. One where I'm missing all the clues.

"I'm just tired," I reply, which isn't a *total* lie. I pat down the horse one more time—this one I've taken to calling Prince Varun, because of his stately appearance and his taste for only the best grass around.

Outside, I find people entering the open gates. It reminds me of Diwali night, the only night the palace is normally open to so many guests. But tonight is special. Tonight is my first real event, my first appearance as Princess Ria, outside of the small palace celebration we hosted two weeks ago.

The night before Saeed left.

"Rani, what if I'm not ready?" I asked my sister a few days ago as we practiced fencing in the courtyard. It isn't my favorite activity,

but Rani insisted. Apparently, there are some things "a princess should know."

"You'll be all right. Just remember that it's not about your title. It's about showing who you really are. Who *we* really are."

The memory fades away. Rani is glancing around the stables now, twiddling her thumbs nervously. I've never seen her act like this. It's so . . . unpolished.

"Is something wrong?"

"Oh." Rani pauses her movements, then smiles. A forced smile I recognize all too well. One I wore when I pretended to be her, the night of our sister switch on Diwali.

"You can tell me anything, you know." I mimic a line she said mere hours ago, before I left to see the woman. She rolls her eyes.

"I just spoke to the man from Anari Square."

Ah, Baljeet, Shima says.

Prince Varun neighs, and I pat his dark-brown coat to steady him.

"So, what'd he say?" I reply, brushing the horse absently with my fingers.

"Well . . . he's well versed in different kinds of snakes and poisons," Rani admits. "But the strangest thing was what he asked me last."

"Which was . . . ?" I prod.

"He asked me about the story of the world's creation." Her eyes darken. The most I know of the world's creation is from stories Mama Anita told me. Supposedly, our world was born from a snake, its body shaping our rivers and plains, mountains and deserts. I don't know much more than that.

"Anything else?" I ask.

Rani shakes her head.

"So . . . my turn, I guess." I square my shoulders. I don't want to talk about the dreams and make Rani worry, but . . . "That stranger I met up with . . . she was a mindwielder. She was able to help me . . . with Amara."

"She did?" Rani asks. She seems more skeptical than surprised.

I nod. "If she's right, if Amara is alive, she is in Amratstan. The White Mountains, to be exact."

"What would she be doing there?" Rani paces the stables, and my fingers tense on the horse's mane. Skies, I can only offer my sister a half-hearted shrug.

"You know what will happen if she uses the Bloodstone," Rani says. "You know what she told us she wanted. Becoming the Soul Master isn't simply heinous—it's unnatural."

"I know," I tell her. As if she hasn't reminded me a thousand times over the past week. My mind flits back to last night's dream-turned-nightmare. It was Amara, as usual . . . but there was another voice there. One that's hauntingly familiar.

"Rani, if Amara *does* become the Soul Master, then what?" I say. "She just wants her husband back. If that's truly all she's going to do . . ."

"She tried to destroy an entire kingdom, putting thousands at risk," Rani retorts. "With the power of the Bloodstone, there's no way she'll stop there. Think of it this way—she's trying to *bring the dead to life*! That kind of power is unnatural. It could throw the entire world off-balan—"

Before she can finish her sentence, Prince Varun neighs again, more insistently now. Rani grabs a bag of carrots from the corner and begins to feed him.

I harrumph. "Why does Prince Varun always get what he wants?"

"Because he's a prince," laughs Rani. She expels a breath, turning serious. "And you are a princess. We can speak more about the Soul Master later. You really must change." She eyes my clothes. When I glance down at my mud-trodden outfit, I laugh. Because it's so *me*.

We rush back to the palace, and Shima returns to the palace terrarium.

I clumsily get changed. My lehenga matches Rani's exactly, making our twin features that much more enhanced. Our matching snake armlets wink in the light, resting above the birthmarks on our inner arms. Together, the birthmarks form the shape of a rising snake. *Sisters of the snake.*

Once I'm ready—in record time, I might add—Rani and I wend our way down the stairs. We match each other's pace, almost unconsciously, until we reach the throne room. Aditi waits near the entrance, smiling. I grin at her—at Mouse, a girl who reminds me of my younger self, of moments spent in the Vadi Orphanage with Mama Anita and nothing but a blanket of stars.

"It's time," she whispers to me. She flits around me, fixing my chunni and bangles. Then she steps back and nods.

"Thank you, Aditi," Rani says. At that, Rani takes my hand, and we step outside.

The courtyard is overflowing. Dignitaries from all over Abai are here, nobles from within Anari and even shop owners from the outskirts. They wear clothing of all colors and sizes, lehengas and kurtas, even tunics once popular in the wasteland kingdom known as Pania. Tonight isn't just for the higher ranks.

"Over there is Ambassador Sana," whispers Rani, subtly jutting her chin at a woman with talkative hands and braided waist-length hair adorned with rose petals. "She's in charge of overseeing incoming guests from the far reaches of the kingdom." Rani rattles off more important names and cities I haven't even heard of. Servants weave between the guests, offering trays of mango lassi and freshly fried pakoras.

"Attention, guests!"

It's the raja. He's dressed as imposingly as ever, in red-and-gold fabrics dripping in jewels, and wearing matching pointed jutti on his feet.

"Thank you all for coming tonight. I'm sure you're all excited for tonight's celebration, when we formally introduce our daughters, *both* of our daughters, to the kingdom."

Whispers fly through the guests. Fingers hover, pointed at me and Rani. My hand shakes in Rani's grip. I don't think I'm ready for this. She holds her smile while mine melts like the candle wax in the tavern, and I turn into a puddle of despair.

"Rani, I don't know if I'm—"

"You are," Rani finishes for me through a steady smile. She waves at the crowd in a practiced manner. "Just wave."

After the raja—our father—finishes the introduction, I raise a weak hand. I catch sight of familiar faces—Sanya, Amir's sister, who I've spent some time with this past week, along with Jas, an older woman Rani has confided in often over the past several days. Next to them stands Amir, who gives me and Rani a shy little wave. But even the sight of them—*friends*—doesn't give me enough strength to counter the crowd's roaring excitement.

Skies be good. The scene drags up a memory from my mind: the night I came to the palace, when the king and queen announced Rani's engagement to Saeed, and I stood in her place, our swap a secret, or so we believed.

Amara came up to me, muttering blessings—all the while knowing that both Rani *and I* existed. *Knowing* the king and queen had twins. At their request, she wiped me from their minds forever using the Memory Master's talisman.

My cheeks burn with anger at the thought, even though, with Shima's snake venom, we managed to return to my parents their memories of me.

How dare Amara play with our lives like that?

It was supposed to be happily ever after. But with Amara's survival now more and more likely, it sure doesn't feel like a fairy-tale ending.

"Here she is," the queen begins, marching up to me. My mother is wearing a pink sari with a matching bindi between her perfectly plucked brows. "She has been long lost to us, but we are so pleased to have her back in the palace, where she belongs. Please welcome my daughter Princess Ria!"

Claps echo through the air like the beat of a drum. I step forward, inching my way into the crowd. People *ooh* and *ahh* like I'm some kind of shiny bauble. I look to Rani for help, but she merely tilts her head. *Go on.*

Raja's beard. I paste on a smile, then spin around, making my gold lehenga swirl. The beads flash in the moonlight, turning me into a sparkling orb.

"Princess Ria is our daughter. And she should never have been away from us or our care." The raja's eyes darken before he calls for a servant with a snap of his fingers. A boy with a yellow kurta rushes over, gently holding a long scroll in both hands. The raja gingerly releases the scroll, and the crowd gasps. It's a family tree, tracing my ancestors all the way back to . . .

The Snake Master.

"While much of our history was lost in the Great Fires," the raja says, pointing at a section at the beginning of our timeline that has been singed off, "we continue to preserve our history today."

The servant hands the raja a bamboo pen dipped in ink. Lines connecting Rani to our parents have already aged, and the raja inscribes a new branch on our family tree.

Me.

The crowd claps righteously as the servants take the scroll away. I'm officially a part of the family, the royal lineage of Abai.

So why do I feel like a fraud?

"Princess Ria is a highly gifted snakespeaker," my father says as the applause dies down. "With hardly any training, she successfully bonded with a snake and performed the Bonding Ceremony."

Gasps sound from the crowd, each one a harsh slap to my ears. But as my eyes glaze over the guests, something makes me pause. A woman stands on the fringes of the crowd, alone, facing me.

Eyes red as rubies, lips shining with blood.

Amara.

I stumble back. She's grinning, hands gripped around a long staff topped with a bejeweled snake's head. The Snake Master's talisman.

Our father's staff.

Rani, I try to gasp, but it's like the name is stuck in my throat. A booming voice breaks the silence, and I involuntarily break eye contact.

When I glance back, Amara has vanished. Just like she did that night in the Snake Pit.

"Almost as gifted as the Great Snakespeaker, Your Majesty?" someone asks from the crowd. The raja chuckles. My mind spins. I squint, but Amara isn't there.

A hallucination? Are these visions going to start haunting me during the day *and* in my dreams?

I refocus myself as I stare at the crowd that awaits the king's answer. *Am I* anywhere near as powerful as the raja? I opened the Snake Pit all on my own. And once, with Rani's help, we even called those snakes to attack Amara in hopes of getting the Bloodstone back.

A failed attempt.

I recall the way I felt that night, my blood coursing through me, cold and icy as a snake's. I'd never felt so much power thrumming inside me. I almost lost myself in it.

"A demonstration, then?" the same guest asks. People murmur in agreement, although some look wary. My father has used snakes to kill. But I know now that there is so much more to them.

If they want a performance, I'll give them one.

Shima, I call. My snake friend—and familiar—slithers into the courtyard, joining me by my side. Her scales flicker with color—yellow for curiosity, pink for love and lust. I switch my emotions on and off, letting them show on Shima's scales. The crowd roars.

It's time to take it up a notch.

My mind splits from the real world, dragging me into a pool of memories. I dive in, relishing the tingle in my fingertips as I call upon my snake magic. It's heavy, weighing on my shoulders like a rock. Almost as heavy as the crown I now bear. But with one twitch of my fingers, my magic lifts, circling around and within me like a hundred threads of light.

No, not light. Dark.

It springs forth like a cobra, fangs sinking into my belly. A voice drills through my mind, so dark and smoky it's like a snake's hiss against the shell of my ear.

"Power is a delicious thing."

The voice is like honey to my ears. An image leaps to mind, of all the energy searing through my veins, buried within me. I imagine fitting a key into a lock and opening a door to the full potential of my magic, letting all that power loose.

"Keep going . . . ," that voice says.

And my magic does. I let the cobra within me, fangs and all, take the reins. It fills me, snakes through my veins. I let it flow like water breaking through a dam. I let it roar.

"Ria, stop!"

Rani's voice snaps me back to the present. My newfound parents are staring at me in alarm. I turn, watching my sister's face go slack at the sight of them.

Snakes.

They've poured out of the throne room and into the courtyard, slithering into the crowd. Nobles cry out and drop their drinks, crystal glasses falling to the floor. Pandemonium follows: the crowd shrieks as the snakes continue their trail, slipping between people's legs.

"Ria, what are you doing?" Queen Maneet rushes up to me.

"I—I—" *I didn't mean it,* I try to say, but I'm still reeling from what's going on. How am I doing this? Calling upon snakes by accident?

"I thought they were locked in the terrarium!" Rani calls. She tries to calm the crowd, but they're already making a beeline for the gates. The courtyard is nearly empty now; I see shocked servants' faces, the foods they were holding on trays now fallen to the grass. The snakes hiss, a hundred voices overtaking my ears. I cover them.

"Make them stop!" Rani says. Her eyes, fear-flecked, find mine. But I can't. My magic is a leash that can't be tightened.

"Quiet!" Father booms, his snake magic lining every word, but even his voice cannot silence the serpents. I'm ready to try and call upon my snake magic again, but suddenly, the voices stop.

With a strange, synchronous movement, the throng of snakes turns and heads for the Fountain of Fortunes near the gates. But why?

I have no time to think of an answer. With slow steps, I follow them.

The snakes huddle next to the strange fortune-telling fountain, hissing. *Speaking.*

I hear them, their language all too familiar to me now.

Lissssten. Lissssten.

I do. Because the fountain is boiling—its sound loud as a clap of thunder.

And the water is as red as blood.

4

Rani

"What is happening?" I ask.

Mother and Father crowd around the fountain, and Ria shivers by my side. Is the deafening hiss in my ears the roar of my own blood, or the sound of the snakes all around us? It's impossible to tell. I've never heard so many at once, not since we brought the snakes out of the Pit the night Amara disappeared.

The Pit that hasn't been opened since.

The Fountain of Fortunes, which looked so calm just under an hour ago, is now gurgling like I have never seen it before. When I was a young child, I thought the fountain to be nothing more than a ruse. I would gaze into its shining blue waters and stare at my rippling reflection, wondering why in Amran's name anyone would wish for a fountain to foretell their future. But as I grew older, my intuition sharpened. I would see poor villagers from all over Abai duck their heads close to the water and send prayers to the Masters above.

Tell me my boy will be strong again someday, I remember one woman saying. And I could've sworn I saw something in the water—an answer. But with each prophecy the fountain gave, the water looked the same: crystal clear, shining like a diamond.

Now, the fountain is streaked with crimson. Shadows fill the water, dark as midnight, pulling me forward until I'm leaning over the edge.

"I have never seen this before," Father whispers, hands grasping the fountain's stone rim with a pale-knuckled grip. "Like it is . . . *angry*."

Angry? A frisson of ice skirts down my back. The Memory Master provides a glimpse into people's futures, if they wish to see it. But their fortunes are usually strongest on Diwali night. And they never look like *this*.

Like a pool of nightmares.

Like fresh blood.

Footsteps echo all around us. People are still running from the palace, as if the snakes will eat them whole if they stay put. A myriad of Charts, dressed in their royal red uniforms, are standing at the gates, calming visitors who are trying to flee. I dip a hand into the fountain and lift it, watching clear water run down the palm of my hand.

"How is this happening?" My twin's cheeks pale as she takes in the horror on my face.

"The fountain has never done this," I say. Something tickles my feet, and I look down, finding the snakes still surrounding us.

Ria inches closer to me until she is at my side. "I think I lost control of my magic. I called the snakes, by accident." She looks at our parents, the golden barrette glimmering in her hair. The ruby-red jewels inside the hair clip remind me of something. A gem as red as the fountain's waters.

The Bloodstone.

"But I didn't call them to the fountain." Ria blanches. She gestures to the pool. "Do you think this could be our magic?"

"Snake magic does not affect the fountain," Father says, examining the pool. I watch his serious face contort in the rippling red waters.

The fountain emits a burst of warm light, so blinding I have to turn away. Even the snakes shrink at the sight, slipping over our feet, back up the palace stairs, fleeing for safety.

A voice begins to speak in a haunting timbre:

A missing heart to be restored
A moon with tears as red as blood
Without the stone, this shall not be
And the Key of a Master shall set souls free

As sisters journey to new lands
Objects of power will be friend or foe
Souls will perish from a land soon lost
By a woman whose ambitions a Master's match

The voice fades away, but I still hear it echoing in my ears, rooted to my brain. A missing heart? A moon with tears as red as blood?

The fountain has given cryptic prophecies before—it surely did when I heard it on Diwali night when I began my search for the Bloodstone.

I thought it meant to direct me to the Mailan Foothills. Instead, our journey took us to the Glass Temple—to the flametalkers, those with ancient fire magic thought to be wiped out of existence. It was they who told me the Bloodstone wasn't in the lost temple but in the place where two kings made the Hundred-Year Truce: the Var River.

All to say, any prophecy the fountain has rendered is . . .

"Mysterious," Father says, eyes meeting mine. I see myself in him, in the faint wrinkles on his forehead, the worry lines etched around his mouth.

"It was talking about us . . . wasn't it. The sisters." Ria's statement hovers in the air. All I can do is nod. It must be. But what does this all mean?

Ria's face pales. She looks like she's seen a ghost.

"Come inside now, Ria," Mother says. She flourishes a manicured hand, calling for a servant who waits with a shawl. Mother places the dense fabric around Ria's shivering frame and ushers her back into the palace. The courtyards are eerily quiet now, Charts having brought the visitors inside, and no stragglers are left to be seen. Even the snakes, so loud before, have grown docile.

"Perhaps you and Ria have yet another adventure before you," Father says grimly.

I scoff. Our last *adventure* nearly ended in a war between two countries.

"We don't even know what it means," I whisper. "Besides, Saeed is with the Charts looking for any trace of Amara. You're drawing up plans for the new treaty to be signed at the peace summit with Kaama. We're fine. Everything is *fine*."

My voice cracks on the final word. I'm far from fine. This past week should have been a dream after being reunited with my sister. But it's more like a sweet mango gone rotten. Glistening and dewy on the outside, and sour in the middle.

Father raises a brow. "Tell me. How is Ria doing? Is she all right?"

I shrug. "She's still getting used to the palace." Truth be told, I've been worried about her. Some mornings I find her looking more tired than ever. I've chalked it up to fencing practice, riding, all the different activities we've gotten her into that she's never done. But maybe there's more to Ria's tired gaze than she's let on. Or it has to do with the stranger she met and still tells me nothing about.

As if my father can sense my thoughts, he takes me by the shoulders. "Rani, you know you can tell me if something is wrong. I haven't always been there for you, but . . ."

"I know, Father." I embrace him. But when I let go, I realize he trailed off for another reason. He's staring at his empty hands, like a fire might implode from within them.

"Father?" I ask.

"My scepter—" Father spins but finds nothing. "Where is my scepter?"

"Were you holding it during the speech?" I circle around him, but after the wave of snakes and the fountain's prophecy, I remember little.

"I thought—but I must have left it in my chamber." Father lowers his hands and attempts to give me a smile, but I can tell when something is bothering him. He almost *always* has his scepter on hand; I should have noticed something amiss.

"We'll find it," I tell him, reasoning that it must be inside. Father remains outwardly calm as he urges one of the nearby Charts to go looking and spread the word.

I understand his panic: Father's scepter isn't simply an ornament. It is an heirloom passed down from the First Descendant of the Snake Master—a talisman of snake magic.

I slam open a book on Abai's history, and the sound echoes through the empty library.

"Abai's sun," I cough out as a cloud of dust rises from the pages. I swat the dust away until it's clear. I'm not exactly one to haunt a room like this—unlike Ria—but I'm desperate to find answers to the fountain's riddle.

I'm so busy flipping through the yellowed pages that I jump at the tap on my shoulder. Startled, I turn around. When I spot him, I sigh, "*Amir.* You scared me."

Amir shrugs as though in apology, though I know he isn't sorry. "I just hoped you hadn't had enough of me tonight." He winks, ever a joker. Only then do I notice the fatigue behind his deep-brown eyes. "I helped the workers return the snakes."

"*All* of them? It must have taken hours!" He nods, and though I am grateful to him, I can't resist teasing him nonetheless. "*You* touched a snake? I find that hard to believe."

"I'm not sure what you're talking about," he boasts, tossing his head back. "A thief fears nothing."

"Nothing except Sanya, maybe," I snort.

"That just makes me wise," Amir says with a grin. "Everyone knows older sisters are scary. You just don't get it because Ria is younger than you."

"By minutes, maybe," I say, giggling.

"It *still counts*," Amir insists. "Don't tell Ria that I think you're more fearsome than her, though . . . she'll take it as a challenge."

I laugh again, feeling my spirits lift just from his presence. Already the night's worries seem further from me, easier to handle.

"Thank you," I whisper, folding into him. My next words are muffled against his kurta, and I breathe in his scent—melon, tree bark, and a mix of familiar warm spices. "Tonight was . . . a disaster."

He pulls me back and looks me deeply in the eyes. Amir isn't a serious person by nature, but he looks so right now. "How were the snakes let loose? I thought they were all locked up." His voice trembles with fear. But I remind myself that he isn't afraid of *me*, or my magic.

"I'm not sure," I say truthfully. On the one hand, a single look at Ria's frightened gaze held all the answers—but those answers only lead to more questions. "They were attracted to the fountain outside. It gave us a prophecy."

"Another prophecy?" he echoes, intrigued. "What'd it say?"

"That's what I'm trying to figure out." The book I hold is fragile and cold. *The Complete History of Magic* by Suneel Nanda. Father's archives aren't exactly open to the general public, and I've never had much of an interest in dense textbooks. Tonight, however, is a different story.

Amir gently takes the book and inspects the front cover. "What're you looking for? Maybe I can help. Ma always told me reading was important."

At the mention of his mother, long since passed, his face goes drawn. I clutch his hand. "I'm looking for something that could help me with the opening of the prophecy. *A missing heart to be restored / A moon with tears as red as blood,*" I recite.

Just as I finish speaking, my breath stops in my chest. I think of what Baljeet brought up.

Hurriedly, I flip to the correct page, fingers stiff as I stare down at the parchment.

An illustration fills the page. *A crimson orb, twisted faces recoiling in horror at the sight of it.*

"The Blood Moon," I whisper. Baljeet had said he saw the reddening rim of the moon, but I had dismissed it in my mind. Even if we snakespeakers hold the legend true, the Blood Moon doesn't exist anymore. It's a relic of an ancient time long past—a myth that has faded into obscurity for most. Not many know the full story of the Blood Moon except royalty, nobility, and learned scholars.

I skim past the legend, then continue reading:

"Scholars speculate that only a nefarious force could cause the moon to return—and its poison with it. As the Blood Moon rises, its effects will be felt everywhere on the earth, and an unstoppable tide of destruction shall approach as the moon grows full. Some, superstitiously so, say the bloodred full moon will come on a night when pacts are forged or broken."

The rest of the page is filled with more lore about the Creator and the creation of the Masters. I know that the elemental Masters were created to wipe away the poison from the land. But there's more I'm certain Ria does not know.

Even my own knowledge, that the Masters—and their magic—had been banished by the Snake Master, is muddled here. No one knows how, or even why, the Snake Master began the Great Masters' Battle. It wasn't until I *spoke* to the Fire Master in the Glass Temple that I learned not everything about their banishment was what it seemed. That the Snake Master might not have been entirely to blame, as all the legends say.

What is the true story?

"The Blood Moon is a myth. A story to scare children," Amir admits, cheeks flushed. "Before I made a life as a thief, it scared me."

His solemn eyes catch mine. This is a side to him I've rarely seen, so honest, so open.

A Blood Moon returning will cause alarm not only for Abai but all kingdoms. While things with Kaama are beginning to look up, I wonder what Amratstan and Retan will think when they notice the reddening moon.

"The fountain spoke of a 'missing heart' that needs to be restored. . . . How is that connected with the Blood Moon?"

He shrugs. "It's all pretty vague."

That's true. But the Memory Master wouldn't offer such a prophecy—in waters red as blood—without reason.

And that's exactly the problem. Prophecies are never simple—and unless deciphered correctly, they can lead to dangerous mistakes.

Not all of them, I think. *Ria and I never fulfilled the first prophecy about us.*

But instead of comfort, I feel a creeping unease. Could this prophecy be false, too?

I shake myself. Whether it will come to pass is irrelevant. If it *does*, it could destroy everything I hold dear. I need to act as if it *is* true, like the prophecy that sent Ria and I swapping identities.

"I never took you two for bookworms. Why are you still up?"

Amir and I whirl at the sound of a voice, rough around the edges and soft in the middle. Amir's sister looks like a picture-perfect noble, from the delicate chunni over her head to the smooth light-brown hair trailing down her back. A star-shaped birthmark sits on her cheek, pronounced in the candlelit darkness. Her brown eyes are soft, but when she wants them to be, they can transform into two sharpened spears.

Sanya strolls in with Jas Auntie. I've taken to using the familiar title for Tutor's wife. While we're not related by blood, she's the closest thing I have to my old tutor. And he was always family.

"Good evening, Princess Rani," Jas Auntie says. She wears a shawl draped around her shoulders, but the outfit beneath still sparkles through—a teal-blue salwar with white beading.

Over the past week, Jas and Sanya have enjoyed their stay at the palace, delighting in the spreads of food and copious clothing at their disposal. At first, Sanya pretended not to be impressed, but both Amir and I knew how happy she was to have her own bed, fresh sheets, and full meals.

Irfan, on the other hand, has been like a brick wall. Nearly invisible in the palace, he prefers spending time outdoors with nothing but his bow and quiver.

"Is your sister okay? We were outside when it all happened," Sanya says. "We lost you in the crowd."

"She's fine." *I think.* "Thank you for asking. And, Jas Auntie, I'm just—"

"Rani, I know," Jas says with a twinkle in her eye. Her gaze finds Amir. "Well, it looks like you two might want to be alone."

"Jas Auntie!" Sanya groans as Amir says, "No, um, actually—"

"We need your help." My voice weighs down the lightness of their conversation. "The snakes led us to the Fountain of Fortunes. It told us another prophecy." I recite what I can of the prophecy from memory. Sanya's and Jas's previously teasing faces turn serious.

"'Objects of power will be friend or foe,'" Jas says. "That is indeed dire."

"Why?" Amir and I say at the same time.

"In our time searching for the Bloodstone," Jas begins, her mouth set in a grim line, "and while at the Academy in Retan, my husband and I learned much of magic. I'm afraid that these objects of power can only be one thing."

"The most powerful objects in the world are . . . the talismans," I realize. "Amara has the cuffs. And Father's scepter is—" I cut myself off. I don't want anyone else knowing about his missing staff. I had assumed it had simply been misplaced. Now I worry there may have been a foul motive behind its disappearance.

"The last line of the prophecy mentioned a woman," Sanya says. "Do you think it could be . . . Amara? The prophecy also mentioned souls. Maybe it's referencing her wish to become the . . ."

"Soul Master," I finish, shuddering. Sanya nods solemnly.

"Somehow, she must have escaped the Pit," says Amir.

My worst fears have been realized. The prophecy was referring to Amara:

Souls will perish from a land soon lost
By a woman whose ambitions a Master's match.

Jas nods, her mouth twisting with disdain.

"If the prophecy is true, then . . ." I find myself looking inexorably toward the window near me, and at the slim crescent of the new moon hanging in the night sky. Next to me, I hear Amir draw a sharp breath, and Sanya's shocked gasp.

"Raja's beard," Amir whispers.

Baljeet was right. It's not white. The crescent moon is tinged pink, sending ice coursing through my veins.

"Then the Blood Moon will reach its full potential in four weeks' time," Jas says. "My husband spoke enough about astronomy for me to know."

The moon tonight is just a sliver, the first of the moon's natural phases, until it will become a full, red orb. "Which means the spectacle will align with the peace summit in Kaama."

We're all silent. Amara wanted war with Kaama. If all of this is connected to her, if she is somehow not only alive but gaining in power, her appearance on the night of the Blood Moon could very well achieve her goal.

I slam the book shut. Exhaustion floods me, and suddenly I need to sit. I take a seat on the bench next to the windowsill, letting my head fall back. Jas and Sanya excuse themselves for be Amir stubbornly remains by my side.

"I can stay here," he says. "There's enough room on the b but I don't move.

Images flash through me from the past day: me kissi Ria losing control over the snakes. "I think I just need alone." I don't meet his gaze.

"You sure?" Amir asks.

A thousand thoughts race through my head. Ho Amir to stay. How foolhardy it would be, after wl and I spoke of.

Carefully, Amir twines his hand with mine. H

palm once and takes his leave. Once he's gone, I loosen a breath, and then, too tired to move, I lie down and shut my eyes.

Before I know it, I wake to morning light filtering through the window and the sound of clopping hooves.

I rub my tired eyes and peer out the circular window. There's a man outside dismounting his stallion. I gasp, and the book falls off my lap at the sight of him.

I rush out of the library and to the front of the palace, legs aching from my runs with Amir.

The man's already beat me there, pack in hand, curly hair stiff from the wind.

Saeed. My former betrothed.

He has returned.

5

Ria

I shouldn't be this nervous—yet here I am, twiddling my thumbs and talking to a snarky serpent instead of walking forward ten paces into the library's meeting room.

The former is not so bad, Shima says. *Talking to snakes is therapeutic.*

"Says who?" I ask my snake familiar.

Says me. She slips closer, her scales shifting to an orange yellow, like an Abaian sunset. *You must not be late for your meeting.*

"Too late for that," I mutter. I stifle a yawn. I barely slept last night. How could I relax after yesterday?

Yesterday, when everything went so wrong. A thief isn't used to the spotlight, to performances, to standing before a crowd. Thieves prefer the quiet dark of night, the shadows in alleyways, the thrill of no one ever truly knowing their real faces.

When my mother brought me back into the palace, she warmed me with a hug and said, *"Your power is a gift. But it also needs to be controlled. Wielded."*

I'd scared off almost every palace guest—the perfect way to introduce myself to my kingdom. I can imagine the whispers: *Princess Ria, the girl with so much snake magic she's a danger to everyone around her.*

Then Aditi woke me with the news: Saeed, Amara Gupta's son and Rani's former betrothed, had returned.

I step toward the meeting room and rest my hands on golden door handles shaped like twin snakes. Inhaling deeply, I shove the doors open and barrel inside. The first thing that greets me is the crimson rug. Red as the Bloodstone Amara disappeared with.

Rani and Saeed's chatter stops. At the sight of me, Saeed rises hurriedly from his chair, nearly making it topple over. "Ria."

"S-Saeed." His hair is thick, unbridled in the dewy morning light. He must have changed once he got here—his clothes look fresh, and I can faintly smell lavender floating toward me. Maybe he'd spent time in the gardens before coming inside. "You're really back."

"Yes, thank Amran," Rani says, sighing as she speaks. She doesn't look nearly as rattled as I feel; her simple garb and the saffron-colored ribbon tying the bottom of her braid exude calm.

Meanwhile, my palms turn damp as I inch toward the nearest seat and settle in, blinking away the sunlight that faces directly at me. I clasp my hands together. "Sorry I'm late. What have I missed?"

"Well, your sister told me about the fountain and its latest prophecy." Saeed takes a seat across the table, hazel eyes flickering from Rani to me. My heart backflips. This is the first I've seen him in a week, and suddenly I'm a jumble of nerves. Hadn't the stranger in the tavern told me he was nearby? I should've anticipated his return.

Saeed slouches forward, as if his body is whittled down by regret, trauma . . .

By the absence of his mother.

"Tell us about your trip," Rani says carefully. "You traveled to western Abai?"

"I was with a few men on Kavya Lake," he explains, straightening himself. I feel his foot accidentally brush against mine as he scoots in. My cheeks rouge as I jerk my leg away. *Get it together, Ria.*

"I traveled to the lake because Mother and I spent time there when I was younger. It's one of the most beautiful spots in Abai. I thought . . ." He trails off with a shake of his head. "I found a couple sailors and stayed with them. They were helming me toward shore, back up to northern Abai," he continues. "You know sailors; there's not much to talk of besides the ocean. So I pretended I was a noble and . . ."

"And Amara?" Rani presses, gripping the table with pale fingers.

Saeed nods, as if to say, *I'm getting there.* "I told them I'd heard about the war coming to a standstill, talks of peace negotiations between Kaama and Abai, now that the Hundred-Year Truce is over. Next thing I knew, the men were interested in me; after a few moments, they said I reminded them of the woman on the wanted posters."

I gulp. The raja—my father—has been ordering his soldiers to put up posters of Amara everywhere, the red-haired woman whose face haunts my dreams. Nightmares. And the voice, not Amara's but clear as glass.

She's listening.

"The sailors, had they seen her? The real her?" I ask.

Saeed shook his head. "They hadn't." Relief floods through me, even though I can hear the sadness in his voice.

"How've your visions been?" I ask, leaning forward.

"Clear," he says. "No more tonic, right?" He pushes through a half-hearted laugh, but Rani and I are silent. It was Amara who gave him the tonic to control his visions.

"Do you . . . still see her?" Rani asks.

Saeed nods. "Yes. At first I saw her staring at her reflection in a pool of water. But her eyes were different—I don't know how to describe it. Like she's . . . changing." He pauses. "I've had that vision before. The water was what made me think of Kavya Lake. But it seems I've come up short. And then . . ."

"Then what?" My heart thumps.

Saeed's lips form a thin line. "I had a new vision this morning, soon after my arrival. I was in the gardens when I saw her. It was like she was standing right in front of me. I wasn't even sleeping. It was the strongest vision I've ever had."

I hold my breath, remembering the moment I saw Amara in the crowd last night. "She wasn't actually *out there*, was she?"

"No," Saeed replies firmly, "she was not."

"But your mother . . . is definitely alive," Rani says hesitantly, less a question and more a confirmation.

Saeed presses his lips together. "I saw her staring at me, telling me everything was going to be all right. That she and my father and I will be reunited again. Then I saw her walking off toward a snowcapped mountain."

A gasp escapes my throat. The Winter Witch's words echo through my memory.

"*She who holds the stone will cross rivers and scale the White Mountains to find the treasures she seeks*," I recite. Everyone turns to stare at me. "I met a woman at a tavern yesterday who told me that. She was talking about Amara. Which means Saeed's mother is—"

"Headed for Amratstan, if not already there," Rani concludes. "And there's more, Saeed. The fountain spoke of the 'moon with tears as red as blood.' Amir and I pored over the old texts. We believe it refers to the Blood Moon. Your mother was mentioned in the prophecy, too."

She was? I recount the final line of the prophecy and shudder.

Saeed blinks. "*Mother?* Are you certain?"

Rani nods solemnly.

"And what of this Blood Moon?" Saeed counters. "There hasn't been one since . . ."

"The beginning of our world," Rani finishes.

"So the Blood Moon really *is* coming back." I clench my hands into fists.

"You know the story?" my sister asks.

I nod. "Mama Anita at the orphanage. She must have realized that I needed to know."

"The moon will become redder as we get closer to the Blood Moon," Rani states. "As the moon grows, its poison will too. By our estimates, we have four weeks before a full red moon. Which means it will align with the treaty signing at the peace summit in Kaama."

My stomach turns. "That's not much time to stop a prophecy," I mutter.

Saeed is still, and I feel myself blush as his gaze remains on mine. But it's not a gaze of wanting as in our past. Tension grows in his shoulders; a crease pulses between his brows.

"What proof do you have that my mother has anything to do with this Blood Moon?" he says, voice low and gravelly.

"Little," Rani admits. "But the visions and the prophecy all together seem to be pointing in one direction. We can't forget—it was your mother's intention to raise your father from the dead. In essence, to become the Soul Master. If she gains power, if she can harness the darkness that will accompany the Blood Moon, who knows what she can achieve."

We all sit there, stunned into silence.

"But how would she do it?" Saeed asks. "How would she succeed when she failed before?"

I've wondered about that, too. Amara attempted to see her

dead husband once before, using blackened roses in her shrine room. She found a way to trap a memory of Kumal there, thanks to information she gathered from Retanian scholars. But that wasn't enough. Now she has the Bloodstone. But those who wish upon the stone must endure consequences, unless the wisher has a special antidote—the lifeblood of Amran. Amara told us her plan before she fell into the Snake Pit: *Once I extract a droplet of his lifeblood and pour it into my veins, I will be immune to any ill effects.*

But how does she plan on extracting the antidote?

"I don't know. But there's something else. The fountain spoke of powerful objects," Rani tells him. "Jas thought of—"

"The talismans!" I finish, thinking of what Shima taught me. "Each is powerful on its own. But what do they have to do with Amara's plan?"

Amara's chilling words from my nightmare float back to me: *I'll get what's mine. We will find all the—*

A dark voice had cut Amara off before she could finish. Before I could hear what she wanted to say: the talismans.

I think of the mirage of Amara last night, holding the raja's scepter.

I speak my worries aloud to Saeed and Rani, admitting to my nightmares and Amara's strange appearance at the celebration. "She somehow knew I was listening and didn't want me hearing her plans. As for last night, I don't even know how she got the scepter." Rani and Saeed exchange troubled glances.

"Ria, why didn't you tell me earlier?" Rani asks. Her sisterly concern has increased tenfold since last night's events. I don't need her fretting over me right now—not when we have bigger problems to deal with.

I ignore Rani's comment. "You were right to be worried about Amara. If she becomes the Soul Master, she won't just resurrect her husband. She could destroy the entire nation of Kaama." My voice wobbles.

Rani's mouth sets into a grim line. "I will tell Father to warn King Jeevan. We *must* find Amara, figure out why she wants these talismans, retrieve the stone from her, and . . ." She heaves in a deep breath. "Destroy the Bloodstone."

"*Destroy?*" I cry. "Rani, it's a *magical* stone. I don't think you can simply destroy something that powerful."

"I didn't say it would be simple," Rani says, frustration lacing her voice. It stops me short. My sister doesn't usually get cross, especially not with me.

"Destroying the stone might be the only way to stop my mother from using it," Saeed agrees, his shoulders hunching, head hung low. "Such knowledge doesn't exist—or if it does, it will likely only be known to scholars in Retan, and they guard their knowledge viciously."

Rani stands abruptly, facing me. "I must meet with our parents right away to make a plan. Meanwhile, you can . . ." She eyes Saeed, who's turned his head toward the window, staring out at the dewy gardens. Then she grins at me and sweeps out of the room.

Way to be obvious, sister.

Once Rani's gone, Aditi enters, two braids hanging cheerily down her petite frame. My friend, nicknamed Mouse for the way she scurries about the palace, is carrying a silver tray. A teapot and three teacups sit on the decorated dish, which is embossed with Abai's crest. She sets the tray down on the table, turning to smile at us both.

"Master Saeed! It's so good to see you."

Saeed smiles. "And it's good to see you, too, Aditi." He gets up and approaches me, pouring me a cup of chai. My fingers brush his as I take the steaming cup, his hand warm against mine. I'm as frigid as an Amratstanian icewolf. Saeed must notice it, too, because his fingers linger for a second too long.

I pull away and sip.

"Thanks." I'm grateful for the tea's warmth, the calming spices that reset the magic in my blood. Or at least, Shima told me that's what it does. Either way, I don't want what happened last night—all those snakes slithering amok—to happen again. Looks like I'll need a magic lesson from Shima on how to control myself and my newfound powers. And a lot more tea.

Aditi sneaks off, leaving me and Saeed alone. I sit across from him at the table and continue sipping so I won't have to speak, but the silence becomes thick and uneasy.

"Ria."

I swallow a too-hot gulp of chai, avoid his bright-hazel eyes. "Yes?"

"I'm . . ." He inhales deeply. "I'm glad to see you."

I can't help myself; I look up. A hopeful glint reaches his eyes, and memories flash before me: the night before he left, a week after Amara's disappearance. We'd shared a dance that night—a bittersweet one, knowing he'd be gone for who knew how long—before he packed his things and disappeared the following morning.

Somehow, I've felt off since. My thief instincts not so strong. My vision not so clear. My mind unfocused. Despite my family coming together again, it still feels like something's . . . missing.

Too many loose ends.

I fiddle with the hem of my blouse. "I'm glad you're back," I reveal, though I don't say more. Somehow, knowing his mother is out there doing Amran knows what, it doesn't feel right. . . . I'm not sure how much he wants to think about her or my nightmares. Or *me*.

Bile rises in my throat. I pull my focus away from those dark thoughts and glance up at Saeed's hair. Another curl has whitened, contrasting with the hazel of his eyes. I want to reach out—but I shouldn't. Somehow, after a week apart, something sits uncomfortably between us. Thick as a block of ice.

Why am I suddenly nervous around him? How can a week have changed so much?

I find the courage to meet his eyes. "You've had a long journey. You should get some rest."

"*Rest* isn't exactly in my vocabulary." He smiles. "When I sleep, I dream. When I dream—"

"You have visions." Suddenly, I wish the table wasn't between us. I want to comfort him. Tell him about *my* strange dreams, too, the fuzzy figures I can't quite get ahold of.

Saeed reaches his hand out across the wood, palm up. Nervously, I take it. He lifts my hand to his lips and places a kiss on my knuckles.

"I'll try to rest. For you, Princess."

And with that, Saeed exits the room, leaving me with a still-steaming cup of chai and my blurry thoughts. I don't know how long I ponder his words, or the feel of his touch, or everything we've just figured out about Amara. She's like water, always slipping out of my grasp. And somehow, she's already one step ahead of us.

6

Rani

Mother and Father wear matching veiled expressions.

"Are you sure this is the meaning of the fountain's prophecy?" Mother inquires. She paces my bedroom, wringing her hands together all the while. This is not a formal place of discussion, but I had wanted a private conversation with my parents—not a meeting of the heads of our nation.

I nod. "The Blood Moon will be here soon, Mother. Which means Ria and I have to leave. We've spoken with Saeed about the prophecy already, and I believe we must head . . ." I swallow thickly, knowing Father won't like my next words. "*Outside* of Abai."

Father settles onto my bed, lacing his fingers together. "I know the prophecy mentioned sisters journeying to new lands, but after all that's happened with Amara, you wish *to travel away*? That could be very dangerous, Rani."

I purse my lips. "Amara told Ria that she visited Retanian

scholars to learn about the Bloodstone," I say. Retan's deserts are famous here in Abai, as are their scholars at the Academy. "If I traveled there, I might be able to learn more about the stone and how to destroy it. Amara is still out there somewhere. And I am capable enough, Father."

Silence rings through the room, deafening to my own ears. My parents remain wordless for a few heart-pounding moments.

"You know our relations with Retan haven't been the . . . *strongest* over the past several years," Father says, his tone grave. "We might still have our trade routes, but with Retan's pacifist ideals, we haven't been a trustworthy kingdom to them for centuries."

"Which is exactly why I must go," I say determinedly. "If we can fix our relations with our neighbors to the south, we can heal our lands. With more allies, we might just stop whatever cruelty this prophecy will bring on the night of the Blood Moon. We could shape our own futures."

Now Mother is the one to purse her own lips. "And what of Ria? She's still getting used to the palace, let alone traveling outside of it."

I know what Mother is truly thinking. After years of neglecting the one daughter she did have, she wishes to rectify her past actions and make up for them. Through *Ria*. She's worried for Ria, my mother. Worried her long-lost daughter will slip away from her again.

"And she is just as capable as I," I reply. "More, even, with her practical smarts and cunning. We cannot sit idle while Amara is still out there. We believe she is in Amratstan's White Mountains—"

Father stands suddenly. "You mean . . ."

I nod. "The Winter Palace." I think of the cold Amratstanian climate, their main palace and villages all set in and around the gargantuan White Mountains.

"We have to leave soon. Perhaps Ria could travel there and look for her."

"You know we already have guards searching every corner of the continent for her." Mother shakes her head. "We don't need you both in any more danger."

"Please, Mother," I say, more desperately than I wish to. "We need the Amratstanians' help if we want to stop her."

Small wrinkles form around Mother's mouth. "Amara is not some rogue thief. She is—was—a friend. And she is all the more dangerous for it."

"That's why I suggest we bring company. Saeed and Aditi can go with Ria. And I'll fare fine on my own in Retan."

Mother raises a brow.

"Or perhaps with a . . . friend. I could bring Amir along."

"Ah, the helpful boy," Mother remembers. "If he agrees to go—"

"He will," I say, perhaps a touch too fast. I remember the taste, the feel of his lips brushing against mine. The secret burns on my tongue.

I'll have to tell someone eventually. But the thought jolts

through me, sour and unpleasant. There is more expected of me than a dalliance with a commoner—even if he is a very special one.

Unbidden memories flood back to me. Mother asking me about the status of my engagement with Saeed. I had told her it was over between us—and had been for some time. But I didn't tell her about Amir.

"Political alliances are like friendships," Father is saying now. "And strengthening our bond with Retan will only help us unite our kingdoms. Unite *all* the kingdoms. The upcoming peace summit is not only about fixing what's between Abai and Kaama."

"Yes, Father." My voice goes cold. "Speaking of Kaama . . . We think Amara plans to destroy it altogether as revenge for Kumal. Now that we know she's alive, she'll have her sights set on nothing less. You must send word to King Jeevan by messenger hawk." I don't dare tell Father about Ria's seeing a mirage of Amara having stolen his scepter. I don't want him worrying any more than he already is.

My stomach churns as Father registers this. "Are you sure, beta?"

"Indeed," I say grimly. "Better to be on guard against an assault than be taken by surprise."

I turn to Mother. "I promise I will be safe. Amir, he's . . . he's more than helpful. He's—"

"Amir is a great asset to us. To the palace, and to our family. I trust he will keep you safe, and you him."

I settle onto my bed. *Amir isn't a friend, or an asset. He's my . . .*

What *is* Amir to me? We've formed a friendship, and then more, on our journey to find the Bloodstone. Ever since we welcomed him to the palace, we've shared stolen kisses and secret embraces. I never found the courage to tell Mother and Father what he truly means to me.

A princess kissing a thief? The whispers would spread like spilled wine. I can practically hear the newsboys shouting blasphemy in the villages: *Princess Rani entangled with former vagabond!*

"You shall leave tomorrow, then," Mother says. "But I want you home before the peace summit in Kaama. Will you promise me?" She tucks a lock of hair behind my ear. Mother hasn't been so warm with me in the past, but since Ria returned, since the forgetting spell was broken, I notice the effort she's making. And I'm glad for it. I lean into her touch.

"I promise."

"I will send a messenger bird to Amratstan's king Rohit and Retan's queen Meeta right away to prepare for your arrivals." Father approaches the door. "But if you are correct about this Blood Moon, Rani, it will take place exactly as I meet King Jeevan in Kaama for the peace summit. Should we proceed after learning of Amara's . . . goals? The last thing we need before the summit is to have King Jeevan think Abaians are responsible for losing the stone, or worrying about the fate of his kingdom in allying with us," he finishes, voice grave.

"I know, Father." I gulp. "We will get the stone back before the summit. I promise."

As the meeting finishes, Mother and Father take their leave. I ask the maids to pack my things before rushing back downstairs. We must leave soon. Every night that passes will bring us closer to the Blood Moon.

I head downstairs, looking for Ria to inform her of our plans. But my eyes land on the late afternoon sun shining over the courtyards. A figure stands with a bow and arrow, facing a grand banyan tree. One etched with the numbers of Charts past and present.

My parents are right. Looking for Amara in Amratstan's mountains will be dangerous. But I know a friend who can help.

"No." Irfan's tone is sharper than his arrows. He aims for the center of the tree—a knob marks his target. He's been using this tree for practice all week.

"Are you refusing a princess?"

The arrow flies and lands just shy of its aim. Irfan sighs before turning to me.

"I swore I'd never return to Amratstan after my parents were killed. You know this. And you must understand."

Irfan sports a glimmering green silk kurta and matching pants. His gold jutti sparkle in the sunlight. But nothing compares to his eyes, a shocking silver, like so many people from the North. They were the first thing I noticed when I met Irfan. The second thing I noticed was his build, which would easily get him into the Amratstanian army—the Sentinels. It turned out he wasn't a Sentinel, but a Chart-turned-deserter. The first to leave his position, and he paid a steep price.

The Charts are forced to take an oath before this very tree, which magically binds them to their place and sears their numbers into the bark. Ever since Irfan deserted his station, he's experienced a never-ending pain, right beneath his branding, one that only Amir's sister could help heal.

"I do. But this isn't a favor for me—it's for my sister. I promised my parents her safety as she travels to Amratstan to search for Amara. And you know Amratstan better than anyone else I could ask."

"The missing woman," Irfan remembers. He's preferred to keep out of palace affairs as much as possible, especially since I convinced Father to let him stay. I'm not sure how much longer Father's promise will hold. His kindness and warmth shine through once again now that he's free of Amara's cuffs—the Memory Master's talisman—that were controlling his mind. But he's not so changed a man to completely forgive a deserter from his army.

"Then you understand? Amara will do anything to fulfill her wishes—even hurt Ria. You know your home—the palace, the guards. You could provide immense help. I'm not asking you as the princess of Abai. I'm asking as . . . your friend."

"Is that so?" Irfan nocks an arrow again. This time, it lands on his target, quivering in place.

"Tell you what." I shift in front of him, blocking the tree. He lowers his bow with a dramatic sigh.

"I can get you whatever you need. Lodging, food, money. The

best medicine for your shoulder. Even a job, if you wish."

"I already had a job at the palace. And I left. I appreciate your help, Princess Rani, but to be quite honest with you, I sometimes wonder what I'm still doing here." I silently fill in the rest of his words. *The one place he ran away from.*

"Then don't stay."

This puzzles Irfan.

"And where will I go?" he asks, working his shoulder. "I can't go back to the Foothills."

"Why not?"

"Because the Foothills aren't home. I don't know what is anymore. I've been running for so long that I've forgotten how to stay still." His voice turns thick with remembrance, silver eyes dimming.

Gently, I take the sun-warmed bow from Irfan's hands. "Then don't. Go where your heart tells you. And if that's to Amratstan— I'd be very gracious." I even bow my head, which brings a bubbling smile to Irfan's face.

"We're leaving tomorrow. Join us at the palace gates two bells past sunrise if you choose."

I return his bow and then walk off, heading for the fountain. From here, I see the sun beginning to set—reds and oranges blending like the fabric of a well-stitched sari. It might be one of the last sunsets in Abai I will see for a long time.

7

Ria

Tonight is my last magic lesson with Rani before we leave, and my sister isn't taking it easy on me.

Moonlight filters through the throne room as midnight approaches. And tomorrow, I set off to Amratstan in Saeed and Aditi's care.

Our goal is set. Find Amara. Find the scholars. Learn how to destroy the stone for good. But first, Rani and I need practice.

Remember, Shima says, noticing I'm distracted, *we are doing this so you won't lose control of your magic on your journey, Ria.*

As if I could forget. Last night the crowds were supposed to be chanting my name, not running like street rats. But Rani's never been one for control, either, and I flush at being the only one censured.

As if she can sense my thoughts, Rani presses the pads of her fingers to the throne room floor. "Focus, Ria. Remember when we opened the Pit. We can do it again, together."

"Together," I repeat, not sure if I entirely believe it. What if that was a fluke? Still, at Shima's insistent stare, I shove my thoughts aside and call upon the magic in my blood, drawing it forth like a tiger to prey. I feel that shift inside me again—the cobra, ready to strike.

The empty space rumbles between us. The marble above the closed Snake Pit ripples. We haven't opened it—and neither has the raja—since the night Amara disappeared. But we can't avoid it forever.

I prepare myself. Shima's voice slithers into my mind.

Don't react; act.

I mimic Rani's movement and slam my hand to the ground, causing the marble to flutter. Both our opposing forces push against each other, and the Pit slowly inches open and shut, like a wound fighting to close. Sweat beads my brow. I relish the vibrant stream of magic in my veins.

I press my fingers deeper into the marble, memories flashing through me. The last time we opened the Pit. Amara, falling. The snakes, whispering—

Gone. Gone. Gone.

"Raja's beard," I bite out, trying to focus. Cursed memories.

Shima doesn't let up on her stance, even when she feels my thoughts scatter. *Feel each other's magic. Let them flow together. Don't fight it.*

But our magics tangle and writhe and, unable to hold out any longer, I let up on my touch, and see Rani do the same. The floor settles down, like it's letting out a relieved breath.

Now Rani stares intently at the floor, at a line of cracked marble that leads from her hand straight to mine. I feel her magic, sharp and sour as a lemon, rush toward me along the crevice. It stings my hand, and I jerk back.

"You need to work with me, not against me, Ria," Rani says. She gives a pointed look at Shima, who nods. Rani's gotten years of formal training with snakes. My magic might be strong when provoked, but I don't have years of practice and refinement. How am I supposed to grasp all these lessons in the short time I've been at the palace? The only person who's taught me magic and history lessons outside of Shima is . . .

Warm hazel eyes. Black hair with white streaks.
Saeed.

No. I can't get distracted. I work to conjure a different thought: Rani and I coming together instead of apart, rising from the Pit, the snakes guiding us forward. A moment when we *proved* we could work together to create wonders.

"You're a snakespeaker," she'd told me, the first night I'd slept in the palace as my true self. "And we can always trust our serpent familiars."

My gaze finds the two faded bite marks on my wrist. She's right. My connection with Shima is stronger than ever—and with Rani, too. My sister. The future queen.

Maybe. I don't know what Rani wants. I don't know what *I* want.

Doubt creeps in. Instead of opening the Snake Pit with Rani, I shrink back. Shima sighs, shaking her head.

And I thought I had a short attention span, she huffs.

I scramble up. "This isn't working." My magic is like a stray cat, choosing to come and go as it pleases. Uncontrollable. I imagine Barfi, the cat at my old orphanage, prowling between rooms, circling my feet, but never quite obeying my orders.

"You're overthinking things again," Rani says, twisting me around and taking hold of my shoulders. Her plumped lips are pursed with a glossy sheen, her hair isn't an inch out of place, and she looks twice the princess I am right now. "Just feel the magic in your blood. Call to it like . . . like a bird singing its morning song."

"I'm not very musical," I hiss. "And I've got a lot on my mind."

Rani pauses. "Is this about the celebration?"

I shrug. What I didn't tell Rani last night was how scared I felt. All those eyes on me, and I had nowhere to hide, to pretend. I'm not Rani anymore; I'm just *me*. And I'm not sure who I want to be, or who the people want me to be.

"What if I can't measure up to you? What if our parents—"

"Mother and Father love you, Ria. Yes, there is still much they have to atone for, and I know you—and I—still expect more from them as we work to aid our kingdom and the treatment of its people. But first, we have to stop Amara from creating even more destruction. As for your magic . . . maybe we just need a new tactic." Rani paces the marble floor, then glances down. "Talk to it."

"To the *floor*?" I snap.

"To the Pit," Rani explains. "Speak to the snakes within. They'll help you."

"Fine. Um, Pit thing? Knock knock. Could you open up?"

Rani huffs. "I mean speak to it *seriously*. Focus, Ria. We can't take down Amara like this."

"Like what?" I counter. I don't know why, but that cobra inside me that I first felt last night suddenly rears up. Anger pushes its way to the forefront of my emotions, turning Shima a haunting crimson.

"Like . . . *this*!" Rani shakes her head, her arms spread wide. "Like you. Ruling a kingdom and possessing magic is no laughing matter."

Silence stiffens the air between us. I remember the Fountain of Fortunes's prophecy about Rani and me—the reason we were split at birth. Its waters showed us nearly pressed together, eyes dim, as though entering a battle.

Twins of opposing forces, one of light and one of dark.

"I'm sorry. I didn't mean that," Rani says, her voice contrite. "I suppose I'm still not used to having a sister. We're supposed to be helping each other, not—"

"No. I get it. But maybe taking magic seriously isn't my thing."

Rani's brows draw together. "We worked together before. We can do it again." She crosses her fingers over her chest, a gesture we made last week to signal one another if we ever needed help. *Anytime we need each other, here's how we'll know*, Rani had told me.

"I'm beginning to doubt that," I tell her, my words biting. My frustration and anger crest inside me and I begin to feel a rumble in my bones and beneath my feet. I listen as my mind forms a thread, connecting to the minds of the snakes beneath me.

She is changed. She is changed.

I gasp and stumble back. The voices roar in my ears, then become still.

The same words Shima spoke the week after Amara disappeared. She had told me more I couldn't decipher—about someone biding their time in the Pit—but even after prodding the snake for answers, she hasn't offered any more information. It's unlike Shima to be so unhelpful, and it had only made Amara's disappearance more sinister.

My mind flits back to that strange man who fell to the ground at my feet, the one with the snake mark on his palm. *I am honored,* he'd said, *to have a snakespeaker in my presence.* I shudder, but Rani mistakes it for a shiver, moving to wrap a hand around mine.

"Don't worry," she says. "We just need more practice. We *can* do this."

I can't quite look at her, but I squeeze her hand back tentatively. If nothing else, Rani's faith in me makes me want to keep trying.

"Oh, and I got you something." Rani pulls a set of jewelry out of her lehenga pocket—matching anklets with beady-eyed snake charms. "Wear this during your trip. I'll wear one, too. It's imbued with snake magic, thanks to Shima. It should keep us connected . . . a reminder our magic is stronger together."

I relax, clipping on the anklet and thanking my sister. She's been there for me lately the way only Amir has in the past. Rani's steady strength, along with Amir's warmth and Aditi's quiet support, has kept me sane these past weeks.

Aditi! I shoot up. "I totally forgot I'm meeting up with Aditi in the library! What time is it?" I gather my skirts. At that moment, a shadow appears in the entrance to the throne room. Amir, quiet as a thief, sways into the room, holding a finger to his lips. I giggle, ruining the surprise. Rani spins around. My heart swells at the way Rani and Amir look at each other. Despite spending so much time in the jungles, Rani still looks and walks like a princess should. Except around Amir, where her perfect poise slips in favor of a smile. A *genuine* smile.

"Gotta go," I tell them. I give Amir a nudge in the torso before sauntering off, but Rani catches my arm.

"We'll find a way to make our magic work again. I promise," Rani says. I nod, but I can't quite meet her eyes.

In the palace hallways, moonlight casts slivers of light and shadows over the floor. I avoid the light and opt to feel the cool touch of the shadows on my feet. It's a game Aditi and I started playing a week ago. *Avoid the light.* It's been easy enough to play, especially in my dreams.

Those have been filled with nothing but darkness.

I find my way to the library easily. Aditi's already inside, nose-deep in a book. Just like old times.

"What're you reading?"

Aditi drops the tome. I recognize the title—it's my name.

Our names.

I pick up the book from the floor and flip to the first page. "'The story of Ria and Rani, a tale of tragedy and triumph' . . . who *wrote* this?"

"A palace scribe," Aditi says quickly. "It's why I wanted to call you here; we haven't much time before we're due to leave."

Right. Not to mention I still need to sleep. My practice with Rani ran long, and our journey creeps closer every second.

"Word travels fast with servants," Aditi adds. "Dignitaries from all over Abai say you're—"

"The talk of the town?" I finish. "Or *kingdom*." I flip through the book. The tome isn't yet complete, but it explains the horrors of what Rani and I discovered. Our birth, the prophecy that separated us—and our eventual rediscovery of each other.

But there is so much we haven't been allowed to speak about. Amara's plans, the Bloodstone, the Glass Temple, even the prophecy that led us to each other. So much is too dangerous to say aloud.

"It's missing some key details," I say, passing the book back to Aditi. She nods, shivering.

"Mistress Amara's wish to become . . ." She shakes her head. "How was your magic lesson?"

"A dud." Just weeks ago, I was mastering my magic unlike any other. Now I'm shivering at the thought of letting loose my magic fully. What if I'm just not cut out for this magic stuff? What if I'm not cut out for *any* of this?

As if reading my thoughts, Aditi leaps from her chair and says, "You infiltrated the palace, escaped the Snake Pit, battled a noble-turned-traitor—"

"You got all this from the book?" I smirk.

But Aditi's words rattle in my brain. Noble-turned-traitor is a good way to describe Saeed's mother. Even Saeed seems petrified of her.

Or maybe of the thought of never finding her again. I haven't been able to tell exactly which.

I check Aditi's newly fashioned timepiece; a gift to all the servants-turned–*palace workers*—along with their new chambers and freeing clothes. Now that Aditi isn't under Amara's orders, no longer her personal servant, she looks happier than ever.

"It's getting late. You should go to sleep," I tell Aditi.

"As should you," Aditi bites back playfully.

"I haven't finished packing my trunk."

"I will help you. I'm already packed for our journey." She shivers with excitement. "I've never, ever left Abai. Maybe stepping into a new kingdom will finally help me grasp my magic. And maybe in a new land, you'll be able to talk to Master Saeed."

"Talk—" I start. How does Aditi know I've been avoiding him since our chat?

"He's probably already asleep," I say. "I don't want to disturb him."

"Mm-hmm," she says, a bit of a singsong tone to her voice. She clasps my hand with hers, and suddenly she looks older and wiser than her twelve years.

"You know I like him?" I blurt out. *Maybe too much?*

She levels a look at me that clearly says I have not been subtle.

"Does liking him scare you, miss?"

My gaze locks on hers, the answer plain as day. "He's my sister's betrothed. *Former*, but still." My parents don't yet know of my feelings for Saeed; but if they had been paying attention, they'd see I haven't yet plucked up the courage to take this ring off, the one Saeed gave me the night of the engagement party.

The night we kissed.

"Doesn't matter," I answer. "I really should get packing. It'll be snowy in Amratstan. I've never seen snow."

"Mama Anita told me stories about snow. She said it melts on your tongue like ghee. But cold!" She smiles a warm smile, one that reminds me of Mama. Our connection to our mother, the one who raised us both in the Vadi Orphanage with stories and starlight on her tongue.

Aditi left the orphanage at the age of five, and I never got to know her during my time there. It was surprising to find we shared elements of our past. As was the fact that the Vadi Orphanage kept kids with magic. And *buried* that magic. Because the only ones allowed to possess magic in our kingdom were the royal family. But with my father, the raja, finally beginning to change his ways, I've swayed him to help me with a project: to aid the orphanage children and bring them into better circumstances.

As we exit the library together, I wonder to myself what kind of magic Aditi might manifest. If she's sensed any sparks of flametalkers' magic from the Fire Master or felt the hum of a stonebringer's magic from the Earth Master.

Within minutes, we arrive at my room. I pull out the hefty trunk littered with my things. All I once possessed was a pack with meager food and coins. Now the trunk holds rivers of fabric, clothes and purses and jewels of all colors and shapes.

Aditi folds my clothes neatly and piles them into the trunk. "You know you cannot avoid Master Saeed forever, Lynx. And who knows—maybe the fresh mountain air will do you both some good."

I purse my lips. Tomorrow we leave for Amratstan. A tingle of nerves and anticipation flutter from my stomach to my throat—and, like Mouse said, a little bit of optimism, too.

"I hope you're right."

8

Rani

Today is the day.

Morning light scatters across the pavilion outside the palace gates. Amir and I stand with our trunks at our sides, facing Ria, Mother, and Father. Ever the king, Father has smoothed the concern from his brow as he reminds me of how important my journey to Retan is. Though I must halt Amara's sinister plans, I face another task as well, one perhaps equally important: to aid our kingdoms' relationship further and create a political alliance.

"We'll be back soon," I promise Father. Though there is much my father has to atone for, I give him a parting hug, then hold Mother's hands. Ria hovers awkwardly nearby. After one glance, she hugs our parents.

"I'll be fine," Ria assures them.

"Keep Saeed and Aditi safe, too. And Shima, of course," Mother says as my snake familiar glides down the palace steps and through the gates with the grace of a decorated stallion, her scales a blushing ivory. It isn't hard to tell how we both feel, nerves jangling through us, and Shima's scales tell all. My snake familiar and I decided last night that it was best she joined Ria to ensure her magic does not spin out of control again.

A moment later, Saeed joins the group outside. He's wearing a long white kurta that accentuates the white stripes in his hair and shining gold pointed shoes. He's carrying his pack, along with a few fur cloaks. They will need them where they are headed.

Saeed firmly shakes Amir's hand in farewell. While they haven't spent much time together, they are already friendly, even brotherly, with each other. The thought makes me let loose a protracted breath, grateful Saeed hasn't held any ill will against me since breaking off our engagement.

To my surprise and delight, a third figure steps into the light after Saeed, his silver bow glinting.

"You came." I smile at Irfan, already dressed in royal blue: the Sentinels' signature hue and the color of the Amratstanian flag.

"Couldn't miss a trip home," he tells me, silver eyes alight like I've never seen them before. Perhaps he really does want to return to Amratstan, despite his mixed experiences there. I cannot imagine how painful it must have been for him to leave his home behind—even with all the terrible things that occurred there.

"We couldn't, either." Sanya and Jas appear with trunks in hand, the gilded morning light making their eyes sparkle.

"Wait—you're coming?" I ask, jaw slackening.

"Not exactly. We're going home. The Mailan Foothills. I already spoke to Amir about it last night." Sanya smiles at her brother.

"You're returning . . . permanently?" My throat goes dry.

Jas squeezes me in a hug. "We'll return to visit, of course." She strokes my hair, her motherly touch as warm as the Abaian sun. "We left in quite a rush . . . many of my husband's belongings are still there."

I'd nearly forgotten how many years Jas spent in the Hidden Lands, where the Mailan Foothills are located, with Tutor. It was unfair of me to think she'd stay in the palace with the rest of us after our quest to find the Bloodstone was over.

Now, after spending weeks with Jas and Sanya at the palace, my eyes well with tears. I wrap my arms around Jas and Sanya fiercely. "I hope to see you soon." My voice cracks on the final word, and before my resolve can falter, I square my shoulders and turn to my sister.

"Ready?" Ria asks me. I stare at my reflection in my sister's eyes, like looking into a mirror. The early morning sun picks up the deep brown of her irises, making them look almost golden. It seems we have much to learn about the minute differences between us. I can only pray that, once we destroy the stone and defeat Amara, we will have all the time in the world.

I take my sister's warm hand into mine and cross my fingers over my chest. "I am if you are."

The air swelters with salt and sea spray. Father's gold-plated vessel, usually accustomed to transporting luxurious goods like fabrics and wool, now carries two new travelers, as opposite as fire and ice: a would-be queen and a thief boy.

Amir stands far from me, stiff-backed, facing the water. I approach him and settle a hand on his shoulder. He turns, his lips tilting into a crooked smile.

"Feeling okay?" I ask him.

A strong gust of wind makes Amir's kurta billow. He grips the rail with pale-knuckled fingers. "I've never been on a boat," he confesses. "It's . . . strange."

"You're not seasick, are you? The boat ride is hardly longer than several bells. After that we'll be on the horses. Like it used to be."

Like we *used to be*, I think, but I rid myself of the thought. Amir does not yet know of the turmoil I hide, nor the words that Mother spoke to me, pounding through my veins.

Amir chuckles, removing my hand from his shoulder and warming it in his. "That's not what's strange. It's the fact that I used to *dream* of taking a boat out of Abai. And now I am. But for a different reason. Before, it was all about starting over."

"To escape the war." I nod, thinking of Ria's conscription. "The Kaamans will sign the peace treaty, I am sure of it." I have to be. When I am older, my title will be more than princess. My words will carry the weight of a queendom.

"That's not all." Amir shifts closer, his arm brushing mine, sending a cascade of warmth through me. "You seem nervous about Retan. Raja's beard, I am, too."

Nervous is one way to put it.

"How'd you convince your parents to let me tag along?" Amir asks, turning away from the railing and facing me. The breeze cools, but I am certain that is not why I am shivering.

"I didn't have to. They said you would be a good help."

While I'm not lying, Amir's lips frown with uncertainty.

"Have you . . . told them?" He bites his lower lip. "About us?"

"They . . . have seen us." *As friends*, I amend silently. My tongue tastes like the briny, salty ocean. Mother's words fill me to the brim, as if I am the sea itself. *You know what a clever and well-considered political alliance could do for our kingdom, Rani.*

I hadn't dared bring up Amir's name, after that. I imagine telling Mother about Amir at some point, the truth whole and complete. But I don't know if that moment will ever come.

I turn away from him and grip the railing. "My parents are grateful to you. They know how much you helped me on my journey outside the palace. Without you, I never would have found the Bloodstone."

Amir's throat bobs. "I guess that's true." He fiddles with the timepiece hanging around his neck, pulling it out from under his kurta. "But I never would've found my sister again without you. Never would've tried."

The timepiece glints in the sunlight. A keepsake of his father's, held in Jas's possession even after Amir's parents died on their mission to find the stone.

I turn back to him and wrap my hands around his, concealing the timepiece. "I know how much you miss them."

"They once told me stories about Retan. About the mines full of nuggets of gold. The spice routes that traveled all across the sands, up through Abai and right into Kaama. My father visited the mines once, as a child. He dreamed about going back again."

A nostalgic smile touches his lips just as a wave crashes against the side of the boat. I stumble forward, breath knocked loose from my chest. Amir lets go of the timepiece and catches me in his arms. Against him, I breathe in his scent: clove and cinnamon. The world blurs before it comes into sharp focus, and I glance up.

Amir, staring down at me. Amir, the first boy I've ever truly loved.

And I couldn't even tell my parents about him.

Amir's hand travels to the back of my neck, keeping me steady. My breath catches in my throat as I stare at his deep-brown eyes, so full of promise. Of desire.

He leans down, his lips close enough to brush mine. I ache to give in, let myself kiss him again. But a warning bell goes off in my mind and I jerk back, nearly smacking my forehead against his.

Abai's sun.

Amir blinks as I push myself away and smooth down my vestments, surveying the boat as if to look for anyone watching. A habit I've formed over the past two weeks of living with Amir at the palace, fearing a guard might see me. Or worse . . . Mother.

"Something wrong?" Amir touches a finger to his lips.

"No!" I clear my throat. "I mean, I'm not sure if I brushed my teeth again after my morning meal." My throat burns with unspoken words, with a sea of lies.

"Um . . . okay." Amir gulps and hovers by the railing, gently facing the sea. He turns his head once back to me, then glances away as I leave him.

How can I tell Amir the truth? That any love I find is expected to be . . . *clever and well considered.* A match for my kingdom, not for me.

While I believe in my own destiny, and taking fate into my own hands, there always seems to be one more obstacle in the way. Does this love with Amir have an expiration date? Love, according to Mother, is not about feelings—it is about duty. The kind of love Saeed once felt for me.

How hypocritical, I remind myself. Just two moons ago, I was angry at Saeed for not loving me as he should, in a way that *transcended* duty.

Now, I'm the one unable to promise more.

My thoughts churn like the raging sea, and I retreat to my corner until we arrive at the shore.

When Retan comes into view, the land looks like a haze of red. The sun is a brilliant orange orb, casting a deep glow over the scattered villages. Rising like a strong tamarind tree is the palace—or three palaces, I should say. Each a tall sandstone building with sparkling towers, facing each other in the form of a triangle. Domed buildings surround the palaces—the prestigious Retanian Academy.

I gasp at the beauty of it all, and beside me Amir is silent, his mouth open in awe. I remember he has never seen such a thing before, has never even traveled outside of Abai. I take a moment to relish in the sparkle of his eyes, the excitement in his hands as he clutches the boat's side.

I myself have only ever been to one other kingdom: Amratstan, to visit Father's once-close friend King Rohit. And Retan, even at a glance, has a beauty all its own—nothing like Amratstan's icy grandeur.

Amir and I disembark. A man waiting for us at the shore waves a wrinkled hand, wearing a kind, toothy smile very much like Tutor's. I smile warmly back, finding comfort in the familiarity.

"A pleasure to meet you, Princess Rani of Abai." The man bows, and when he rights himself, I notice the crest on his shoulder, pinned to his red-and-gold sleeveless shirt: an eagle soaring over the desert dunes. A common Retanian symbol, of knowledge spreading its wings and taking flight across Retan.

"The pleasure is mine, sir."

"Call me Ranjit. Palace keeper. I'll help you load the horses with the aid of your hand," Ranjit says, nodding toward Amir and gesturing for him to pick up the trunks.

"Hand? Oh." Amir clears his throat before giving a clipped laugh. "No, I'm actually—"

"A dear friend," I cut in for him, smiling at Ranjit. "And he's . . ." I hesitate before tacking on, in a moment of weakness, "a companion of mine. He is a guest as much as I am."

Ranjit makes his apologies quickly and thoroughly, eyes shifting between me and Amir as he takes in the differences between us. And though Amir is friendly as ever as he helps Ranjit load the luggage, he doesn't quite meet my eyes.

While we wait for Ranjit to finish piling our packs into a nearby carriage and preparing the horses, a strained tension sits between us.

I try to focus. I can't forget we're here to learn more about the Bloodstone . . . and how to destroy it. To gain an alliance with this southern kingdom.

As Ria would say, *No pressure.*

Together, we mount our horses and head deeper into Retan.

Retan's capital is like a tiara filled with jewels. Literally. Jhanswa City is shaped like a crown studded with shops and huts, each a halo of color, from deep blues to verdant greens. Peppering the city are the Academy's buildings, just as Tutor taught me, where the scholars reside. They are famed for having saints as ancestors, ones who were believed to have had communications with the Masters themselves. But most beautiful of all are the jutting points of the crown: the three glittering palaces.

The palaces we now stand before.

Ranjit and Amir lug our trunks up the stairs until we stand before the first palace, made of white marble and veined with blue. A long sandstone pathway marks the entrance past the gates. Rows of vibrant green shrubs line the path, and standing attention at the front are guards who flank the building, wearing red robes and holding gold-tinted spears. They each turn as Amir and I pass, then part at our entrance in polished synchronicity.

At my first step inside, I can barely hold in my breath at the beauty of it all.

"Welcome to the Blue Palace," Ranjit says. The interior is entirely made up of hues of blue: a ceiling made of sapphire, rugs threaded with gold and azure, curtains shaded lapis lazuli. My smile widens as I take in the scene. Every servant wears a gold tunic or sash. Some carry plates of sweets, like candied almonds and golden raisins. A servant offers me one as soon as I enter, and I accept, tasting the sticky sweetness of a raisin against my teeth.

"Raja's beard," Amir says after he has tasted one, "these are good." He grabs more from the servant's tray before she leaves.

Ranjit leads us deeper into the palace, pausing at a tearoom.

"Ranjit-ji, if I may ask," Amir says, "where is the queen?" To me, he whispers, "That is who we're supposed to meet with . . . right?" He pops a raisin into his mouth.

"Yes, Amir." Turning to Ranjit, I say, "The Blue Palace is beautiful. We are very excited to meet Queen Meeta."

"Oh, Princess Rani." Ranjit chuckles to himself. "The Blue Palace is only where the queen takes her tea. She'll be at the Gold Palace right now, most likely."

"The queen has a whole palace for *tea*?" Amir whistles in disbelief.

And Ria thought *our* palace was big. I snicker, and though I knew the fact that there are three palaces in Retan, the halls before me look daunting. I'll need a map to get through this place.

Ranjit nods. "Don't worry, I've arranged for you to meet with Dhruv first. He'll help you around the palaces."

"Dhruv?" I wonder.

"Yes, he's—why, there he is!" Ranjit says just as a boy appears, no older than eighteen summers and wearing simple clothes entwined with silver beading. The rope necklace at his throat gleams with what looks like a Retanian firestone I've seen only in textbooks, a gem from one of their famous caves. His mop of hair, black as a jungle crow's needle-sharp feathers, falls into his equally dark eyes. He rubs his slightly crooked nose, as if nervous.

I have that effect on people. Palace hands, maids, even villagers. I've been given names before: *Snake Princess. A girl with fangs for teeth.* I feel a pang at the thought that the rumors may have spread this far.

"Are our guests ready for a tour, Ranjit-ji?" the boy asks, directing a kind smile at the palace keeper. How considerate that the queen already arranged for us to be given a tour by a palace hand.

The older man nods. "I'll let you take it from here, Dhruv." Within moments, he disappears into the blue-veined halls of the palace, taking our luggage with him. The boy perks up, back stick-straight.

He begins, "I hope you both find the Blue Palace comfortable." His eyes bounce between the two of us as he leads us into the nearest corridor. "When we received correspondence from King Natesh, we knew we'd need to offer you both a respectable place during your time here. So, this is where you'll be staying. Only a few palace hands live here in individual chambers, so there will be plenty of room for you each to pick out your suites."

"Suites?" Amir's jaw drops. He takes in the domed ceiling

above us, still in awe of all the extravagance.

Dhruv chuckles warmly before stopping by a large room. When I peer inside, I see a grand table, surrounded by bookcases. "In here are several history books, though you'll find a much larger collection at the Academy—in case the two of you have a thirst for knowledge. I know I always do."

I quirk a smile. His voice is high and polished, contrasting with his simpler attire. I suppose the palace hands here truly do get the same treatment—and education—that the royals do. Perhaps a system that we can introduce back home.

"I am well versed in Retanian culture and traditions," I tell Dhruv respectfully. "Though I have only recently begun studying its history." I chance a step into the room, recalling the pages of the history books I dusted off before our journey. "There are three palaces in Retan to represent the triplet sisters who created the kingdom. *Queendom*," I correct, gazing up at a portrait on the wall. The painted woman sports a glittering crown and intelligent eyes.

"That is Queen Meeta, the current monarch of Retan," Dhruv says. "Our matriarchs are indeed all descended from the triplet queens."

He leads us out of the room full of books, and I catch Amir glancing back in longing. My gut twists when I remember how little he knows of this place, of the small amount of schooling he likely received compared to my private tutors (which I complained about). I gently tug on his hand as we continue the tour.

"What's this?" Amir says, pointing. I didn't even notice the strange small door as we passed—it's nondescript, a pale beige with only a faint outline to differentiate it from the rest of the wall. There's no doorknob, just an empty keyhole shaped like a triangle.

"It's an old passageway," Dhruv explains. "Supposedly. No one's ever been able to open it. Not since the Three Blessed Sisters passed on, Amran rest their souls." He lowers his head in reverence, and I do the same.

"Where does it go?" Amir tries peering into the keyhole. I press a hand to the door, trying to nudge it open, but it won't budge. On it is a symbol of the sun, a triangle painted within the center. Instead, I feel something strange slithering from the concrete and into my fingers, tickling my senses. *Magic.*

"According to legend, it leads to a chamber built by the sisters that exists beneath the three palaces. Some say it's where they studied all kinds of subjects. Others say hidden treasure is buried down there. And *others* . . ."

I raise a brow.

". . . a dungeon that holds a thirty-foot-long snake. You know, for enemies." He winks directly at me.

I cut him with my eyes. "Somehow I doubt that."

"Why?" Dhruv asks playfully. "Dungeons could hold all sorts of creatures."

"Because my snake magic would have sensed a giant serpent by now." I shut my eyes, wishing I could feel Shima beside me.

The smoothness of her scales, the familiarity of our blood bond. It had taken five years for me to master my magic with her—and by master, I mean *just barely grasp*.

"I guess it's a good thing we have a snakespeaker in the palace, then," he says, flitting a smile my way. I return it, and we leave the strange entranceway, turning in to a new hall.

"And here," Dhruv says as we approach a set of silver double doors embossed with a soaring eagle, "is the Blue Palace's kitchen. My favorite place."

"So you work in the kitchen?" I wonder.

"You could say that."

Dhruv leads us inside, and I have to hold in a gasp.

Because the entire far wall is covered in spices like I have never before seen. Warm smells tickle my nose, whisking through the air, and I know Amir can smell them, too, by the pleasant smile that crosses his features.

"Raja's beard," he says.

"Raja's beard is right," I chuckle.

Though I am used to turmeric, fenugreek, garam masala, and other spices, there are some here I've never heard of before. Pomegranate and mango powders, floral spices peppered with citrus. It's all true; Retan is a land of flavors.

"Try this." Dhruv reaches for something on the counter, shaped like a lotus flower, and places it gently on my palm. I take a bite. It's a cake steeped in rose syrup. Crushed bits of pistachio burst in my mouth like fireworks.

"This is *divine*."

Dhruv offers Amir one of the delicious rose cakes. He pops the whole thing in his mouth, eyes widening. He's certainly never had anything like this in Abai.

"If this is what you make every day, I think I'm gonna stay awhile."

Dhruv laughs. "I cannot take all the credit. I'm not the chef."

"You should be," Amir says, mouth full of another cake.

Dhruv blushes. "Well—"

"Prince Dhruv," a voice proclaims from the Blue Palace's kitchen entrance, where an aproned woman bustles inside. "There you are."

Wait. *Prince* Dhruv?

The
Hunt

The Hunt

Sahil

What did I do so wrong, brother, to make my other brethren turn on me?

I starve for something so simple, so natural. Is it wrong to want, to desire? I am one of them, am I not? I am a Master.

It seems being a Master is not enough for me. That should not mean I am a villain.

But every story has one.

Now, as tall as a willow tree and thinned to the bone, I return to a sprawling river that slinks like a snake. This is the Tide Master's domain, but she is not the only one with a connection to these particular waters. I watch my reflection shift in the water, the light of a full moon behind me: furrows crease my brows together, and my flat nose flares. In certain lights, the scales of my skin are visible, but to most, my snakeskin is only seen with a flash of sunlight, like a fish's skin catching the first rays of dawn.

I speak to the river as I would a snake. With one touch the river bends to my will, water rushing forth and dragging itself back. Ripples scorch my fingers as I let my magic seep into the water. Its waters hiss back, spraying me with sea salt. A few moments later, the water parts, revealing a stairwell made of earth and salt. I descend into the river, water surrounding me like a whirlpool but never touching my skin, and enter my home.

It is not much—an underground hideaway for myself and a few others. But it is mine.

"Already back?" Raya says, gazing at me with eyes green as the weeds caressing the riverbed. "I thought you were traveling."

"I do not wish to speak to Preethi today," I sigh. I fall into a meditative pose right there in the middle of the Snake River, where the pull of my magic and the moon is the strongest. Small sea snakes slip past me in greeting, fangs stained with blood, before they return to the shadows behind Raya. They always do like her more than Ruhanya.

I give myself to the water, to the shape of the river, but never dare ask myself why the river and myself are practically kin, bound together as one.

"It would be good for you to speak to the other Masters," Raya continues, coming to my side and resting a hand on my shoulder.

"As if any other Master would listen to me," I scoff, turning away. It does not matter that I have little idea why my brethren see me in such a way. They scorn and shirk me with no need for reason.

"Preethi is kind," Raya reminds me. "Kinder than the others."

"No kinder than the brother I lost."

We are both silent after that. Silent with rage, sorrow. Silent with *thoughts of an unlived life, of someone lost too soon.*

They were afraid of you, brother. Of your power.

So they Unmade you.

But there are fragments of you that still exist. A Master can never truly be gone. I felt your magic myself, the moment Amran took you away. That day, even the clouds gathered to see you off. Rain spat down, an offering of goodbye. I felt the earth rumble as you disappeared, but your magic remained, broken into pieces and scattered across the continent.

Even still, a piece of you resides in my daughter—a piece of your soul magic lodged within her.

A part of you lives on.

She hasn't forgotten you, either. I don't bring you up often anymore, but Raya still plays your favorite game. The one you played together. Making wishes on stars is child's play, I thought at first, but you, too, were born as a child instead of a full-grown Master like the rest of us. Sometimes I forget that simple fact, just as easily as I'm beginning to forget the shape of your chin, nose, and eyes.

At Raya's anger, a whorl of sea snakes rises from the dust of the sandy ground. The snakes hiss and jeer, echoing the storm of emotions in my chest. A blush rises to Raya's cheeks at the exertion of her power, pulling forth so many sea snakes from the riverbed. A power I recognized from her birth—one full of strength and might, even more powerful than . . .

"Where is Ruhanya?"

"Right here," a voice answers. She enters, her hair dark as night *like mine, her skin a tawny flush of deep brown, her eyes an echo of my own.*

Wide and reptilian, full of a thousand questions and never enough answers.

Raya goes to Ruhanya's side at once, two opposites yet irrevocably linked.

Unlike the other Masters, I was blessed by Amran with more than one First Descendant. And yet that seems to only ostracize me more from the others.

Let them fester in their envy.

"I have made up my mind," I say, rising to meet them. "I wish for a new home. Something I can call my own." Something the other Masters can never know of—a place where I can be free from them entirely.

"Where, Father?"

I gaze at the ground. I don't know where we will find a home where we are not ridiculed and scorned. But it must be somewhere far away from this place, this river, where I have hidden for so long.

"Then we will find one," Raya says, placing her hand on my chest. Ruhanya joins her, watching as our power coalesces into blinding light, bright as the moon above our river abode.

I stare down, eyes hardened. My blood does not respond in kind, nor does it pump the way my daughters' do. My twins.

Even the Masters' hearts flutter, beat, and bruise.

Mine is nowhere to be found.

9

Ria

"Come, Ria," a voice tells me. *"Come."*

I obey, a tall, flickering candle balancing on a plate in my palm. I don't waver. I step, once, twice, toward the voice. I head deeper into the narrow corridor of the boat, wooden floors creaking beneath me. Each room I pass is quiet, the passengers of the boat fast asleep, unlike me. A door at the end of the hall emits a fiery glow, and I sense a strong presence. As thick as fur, slippery as snakeskin, and familiar as a friend.

Yet every hair on my body stands on end.

"I'm coming," I tell the voice, but I don't hear myself. All I see is that door before me, locked, craving to be opened. I reach out a hand holding a rusted key, imagining myself opening the door, *finding* the person beyond it. . . .

"I can teach you so much. Come . . ."

The voice is so compelling, like sweet honey. Only one thought runs through my mind: *I want to meet this presence burning inside my head, I have to—*

"You're smart, Ria," a woman's voice says.

I spin to face her. She's approaching me, face shadowed, but I swear her feet aren't touching the ground. "Already on the way to Amratstan. You know about the talismans, too, hmm? Perhaps you think you can stop me from finding them."

My breath is caught in my throat. I can't think; my brain is fuzzy and the door behind me beckons. I want to turn back. I want to see who that first voice belongs to—

"Has Aditi brought me my roses?" Amara asks me sweetly. "I need my roses," she continues, until she comes into sharp focus.

I gasp—her face is a picture of horror. One side of her nose has flattened. Her eyes flash crimson. As she speaks, blood drips from her lips. *"I need my roses."*

My eyes fly open. I'm greeted by the lulling rock of the boat beneath me, the smell of the briny sea air even from within my cabin. The air is damp and humid, and sweat clings to my skin.

I'd seen that strange door again, the one with the lock begging for a key. The same one I'd imagined in my head during the celebration. What does it mean?

Every time I blink, I see those red eyes. *No*, I think. This nightmare wasn't like the others. This one was hazy and hypnotizing, less . . . *real.*

Not to mention Amara has never spoken to me directly in a dream before. I shudder, running my fingers up and down my arms to calm my nerves, but instead I feel like a frayed rope, my thoughts scattered like pebbles.

You know about the talismans, too.

So she really is looking for all the talismans. Somehow, she's aware that we're onto her. But if she's taunting me this way, it means we're on the right track. We need to figure out where the talismans are and stop Amara from destroying Kaama. Fast.

I want to collapse back onto the bed, erase that strange dream. But I already know no slumber will return for me tonight.

I lift myself from my cot and tug on a pair of Rani's silken slippers. Padding out into the corridor, I make my way to the deck. Even this *boat* feels fit for a princess, the hull and interior corridor walls each decorated with Abai's crest—a snake slithering up to a crown. Red velvet curtains warm up the space. Gold-paneled walls make up the vessel, and even my own cabin is decorated up and down in royal purples to mimic my and Rani's bedrooms back in the palace. All of a sudden, it's too much, and claustrophobia has me hurrying up the stairs.

Once I reach the deck, the night sky greets me. I breathe in the cool, salty sea air. I'm a girl made for land, not the sea—though I can remember a time when ocean spray and seawater were all I ever dreamed of, back when I thieved with Amir. Freedom, clasped between the ocean and the sky. The sparkling navy-blue waters of the Satluj Sea, sprawled out before me, is so big I can barely take it all in—but its beauty doesn't touch me now. The seafoam is tinged pink, reflecting the changing moon. I clutch my churning stomach, nerves flooding through me.

I approach the railing and grip the wood tightly beneath until my knuckles turn pale.

The mysterious voice echoes deep in my skull. *"I can teach you so much. . . ."* Like it wanted to tell me something. A secret only the two of us could share.

"Raja's beard," I mutter to myself. My stomach roils from the little food I ate for dinner, mostly dried apricots. The fruit was tasty, reminding me of nights where we had so little to eat on the streets of Abai, clinging to pocketfuls of stolen nuts and seeds to get by. Back then, dried mangoes and apricots were a treat.

Part of me is still that old Ria. I cling to that, ridding myself of all thoughts of Amara.

"Can't sleep?"

I startle, nearly jolting out of my skin before I see him. Saeed stands beside me, dressed in a sleeveless nightshirt and billowing trousers. He's barefoot, I notice.

"You neither, huh?" I say, peeling my gaze away from his muscled arms.

"It wasn't a bad dream, if that's what you're thinking," he says, joining me at the front of the boat. He stares out at the water, the sparkles reflecting off the sea shining in his hazel eyes. He turns to me. "I hope you weren't having a . . . nightmare?"

I purse my lips. Part of me wishes to confide in him; the other part still belongs to a distrustful thief. I close my eyes, but I can still feel his gaze burning into mine.

"How did you know I was having a nightmare?"

"I know a lot about dreams, remember? You can tell me more," he says, inviting me to speak. But my throat closes up and I look away from him and back toward the dark sea surrounding us.

After a moment of silence, he thins his lips. "Then again, I would choose to forget every nightmare I've had of Mother if I had the chance. Especially lately. There's something wrong with her. Something . . . different."

Saeed runs a hand through his hair, a few whitened locks lit by the stars in the sky. "I don't know about you, but I've never been good with boats. It's no wonder we're both having trouble sleeping."

I let out an incomprehensible noise. "You're afraid of boats?"

Saeed rubs the back of his neck, gazing downward. "I mean . . ." I've never seen him, such a princely gentleman, look so flustered. "I got terribly seasick as a child. The only person to comfort me was—"

He cuts himself short, but I can guess the rest. "Your mother."

At those words, his startling eyes find mine. I feel transparent as a phantom, as if he can see right through me. Right into my nightmares, where Amara haunts me.

"Ria," he says, "I have something for you. I meant to give it to you earlier, but . . ."

But I've been avoiding you on this boat, I want to fill in.

"Follow me," he says. Saeed doesn't give me a chance to respond. He turns and I do as he commands, heading deep into the belly of the boat.

* * *

Saeed's cabin is suited for a king, decorated lavishly in reds and purples. I can't help but find it fitting, a reflection of the two sides of Saeed—Abaian and Kaaman. The whole room seems to have an air of royalty, and even after weeks of palace life, this kind of lifestyle still surprises me.

I guess weeks of royal living don't erase the moons after moons spent in slums and on the streets.

I shut the cabin door gently behind me and then take a seat on a stool perched next to a furnished wooden desk. An oil lamp next to me casts eerie shadows on the golden walls.

As Saeed rummages through his pack, I say, "I'm glad we're finally on our way to Amratstan." *Raja's beard.* I want to smack my own head. Small talk isn't really a thief's strong suit.

But Saeed is nothing if not cordial, and he responds in kind. "The weather will be a refreshing change."

"Exactly," I say. "I despise the heat of high summer."

"Well, you won't find any of that in Amratstan. Their palace is carved out of ice," Saeed reveals, glancing back at me. At my gawking, he smiles. "So, I brought you this."

He sweeps a furred cloak from his pack, like a stage magician pulling rupees out of a hat.

My eyebrows rise as I lift myself from my seat. I take the cloak into my hands, a brilliant, plum-colored cloak with diamond patterning. A haze fills my mind when I bring the cloak to my nose and breathe in Saeed's sandalwood scent.

"For the Amratstanian chill," he says. "I brought some for Irfan and Aditi, too. I'll give those to them soon, I just . . . wanted to give you yours in person."

I hide a smile at the gift. "You thought of me? Us?" I tack on too fast. A flush steals over my face—just because I can't get him out of my head doesn't mean he's the same.

"It got lonely on my trip," he explains. "I was glad to be back at the palace, even if only for a day. But it seems we won't have a respite for a while yet."

"Magic doesn't take a break," I mumble bitterly to myself.

I don't want him to pull away, but he does, leaving the cloak in my hands so he can fiddle with a few stray papers on his desk—maps of Amratstan, given to each member of the crew by Captain Jai this morning. I gather my courage. "You were right, you know. About the nightmare."

Curiosity piques in his gaze as he turns back to me. "How so?"

I sidestep him and drop the fur-lined cloak onto the wide, red-linen bed. "Your mother seems to know we're in a race after the talismans, too." I describe what I dreamed, though I'm careful to leave out the monstrous apparition I saw—Amara's face bloodied. I'm loath to hurt Saeed further, even just as the messenger.

Saeed's skin pales. "We knew she was headed to the White Mountains . . . which means she's likely searching for the Earth and Sky Master's talismans. Those Masters' descendants made the land of Amratstan their home. The Amratstanian royalty are descendants of the Earth Master himself. As for the Tide Master . . ."

"Go on," I prod him, though it looks like he doesn't want to.

"Mother would often speak of the talismans," he says. "Though she never once told me the cuffs on her arms were the Memory Master's, I had my suspicions of why she kept them so close. I asked her questions, and I don't think she liked that."

"What kind of questions?"

Saeed sighs. "All about the talismans. She didn't like to answer me. I myself never taught Rani about the talismans because so many of them have vanished or . . . been hidden. Outside of the raja's scepter, of course. The Tide Master's sword is one such lost talisman." His voice turns grim. "A sword believed to be able to cut through any element. Legend has it, it was washed away in a mystical river somewhere in Pania."

"But Pania's a wasteland now," I say, remembering what children in the orphanage used to say. That the kingdom had been mysteriously and wholly destroyed. There's no one alive to truly tell the tale of what turned Pania into a barren, inhospitable land.

"Indeed. But some say the sword is always drawn to water, even after the Tide Master disappeared. The last time it was seen was somewhere deep in a river in Pania, and this river ends in Amratstan's mountains. If the legend is true, the sword could have been swept to the North after all these years."

"And do *you* believe the legends?" I ask playfully. Legends and stories were my favorite growing up. But as I've learned firsthand, that doesn't mean they're all to be believed.

Saeed smirks. "It seems foolish to doubt any of these myths.

So many of them have been proven true these past few months. There's always more to magic than meets the eye," he says, voice low as he steps closer to me. "And I would've never discovered my own magic without you, Ria. . . ." He trails off, as if battling what to say next.

My cheeks warm. "You know, I've never told anyone this, but I used to sleep like a baby on the streets. Getting through the days was the real struggle. So having nightmares is . . . different. New. I won't lie; they scare me. So much in my life has changed recently. I'm still not sure who I'm supposed to be. I'm not even sure who I really am, on the inside."

He comes even closer now, stopping a few breaths away. "You're Ria. No one else."

"Are you sure? For a good long time, you believed I was Rani," I point out.

He smiles. "And I will never judge you for your deception. Your switch with Rani was . . . brave. And to be honest, I'm grateful you switched. If you hadn't, I never would have met you."

Tears spring to my eyes at his statement. I take in his soft gaze, the deep flecks of gold in his eyes, the strength of his chin and the cut of his jaw, proudly bearded and even a little roughened up after his trip.

"I'm grateful you found a place in the palace, with your sister at your side," he continues, noticing me staring. "A home."

Home. "And you? Do you still think of the palace as home?"

His gaze softens. "Yes."

My fingers suddenly itch to do something—steal a jewel, sweep away an apple from a pile of fruit before a crowd of unassuming villagers. Thieve. Instead of standing on this precipice—staring into Saeed's eyes and feeling myself fall further.

"I was wondering—" I begin.

At the same time, he says, "Ria, I'm—"

We both stop and laugh. When we're finished, I shiver, despite being indoors.

"Here," Saeed says, stepping behind me and taking the fur cloak from the bed. As he places it around my shoulders, his breath feathers my ear. I crane my neck so I can look at him, entranced by his hazel-eyed gaze. Do I want him to move closer? I shiver again under his warmth, and he takes that as a sign to bundle me up further, pushing the cloak tightly around me.

"You'll get cold, too," I warn him as he moves to stand before me.

"Well, I've got a little more muscle than you do to keep me warm."

"Oh, really?" I can hear the teasing lilt to his voice, but it doesn't stop me from blushing. I notice his lips are pale; he *is* cold. He just won't admit it.

"You're stubborn, Saeed."

"That's what they call me. *Stubborn Saeed.* The best tutor this side of the Var River. I needed all the stubbornness I could summon to teach you . . . and Rani."

I giggle against the fur of the cloak. It's been so long since I've laughed like this with him . . . since before we needed to worry about Amara, before we knew her plan to become the Soul Master.

The destruction she'll cause from the imbalance of magic.

The smile falls from my lips. "What do you think your mother will do after she brings your father back? Do you think her magic will—"

Before I can finish, Saeed glances down, his curls brushing against my cheek. My breath halts, and as he glances up his breath is against mine. I gasp as his gaze turns deep, thick as honey. He inches closer, examining my features, the differences between Rani and me, until his gaze falls to my lips.

My stomach warms. My head bends closer—our noses are nearly touching—

"No," he says, almost to himself, stepping back.

"No?" I echo, voice squeaky. My heart thumps in my chest.

Saeed clears his throat. "I meant no, she won't bring my father back. We'll stop her before she can, and before she can become—" He doesn't say *the Soul Master*, like he doesn't truly want to acknowledge it. "We've no clue how far her plans truly stretch, or why my mother wants all the talismans. But we'll make sure she doesn't find them."

I nod curtly, my lips cold from the chilled air and the new-found space between Saeed and me. "Do you wish you could see him again? Your father?"

Saeed's gaze grows cold. "I didn't really know him, but from my mother's stories he was a great man. Besides, it does not matter what I want; it's the future of this—*your*—kingdom that matters,

Ria." My name on his lips would have sounded like a sweet caress, if not for his tone. A low one, full of questions and unknown pain.

My brows crease. I'm lucky I got to see, hear, *speak* to Mama Anita one last time, many weeks ago at the palace.

And I know what Saeed is hiding from me. He misses his mother and wants to see his father again. Just as I'd hoped to see Mama Anita.

I lick my lips. "Right," I say. "*My* kingdom." Which means I need to get clearheaded already, stop thinking about Saeed and *focus*. I step back, keeping a safe distance between us. Maybe I shouldn't be here right now. Maybe I shouldn't have left my cabin in the first place.

I fake a yawn and offer a poor excuse for a good night. I should be preparing for our arrival in Amratstan tomorrow. After all, we have no clue what else might lie ahead.

10
Rani

Dhruv.

Prince Dhruv of Retan.

How could I have been so fooled by this boy? He's Queen Meeta's *son*. Mother and Father did mention the prince to me once many moons ago; how could I have forgotten his name?

"You . . . you never told us you were a royal," I stutter as I turn, watching the aproned woman approach. She is a petite woman with graying hair, and she carries a tray full of lotus-shaped rose cakes.

"You tricked me," Amir says, though he sounds more enthused by Dhruv's mischievous nature than deterred. Meanwhile, I find myself cursing under my breath. How had I thought this boy a simple palace hand? He never said so. Ranjit hadn't called him Prince Dhruv like the cook had—right?

"I see you're already eating tonight's desserts." The cook chuckles, trotting toward Dhruv and patting his cheek the way a mother would her son's. "I told you—taste testing once a week *only*."

"But, Siva Auntie," he fake-complains, leaning into her touch, "I couldn't turn our guests away from your famous rose milk cakes."

She tuts. "Is that so? You ate the entire stash of pistachios last night. I had to order more from the market!" She raises her hands and huffs. "Not to mention all those cherries we pitted last week, only—"

"For me to eat them?" Dhruv shrugs. "It's hard to resist a midnight snack."

Siva *tsks*, turning her face serious. "You know our crops aren't faring so well. You must be more careful." I barely have a moment to digest her words when Siva finally turns to us. "Ah, you must be the visitors." She puts down her tray, bows at both of us, then skirts the counter to touch the floor at our feet.

"That isn't necessary," Amir says after a soft laugh, helping the older woman up and bending to touch the floor at her feet instead. I follow in kind.

"I'm no dignitary," Amir clarifies, "just traveling with Princess Rani."

Siva raises her gray brows. "Oh?" Her skin wrinkles, and she looks unsure of how to regard him. "Well. You two look like you've had a long journey! Don't tell me Prince Dhruv was taking you on another one of his tours. He loves to joke around with visitors."

"He does," I say dryly, eyeing him, "doesn't he?"

His eyes sparkle when his gaze locks on mine, and I ignore the flush growing on my cheeks. I've been played, and by a prince no less. How embarrassing.

"I was just going to take them to the suites so they could get ready for tonight," Dhruv explains, looking sheepish at Siva's half-hearted scowl.

Siva flours the counter, nodding all the while. "I have lots of food to prepare. You're all in for a treat!"

"What's tonight?" Amir and I ask simultaneously, but I can't find it in me to look at him right now, while I'm still flushed from Prince Dhruv's ruse.

"Just a little something to welcome the famed Princess Rani," Dhruv explains. "My mother's request. A party will be held at the Gold Palace." He leans in close to me and Amir and adds with a wink, "The Saffron Palace was overbooked."

I laugh, though my heart isn't in it. The prince's presence has me entirely rattled, and I'm usually not one to be stunned so easily.

"Oh, sands," the woman curses, "you look pale, dear princess! She needs sleep."

I paste a smile on my face. "Just a little tired. Lead the way to the suites, *Prince* Dhruv?" I scold myself silently. I'll need to be smarter than this if I'm going to present myself—and Abai—as an ally for this kingdom.

He nods, his hair sweeping before his eyes in a princely manner I hadn't noticed before. His brown skin shines in the bright sky-lights dotted throughout the ceiling of the Blue Palace as he takes us to the suites. I scowl at his back the entire time. I don't enjoy being played for a fool, though Amir doesn't seem to notice the flush of embarrassment heating my cheeks.

Once Dhruv drops us off by the large hall of suites, I bow as politely as I can and take the nearest suite. Amir settles in the suite across from mine. Before I can close the door, I catch sight of Prince Dhruv lingering bashfully outside my suite. His eyes flicker up to mine, a question burning inside them.

My heart hitches in my chest and I close the door too quickly. I pull away from the sapphire door handle as if it's a poker touched by fire. Abai's sun, why am I so riled up by him?

I don't let myself dwell on that maddening prince; I have to prepare for the party tonight—and my first presentation to the kingdom of Retan.

But only minutes later, a knock sounds. I rise from the soft bed and swing the door open, revealing the palace keeper who introduced us to the prince.

"Ranjit-ji," I breathe, relieved. For some reason, I thought the prince of Retan would be back to play another joke.

"I just came to check in. I hope you had a good tour. Dhruv wasn't too much trouble, was he?" Ranjit's eyes sparkle with mischief.

"Trouble? No. But surprising . . ."

"Ah." Ranjit chuckles. "Pretending to be a hand. It's his favorite joke. He'd be a street jester in another life if he weren't a prince."

"I suppose so." I think of the ease with which I laugh with Amir. Perhaps Dhruv isn't so different from him, then.

"If you don't mind, I must prepare for tonight."

"Of course. The queen asked me to bring you this, before the party." Ranjit pulls something from behind his back—a beautiful golden notebook.

"This is too kind."

"A gift to welcome you. Now, I'll let you get ready." Ranjit turns on his heel, leaving me truly alone for the first time today.

I am not ready.

My hair feels limp, my skin still flushed red from the hot bath. The tub was filled with steaming water and sprinkled with rose petals, already set for me at my arrival. But I couldn't fully enjoy it—not while my mind whirled with thoughts.

I face a night ahead of me that could determine not only the fate of my kingdom—but of the world. I'm used to responsibility, but I had hoped not to be in charge of saving the world again. At least, not so soon.

I shudder out a breath and return to my sapphire-laden bedroom. I quickly wrap a gold-speckled sari over my frame—after all, we are celebrating at the Gold Palace tonight, and I want to make a good first impression. I take a look in the mirror.

Staring back at me is the princess of Abai. But she's also a princess lost in an ocean of confusion. I sweep my hair into a plait, forcing it to look presentable, and begin to exit the suite. But I pause, taking a closer look at the notebook Ranjit gave me, and quickly flip it open. On the first page, I inscribe a checklist of all the talismans, most of which I learned about from Tutor. I cross out those that have already been found by Amara:

Earth Master—map

~~Snake Master—scepter~~

Sky Master—unknown

~~Memory Master—cuffs~~

Fire Master—compass

Tide Master—sword

The only one I'm unsure of is the Sky Master's talisman—information on it has been lost to time, with a million theories, each wilder than the next. At least we are in the right place to get to the truth. The scholars here will have the answer—if we can find the right one to ask.

I close the notebook, mind spinning, and open the door to my chamber. There, I find someone's back facing mine, as though guarding the entrance to my room.

"A personal guard?" I wonder as the man turns around. No—not a guard.

It's Amir, dressed in finery that matches mine.

My heart backflips. "Amir," I say, breathless. "You're ready?"

He grins sideways, ever a thief. "As I can be." He leans in close to me and I freeze as he plants a kiss on my forehead. My eyes dart around the hall. Has anyone seen?

When he notices how stiff I am, he stops. "Something wrong?"

The last thing I need are Retanians gossiping about me the night of my arrival. "We—we are going to be late," I say too quickly, heading out of the room, but he catches my arm before I can get far.

"Forgot those?" He nods at my jewelry-strewn bed.

"Abai's sun."

I quickly slip on the earrings and bangles and return to Amir. He's wearing a sneaky grin.

"What?" I ask him.

"It's not like you to forget *jewelry*," Amir drawls. I force a shrug.

"The party is going to be . . . a lot. I don't want to make any foolish mistakes." I think of the tenuous relationship between Abai and Retan, the political alliance Mother and Father wish for me to forge during my stay.

"Personally? I can't wait for the food. I mean, isn't that the best part of every party?"

I snicker. "I suppose that *is* the one thing you can always look forward to."

"Shall we, Princess?" Amir raises a brow and holds out his arm. I clasp my hands around it.

It is time to introduce ourselves to Retan.

If Jhanswa City is a sky, the Gold Palace is its brightest star.

The outside is lit by sconces, and the whole place is illuminated like a giant dome of wonder, made of gold filigree and arched entranceways the color of burnished copper. It sits between the Blue Palace to its far right, slightly smaller in size, and the Saffron Palace, an orange-red and narrow building, sitting to its left. Even the hewn-stone Academy is lit, as if it knows a party is about to begin.

One just for me.

We travel up the path swollen with bejewelled guests and servers. "Date fritters?" someone asks, dressed in a beautiful ivory suit and holding a tray of delectable golden puffs.

"Don't mind if I do," Amir says, taking one for him and me each. I taste the sweet and sticky fruit, letting it melt on my tongue. A pleasant note of fennel lingers in my mouth.

"*That* was heavenly," Amir says after he's finished, wiping his hands on his kurta.

I slap his hands away from his precious clothing. "Amir! You'll get crumbs all over your clothes!"

He laughs while I brush him off, my fingers trembling with nerves. What he doesn't realize is how important tonight is—how much I want the queen to take me seriously. But that thought melts away when I look up, realizing how close we're standing, our noses nearly touching. I clear my throat and step back.

We make our way to the palace entrance, where more red-robed guards stand, though they look relaxed, some even smiling. It's so unlike the Charts' stoic faces—soldiers miserable under my father's iron-fisted rule for so many years.

I'm holding Amir's arm like it's a lifeline when one of the guards steps in front of us. "Apologies, Princess Rani, but your hand is not allowed inside the main ballroom."

"Oh," I say while Amir blanches, "he isn't—"

"You may use the side entrance," the guard says to Amir, pointing at a space where a cluster of hands stand.

Amir's throat bobs. My veins light with ire, and immediately my snake magic surges forth like a weapon. *Enough.* I won't let Amir be confused with a hand again.

I let my voice curl around the guard, lulling him with every word. "I'm afraid you're mistaken. My *friend* isn't a servant. And you shall let him in, or—"

Just when I'm about to say something foul to the guard, a voice calls out, "There you are!"

My connection to my magic breaks. The guard looks a bit befuddled, like the magic only worked halfway. I suppose I'm a bit tired from our trip.

I whirl just as Prince Dhruv arrives behind us. If Dhruv's clothes looked simple earlier, he is now fully decked out like a future raja. He wears a sleeveless top that reaches mid-thigh, gold-threaded and bright as the sun. Underneath, his alabaster pants are veined with gold, matching the exterior of the palace. His hair is like black silk, falling in subtle waves over his forehead.

"Retan's got style," Amir comments, eyeing Dhruv. Indeed—the royals have exquisite tailors. Perhaps even better than the ones we have in Abai.

"Pleasure, Princess Rani," he says, taking my hand and kissing the back of it. Amir stiffens next to me, but Dhruv doesn't notice, instead acknowledging Amir warmly with a tilt of his head. "Glad to see you again, my friend."

"Prince Dhruv," the guard welcomes him, bowing, "I was just telling Princess Rani how—"

"How all guests are welcome inside the Gold Palace?" he says, his eyes never leaving mine. "Come inside, please."

Amir and I follow behind Prince Dhruv, ignoring the guard's stare.

My stomach flutters as we step inside, and I have to keep my jaw from dropping. The Gold Palace is alive with color: the richest red drapes, the brightest orange saris, the gilded golden walls and dripping silvered chandeliers. Directly ahead of us is a grand lobby, where people dance in graceful swirls and hold glasses of honey-colored spirits. I swear even Abai's fireworks couldn't compare to Retan's palaces.

I think of what Mother and Father told me. This is our chance to heal the broken bonds between Retan and Abai, and rekindle our once-prosperous trade. But more than that, it's a chance for me, the future queen of Abai, to finally make amends and care for my people.

I can't fail them.

"Amir, Princess Rani," Dhruv says, turning to us, "I hope you're finding the Blue Palace comfortable?"

"More than," Amir admits, though he still looks slightly off-balance from the guard's comment. "And the food here is much better than the scraps I used to eat," he adds with a forced laugh, trying to lighten the mood.

"Scraps?" Dhruv echoes, confused. I see Amir's eyes widen as he realizes his mistake, and my heart thumps.

I'm quite certain Mother didn't tell Queen Meeta of Amir's former status as a street rat.

"You know what," Amir says, laughing with a strangely high

tone, "I just realized I should be"—he points toward the side entrance where a group of hands remain—"outside. Getting more appetizers."

Dhruv opens his mouth as if to point out the plentiful food inside the palace, but Amir has already offered me a poor excuse for a smile and made his way outside. Too quickly, he's gone, leaving me and Dhruv alone. The presence of the prince next to me sets my nerves on edge.

"Your . . . friend," Dhruv begins, jutting his chin to the space where Amir was once standing.

I pause, hesitating on what is my story to tell. "He isn't used to these kinds of parties," I offer eventually. "Or extravagance, for that matter." My stomach churns. I understand why Amir fled, but selfishly, I wish he'd stayed. I don't want to be alone out here.

"I hope he knows that he is just as welcome here as you are, Princess Rani." Dhruv tips up a half smile, and my frayed nerves ease.

"You are too kind, Prince Dhruv."

"And *you* are one of a kind, Princess Rani."

I can feel my cheeks blushing, and I glance away. Was that a joke? Does he know about the recent discovery of my twin? Or am I simply overanalyzing everything?

The hustle and bustle of the party blurs. I look away, stomach roiling. "It's quite hot in here. Is there a place I could . . . freshen up?"

He nods. "The last corridor on the right."

I thank him and pull away, heading for the corridor. When I'm sure he isn't looking, I turn back and rush toward the exit where Amir left. Once outside, I am assaulted by the heat of Retan, even at night. I pass a group of hands, searching for Amir, and enter a thick copse of neem trees. I lean against one with relief, safely tucked away from the boisterous noise of the party.

"Freshen up, huh?" Amir says, and I jump, turning to see him approaching me. He echoes my position, leaning back against the bark. "I need to teach you how to get better at lying."

"How did you hear me?"

"I'm good at lipreading."

"Oh?" I tease, releasing my anxious thoughts and stepping closer to him, eager to forget the pressures of the party. "What else are you good at?"

I expect him to smile, but he does nothing of the sort. "Clearly, I'm no prince." He jerks his head toward the side entrance.

"I don't want a prince," I say, voice strained, Prince Dhruv's crooked smile flashing through my mind.

Silence. Amir loosens his shoulders. "I'm kidding," he says, stepping toward me and brushing a few stray locks of hair out of my face. He keeps his hand there, planted against my cheek, as if sensing the confusion and questions simmering within me.

"Ever since we got here, you've been acting strange," he murmurs. "Tell me you two didn't switch again and I'm standing in front of Ria. Because that would be *really*—"

"We wouldn't switch on you again. But . . ." I sigh. "There's something I've been meaning to tell you. I never spoke to my mother about us. I lied to you, and I'm so, so sorry." My voice breaks. "Will you forgive me?"

Amir flushes, taking my hands in his. "There's nothing to forgive, Rani. If you aren't ready to tell the queen, you should've just told me. I won't pressure you. I don't want to rush this."

This. I know he won't pressure me; he never has. It's my own mind that's creating a mess, a jumble of knots threatening to unspool.

Amir clears his throat, looking down as he scuffs his shoes against the dirt. "You aren't embarrassed by me, are you? When I said I used to eat scraps . . . I'll admit, I was flustered by the prince's response. But . . . Rani, I don't care who knows I've been a thief. I'm proud of who I've become." He gulps. "I just never want to embarrass you."

The statement hangs in the air, uninterrupted, before a burst of cheers swallows all sound. I glance at the side entrance, where I spot the loud party guests enjoying the sight of their prince. Dhruv swaggers through the room, kissing and shaking hands, obviously used to all the attention. Strange. In Abai, I rarely went out, kept to myself. People didn't even know what I looked like. Here, in Retan, it's like the royals are part of their people.

I turn back to Amir. "I could never feel embarrassed by you. I just don't want to see people treat you differently because of your past."

The side of his mouth quirks up. *"You're* trying to protect *me?"*

"You stayed with Ria for moons, no food, no coin, no anything. I'm just trying to make sure you never end up there again."

"You think I won't stay at the palace?"

"Do you want to?" I breathe. "Your sister is headed back to the Foothills. With Jas. She's like a mother to you both." And a mother to me, too. My last connection to Tutor.

"She is. But—I have plenty to stay for at the palace, too." He leans into me and I into him. One brush of his lips is all I want, one taste to forget everything. But unexpectedly, he pulls something from behind his back and places it in the space between us. A flower.

"Where did you—" I glimpse a bush of night-blooming jasmine to my left and muffle a laugh.

"In honor of a new start. Will you accept this flower?" Amir asks with a flourish, bowing. It doesn't matter to him that I didn't admit I was proud of him. I *am* proud, and, Amran willing, maybe I will find the strength to tell him that. But something about this place, this new queendom, makes me pause. Not everyone sees Amir as I do. And I need to make the perfect impression, for the sake of my family and my people.

I pluck the flower from Amir's fingers just as he whispers, "We have company."

I whirl to my right, finding a woman in a bright-orange sari turning the corner.

Abai's sun. What if this person knows I'm Princess Rani of

Abai? I cannot have rumors starting here, too—rumors of me kissing the boy I traveled with.

The woman's brown hair falls in long waves to her waist, and her face is heart-shaped like mine. She is years older than I, if the small grays in her hair indicate anything, but her deep-brown skin gives off a youthful glow. Her sari matches the Retanian style, raw silk fastened with a belt made of delicate marigolds.

I gasp when I recognize her face from the portrait in the Blue Palace.

"Queen Meeta," I nearly trip over my words, bowing. "I had no idea—"

"Greetings," she says, bowing in kind. I silently curse. I could play off the closeness between me and Amir, but Queen Meeta is too smart for that. She's had to be. A queen for thirty years; a queen ruling a land of people without war, without struggle, even as they are surrounded by it.

"Welcome to the party. I presume that you are the princess I've been hearing all about."

"Yes. Princess Rani," I reveal, stepping closer to her. "And this is—"

"Amir Bhatt." Amir introduces himself, bowing low with reverence. The queen raises a brow at the interruption. I bite my lip. A regent should never be cut off like that. Especially not by a—

Commoner, my brain insists. *You were thinking Amir is a commoner.*

With a quick squeeze of my palm, Amir says, "I'll be off, then.

The Blue Palace is supposed to have a luxurious sauna," he whispers under his breath.

Another excuse, I can tell. Even though there's a hint of a joke in his smile, I know he feels the tension he's created. But once again, I'm all alone, under pressure to perform flawlessly. When he's gone, the queen's eyes settle on mine.

"I read your father's correspondence." Her lips frown, like she's bitten right into a sour lemon. "The raja has told me all about this . . . prophecy. It seemed quite urgent. Abaian royals have not set foot in Retan for many years."

"And we apologize for that," I say. "It was a mistake to cut ties for so long. Our lands are connected, and so are we."

"Are we?" Queen Meeta counters. I expect her tone to sound cold, like mine once was. *Princess Rani. The Snake Princess.* Instead, Queen Meeta just sounds curious. "Retanians do not condone war."

"The Hundred-Year Truce is over," I confirm. "But that does not mean we cannot renew peace."

"Spoken like a true Retanian." Queen Meeta chuckles, and just like that the tension splits. Still, she is clearly not one to let the topic go. "But war's effects last long after peace has been achieved. Retanians have seen how the Creator's ire changed the land even after King Amrit and King Rahul created their truce a century ago."

Queen Meeta fixes me with a suddenly sharp stare. "And I think, Princess Rani, that you, too, must have noticed how dire things have become since this new moon." She gestures to the flower I'm holding.

I stare down at the jasmine flower Amir gave me. Where it was once alive, it now looks shriveled and black, the petals falling to the dirt. Gasping, I drop the flower.

"Why—"

"Those jasmine bushes are much like the rest of our world, affected by the coming Blood Moon. These flowers are a reminder that life can prosper forever, under the right circumstances . . . but handled without care, might also hit an expiration date."

"The Blood Moon? You know of it? What do you mean, an expiration date?" I swallow thickly and try to calm my frenzied thoughts, remembering the fear in Baljeet's eyes. The reddened moon in the sky, signaling a poisoned world.

"Of course. The Blood Moon is widely regarded as a myth— but all myths spring from some sort of truth. All legends started with belief. When the new moon began to crest, we couldn't deny the proof in front of us." She pauses to smile gently at me. "We are not so different from you, Rani. Much like snakespeakers, we believe that the world was born from a snake's skin: its mouth, its eyes, even its heart. And we know that its heart is our earth's very core—and its essence. As the Blood Moon grows nearer, we feel this essence more than ever before. Our crops and rivers are dying at an alarming rate. We don't have tidesweepers to aid us the way our continent did centuries ago."

Siva Auntie's words pour back to me. *You know our crops aren't faring so well.*

"Snakespeakers have been lucky," I respond carefully. "Our

magic has thrived for centuries. But it shouldn't have been only us thriving." I step closer to the queen, bowing my head slightly. "My hope is that our time together will heal our lands, and the poisoned core of the world, to make our countries strong."

Queen Meeta hums to herself, as if not entirely believing my words. My *proposal*. Suddenly, I feel foolish—what can I, a runaway princess, do to help heal a rift between two disparate countries? I have to do more—I have to offer my trust, as true allies would.

"Queen Meeta," I begin, "there is something you must know." I say the words slowly, knowing the risk I'm taking, and explain in thorough detail what Ria and I have discovered about Amara, and her wish to become the Soul Master.

Queen Meeta's facial expression is inscrutable, a puzzle for me to unlock. "A threat indeed. And quite the task ahead of you." She places a warm hand on my shoulder. "You have come to the right place. In Retan, we appreciate all magic and all Masters, and you will find scholars to give you the answers you seek—though I warn you that, after our long silence from Abai, not all will trust your intentions."

"It is as I said," I begin. "Retan and Abai can reunite. We will be stronger, once we bring our countries back together. I can prove it to anyone who asks," I tell her, more forcefully this time, even if just to make myself believe my own words.

I am not sure I have the queen of Retan entirely convinced, but she does seem surprised by my courage. "You are a headstrong princess. A bit like me when I was younger. I've always admired bravery." A considering smile flits across her face. "There is something I wish to show you." Queen Meeta draws me away from the flowers, leading me back into the Gold Palace, away from the revelers and down a series of hallways.

The sounds of the party fall away, and we pause in a corridor holding three portraits: I recognize them as the three sister queens of Retan, enshrined in my textbooks as they were. The *first* queens of Retan. They each wear their hair in an intricate bun, swept back from their faces, revealing round countenances and thin lips. Yet their eyes are like dark pools, harboring secrets.

"Do you know of Retan's history?" Queen Meeta asks, her inquisitive brown eyes finding mine.

"I was not the greatest student," I admit. "But I know of the sisters."

I was always fascinated by the idea of sisters ruling jointly. I never realized that one day, I would have a sister, too. Perhaps one to rule alongside . . .

"The Three Blessed Sisters ruled Retan at its inception," says Queen Meeta. "They had a maxim that each Retanian still reveres to this day. *'Protectors three, enchant me, allow our minds and souls to be free.'* They valued freedom and knowledge above all else. Each sister oversaw her own palace and had her own interests." Queen Meeta points at the first sister. "Queen Saira of the Gold Palace loved poetry and stories. She had books full of her writing; all her collections are now on display at the Academy's library."

She shifts to the right. "Queen Sampada of the Blue Palace, the only one of the sister queens to bear a child, loved science and mathematics. She helped establish the Retanian Academy itself, insisting that knowledge is one's most important weapon. That is why the Academy is so close to the palaces."

Finally, Queen Meeta moves on to the third portrait. "And Queen Sunita of the Saffron Palace loved nature. She worked alongside palace gardeners and aided in landscaping all three palaces after they were built."

"That's incredible," I say, though thinking of the Blood Moon's poison seeping into the beautiful natural areas of this land makes me shiver. My eyes catch on a symbol drawn on the wall underneath Queen Saira's portrait: the sun, with pointed tips in black ink, a small triangle painted within the center. It looks oddly out of place on the golden walls, where everything else is so intentional. And I've seen this before—on the sealed door in the Blue Palace.

"Indeed." Queen Meeta sighs, pulling me away from my thoughts. I see her eyes shift from those of a warm mother to those of an examining auntie. I recognize that critical gaze; I've seen Mother use it one too many times.

"I assume you've met my son, Dhruv?"

"Yes, Queen Meeta. He was quite the"—I struggle for a way to summarize our first meeting—"joker," I finish cautiously.

Her brow smooths in fond understanding, a small smile pulling at her lips. "I will tell you that my son is one of the most kindhearted people you will meet. But he is also a troublemaker." She chuckles. "I trust you will get to know him better during your stay? He, like Queen Sunita, is a lover of nature. If you wish to address the poison of our land, and heal the rift between Abai and Retan, then I hope you shall turn to him for advice."

Turn to *Dhruv* for advice? "I will," I say, if only to get one step closer toward our plan to heal our lands.

"I'll have you meet properly with my son soon," she says, drawing my attention back. "And I'll arrange for you and your friend to be taken to the Academy tomorrow. But I must tell you, scholars do not speak to citizens so easily. Even royals are discouraged from speaking of magic with them."

"Why?" I ask.

"Because, Princess—magic holds many secrets. Knowledge is deadly, no matter what."

"Thank you for the warning. But we must speak to the scholars. There is no other choice—I will find a way to earn their trust."

"I would expect nothing less from you, Princess Rani."

Queen Meeta leads me back to the party, where we part ways. She elegantly sweeps toward a raised dais in the center of the room. The dais, shaped like a blooming flower, is a spectacle of art. Conversation withers away as she ascends the dais, commanding attention with her fierce-eyed gaze.

"Welcome," Queen Meeta says. "I am grateful for all in attendance tonight, especially those from far and wide. We have much to celebrate. Our northern neighbors, Abai and Kaama, are in talks to end their centuries-long feud." Her eyes flicker to mine, and her words ring in my ears. *Can* I heal our lands? If Queen Meeta is correct, then even just to bring Abai and Retan back together, we need to heal both our lands and the poisoned core of the world. Which means stopping Amara from finding the talismans and using the Bloodstone.

One step at a time, I tell myself.

"Tonight also marks the Night of the Sisters. The birth date of the three sister queens who founded Retan and led us to be a peaceful queendom, a knowledgeable queendom, and a happy queendom."

Retanians clap, and joyous applause echoes through the palace.

"Of course, their journey was not an easy one," Queen Meeta says darkly. "It took the sisters time to come together—to realize a country is not led by one ruler, but by its people."

The roars continue. I shiver, a curl of shame winding through me. I had always taken Father's rule as law, until I met Ria. It has taken me too long to learn the lesson Queen Meeta now openly embraces.

"And while our sister queens died young, their journey remains. The sisters always said: knowledge is the greatest magic of all. So tonight we raise our glasses to them. We honor them. The Three Blessed Sisters."

I swear I see the queen's eyes land on mine, as though she is speaking directly to me. Not only of the tasks ahead of me, but of my and Ria's future together as queens.

"Speaking of sisters," Queen Meeta says, "we have a very special guest. Some of you may have already heard the rumors . . . Princess Rani of Abai is here with us. Come join me on the dais, Princess."

My cheeks burn as the crowd looks around. When I finally step forward, I hear quiet gasps spread throughout the partygoers.

"*Is that her?*" one girl inquires.

"*Don't make her fangs come out,*" a boy laughs behind bejeweled fingers.

Once, I would have fumed at such a statement. Now, I push my shoulders back and stride toward the dais, every inch the princess I know I am.

"Princess Rani has traveled far; all the way from the Abaian palace. I trust you will show the princess the kindness and strength of our people—Retanians, united by the sands."

"United by the sands," the crowd echoes.

After Queen Meeta finishes her speech, most guests head back to their discussions. But several eyes are still pinned on me. Watching me. Peeling back the layers, as if hoping to reveal a second snakeskin underneath.

I rub my arms from a sudden chill, pausing when I find a familiar face gazing at me from across the room. Prince Dhruv raises his glass toward me with a smile—not joking, but genuine.

It seems my time in Retan is going to be much more complicated than I thought.

11

Ria

Disembarking the boat is like unlacing one of Rani's suffocatingly tight blouses. Freeing, refreshing—and I can finally breathe easily again.

I could kiss the solid ground under my feet, if not for the mud and dirt and . . .

Snow.

When Mama Anita taught me about the mountain kingdom of the northwest, I'd imagined sheer rock touching the sky like the brush of fingers, an endless expanse of sea and stone. Now, before me, it's like my childhood wonders come to life.

Fat flakes of snow salt the air. Aditi and I are standing side by side at the top of the biggest rock I've ever seen, before the icy mouth of a palace entrance.

Saeed wasn't kidding when he told me this place was a literal *ice palace.* The palace is carved right into a mountain, part of it sculpted from what looks like magicked ice. The whole structure gleams with icy turrets and freshly fallen snow. The right side of the palace juts sideways out of the rock and floats over a frozen river that winds back and forth, almost snakelike.

I open my palm, expecting to feel snowflakes land on my hand, icy as a cool lake—but instead the frost warms me. A pleasant burning sensation tickles my fingers.

"This is . . . incredible," I say as Aditi grasps snow between her fingers, eyes bright like a child's seeing the world for the first time. "Is it always like this here?"

"Not near the Summer Palace," Aditi informs me. Must be somewhere in southern Amratstan. Here, at the most northern tip of the continent, I feel colder than I ever have before. My toes threaten to turn into ice cubes if I stand out here much longer. But I don't know if I can muster the courage to step into the palace.

"Are you scared, Princess?" Aditi wonders.

I don't realize my hands are tightened fists. I loosen them, but they're stiff from the Amratstanian snow, and I shake them out. Cold isn't exactly a friend to thieves. Or royalty, apparently.

"Never. Nervous, maybe," I say. "Not scared." Not after what we went through together with Amara.

Aditi offers me a warm smile. She relaxes a little and puffs her chest, straightens her shoulders, shifts her features.

A mouse finding a home in a lynx's world.

Slick, warm scales find my feet, and I glance down to find Shima coiled there. Her scales flutter, a mix of red and blue and white, a combination of colors I don't yet understand the meaning of.

Look behind you, Princess, Shima purrs.

Brow perked, I turn. Saeed and Irfan approach from behind me, both of them looking chilled but also thankful for landfall.

Irfan's icy eyes somehow look warm, and he gives me an encouraging nod. My eyes slide to Saeed, whose midnight-black curls sway loosely over his brows as he comes to stand next to me. I shiver once he's at my side. *The snow again,* I tell myself. I haven't spoken much to Saeed since last night in his cabin, instead opting to practice my magic with Shima.

Shima's scales flash the color of a stormy sky. Nerves roll up my spine while my cheeks redden from both the chilled air and Saeed's noticeable warmth.

You might want to unclench your jaw, Princess, Shima teases.

I do as she says. Snakes shouldn't be so good at reading thoughts.

I twist toward Saeed, wondering what to say, when a flash of black in the corner of my eye captures my attention. A shadow stands on the cliffside, its cloak rippling in the wind. I blink, wondering if it's her, my nightmares come to life. But the figure looks too square-shouldered. In an instant, the shadow is gone, taken by a sudden gust of snowy wind.

Aditi takes my hand, grounding me. "Ready, miss?"

I stand taller, facing the palace. "As I'll ever be."

When we step inside, my breathing stops. Because the inside of this ice palace is like a glass globe.

High, ornate ceilings and patterned walls carved from rock and crystals shimmer around us, forming a sphere. The floor itself is smooth as ice, but nowhere near as slippery. How is that possible? I test my feet along the floor, grasping Aditi's hand, as we head deeper inside. The inside of this place must be magicked like the outside—is this tidesweeper magic? Stonebringer? Both?

Two winding staircases facing opposite each other lead to a grand landing, where a pair of guards stand. Their fine blue gear makes me think of only one thing.

"Sentinels," Irfan says before I can. I don't know much of his life—only bits and pieces of what Rani told me—but I do know of his time as a child in the training camps, right here in Amratstan.

Irfan's fingers loosen on his bow as he gazes around the grand foyer of the palace. Coming back here must be opening the flood-gates of his memories.

Irfan steps ahead of us. His eyes won't move away from the soldiers standing tall and proud above us. Soldiers who look, I realize with a rush of shock, identical—cutting silver eyes and deep-brown skin, neat braids and decorated blue uniforms.

"Who's this?" a curious voice asks from a nearby corridor. A girl around my age approaches us, hips swaying in a stunning onyx sari embedded with beads like shimmering stars. Raja's beard, does she look like a princess. Her raven hair is swept into an intricate bun, a loose curl framing her long face. Next to her appears a man of many years, with a trimmed graying beard and a bone-white scar biting his cheek. It doesn't take me long to remember his name. I've been practicing.

"King Rohit," I greet him, bowing. Aditi follows suit to my right and Saeed to my left. Irfan is frozen still, staring up at the Sentinels, and I have to clear my throat to get him to move. Finally, he bows—but he doesn't look happy about it.

I wonder if King Rohit recognizes him after all these years.

The raja—*my father*—told me about his relationship with the Amratstanian king before I left. They were boy princes, growing up together on trips to Amratstan's Summer Palace closer to the Abaian border. His daughter and Rani used to play together as children . . . that is, until our father became obsessed with the war. And some other mysterious reason he wouldn't name.

"Oh, Rani!" The raja looks surprised, as if unsure if we would show up. "It's been so long, beta."

Child. He must think of Rani as his own child, from the closeness between our parents. Before I can respond, he takes me into his arms, and I stiffen instinctively. "Something the matter?" he asks, pulling back.

He doesn't know, I panic. But didn't the raja send a messenger bird to tell him the news? About me and Rani?

The girl beside the king narrows her eyes as she stares at me. Her sharp silver gaze finds mine. The gem of a bindi between her perfectly plucked eyebrows sparkles.

"Apologies, King Rohit," interrupts Saeed, "but this is not Rani. I assume you received our letter delivered by snowbird?"

"Snowbird?" The king lets go of me and steps back. "I apologize, but our snowbirds have been less reliable of late. This weather has been unpredictable. Now, Rani—"

"It's Ria," I blurt. I want to slap myself. Did I just interrupt a king?

"What's going on?" The girl flicks her gaze to the snake at my feet. Shima offers a low hiss, her scales reddening like my cheeks.

"King Natesh," I begin, "is my father. But I'm not Rani; I'm his long-lost daughter. Rani's twin."

At first, the king's lips remain pursed. Then his laugh echoes off the stone walls as his gaze bounces between me, Saeed, and Aditi, then to the snake at my feet. "You cannot be serious! Natesh always had a good sense of humor, hmm?" I notice an edge to his words; there's something he's not saying about my father, if my instincts are right.

"If I may," Irfan says, stepping forward, "this is not a joke, King Rohit."

Rohit finally plants his eyes on Irfan, as if noticing him for the first time. His smile melts at the presence of the ex-soldier, the silver in Irfan's eyes and his soldier's build a telling sign.

"Sir," Irfan continues, bending down onto a knee and pressing three fingers to his forehead. "I am Irfan Gill. May the mountains move you."

The king looks intrigued. He touches three fingers to his forehead as well, though his gaze stays wary. "I rarely forget the names of my soldiers, whether former or current. May the mountains move you as well, Irfan. It has been . . . some time, hasn't it?"

"I was but a child." Suddenly, Irfan sounds different; the usual warmth in his tone abandoned, a winter soldier to the bone. "Things have changed here, I pray?"

"They have," the girl interjects, looking at me. It's like her silver eyes have latched onto mine, inviting, calculating. Begging for a challenge.

Thieves love a good challenge.

"You speak the truth, then?" she adds, sauntering toward us, pausing before me.

I nod, forcing myself to speak. "Rani and I found each other over a moon ago. We were separated at birth because of a prophecy. I . . . thought you might've heard the rumors."

King Rohit barks a laugh. "King Natesh had one child." His voice is deep and dark, grim and controlling. The ivory scar that cuts across his face seems to pulse. The scar is similar to Amir's but thicker, as if cut from a large blade. A dull, painful blade.

"That's what we thought," Saeed says, planting a hand on my back. "But there's much more to the story. King Natesh wrote it in his letter."

"The one I happened to never receive?" Suspicion laces his tone.

Aditi glances at me before stepping forward, quiet as a mouse. "If I may, King Rohit-ji, it's all written in this book. . . ."

She extends her hands, holding the book she was reading in the library. The one all about my and Rani's life. King Rohit flips it open, skimming the pages, lips shifting from pursed to a dark scowl.

"A woman wiping your parents' memories of you clean? Twins separated because of a prophecy?" The king scoffs, practically throwing the book back at Aditi. "The ink looks only days old! *This* is your proof?"

"Please, sir," I say, stepping forward. "It's all true." I lift my sleeve to reveal my snake birthmark—the half that connects to Rani's. "My sister's is on her left arm. They connect."

The girl raises a brow.

"You remember?" I ask her.

She looks at the floor. "I noticed it when I was a child." A few seconds pass before she finally looks up—I watch as she takes in the differences between me and Rani. She presses three fingers to her forehead. Must be an Amratstanian greeting. "Then I suppose we have never met."

I nod. "I'm sorry, but I don't know your name."

"I am Princess Zoya," she says. "And they are . . . ?"

"Saeed Gupta," Saeed says from my left, bowing, and recognition dawns on Zoya's face.

"Rani's betrothed?" Her eyes bounce to mine. "She used to tell me as much, when we were children. That you two—I mean, Rani and her betrothed—would get married. Fall in love."

I nearly choke on my own spit. Saeed only offers a thin smile.

Zoya looks intrigued.

"Is there someone who could take our bags?" Irfan says, cutting the tension. "We've had a long journey." He looks back up at the balcony—at the soldiers.

Rani did tell me Irfan is like a box of sealed secrets.

"Ria can stay with me," Zoya says. "She's practically family."

Something about her words doesn't make me feel like family, but I'll play along.

I smile tightly. "Sure. And Aditi . . ."

Before I can finish, a horde of servants approach, notice our luggage, and begin picking up our things. "Our servants will be happy to attend to you," Zoya says, nodding at King Rohit. "Isn't that right, Father?" Before she can even let the raja reply, she continues: "What is the reason behind your stay, if I may ask?"

"We didn't come for a vacation," I say slowly. "We're here to search for someone. Someone we believe is right here in the White Mountains, seeking the Masters' talismans."

King Rohit sneers. "Talismans? Your family is one to say something about—"

"Father," Zoya cuts in. She turns her gaze to me. "We assume this is another thing you had written in your *letter*?" Her tone is slightly colder than before, as if I had erred in bringing up the talismans.

Saeed nods for me. "We would be happy to explain more thoroughly. We would greatly appreciate your assistance in helping us to find this . . . *person* faster. They seek all the talismans. If they find them, our very world could be in danger."

This makes King Rohit's *and* Princess Zoya's cheeks pale. Before either can answer, the two Sentinels—*twins*, they must be—come down from their station. "Shall we escort the visitors to their chambers, Your Highness?"

"Please," Zoya says, her eyes searing into mine.

Zoya's chambers are almost as large as the Abaian palace's gardens and soaked with pink. It's like I'm floating in sunset-colored cotton clouds, my awe and delight coloring Shima's scales a curious yellow as she glides into the room beside me. These chambers are even bigger than Rani's; so large, in fact, that the room is separated in two, with four-poster beds on either side.

I can't believe I'm in an *ice palace.* I can't believe I'm actually surrounded by threads of blues and golds, instead of sleeping on the streets like I was just two moons ago.

A part of me is still waiting to wake up on those streets, belly aching with hunger, huddled next to Amir for warmth.

"I would think you were caught up in memories, but you've never stepped foot in here, have you?"

Zoya's voice catches me off guard, and I whirl. Behind her are the twin Sentinels, who have placed my luggage on the bed on the left side of the chambers.

I flush. I was so caught up in the grandeur in front of me that I forgot Zoya was following right behind me.

"Memories of a sort," I respond, flustered as I face her cool demeanor. "I didn't mean to—"

"You were only excited," Zoya says, heading deeper inside the room. "I might do the same, if I were you."

Though her tone is light, there's something darker creeping around the edges of it, like a feral snake.

Rude, Shima bites at me, coiling herself tightly on the bed. *And stereotypical.*

"How strange," Zoya adds, approaching me. "You certainly look the part of Princess Rani's twin, yet you act quite differently."

"I grew up on the streets," I reveal, meeting her challenging tone with my own. "Rani and I haven't exactly had time to pick up each other's habits."

"You're a twin?" the twin Sentinels interrupt simultaneously. I'm startled into laughing, and for a moment, both of them drop their guard. The connection between us is instant; finding another pair of twins seemed so unlikely once, and now with these two—Neeta and Neesa, they tell me—in front of me, I feel a spark of excitement run through me. Perhaps there are other twins—friends—I could discover one day.

"What a treat," Neesa says, eyes sparkling once I explain my abridged story to the Sentinels and Zoya. "I suppose you're not the only princess with an unlikely past."

"What do you mean?" I ask.

"Princess Zoya," Neeta explains with a sly smile toward the princess, "grew up with specialized training. She knows how to swing a sword like any soldier. Don't you, Your Highness?"

Zoya only shrugs, staring far away. But Neesa doesn't seem fazed as she inches closer to me. "Don't be fooled by the beautiful princess," she says in my ear. "If she weren't a royal, she'd be a soldier, or even a guard like us."

Zoya clears her throat. "Is that all, Neesa?"

"Yes," the other twin replies promptly. "We will leave you to rest and recover your energy. Dinner with the king tomorrow night will be a divine affair."

Neeta nods in tandem, and seeing them side by side makes my heart swell. "There's so much of our palace and capital to explore."

"We've got Irfan to help with that," I say. "He's a former soldier, you know."

A curious expression steals over Neesa's face. "We know."

I halt, sensing tension thickening in the air. Zoya's cheeks flush, though I don't know why. "Sorry," I say quickly, too quickly. But my words have already done the damage, and the tension that broke with the twins' interruption is back in full force.

"So," I say, after Neeta and Neesa have left.

"So," Zoya echoes.

"I'm guessing you and the king aren't fans of Irfan, huh? A deserter, back at the palace?" I try to laugh it off, but Zoya doesn't look too happy.

"Father has always taught me deserters are traitors to all we value. And anyone who associates with them are, too." She sucks in her cheeks. "Then again, it seems your plight is more than enough warrant for you to stay. And we are not ones to deny company."

She doesn't exactly sound like she *wants company* after that spiel. Nor after what we told them about someone seeking the talismans. What is up with their reactions?

Zoya says, "Get settled, like the twins said. I'm sure hearing the full reason for your visit will be . . . enlightening." She gazes out the window at the quickly arriving moon. It's only late afternoon, but this far north, darkness arrives faster than night, and the red-tinged crescent moon is beginning to appear in the sky.

"Actually, that's why we're here," I say, joining her side as we both look up at it. "The Blood Moon. Have you heard of it?"

Zoya's gaze hardens. "In Amratstan, we hold little faith in such myths. A bedtime tale, and not a very happy one. What of it?"

Her dismissive tone rankles me once again. What is her deal with me?

"It's not such a bedtime tale when it's literally in the sky above us," I retort, my tone sharper than intended. *So much for diplomacy*, I lament.

To my surprise, though, Zoya seems to enjoy the challenge. She nods at me, a new glimmer of respect in her eyes.

"It's true, and we *have* noticed this strange phenomenon. Father has made sure our kingdom's most respected astrologers are keeping an eye out. They say there is no explanation for it; that the moon is turning redder day by day. Some say it is an eclipse. But I will admit, strange things have been happening of late. Lakes drying up, crops parched. Usually the ice gets to everything first, but this . . . this is different."

She looks to me as if I'll provide an answer. I have little to tell her, but with the Blood Moon just a few weeks away, I can't afford to keep what I do know to myself. We need Zoya's help.

"My sister and I believe the Blood Moon is a sign that the world is being poisoned once more, as it was at its creation," I say haltingly, unsure of how much to reveal. "And that the Blood Moon may be tied to the person seeking the talismans."

Which reminds me. "You and your father seemed to have a . . . strange reaction when we mentioned the talismans."

Zoya's eyes turn into two hard stones. "The Earth Master's talisman belongs to my family. We're his descendants. My ancestors possessed our Master's magic, though of course after the Earth Master was banished, our magic left. But the talisman once gave us a taste of it."

Once? "So you know where it is—"

"If I knew," Zoya interrupts, "my family would have our rightful treasure back. And your father, absent as he's been from my family for the last decade, would have fixed his own mistake."

Mistake? It's too soon to echo her as she turns on her heel and leaves.

What in the raja's mind was *that* all about?

I turn back to the picturesque window, a hundred thoughts spinning through me, and find the snaking river below. The river where I thought I saw a cloaked figure. From up here, it looks almost . . . familiar.

A sudden revelation hits me. *This* was the place I saw Amara and the servant called the Black Viper in my dreams. The place where she spilled her blood into the water, for what reason I still don't understand.

I can't seem to pull my eyes away from the river. I can almost feel the waves sweeping against my ankles.

A sudden vision overtakes me, that cobra within me rising with overwhelming force as a memory washes over me like a maelstrom. Not my own. I'm watching someone else: a girl, sitting within that very river—*the Snake River*, a voice hums in my mind. She's pressing her hand to a man's chest, startling green eyes filled with a strange fervor. Her skin glows, her power echoing through the water, through the sky. But for all I've never seen her, she doesn't feel like a stranger. In fact, this girl I know nothing about feels as close as a friend.

I falter back, ripping my gaze away from the Snake River. My vision clears, but the unsettling feeling—the girl's urgency, her desperation—remains.

Who was she? And why, eerily, did she remind me of myself?

12

Rani

"*Psst,*" comes a sound from behind me. I turn toward it but only find a lonesome tree bearing golden fruit in the Blue Palace's gardens. After scarfing down this morning's breakfast, methi paratha with delicious heaps of butter, I left for fresh air to think. I had too much on my mind after last night's conversation with Queen Meeta, and the strange, poisoned flower Amir gave me.

I approach the tree now with timid steps. One of its fruits lingers on a low-bearing branch, catching my attention. I reach out, but a different hand touches it first, twisting the fruit clean off the stem.

"Morning, Princess."

I feign annoyance as Amir appears from behind the tree. His hunter-green kurta sways in the wind as he lifts the fruit to his mouth and takes a bite with an audible, crisp *crunch*. I must momentarily lick my lips, because Amir offers the apple to me.

"Try it. It's a golden apple. A Retanian favorite." He swallows and smiles.

I hesitantly take a bite from the other side. At first it's tart, making me suck in my cheeks, but the flavor quickly melts into something sweet and floral, like honey and rose syrup.

"Mmm. I can see why. Where did you learn that?"

"You're not the only one who did research before we left." He winks.

I fake-gasp. "Amir? *Research?* I didn't know the two words could go in the same sentence." I smirk while Amir laughs, high and melodic. I wish I could bottle this moment, this simple banter and the sweet taste of the golden apple all in one. For a moment, I nearly forget about last night's affair—the queen's expectations, the way that guard looked Amir up and down. But a new voice breaks into the moment.

"Apologies for the interruption. Did I hear you say *research*? I'm told it's one of my strengths."

Amir's expression falls, though he dutifully takes a step away from me to nod, albeit slowly, at the stranger entering the court-yard. Prince Dhruv enters the gardens gracefully, even a bit bashfully, hands laced together in front of his well-fit red-and-gold kurta pajama. He looks polished, princely to a fault, and once again I kick myself for not realizing his status—*the* prince of Retan—when we first met.

"Your mother said we could visit the Academy and learn from the scholars," I tell Dhruv. "We wish to speak to them about something called the Bloodstone."

"Did she also tell you they're impossible to reach?" Dhruv asks, concern furrowing his brows.

I sigh, nodding.

"Well . . . *almost* impossible," he corrects. "I know a place where you might get the information you need. But you'll have to be a bit . . . sneaky to get into the forbidden section of the Academy's library. Only a select few have access."

"Library?" I echo while Amir says, maybe too giddily, "Forbidden?"

"Is that a problem?" Dhruv raises a brow. Uncertainty fills my gut. I'm here to make a good impression—prove myself and Abai to be a responsible, worthy alliance.

But I've taken bigger risks before. With the Blood Moon nearing, we must do whatever it takes to get information on the Bloodstone and the talismans.

"No," I say resolutely.

"Then it's settled." Prince Dhruv slides on a mischievous smile with ease, and I pretend, just for a brief moment, that it doesn't spark something in my veins. "Next stop: the Academy."

After Ranjit prepares the carriage, we take off. The carriage sweeps through Jhanswa City, past apothecaries and tailors alike, until it finally rolls to a stop at the main entrance to the Academy. The university entrance is a gateway made entirely of gold, leading into a bustling array of buildings with a grand, dome-shaped library at its center. The whole place teems with a river of people, ebbing and flowing in every direction. Students and professors alike wear matching brown robes with the Academy's emblem on the back: a book with a ribbon fluttering around it.

Sound rises from all sides: chattering gossip and nervous muttering—*"Are you sure that's on the test?"*—but what overwhelms me most is the smell. Food stalls are scattered all around the campus, boasting all kinds of fare, from delicate desserts to crunchy street snacks. The smell of slow-cooked potatoes and fried dough makes my stomach cry in protest. Sneakily, Amir veers off and returns with a cupful of mini samosas.

"Didn't we already have breakfast?" I ask.

Amir rolls his eyes. "When has that ever stopped me?" He pockets the extra change—Retanians use copper coins called sikkas imprinted with the Three Blessed Sisters' faces—and we eat as Dhruv takes us down a long, gilded path leading to the library. The entrance is flagged by fluttering banners. While my eyes had glanced over the stark red banners before, I now focus on the Retanian writing threaded within, an ancient form of the modern language that uses tightly packed letters and sloping characters.

The path to knowledge lies here.

But the inside of the library is what truly makes me gasp aloud. It's more than twenty stories high, boasting endless shelves of books as students mill about the tables, either poring over papers or trying to catch a wink of sleep. While I was privately tutored, there's something immediately familiar about the feeling of this library, this trove of books, the camaraderie of the students, that makes me immediately relax.

"This way," Dhruv says quietly, and I keenly note the number of people who stop and stare as we pass. Staring at *Dhruv*, that is. Some girls nudge each other and flip their hair, which Dhruv slyly acknowledges with a lazy smile, and I swear even the nearby librarian peers around the corner to get a glimpse of him.

I suppose we are, quite literally, in the presence of Retanian royalty. I find myself enjoying it more than expected. It's nice, for a moment, not to be the one gawked at.

Dhruv leads us to the fifth floor, each level marginally quieter than the last. We weave through the shelves until we arrive at a quiet section. Although there are technically no corners in the dome-shaped library, this area looks odd, cordoned off by a door. Dhruv fishes a key from his pocket, unlocks the door, and then leads us up a spiral staircase.

"This feels . . . how do I put it? *Illegal*," Amir says. "Which, to be fair, I have no problem with. Just thought I'd mention it, so we're all, y'know, on the same page."

I shove Amir's shoulder as we ascend. But he's right: it certainly feels like we're entering somewhere we're not meant to be. At the top of the staircase, Dhruv produces a card made of parchment with elaborate Retanian writing—*Prince Dhruv Walia of Retan*—and places it in the door handle. The handle twists, and something mesmerizing begins to happen: a flame appears, burning the card until it's naught but ash. The flame douses itself, leaving an inky trail of smoke behind.

Amir's jaw hangs open. "What was *that*?"

"A safeguard, so only those permitted are allowed to enter." The door clicks open. Dhruv raises a finger to his lips and motions us in.

The room is quiet and dark, holding just three tables and numerous stacks of papers and tomes. Something inside me deflates. I'd hoped that today's secret business would provide some grand revelation. A scholar secretly in hiding. A magical trove of books that would flip to just the right page you needed with a swish of the wind.

"Don't worry," Dhruv says, as if reading my mind, "this is only the common room. The actual forbidden section is past that door." He points at a short passage leading to a closed door. "Unfortunately, I'm not allowed to bring anyone with me, so we'll have to be a bit . . . sneaky. Once I present myself to the prefect, I'll make some sort of distraction to lure her away. Meanwhile, you two can stay hidden here until she's gone, and then I'll join you inside once it's safe."

Amir and I eye each other.

"That's . . ."

"A good enough plan," I finish, already knowing Amir's choice of words would have been less optimistic.

Dhruv chuckles to himself. "Something tells me you have a better idea."

"Hide in plain sight," Amir suggests. I swear his mouth twitches before he says, "You and Rani go ahead first. I'll make up some excuse to get in."

"And if you can't?" While Amir and I have pulled off a few stunts before, I am not certain it will work this time. He's already been denied entry once. I don't want to see that happen again. "I'll use my snake magic; it should be enough to convince the prefect."

And yet it wasn't enough for the guards. While I was a bit distracted last night, I promise myself now that my focus will make it work.

Amir nods, albeit slowly. Oblivious, Dhruv leads us down the passage and knocks on the door thrice.

There, the prefect opens the door with a wide smile. "Prince Dhruv! Welcome back." The prefect, a girl sporting long, wavy hair and a simple orange salwar beneath her cloak, touches her chest in a warm Retanian greeting, her fingers grazing the clasp—what looks like a rare Retanian coin.

"Prefect Padma," Dhruv says with a respectful tilt of his head. "I'm here with our kingdom's most esteemed guest."

"Ah, Princess Rani." The girl bows. "I heard of your visit last night. Welcome to Retan."

"Thank you." I return her gesture with a hand to my heart.

"Professor Neel is running his weekly reading circle, if you'd like to join," Prefect Padma says with a strange twinkle in her eye.

Dhruv's shoulders bunch up. "Actually, I'm here on business with Princess Rani. Along with a . . . consultant." Dhruv clears his throat, eyeing me. A signal: it's time to use my snake magic.

I call upon my magic as I always do: by visualizing a chest of drawers in my mind. I tug on a drawer and watch the threads of magic unspool from within, connecting deep to the marrow in my bones, until the magic and I fuse into one.

"He's here to officially accompany Prince Dhruv. Ranjit-ji sent him along," I say, gesturing at Amir, who stands a pace behind me. Strangely, though, the flicker of magic, that aura I usually feel around me, falls back. Like it's shirking away from me.

"Did he now?" Prefect Padma wonders, peering around me to take a closer look at Amir. "I didn't hear anything from Queen Meeta about a consultant." Padma tilts a brow at Amir, looking him up and down in a way I don't appreciate. He fits the part, with clothes made from Retan's finest silks—taken from one of the plentiful closets within the Blue Palace, I'm certain—but he still seems a touch out of place, obviously not used to such linens.

"Is . . . something wrong?" Dhruv mutters to me. I try to call on my magic again, but it feels like it bounces back *against* something. Is there some kind of magical barrier here from the Old Age? A way to make sure no one gets into the forbidden section of the library?

Quick on his feet, Amir notices my plight and pastes on a smile. "Yes, I'm actually the youngest noble adviser in Prince Dhruv's circle. Some say a youthful perspective is needed . . . wouldn't you agree?"

Padma, likely around Amir's age, furrows a brow as her lips

twitch up. Despite the lie, she seems unwittingly charmed. Noting his advantage, Amir presses on.

"Besides," he continues, leaning forward a bit closer to Padma than I would have expected, "it's not every day I get to meet someone so knowledgeable about Retanian sikkas." He points at the clasp on her cloak. "That one's two hundred years old, correct? Only a smart collector like yourself could've gotten something like that."

The prefect's eyes turn doe-like, and my body flushes in response. "Do you collect coins, too? I'd love to discuss—"

"You know what," I cut in, cheeks hot, "Amir would love to discuss *coins* with you another time, but I'm afraid we're in a hurry now." I point to the forbidden section.

"Of course," Padma says distractedly, twirling a finger through her hair and still staring at Amir, who's offering her a quirked grin. "Please, come in."

Prince Dhruv wears an assured smile as we stroll in. I move to plow past Amir, but he pulls me back before either of us can enter.

"It worked!" he whispers with enthusiasm.

"And how did you know it would?"

"The clasp on her cloak was silver, a special edition of the sikka made in remembrance of a beloved Retanian queen. And her badge was fraying around the edges, meaning she's been a prefect for a long time, despite being so young. She would know the significance of this coin."

"More research?" I ask in awe.

"Yup. A thief pays attention to the details," he says, a playful bravado in his voice as though he's some kind of sage. "It makes all the difference in the end."

"You didn't seem to catch on to any *details* that I wasn't Ria during our switch," I quip, forcing myself to forget the look Padma gave Amir.

"That's because I was focused on the mission. And I noticed a few things," he says, feigning hurt. "Plus, you're not a *completely* terrible actor."

"What a compliment," I respond dryly, before stopping short at the room in front of us.

Inside, a colorful collection of books comes to life. Winking lights shimmer from every corner of the circular enclosure, like dappled sunlight on water. It takes a moment for me to realize what they are: firebugs, small flying beetles with tapered fire wings, native to Retan, and known for making an appearance on quiet, romantic evenings.

"Anything you might need to know about the Bloodstone should be here in the Scholars' Archives," Dhruv says. "The firebugs were brought here by the scholars. They'll lead you where you need to go."

Dhruv's eyes flicker to meet mine. Something tells me he wasn't talking about books.

I set off through the shelves, Amir by my side. Amir pulls out three books about ancient relics and flips through them at a nearby table, coughing as he opens a tome and a cloud of dust appears. As he swats the dust away, small, flickering dots of light float across my vision. A swarm of firebugs is flying, no, *dancing* around my ankles and zipping up around my legs and torso. A pleasant warmth flickers from their wings. I study the beetles with curiosity as one rests on my finger, then wanders up to the tip of my nose before drifting lazily to the next set of shelves. I follow the bugs as they form a stream, leading right to . . .

Dhruv.

Dhruv snickers as a firebug tickles his neck. Book in hand, he turns to me and says, "Found anything?"

Only you. I clear my throat and shake my head, finding my tongue numb. It must be all the dust.

"What's that?" I manage, pointing at his book, *The History of Retan's Jewel: Jhanswa City.*

"Something by an old friend," Dhruv says a bit suspiciously as he tucks the book away. The spine clearly notes the name of the author. *Scholar Suneel Nanda.*

"You were friends with a scholar?"

"He's a professor now."

Vaguely, Prefect Padma's words float back to me. She mentioned something about a professor's reading circle, but Dhruv didn't seem too interested. In fact, he had looked apprehensive.

When it's clear Dhruv won't budge on the subject or move away so I can check the book, I switch topics. "How often do you come to the Academy?"

"Thrice weekly, four times during exam season—which it

appears to be," Dhruv says with a small sigh. "But I enjoy sitting in on lectures."

"You're not privately tutored?" I gasp inwardly. Who has ever heard of a royal studying among their people?

"No one is in the capital," he laughs. "But to be honest, I'm still not used to the stares. People have called me a teacher's pet for raising my hand too much. For being so involved they thought every teacher was biased toward the oh-so-studious prince."

"I'm sorry," I tell him. "But I thought you *were* studious?"

"I was," Dhruv says cryptically. "People think that royalty have everything. In a sense, of course, we are very blessed. But that doesn't mean we don't have our own desires, our own wishes for the lives we would like to lead."

I've felt the exact same thing growing up in the Abaian palace. "You're a bird locked in a cage."

"Exactly." Dhruv's eyes light up. "The world expects everything from you. My *mother* expects everything from me."

"My mother's not much different," I tell him. "But when I finally left the palace, I learned that we don't have to be chained to who we are. We can change. I did—and so has Amir. We changed because of each other."

"He seems like a good man. How long have you two known each other?"

"Just under two moons," I tell him.

He raises both brows. "Seems much longer than that. You two must be fast friends."

I smile thinly as the words again call to mind Padma's easy interest in Amir, my mother's cold reasoning. "Friends. Yes."

But other memories surface, too. I remember the time we spent together, searching for the stone, longing for something new. I remember how we found that in each other. I close my eyes and recall the feel of Amir's arms on mine while we kissed on the Stone Terrace. Warmth and light, dissipating any iciness within me.

"He's lucky to have met you. As am I."

My eyes open to find Dhruv's warm gaze fixed on mine. Surprise courses through me at his words—it's rare that anyone has thought themselves lucky to know me, the icy Snake Princess. I clear my throat. "We should really continue looking."

"Of course," Dhruv says, his voice barely veiling disappointment at my abrupt response. I'd be lying if I said I didn't want to continue this conversation, but another urgency takes hold.

We're here to stop Amara, not to make friends, I remind myself, no matter how handsome or similar those friends might be to myself.

I continue my search and follow the firebugs as they form a glittering path to the back of the shelves, almost like an arrow on a compass pointing the way.

Absorbed in my task, I veer around the shelves in a strange zigzag, scanning the spines of books as I pass, until a few minutes later I hit a dead end. A small rectangle of light washes over the space, and voices pepper the air from just beyond a half-open door. One of the firebugs slips inside, and I feel the strange urge to follow.

I peer through the door to find a small group huddled together at their desks, a professor facing them a bit farther away as he unlatches an overpacked trunk resting on a wooden podium. The words he mutters aren't so distinct, but one jumps out.

Magic.

A hand touches my shoulder gently, and I gasp and step back into someone right behind me. Their hand steadies me, gripping my elbow gently.

"Apologies, Princess," Dhruv murmurs. "I wanted to follow the firebugs, too."

"Why?"

"Because they're creatures of fate. I believe some things are destined. Do you?"

"Not always," I tell him, though I feel a strange tug to confide in him after our discussion earlier. No one has ever understood me on that level before, so easily and immediately. Ria and I forged our futures, but there is still so much unwritten—and I get the feeling Dhruv might understand that better than anyone.

"Then we'll make our own destiny," Dhruv finishes, his voice almost alluring in the dim and quiet of the Archives.

Well, almost quiet.

"You there," a voice booms, and we both startle. Someone pushes the door back, letting the musty air of the small sitting room and the flickering candlelight rush over us. "Are you here for the reading circle?"

The group turns around, eyes drilling into mine.

"Um—" I begin, but Dhruv sweeps in with a wave of his hand.

"Hello, Professor Neel. It's been a long time."

13

Ria

I'm standing in the middle of a palace hall, waiting.

Waiting for the voice to return.

A fiery orange light exudes from the space underneath the door at the end of the hall. All of the sconces in the hall have been blown out, as if this singular light wants to pull me forward. Pull me *toward* something.

Or someone.

There is no wind, no coldness, even in this palace of ice. Somehow, even from paces away, I feel the presence of warmth behind that door, of a welcoming heat instead of frost.

I reach for the door, sliding the golden key between my fingers into its lock, but the moment my fingers touch the knob I wrench my hand back with a hiss. It feels as if a thousand suns are burning my hand, and I stumble back from the doorknob.

"Dreams are simply a silenced version of our greatest desires." The voice finally speaks, that familiar, alluring tone echoing all around

me. *"Envision what you want, and let it happen."*

Clutching my burning hand to my chest, I close my eyes. *Breathe, Ria.* I envision this door unlocking, imagine it swinging open, imagine the presence in my head facing me.

"Open your mind. Open your magic."

I command the door to open, but it only rattles in place. "Where are you?" I whisper, mesmerized by the light, by the thirst within me.

The voice haunts me from every corner. *"I am everywhere and nowhere. I am your power beckoning."*

My power. I feel it swell within me, ready to burst with sheer strength, and I look once again at the locked door, directing all my focus its way. The key glows with golden light, yet still the door refuses my wish. Just as anger begins to overtake my thoughts, a vision curls at the edges of my sight. The girl at the edge of the river. Hands pressing against another's chest. The golden light erupts, hot as flames, lethal as a cobra's fatal bite.

Eyes, red as blood, gaze down on me with the unexpected love and care of a guardian . . . before they disappear.

Screams. Endless screams. And—

"Princess Ria?" a voice calls out, echoing in my eardrums. Hands shake my shoulders. I gasp and snap awake, rolling over, hands pressed against the iciness of the Amratstanian palace's floors.

Ice I hadn't felt in my nightmare.

Dreams are simply a silenced version of our greatest desires. So I was dreaming. But why do I feel disappointed now to be woken up? I was so close to something—something that feels like the very air slipping from my lungs, even though I can't put a name to it.

Those same hands pull me up, keeping me righted so I won't fall over. The first thing I make out is the stranger's eyes, an icy blue as unnerving as the Satluj Sea we crossed from Abai and into Amratstan.

"This isn't exactly how I pictured our first meeting," the man chuckles softly. My brows dip in confusion, and he offers a thin smile of apology. "Excuse my forwardness, Princess Ria. It is truly an honor to meet royalty of your kind."

The man offers the official Amratstanian greeting, pressing three fingers to his forehead. I follow his lead, still dazed from the abrupt snap from dream to reality, inspecting him close-up for the first time. He can't be older than forty summers; his hair has a coppery tinge to it and his skin is dark brown and weathered. He's got a few silver hairs sprouting from his neatly trimmed beard, matching the silver specks in his eyes.

"Thank you," I say finally, "for helping me. I don't know how I got here, to be honest." What time is it? I glance backward, finding the door to Zoya's room not far behind me. I've never sleepwalked in my life. And that dream . . . it felt so real. Realer than any other nightmare I've had.

Did I hit my head? I press my hands against my skull, and the man reaches out in concern, eyes widening. "You should get looked over, Princess Ria. I am the palace physician, but you can call me Veer." He bows low, offering a gloved hand, and I shake it.

"I'm fine," I tell myself more than the physician, mostly because as the shock wears off, embarrassment begins to take its place. "How'd you know who I am, anyway?"

"Your name has traveled far since your arrival," Veer explains, and then sheepishly adds with a chuckle, "*and* because Princess Zoya has a bad habit of spilling more than her tongue should allow during her visits."

I permit myself a laugh, too, trying to push away the strange dream and everything I saw in it. But it doesn't work. Everything still feels too close, too real. The pull to that mysterious voice. What does it all mean?

And I'm so tired. I would give anything just for a night's rest.

"Do you carry anything that could help with . . . nightmares?" I ask, feeling the exhaustion truly hit me.

Veer nods. "Of course. I have many tonics back in my infirmary." Still, he lifts a brow. "Though I wouldn't recommend a tonic for the occasional bad dream. Does this have to do with your . . ." He glances around. "Sleepwalking?"

"Possibly," I mutter under my breath. "I've been having strange nightmares of . . . a woman." Though Amara wasn't in this nightmare, I'm sure she's behind them. I shiver as I recall the way blood had dripped from her mouth, the last time I saw her.

"Woman?" Now the physician looks interested, eyes wide despite the late hour of night. "Describe her."

I quirk a brow, unsure where he's going with this. "She has red eyes, red hair, a strange voice—"

"Voice?" Veer leans forward, tucking his hands into his white physician's coat. "Could you explain it to me?"

"It's deep. A voice that belongs to the skies."

Veer bites his lower lip. "I apologize for all the questions, Princess. But you are not the only one to come to me with this problem. I just came from a few, actually, suffering from an issue similar to yours. Nobles, mostly, from the Summer Palace, visiting for the winter." He pauses, shuddering. "They also say they've begun to see a woman in their dreams, similarly described." He barks a laugh. "However, people always have a hard time sleeping this time of year. It's cold and dark here compared to the South, and that's not always an easy adjustment."

"You believe that's all it is?" My voice comes out shaky. There have been others—palace guests, even—who've been having nightmares of Amara?

"I have to," Veer states. "I am a physician. I've seen some strange things in my time here at the Winter Palace. Multiple patients have even come to me with burn marks in the shape of snakes. But there is always a logical reasoning to everything, and a way to heal it."

His words make me shiver. *Burn marks in the shape of snakes?*

"Is there anything you could give me to help with the nightmares?" I say, thinking of something else. Anything else.

He nods. "Lavender and valerian root should do the trick. I'll have it delivered to your room in the morning."

"Thank you." Memories flash through me: Saeed with his sleep tonic; Amara, fogging up her son's visions. I squeeze my eyes against a shudder.

"Medicine is my job," he replies humbly. "I've always thought of magic and medicine to be one and the same, in truth. That is why I've always had a fascination with snakespeakers. Your magic can cull venom from a snake and turn it into the most power-ful potion. Absolutely brilliant." He chuckles again. "Look at me, going on. I bid you good night, Princess. You should get your rest."

Just as he turns to leave, I stop him. "Wait!" I call out. My throat turns thick, remembering what the voice told me. "Do you believe that dreams are a silenced version of our greatest desires?"

Veer offers me a thin smile. "If dreams didn't reflect our inner selves, I don't think we'd have them."

After a relatively quiet day of peace and palace tours, evening descends, bringing with it whispers of a reddening moon. Inside, the dining table is laden with a hundred foods I can smell, taste, and touch. Roasted squash sabji in silver platters, steaming black daal, and buttery saag with corn flour roti. It's a spread fit for a winter harvest.

"Dig in," King Rohit tells us, lifting his goblet of wine. Prin-cess Zoya does the same, both of them sitting across from me in the middle of the large mango wood table. I try not to stare at Zoya's lavish sari. Something like that could pay for years of shelter and food. Something like that could've kept me off the street.

I erase the thought as my belly growls. This dinner looks just as the twin Sentinels described it: *divine.* But I can't help but note how much food there is for so few people; Irfan opted out of tonight's meal, and Aditi's dining with a few kids of palace guests she met earlier today. Not to mention Princess Zoya didn't exactly invite my snake familiar to the dinner table.

Which leaves me sitting before a king of stone and ice, with only Saeed's presence to comfort me.

After we've filled our bellies to the brim, palace staff sweep away the food and offer us hot cups of chai to wash down the meal. I sip. Too sweet. Cane sugar was barely affordable for the Vadi Orphanage. I learned to handle tea with nothing but a splash of sheep's milk. And soon after that, nothing but the tea itself, black as night.

Black as King Rohit's dark gaze.

The king, as if sensing my thoughts, speaks up. "May I ask, ever so politely, for you to explain your full purpose here? How you plan on finding all these talismans you mentioned yesterday? And *who* exactly you are trying to stop from finding them?" His smile is tight, telling. It reminds me of Zoya's words yesterday: *If I knew, my family would have our rightful treasure back. And your father, absent as he's been from my family for the last decade, would have fixed his own mistake.* Somehow, the raja—my *father*—has something to do with the Earth Master's talisman, the very thing Amara is seeking.

Would have been nice for him to give me a heads-up about it.

Luckily, Saeed steps in to cover my hesitation, ever the savior. He takes a small sip of chai before saying, "Actually, King Rohit-ji, it's to do with my mother."

"Your mother?" King Rohit echoes. "Amara Gupta, if I remember correctly?"

Saeed nods. "I came here once or twice as a child with her, King Natesh, and Rani." He looks at me. "*Not* Ria," he emphasizes, as if to convince the king I really am Rani's twin.

"I see," King Rohit says, voice grinding. "And where is she? Your mother?"

"Amara's gone, sir," I say, finding courage in my voice. I sit taller. "She's no mindwielder, but she had a special heirloom—a talisman—that could control one's thoughts."

King Rohit looks at Zoya, brows raised, and Zoya mirrors the movement. Like father, like daughter.

"Nothing has the power to do that." King Rohit's voice is convincing, commanding. The voice of a leader.

But I'm a leader in my own right, too. I have to speak up for myself—for my country.

"I know it sounds ridiculous, but you have to believe me," I say. "Do you know of the Memory Master's talisman?"

Zoya turns to look at her father. "I learned of a few of the talismans during my lessons, but never knew for certain what the

Memory Master's talisman was, or its power."

"The Memory Master's talisman is a pair of cuffs," I explain. "So powerful that Amara could use them to bend others' minds to her will, as she did with my father. She wanted to use him to find the Bloodstone. You must know of the Bloodstone, correct?" I add to King Rohit.

"Nothing of import," he says a little too loudly as a few servants bustle in and take our teacups. When they're gone, he lowers a thunderous brow, the scar biting into his face stark like lightning. "The Bloodstone is a myth. A legend only believed by those chasing power."

"It's as real as the talismans," I argue, and, tired of defending myself, shoot back, "and you've both neglected to tell me why exactly my father is being blamed for *your* talisman going missing."

King Rohit leans back, obvious surprise on his face, and then turns to exchange a look with Zoya.

"You expect me to believe you do not know of it?" he asks.

I flush, suddenly and embarrassingly aware of what little I know of my father and my abrupt change in status. Two moons ago I didn't know my own father's name. Now I'm uncovering a lifetime of secrets, and in moments like these I still feel like a thief playing pretend.

Zoya's voice breaks the silence, her gaze stony against mine. "When your father and Rani last visited ten years ago, our families were at peace. Or so we thought."

She continues, "The final night of their stay, the Earth Master's talisman went missing. Only a descendant of the Earth Master can pass the talisman on to someone else. My father had handed it to King Natesh the night before as a sign of trust. When it disappeared, he was the only possible person who could have stolen it."

Those words land like an arrow through my chest. Boldly, her gaze sharpens on me, and my blood heats. I move to stand when Saeed stops me with a gentle hand wrapped around my wrist.

"Maybe it was a misunderstanding," Saeed offers. But neither Zoya nor King Rohit give his words merit.

"What does the Earth Master's talisman do?"

Zoya hesitates before answering. "It is a map with the ability to lead one to their most desired earthly objects."

"No matter what you believe," Saeed interrupts, "we *know* my mother is in Amratstan, searching for the talismans as we speak, which means at least one of them must be close by. And we have to stop her."

King Rohit's gaze flits between Saeed and me before he leans in. "How do you know this?"

Saeed's expression turns sober. "I am a mindwielder, sir. In my visions, I've seen my mother in the White Mountains. That is why we came here."

King Rohit laughs. "A mindwielder? Such magic no longer exists."

"But it does. My sister has seen fire magic as well, at the Glass Temple. Magic is returning to the world—and there's darker magic on the horizon if we don't find Amara."

Both Rohit's and Zoya's faces pinch with concentration as I explain Amara's plan to use the Bloodstone and become the Soul Master. How she could destroy all of Kaama if she succeeds.

King Rohit tents his fingers. "Let's suppose this is all true, and your mother did travel here," the king tells Saeed. "This is our home. *We* oversee all in the White Mountains. If this woman were here, we would have known by now."

"Not with all your palace guests here visiting for the winter," I interject, thinking of Veer's words last night. King Rohit's mien darkens. Apparently, I have a thing for talking back to royalty.

Saeed plants a reassuring hand on my arm and we swap a long look. Heat flushes my cheeks at his warm-eyed look, but I feel my ire calming. Zoya lets out a little laugh to herself, as if she can sense what's between us. I wish I could kick her foot under the table, but that wouldn't be *princess*-like.

Before I can do anything, Saeed leans closer to me so our arms are brushing. As he's staring at me, he says, "Ria can vouch for my visions. She's the one who helped me see them clearly. It was my mother who wanted to cover them up. Now, they are stronger than ever."

I peel my gaze away from Saeed's, which is hot as a fiery Abai sun. "It's true." My voice is small, a croak against the wide space of the Amratstanian dining room.

But King Rohit looks stubborn. "The White Mountains were built by the world's first currentspinners and stonebringers. Our

Winter Palace only covers a third of it, I will admit, but we have Sentinels watching the mountains at all times. No one has seen Amara Gupta, I can assure you of that."

I steel myself. "Then let *us* hunt after her," I plead. "And ask your Sentinels to warn the townsfolk about this woman, put up wanted posters. She could be deep in the mountains, where not even the Sentinels have seen her."

"*If* she's there," King Rohit says.

"I propose a deal," Saeed pipes up. "We're both seeking the Earth Master's talisman, yes? Then let us search for my mother— *and* the missing talisman. I know the raja of Abai, and he is no thief." He offers me an apologetic look at his words. "Allow us to stay during our search," Saeed continues. "We need to find my mother and stop what she's doing. My mother's plans for the stone, and whatever she wants with these talismans, could cause mass destruction. Change the world as we know it."

"Do you believe this?" King Rohit asks Zoya.

Zoya is quiet at first. "Why would someone lie about this?" She glances at me, the cold frost I saw before in her eyes now melting. "The least we could do is help."

"King Rohit-ji, Princess Zoya, we kindly ask that we have some Amratstanian Sentinels join us on our search. For protection," Saeed states.

"How about Neeta and Neesa?" I say, thinking of the twin guards, the comfort and bond we've already shared despite speaking to each other for only minutes. Saeed nods and agrees with me.

But King Rohit is the one we need to convince—and he is still silent, his expression unforgiving.

Saeed speaks. "King Rohit, we must find Amara if we are to avoid further bloodshed and create peace between our lands again. Such a thing will never be possible with the Bloodstone in the hands of my mother. You would want peace between all our lands again, yes? King Jeevan of Kaama and King Natesh will soon be drawing up a new treaty."

King Rohit purses his lips. "I have heard of the war ending between Kaama and Abai . . . yet I was not sure whether to believe it. To see all of our kingdoms unite once more . . ." He blows out a breath. "Fine. We will help."

Zoya agrees as well. "We're throwing a party next week for my eighteenth birthday, which means there will be a lot of new people arriving in the area. She will be difficult to apprehend—but we will tell the Sentinels to keep a sharp eye out for her. And I was thinking, the soldier . . . *Irfan* could be a big asset to your mission, with his knowledge of Amratstan."

King Rohit grunts, less a confirmation than him relenting. Clearly, there's some bad blood between him and his former soldier. I should probably help to clear the air.

"And we'll agree to put up some posters, if you provide an apt description to our palace scribe," Zoya says. She looks at me now. "You know, it's scary how much you look like Rani. Yet you speak nothing like her at all." She laughs. "We were the best of friends back then. Then King Natesh suddenly stopped visiting after our family's talisman went missing. The rajas . . . they were friends as children, too—that kind of friendship never truly ends." She whispers the last bit.

I smile. She's right. Finally, maybe we can get somewhere with all of this. We can find Amara. We'll—

A piercing pain stabs my temple. "Agh!" I cry, hand flying to my forehead.

"Ria?" Saeed asks urgently. "Ria, what's wrong?"

The room starts to spin. I clutch my head as a voice, taunting, caressing, splices my thoughts.

"Power is a delicious thing."

No, I think. Why am I hearing this voice again? This is no nightmare. I swallow down the bile creeping up my throat, breathing in deeply, and when I turn my gaze up to Zoya and King Rohit—

I see something else. *Someone* else. She's standing in the middle of the corridor by the entrance to the dining hall, her flaming red hair wickedly glowing in the light of the candlelit sconces.

Amara.

I freeze. Someone crosses in front of her. They sport a hooded cloak over broad shoulders. *The Black Viper*, the man from my nightmares.

"We need the girl," the Black Viper says, voice low and alert.

"In time," Amara answers, glancing over the Viper's shoulders. Her eyes narrow on mine as the man departs.

I surge to my feet, sending my cup of chai spilling across the table. Black tea splashes across the wood, landing on King Rohit's tunic. He leaps up and curses.

"Wondering how I'm here, are you?" Amara chuckles, but her form looks ghostly, pale. "Don't worry. Only you can see or hear me. I am in your mind, after all."

"What?" I gasp, looking around the room, but everyone's making too much of a fuss over the king's now-drenched tunic.

"It's just the same as when I held the scepter in the middle of your little *celebration*. I am an illusion of the mind, placed here by the one who is connected to you perhaps even more than Rani." She grins.

This is impossible.

"Poor Ria. It seems you've picked up a few clues, but you're never quite fast enough, are you?" Amara says, grinning. "Too late to catch me now. I wouldn't even bother trying if I were you. I don't waste my time on street rats."

A flicker of movement, and she's gone.

I blink, words stuck in my throat, but Amara . . . isn't there. There's no sign of her or the Black Viper. My heart speeds up; was I hallucinating? No—this is just like the moment I saw her holding Father's scepter in the palace gardens.

Zoya's voice shakes me back to the present. "Ria—"

"I'm so sorry," I say as a horde of servants enter the room, cleaning up my mess. My cursed dreams are bleeding into real life. I grab a cloth and help them clean. "I'm so sorry—" I repeat.

"That's quite all right," King Rohit says, standing now, a servant helping him clean his tunic.

Saeed says for me, "I think we just both need some . . . rest." He gazes at me with confused eyes, and it's taking everything within me not to tell him what I just saw.

"Rest," I say. "Yes. That's exactly it. My apologies."

I glance back at the corridor. There's nothing but two sconces of candlelight. But where both were lit before, now there is only darkness.

14

Rani

Professor Neel's eyes scrutinize mine, then swivel to the prince. "Prince Dhruv. What a pleasant surprise. It's been quite some time since you last joined us."

The small room is swathed in bright curtains and sconces holding balls of fire. Seated students and desks are spread out across the space, and a wide set of stairs leads down to where Professor Neel stands before a podium, like a teacher about to give a class lecture.

Prince Dhruv enters the room coolly, hair windswept despite the fact that we're still indoors. Everyone faces him, drawn like a magnet.

"I'm actually visiting the Archives on official palace duty, but I suppose a detour wouldn't hurt," Prince Dhruv says, the lie rolling off his tongue smooth as silk.

"And your companion?" the professor asks. I peer out from behind Dhruv.

"This is Princess Rani of Abai. My new friend." I flush at Dhruv's choice of words as his eyes catch mine. *Acquaintance* is more appropriate. Right? We don't know each other that well, and I certainly don't know who Dhruv is to me.

"Ah, what a pleasure to meet an Abaian royal. I heard about your visit from one of my prefects. Please join us, Princess Rani. I was just about to start the demonstration."

Prince Dhruv gestures for me to take an empty seat at the front, so I do—though I'm not sure what I'm in for. But those firebugs must have led me here for a reason; could Professor Neel have something I need? Something not available in the Scholars' Archives? His name rings a bell—and then it hits me. *Suneel Nanda.* The name of the man who wrote *The Complete History of Magic*!

In either case, something tells me this isn't a usual reading circle.

The candlelights suddenly flicker and dim, washing the room in semidarkness. Professor Neel opens his trunk, and a few slips of paper rustle to the floor. I bend down to find a diagram of a large volcano that looks vaguely familiar.

"Can anyone here tell me the significance of the Malwan Pass?"

When no one raises their hand, I lift mine timidly.

"Yes?" Professor Neel's eyes light up. His sparse brown hair barely covers his head, but there's a youthfulness in his eyes I haven't seen in a long time.

Not since Tutor.

"It was once a trade route between Abai and Retan. It was originally quite dangerous because of the many volcanoes throughout. But when they became inactive, the Pass was a common trade route. Unfortunately, it hasn't been used in ages, as trade between the two countries has dwindled."

Father hasn't spoken to Retanian dignitaries in a long while, too consumed by the war with Kaama and Amara's all-powerful mind control. Plus, Retan didn't exactly approve of the warmongering.

The professor dons a smile, impressed. "Very good. Retan is a pacifist country, hence their lack of relations with Abai of late. But of course, we're not here for a history lesson. We're here for this."

Professor Neel pulls something from his trunk, glowing red like the Bloodstone itself.

"This is a magma rock from the Pass itself, pulled from the Fire Master's volcanoes. Hence the unusual glow."

Students audibly gasp, leaning closer to get a good look at the relic. Despite my fascination, I stay back. I think I have one too many relics, from the stone to the talismans, to deal with.

"Some say that just holding the rock from the Pass can unlock a fire within us. The Fire Master called it our *agash*. An energy smoldering in our very core, connecting us to the heat broiling in the crust of the earth. Would anyone like to try?"

Students plunge their hands in the air, but it's clear Professor Neel has already made his choice, ignoring them in favor of calling Prince Dhruv to the front.

Carefully, Dhruv steps to Professor Neel's side and grips the relic in both hands. He shuts his eyes and hums. "I think I see something."

"Yes?" the professor prods.

"I see . . . what we're having for dinner tonight. Moong daal." He opens an eye, enjoying the laughter that circles through the room. I withhold an eye roll, but my mouth betrays me with a flitting grin.

"Princess Rani?" Professor Neel calls, taking back the relic with gentle hands. "How about you give it a go?"

"I'm not sure—"

"Someone with magic like you might access something from this relic that we cannot. It would be a great demonstration for the students."

Despite the guilt trip, something inside me draws me toward the rock, this piece of ancient history, of the Fire Master's creation.

I inch toward the front and grasp the rock carefully. Everyone in the circle glances up, pencils poised on their papers like this might be on a test.

I shutter my eyes closed and focus on the feeling of the dust and ash and rock, so strong and aggressive compared to my snake magic.

My gut burns with heat. I feel the *agash* sear through me like a blazing fire, racing through my fingertips and into the rock. For a moment, as fire surges through me, I feel as if I am back in the Glass Temple. That I could open my eyes and look into the Fire

Master's once more. His warm presence feels so close, as though it is pulling at my own fire and redirecting it. When I open my eyes, the rock is glowing in the middle, forming some kind of symbol. I tilt my head. A triangle within the sun.

The symbol I'd seen beneath the Three Blessed Sisters' portraits— and on the door to the sealed chamber.

"Observe!" says Professor Neel with elation, and I faintly hear pencils drop and mouths click open in awe.

My fingers loosen with sudden wonderment, and the relic crashes to the floor. The symbol fades into nonexistence as Professor Neel rushes to scoop up the relic and check for damage.

"I'm sorry—"

"That's perfectly all right," Professor Neel says when he sees no harm has been done. He returns it to his trunk with both hands. "Magic can be . . . overstimulating. It's best we don't overdo it." He clears his throat. "And on that note, that'll be the end of today's demonstration. Thank you, pupils, for your attentiveness. Let's reconvene next week; good luck on your exams."

Groans and sighs. Then the students filter out of the room, leaving me, Prince Dhruv, and Professor Neel in the flickering candlelight.

"It's a delight to see you again, Prince Dhruv," Professor Neel says with sudden pointedness. "How long has it been? One might even say you were . . . *avoiding* me."

Dhruv forces an unconvincing laugh. "Of course not, professor."

Professor Neel smiles, but an uneasy tension remains.

"Professor Neel, if I may ask—why did that symbol appear? I thought the relic was supposed to light some sort of fire inside us. Was that all figurative?" I ramble, hoping to get his attention off Dhruv and on to our plight.

"Magic can be as figurative as a walnut. Sometimes you have to crack it open to reap the benefits within," Professor Neel says, attention turning to me.

Dhruv tilts a brow. "I'm not sure that made any sense."

Ignoring the prince, the professor continues, "That symbol appeared as a result of *your* connection to the magma rock. I can't determine what it means because it pertains only to you."

"I think it means that the Three Blessed Sisters are more important to your journey than you know," Dhruv surmises. "The triangle represents the three sisters, and the equal sides represent their belief that all magics are of the same importance. None lesser, none greater. The sun is their bright reign over Retan . . . until their untimely deaths."

"Untimely deaths? What happened to them?" I ask, surprised. For all I'd researched about the sisters, I'd never heard of anything odd about their deaths.

Professor Neel's lips thin. "They simply vanished on the same day. Their bones were eventually found in the Malwan Pass, but no one could discover *how* they died. Some say Amran brought them an early death so they wouldn't have to face suffering in the future. A kind theory. Now if you don't mind, I have a lecture to prepare for." He begins collecting the fallen papers and returning them to his trunk.

"My apologies, professor, but Dhruv mentioned earlier that you were previously a scholar, and I was hoping to ask you some questions. We came to the Archives looking for answers regarding something of precious value to me. It's called the Bloodstone. I've heard scholars have much knowledge of it—and since you wrote *The Complete History of Magic*, I thought you might be able to help us."

Professor Neel bristles for a moment before returning his attention to his papers. "I can't help you as a scholar. I retracted my oath years ago."

"Yet you teach magic to students eager to learn about the past," I argue. "I believe you're still a scholar at heart."

"That is different. None of what I teach is practical. It's merely curiosity. The Bloodstone is real—too real, and too dangerous. And as I said, I'm no longer a scholar."

"Teachers are scholars," Dhruv says, coming to my aid. "They spread knowledge far and wide like the Retanian eagle. I trust you would help someone in dire need."

The professor thumbs a sheet of paper. "And what dire need would that be?"

"Stopping a woman who wishes to use the Bloodstone to become a Master," I say.

The professor freezes. Intrigued, I lift a brow. "Do you know her? Amara Gupta came to Retan four years ago to research the stone." She'd told me and Ria that she'd used her cuffs on scholars to get the information she wanted . . . was Professor Neel one of them?

I know I'm right when Professor Neel visibly shivers, and I swear his knees buckle as he moves to sit. His age seems suddenly apparent when he rubs the fine wrinkles on his forehead. "I gave in," he finally says, covering his eyes. "It was my fault. I collapsed under her demands. I knew she wanted the stone for destructive purposes—for more than just her husband—but I couldn't even control my own tongue."

"You were under a magical influence—the Memory Master's talisman. It wasn't your fault, professor." I gentle my tone. "Please, I need to know how to stop her. I wish to destroy the stone."

Professor Neel laughs with no mirth. "Destroy the Bloodstone? That is no simple task, Princess Rani. Even the scholars do not know how to accomplish that. I warned the woman, this Amara, of the Bloodstone's harm, but there was greed in her eyes, darker and deeper than any greed I've ever seen before." He gulps. "She wanted something impossible. Her husband, returned to life."

I nod. "She wants that still. She believes she can use the Blood-stone to become a Master capable of bringing him back."

"Because I told her. I told her everything—but I didn't think she would take my theories so far."

For a moment, I think Professor Neel is going to close off from me, but he continues, "The Three Blessed Sisters were very knowledgeable about the subject of the Bloodstone. And highly secretive.

They lived during the fall of the Masters, and within years had become triplet queens of this land. If anyone would know how to destroy the stone, it's them."

"But, sir," I begin, "they're not alive."

"They might not be, but lucky for you, Retan is all about preserving history. There are several articles and books that recorded the queens' obsession with the Bloodstone. Back then, it was considered a holy grail of sorts. . . ." A long pause. "I shouldn't be talking about this."

"Please, professor. I need to know whatever I can to stop her." My voice cracks in earnest. *Her.* Amara. The monster both inside and out.

Professor Neel gives in to my and Dhruv's equally pleading gaze. Clearly, the two have a shared, albeit likely rocky, history. "I studied the sisters at length. Each sister knew about the Bloodstone and its properties. Queen Sampada, a science fanatic, attempted to formulate something that could destroy the stone. This we know with certainty from scientific papers in the Academy."

Professor Neel gestures at the school. "Queen Saira's poetry spoke of her desire to find a stone and break it, in much more lyrical language, of course. She also consulted all manners of folktales and oral histories to discover any possible clues to the Bloodstone's whereabouts, and wrote about the night the Masters disappeared by means of the stone. And Queen Sunita believed nature was the answer to destroying the stone, and pursued every possible option vigorously. But upon their mysterious deaths on the same day, rumors spread that the sisters had hidden away their discoveries where no one could find and use them for ill."

That doesn't narrow it down much. But I had seen the Three Sister's symbol in the stone. That had to mean something.

"The symbol that appeared in the stone," I begin. "It was on the door in the Blue Palace, right? Do you know what's behind it? Why the sisters built the chamber?"

Dhruv raises a curious brow. "Mother always believed it was a place for the Three Blessed Sisters to privately work on their creative endeavors. Or . . . their more secretive ones."

"Secrets about magic," I say. What if their findings are all hidden in the chamber? What if it holds the answer to destroying the Bloodstone?

"Professor Neel," I ask, mind circling back to Amara, "what do you know of the Soul Master?" I dig through my small purse until I find the crinkled page about the myth of the Soul Master, offering it to him.

Prince Dhruv looks intrigued.

The professor casts his gaze to the floor, not taking my offering. "Too little and too much, apparently." At my confusion, he elaborates, "Many believe the Soul Master was intended to be the seventh and final Master. Others believe a Soul Master's power, of controlling life and death itself, was preposterous—something only Amran could perform or will."

"What do you believe?"

Professor Neel taps his fingers on his desk in an insistent

pattern. "I believe the Soul Master was indeed made as the seventh Master. There are even references to such a person in ancient texts, and the name of what would have become the Master's future descendants, called specterwalkers, capable of wielding this soul magic. Why the Soul Master might have been Unmade by Amran himself, I do not know. But there is evidence that this Master, and this power, once existed, if only for a short period of time."

"The empty portrait in the Glass Temple," I remember. There were portraits of all the Masters in the Temple, but the seventh and final one was empty.

"So if someone *wanted* to become a Soul Master, and achieved such a thing, how could one . . . *stop* them?"

"A Master cannot be stopped," Neel says darkly.

"But several were. By the Snake Master."

"Yes. By another *Master*," the professor retorts. "We are mere mortals, Princess Rani. A rogue Master would have too much power for anyone but another Master—or Amran himself—to stop."

I swallow hard.

"Amara won't be a mere mortal for long. She's seeking all the talismans—might you have an idea why?"

Professor Neel pinches the bridge of his nose. "This is dangerous. No one alive has seen the power of the talismans together. To access a talisman's magic is to access Amran's own powers. If all the talismans were brought together, that would be enough to unlock the lifeblood of Amran from within the stone."

Silence fills the air, heavy as a veil of fog. *This* is what Amara desires. The ultimate power necessary to make her wish.

"We have to stop her," I say, numb. "Amara already has two of the talismans, and she'll harm anyone who gets in her path to find more."

"T-two? Amara has two of the talismans in her possession already?" Professor Neel's pallor lightens at my nod and his knees weaken. "Sands above. This is much worse than I thought."

"What is it?" I press.

But Professor Neel says nothing, only pulls a nib of chalk from his trunk. He jots something down and hands me the note.

"Head to the Island Market and ask for Jujhar. Tell him my warning. It's written there, on the back of the paper."

"Warning?" I say, confused. I flip it over. *The Sky will darken if the feather is not protected.*

"He will understand its meaning. Hurry. You must find him soon if your search is truly so dire. He will have information on the talismans for you." He sweeps up his notes and places them back in his trunk, fingers trembling as he latches it closed. "I apologize for my tone, Princess Rani and Prince Dhruv, but I really would not like to be involved in this any further. I wish you the best of luck."

"Of course." I cling to the note, wondering who this person is that I will meet, and what he might have for me.

15

Ria

Frost kisses my gloved fingers as I leap down the crags in the mountainside, taking in the sights and smells of Amratstan.

The capital, Kalpur, is more beautiful in the morning than I expected. People dressed in blues and golds bustle around, carting slabs of carved ice; others cook gobi in pots over flame. The hustle and chaos invigorate me. Something about being by myself out here reminds me of mornings in Abai: just me and Amir chasing jewels and naan, stealing from vendors, craving freedom like a hot meal and a warm, crackling fire.

I make my way to the bottom of the mountain, jump from the rock, and land on both feet, arms out for balance. I smile to myself. I've still got it.

Some part of me misses the old days. The other part remembers my hunger and thirst—for food and for shelter. For a life I could claim as my own.

Thank the skies Veer's potion helped me sleep last night, or else

I wouldn't have an ounce of strength this morning. Not after what I saw last night—Amara. Her words burn through my memory. *I am an illusion of the mind, placed here by the one who is connected to you perhaps even more than Rani.*

Who could possibly be connected to me *more* than Rani? It feels impossible—only my bond with Shima comes close.

But I don't have time to unravel Amara's cryptic words right now. The whole world hangs in the balance of my and Rani's actions—and I need to do my part and find the Earth Master's talisman before Amara does.

I head for the outer rim of the village now. Sentinels have already checked the palace and its base for Amara, at the urging of King Rohit and Zoya. No such luck. So we're taking our search to the woods today.

Snow falls gently from the sky as sellers ready their products in tightly packed stalls. Fresh-caught fish laid out on carts of ice; karela piled into sky-high crates. I've never had a tooth for bitter melon, even though it was often all the orphanage could afford for the week's vegetable supply.

I wind through the stalls, chunni pulled over my head, a simple salwar kameez for my morning garb. Amratstanians probably wouldn't recognize Princess Rani out here, but it can't hurt to be careful. And there's something freeing about having no identity for a moment, to have no name, no face.

"Looking for something?" a voice calls from behind me.

Moment over.

His curls, struck through with bone-white streaks, are the first thing I notice. Then the hazel eyes tucked beneath thick brows, the glimmer of what looks like a tiny gold bead studded into his right earlobe.

"That's new," I tell Saeed, voice breathy. Somehow, in the dewy morning glow of sunlight, he looks even more handsome than he did last night at dinner. My stomach warms as his gaze settles on me.

"Amratstanian tradition," he says, pointing at the earring. "King Rohit's gift, according to the palace staff. Just put it in after dinner. It's . . . well, good luck, for soon-to-be newlyweds."

I blanch. "Oh."

"I didn't have time to correct them," he adds quickly. Something about him out here, looking even the slightest bit out of place where he's usually so unruffled, makes my lips quirk upward.

"Another charade, then?" I quip. "I'm good at those."

He glances down, a slow smile creeping onto his lips. Today he's dressed in a fine blue kurta pajama under a white coat emblazoned with Amratstan's crest—a snowbird. They're good messengers, according to my parents, even though King Rohit never received his letter.

Strange.

Saeed scrunches his nose. "Maybe we should talk somewhere away from the fish."

"You don't have to tell me twice."

We pause at the woods' entrance. I spot Neeta and Neesa, and a pleasant warmth surges through me. They're dressed in equally fine blue coats with gold buttons, also threaded with the Amratstanian crest. Below them, two wolves paw at the snow. But they're not regular wolves. The tips of their fur are coated with ice. *Icewolves*. As they shake their heads, a melodious tinkle fills the air, and they nudge their heads playfully against the Sentinels' boots.

I turn my attention to Irfan, standing beside the twins. He looks fit to be a soldier, dressed in black boots and a fur cloak that covers equally dark clothes. Rani did tell me he likes to blend with the shadows.

There's one last person here who I hadn't expected.

"My ma loved these woods," Zoya says by way of explanation when she sees me. "And I thought you could use another pair of eyes."

At least she looks like she's forgotten about last night's disaster at dinner. I shiver remembering it.

"Your mother?" I say.

Zoya smiles wanly. "We used to take walks together in these woods. They were her favorite place, before she passed. She said the spirit of the Earth Master watches over these woods still." Her smile dissipates. "But if he does, I wonder why the woods would have taken her away."

I didn't know Zoya's mother passed in these woods. A hazy image of Mama Anita floats back to me, reminding me of our last conversation together. A final goodbye. I wish Zoya could have had that. Maybe there is something connecting me and Zoya after all.

"What if the woods didn't take her? If this really was her favorite place . . . maybe they were welcoming her. Allowing her to rest peacefully."

Zoya's eyes well, but she blinks the tears back. "Maybe," she agrees. "Ria . . . I want to apologize. I haven't welcomed you here as I should. With our fathers' feud, I assumed . . . But our heads have been clouded with anger for years. It's time we clear them."

"I'd like that, too." I extend an arm, hoping she'll clasp it in kind, and she does. A warm Amratstanian greeting, I've learned, to welcome a friend. I hope that's what I can become with Zoya.

The soldiers' talwars gleam in the sunlight. Trees proudly flank the entrance to the forest, bending toward the ground as if waiting for us.

Waiting for the first day of the hunt.

The soldiers enter the forest first, Princess Zoya behind, dressed in sunset pinks that contrast with the soldiers' sapphire coats, with me and Saeed helming the rear. I'm grateful for the snow boots laid out for me this morning—already inches of snow have filled the forest, with snowbanks rising high and nearly covering tree trunks by our sides.

Still, I feel bare out here without Shima. But I knew bringing her out here wouldn't help. Snakes are like thieves: neither are made for cold weather.

My breaths come out in thin, puffy clouds as we trek deeper into the woods. Looming trees cast shadows all around us, making the whole forest that much darker and more terrifying.

Something on my right catches my eye. I twist to take a look, but my foot catches on a root and I stumble—

"I've got you," Saeed whispers, clutching my arm to help me right myself. His hazel gaze doesn't leave mine.

"I . . . ," I start to say. But a tranquil whirl of snow descends from above, landing in Saeed's hair and blending with the white streaks. He glances up, and I do, too. There's something magical about the snow. Not any snow—but the gentle kind, swirling in a soft vortex all around us, as if made just for this moment.

Zoya's voice interrupts my thoughts.

"Hurry up, snowbirds!" I catch sight of her shaking her head and winking at me. My cheeks burn—from the wind and Saeed. Damn, he's good at sweeping a girl off her feet. Literally.

We continue through the snow. "If we find her," I whisper, "what do you think will happen?"

"I've dreamed of that moment over and over. *Actual* dreams—not visions," Saeed corrects. "Sometimes I face Mother with courage. Others . . ." He shakes his head. "I haven't told anyone this, but sometimes, in my dreams, I *want* her to become the Soul Master. I want her to bring Father back, just so I can see him one more time. Have them both back." He laughs, but it sounds pained. He glances sideways at me. "Is it wrong of me to want that? To get what I've never had?"

A father.

I purse my lips. "You shouldn't be afraid of how you feel."

"That's the thing. I *am* afraid." A snowflake lands on his face and melts into a teardrop. He wipes it away with a finger. "When I have visions of her, she looks terrifying. Wrong. Like she's no longer herself."

Her face comes back to me: hooded eyes, bloody lips. He's right. She is terrifying. And Saeed should know the truth—should know that I saw his mother last night with the mysterious Black Viper. *We need the girl.* What if that girl is . . . me? But I can't bring myself to tell him, to add another weight to his shoulders.

I know all too well how long these visions can linger. My own nightmares cling to me like a second skin; how much I want to find the mysterious voice in them, that girl I saw in the Snake River. . . . I fear I won't be able to escape them soon.

"It may not be as bad as we fear," I venture, hoping that what I say is the truth. "I believe we can find her before things get worse."

Saeed only shakes his head. "I know you're trying to comfort me, Ria—but I don't know how much I can believe that. She's deceptive. Cunning."

It's true—Amara seems one step ahead of us at every turn, and her ruthlessness has never abated. What can I offer in the face of that?

We reach a tall snowbank and pause for a moment, catching our breath.

Steeling my nerves and reaching out, I grasp gently on to

Saeed's hand and clasp it between both of my own. Saeed turns to look at me fully, his eyes softening as they land on mine.

"I know it feels hopeless," I say. "But whatever happens . . . we'll face it together. You won't have to do it alone." My cheeks flare at the admission and I try to hide my thoughts, but I feel like Saeed can see every emotion written on my face, just like Shima.

"Thank you, Ria," Saeed murmurs. He's so close that the fog of his breath in the cool air meets mine. "You have no idea what a comfort that is."

I squeeze his hand between mine once more, feeling the warmth between us, before I reluctantly let go and we begin to follow after the others.

"We *are* quite good at working together, aren't we?" Saeed continues, a smile playing around his lips as we crest the bank. "Ever since you convinced me to climb up into the rafters with you and spy on a war council."

I gasp in pretend affront, though it's nearly ruined by the laugh bubbling up inside of me. "Me, convince *you*? I'll have you know I never did a dishonest thing in my life before I met you. You obviously corrupted me."

"My plan all along," Saeed intones gravely, before turning to grin at me. "Luckily, it didn't take long."

"Hey now," I object, halting in my steps so that we're facing each other. "I wasn't *that* easily swayed by all your charm."

I mean, that's definitely a lie. But *he* doesn't have to know that.

"Then tell me, Ria," he says, some of the teasing leaving his tone. "When did you first start taking a liking to me?"

"O-oh." Whatever I was expecting him to ask me, it wasn't that. "Well," I say, adding a veneer of false confidence to my voice, "it definitely wasn't when you first kissed the back of my hand on Diwali night."

"Oh?" he says, thinking back. "Ah, correct. I was a stranger to you then."

"And it definitely wasn't when you gave me that lesson on the Rao Raja," I continue, though I remember blushing before him that day in front of that damned snake. Shima is a good match-maker. I'll give her that much.

"Ah, so it *did* take me awhile, then?" he asks, still not making any move to advance, despite the soldiers and Zoya disappearing up a steep slope ahead.

But it's like his stare becomes too much, reminding me of what we are. Heat and ice and everything opposite—everything that isn't meant to be together. Yet somehow, it's all I want.

"I don't think it was just one moment," I reveal to him. "I think it was all of them. I didn't know what I was doing back then—I just knew I had to act as Rani," I admit. "I'm a thief. I sneak around and steal food and money when I can. I'm not used to pampering or being looked at by nobility. It was all so different. But every step, every moment—you were there for me."

Saeed smirks, gestures at the frigid air around us. "And this is pampering? Walking on foot in deep snow?"

"Snow is a relief from Abai's heat. But you're shivering," I realize. I pull the glove from my hand and press it to his cheek as if to warm him from the outside in. His honeyed gaze pierces mine. "Your cheeks are red. Does this help?"

"I don't think they are red from the cold," he says in a whisper.

My stomach flutters. I pull back, but he catches my hand and presses it against his cheek again. My fingers creep closer to his hair, finding purchase in the curls that bounce above his thick brows. My whole body tingles, telling me to close the distance between us.

As Saeed leans down, my lips cool and burn at the same time, aching both for his touch—and wondering if I'm doing the right thing. His lips brush against mine, and I withhold a gasp as his teeth gently bite my bottom lip, tugging me nearer. I'm so close to melting into him—

But Saeed pulls back all too quickly. He gasps, bringing two fingers to his temple before focusing on a spot behind me, eyes glazed over.

"Saeed?" I wave a hand in front of his face, cheeks suddenly cold. "What's wrong?"

He shudders in another big breath, eyes snapping back to mine.

"Over there," he whispers, hoarse. "By the fallen tree."

I open my mouth to speak, but Irfan interrupts. "Something the matter?"

The others have paused to watch us.

Saeed says, "I—I had a vision." He points at the tree next to Irfan.

Irfan turns, inspecting the branches. He whistles to the ice-wolves, who've already begun to search the area surrounding the large banyan tree with a broken trunk.

"Saeed, what did you see?"

Tension feathers his jaw. "It's under the snow."

An icewolf yelps, its bark reverberating through the forest. "It?" I repeat to Saeed, but he doesn't say anything else.

Mind scattered, I leave Saeed and rush toward the tree. The icewolves sniff the pale snow. Irfan extends an arm as I draw near. A sign.

"Don't move any closer."

He bends down and brushes away the snow at the base of the tree. His hand halts as it connects with something hidden beneath the snow, something frozen stiff. A feather? He pushes the snow back more until I see it. Them.

I nearly heave.

"Frosts below," one of the twins gasps. Sentinel Neeta. "Now we know where our snowbirds went," she says, eyeing Zoya.

Our snowbirds have been less reliable of late, I hear King Rohit saying.

The snowbirds' eyes are closed, their wings broken and mangled as they lie in a mass. I want to look away, to forget this grotesque scene, but a part of me can't.

"W-who could've done this?" I ask, turning back toward Saeed. He's still on his knees in the snow. But part of me already knows the answer.

"My mother was there," he says, loud enough for the Sentinels to hear. "She passed by here not too long ago. I saw it."

I approach Saeed carefully. "D-do you mean she . . ."

Suddenly, he's red-faced from what looks like anger.

"No! My mother isn't a killer," he says, as if to convince himself, even though we know otherwise. He lifts his gaze to Irfan, but the soldier doesn't look so convinced.

"She may not be in her right mind," I tell him, letting all my worries loose from my tongue.

Saeed's eyes crinkle with concern.

"There's . . . more I haven't told you," I begin. "I saw her last night. She was talking to me, saying only I could see her. That something was . . . connecting us." I almost gag at the thought of the dead snowbirds, pressing a hand to my mouth instead.

"Princess Ria," Irfan says with dark eyes I haven't seen from him before, "please tell me you haven't been keeping secrets from us about Amara."

The accusation sends a spike of anger through me. As if I haven't been *trying* to decipher these dreams ever since they started plaguing me. As if I'm not as lost as they are.

"I never saw these birds in my nightmares, and she never mentioned them last night," I say, unable to muster more energy to defend myself. "I swear."

Dead silence fills the air.

Eventually, the twin Sentinels pick up one of the snowbirds and wrap it inside a cloth. "We'll take the birds to the palace for a proper burial. The icewolves will continue on the trail, and we'll see if we can find anything more."

The Sentinels leave, Zoya following close behind, though I catch her looking at me warily. Unbidden, my thoughts flash back to the night of the party; my power surging out of control, the guests looking at me with the same wariness and horror. As though I'm a snake about to bite at any second.

Irfan, a thousand questions flitting across his face, follows the Sentinels, leaving me alone with Saeed.

I begin to move toward him, but he holds up a hand.

He exhales shakily, his usually reassuring gaze now cold. "Ria. You should have told me what you saw of my mother. I deserved to know."

I want to reach out, comfort him somehow, but the spark that was just there a moment ago has been replaced by ice.

Maybe that's the way it's meant to be.

We leave the forest in a tense silence. I think back to the horrid discovery of the birds, buried under freshly fallen snow. I'm not sure why Amara would have targeted them in the first place. Which means the dead snowbirds are just the beginning.

Amara

The taste of blood is not so bad any longer.

In fact, it tastes like ripe pomegranate, native to Kaama's shores. It tastes like a childhood spent along frosted beaches and around ever-growing fruit.

It tastes like home.

"They've found several of the snowbirds," the voice from within her says. She looks down from a crag in the mountainside, watching the girl and boy exit the snow-blanketed forest. A spark, a flare, spreads through her. Her son is so close. Soon, they will be reunited.

Once she accomplishes her task.

"It's no issue. The Earth Master's talisman is close." Amara turns to their confidant, the snake tattoo on his palm flaring with light.

He shall be a great help, Amara thinks. Once she finds the talismans, she will get the power she has waited for.

She will finally make her wish.

She'll see Kumal again, holding roses and offering sweet kisses.

She'll have the kingdom of Kaama at her mercy. Her long-awaited revenge, so sweet.

Kumal. My rose. He never deserved his death. For years, wearing the Memory Master's cuffs, she felt powerful and powerless all at once. She couldn't manipulate the raja of Abai without remembering the manipulation her father once wrought on her. The scars that never faded on her hands. The jeers from her husband's family when they discovered what—*who*—she was, half Kaaman, half Abaian.

A memory surfaces of a girl running through her small village, Zira, at the edge of Kaama's eastern border. She waves her freshly woven coconut-palm fan in the air, watching it flutter. She can almost hear the whistle of the palm fan against the air, as melodic as birdsong.

The sea stretches out beside her, lined with jagged rocks. She'd been told to never visit the sea, for the waters beyond were unforgiving.

But from afar, the glittering sea was harmless. Inviting, even. For a brief second, she feels euphoria. Hot sun on her skin. Grainy sand between her toes.

Sunlight bounces off the waves, hitting her eyes and making her dizzy for a moment. Purple spots float beneath her eyelids. But before she can stop running, she trips and crashes onto the sand, face-first. Sparks of pain explode in her head.

Amara's head.

She growls now, remembering the rumors. That day, no one blamed the boy who left his taut rope along the beach's sands. A trap? No. She had been running too fast. She had been too happy. She should have been inside.

But she remembered what the boy said, looming over her when she opened her eyes, his lips scrunched up with spit. "Filthy pupa."

She'd heard the word many times. Not a caterpillar nor a butterfly, but in between. That was all she was. Neither fully Abaian nor fully Kaaman, but half. Never whole.

She would remember that pain, the word stabbing her harder than the jagged rocks. And when she came home, hiding her bruises with her frayed chunni, she saw her father waiting for her, his cuffs glowing with golden light.

Amara breathes in deeply, willing no tears to fall. She can still smell the salty sea spray. She can still feel the hundreds of cuts on her arm, stinging in pain later that night, as though she'd been cut by glass instead of seashells.

Her whole life, she had been cut and molded into the person people wanted her to be. She had been cut so many times she was no longer human but a shattered shell.

This is my second chance. Kumal's *second chance. I will not waste it.*

"Well, what are you waiting for? Inform the others," Amara tells the man at her side, more determined now than the moment she left Kaama, more determined than the day she decided poisoning her son was a small risk in her greater scheme. *This is for them.* For her family and a love so great it burdened her into wickedness.

This would be her story, rewritten and reclaimed, and she *would* have her happy ending.

16

Rani

The isles before me rest in the sparkling sea like the inlaid jewels of a crown.

Before me, Amir, and Dhruv is what looks like a tropical oasis, with floating islands peppered amid the still waters. Stars crowd the night sky, filling the air with dusky light, but it's the oil lamps of all hues that make the oasis come alive, dangling in midair as though they're drifting firelarks coasting on the water.

This is it. The place where we are to meet this mysterious Jujhar.

The Island Market, Professor Neel's note had told me yesterday. *Meet Jujhar at the Night Tavern. Walk to the hearth and ask for him.*

Now that we know why Amara needs the talismans—to obtain their combined powers and become the Master of Souls—our mission has become ten times more urgent.

It also means we don't have the time to linger in these breathtaking surroundings.

Ria would love it here, I think, and resolutely plan to bring her here one day. After Amara. After our world is safe.

"This," Amir says, echoing my thoughts unconsciously and licking his lips as a woman with a basket of papayas on her head passes by, "is a thief's paradise."

Indeed, if I were a thief, I would be just as captivated. Thick crowds fill the market, where customers haggle for what I can tell are fake silken scarves, and children slurp on mangoes at the feet of their grandparents. The smell of fresh fish and curried crab rises from the stalls, where workers cook with searing flames nearly reaching the sky.

We walk through the main passageway, wedged between tightly packed stalls. I hear the crackle of frying onions, the sizzle of steaming pakoras. My mouth waters at the incredible smells that drift our way. A woman nearby flips dosas on a steaming thava, the turmeric-spiced potato filling oozing out. We pass stall after stall of tantalizing sights and smells, until finally we arrive at the dilapidated doorway marking the Night Tavern's entrance.

"Fireglobes," Dhruv explains from my other side, pointing upward. "They're magicked balls of light, made by flametalkers of the Old Age. Flametalkers once used their fire magic to sweep the sands, blow glass, and cut gems. We have many remnants of magic here in Retan. If you look closely, you'll find a bit of it everywhere."

Not oil lamps, then. I find an easy warmth in his eyes as I turn to him, and my belly burns pleasantly.

I spin to Amir to avoid gazing at the prince, but Amir is munching on fried dough, crumbs staining the corners of his lips. I elbow him. "What? I didn't *steal* this. I just paid less than the sale price."

I giggle warmly, enjoying being outside of the palace with Amir—free of the pressure to hide our affection or perform as a princess. And especially not having to watch Amir charm Prefect Padma, no matter that it got us into the library. I flush. Why am I thinking of that now? It meant nothing to me . . . or Amir. Right?

Dhruv doesn't appear to have heard Amir, and swings the door in front of us open with a grin, like he's done this a thousand times before. Perhaps he has. As prince, he seems to know his kingdom well. Better than I did mine.

Within moments, sound washes over me: the thump of dancers dressed in vibrant salwars; their claps to the beat of the tabla; the jeers of patrons sloshing over cups of drink.

"Honey brew," Dhruv points out. "Honey is one of Retan's most sacred and lucrative exports; honeybees were Queen Sunita's favorite."

As he speaks, my eyes scan the tavern. The wooden space is small yet full of people swinging left and right, celebrating nothing but a starry night and good fortunes. A month ago, I would have thought this place bawdy, but now, the sound of coarse music drumming over my thoughts makes me relax. *Try to have a little fun, sis*, Ria told me the moment we parted ways for our journeys. Well, fun is certainly accessible in Retan.

In the back corner of the tavern, we find a lit hearth where two chairs are perched, their wooden legs beginning to warp from age. As we approach, a woman smoking a pipe looses a breath and says in her husky voice, "You three look like trouble." She grins, sitting back, not even the slightest bit fazed by the prince in her midst. Her hair tumbles in coiled ringlets, dyed a deep red with mehendi, like Amara's. But her face is more soft and subtle, with a smile on her thin lips and crinkling her kajal-rimmed eyes. "Would you like to smoke?" she says, offering the pipe.

I respectfully decline. "We're looking for a man named Jujhar. Can you help us find him?"

"Jujhar," the woman says, practically scoffing. "The man never leaves his study." She points behind her, breathing in the smoke. "Good luck. He won't see the likes of you," she says, looking me up and down, and then eyeing the prince. What does that mean? That Jujhar is not a fan of royalty?

We skirt past the hearth and up the stairs of a nearby corridor. There stands a navy-blue door, shoddily painted. Dhruv knocks thrice. Footsteps sound, and the door whirls open.

Jujhar does not look anything like I expected. I thought I would meet a man of Professor Neel's age, but he looks only a handful of summers older than I. His thick brows frown when he gazes at us, and surge even lower when his eyes land on Prince Dhruv.

"No thanks," Jujhar says, about to slam the door, but I catch it at the last moment.

"Halt," I command, using my most haughty princess tone, and Jujhar does, shocked into stillness. "I am the princess of Abai. I have spoken with Suneel Nanda and he told us to come here and meet you."

"About what?" Jujhar scoffs. "How to interrupt someone's night?"

"About the talismans," I say, anger rising at his dismissal. Jujhar turns slack-jawed.

"What do you want with those?" he asks, suspicious. Standing under a fireglobe, eyes hooded, he reminds me a bit of Irfan when we first met. Wary and uncompromising; a steely exterior that hides any true feelings from view.

"Whatever you can tell us." My eyes catch on something drifting through the room behind Jujhar. A bird settles on his shoulder, chirping melodically. Its wings are iridescent, indigo and midnight blues all at once—I've never seen anything like it.

"This is my skyhawk, Sahara." Jujhar turns to the bird, which quickly takes flight. "Don't be fooled. She can grow up to the size of a tiger when she wants. Helps if I need to travel quickly." This whole statement also sounds a bit like a warning.

"Yet you seem to stick to your study." I raise my eyebrow.

Jujhar only grumbles. "Come inside," he says. Not exactly the best welcome, but if it allows us to talk with him, I'll hold my tongue.

The inside of Jujhar's study is like a treasure trove. But instead of treasure, Amir, Dhruv, and I are surrounded by books, nuggets of information as precious as any piece of gold.

My eyes trail upward, absorbing the seemingly endless shelves and a ceiling that could touch the clouds, where Sahara flits about. But, I realize, there are no stairs, nor a ladder to reach the books perched on the highest levels.

"Whoa," Amir breathes. His eyes widen, and papers shuffle on Jujhar's desk as a fierce wind passes by, cold to the bone. I shiver, looking around for an open window or draft, but find nothing.

"You wanna know about the talismans?" Jujhar asks.

"Yes. We need to find them, and we need to know *what* some of them are, too," I say.

I dig into the satchel I brought with me and pull out the notebook the queen gifted me. I flip it open to the first page, where I wrote the list of the talismans, and offer it to Jujhar.

"Impressive," he says, handing the book back to me. "But it seems you don't have the Sky Master's talisman listed here."

I shake my head. "That's the thing. We don't know what it is. But we do know that it's in danger."

Jujhar goes silent for a moment. "The talismans aren't simply objects on a list. They're connected to the people they represent. And, well, you can only really learn this stuff from people like me."

"People like you?" I wonder.

Jujhar nods. With a flick of his hands, books tumble off the shelf. I raise my hands to protect my head, gasping, but the books halt in midair just before they can crash down, a gentle wind keeping them aloft. I gape when I realize *Jujhar* is doing this, all by himself. Nearby, an enchanted pen begins to sign documents, and each page moves into a new pile, as if swept by a sudden breeze.

"You're a currentspinner," I breathe.

Jujhar nods, then flicks his hands, and another gust of wind sends the books right back to their places. "My family is descended from the Sky Master. I haven't told many about my magic. Professor Neel is one of the few who knows. Only he—and the royalty—know about my keeping . . ." He trails off.

"Keeping what?" Amir says.

"Nothing."

"But then you would know about the Sky Master's talisman! Right?" I feel the excitement rush through me. "Do you know where it is?"

Jujhar's expression closes off further at my question.

"The Sky Master's descendants had our talisman for only a few generations," he says, his eyes focused oddly on Prince Dhruv. "The Sky Master was very close to the triplet queens before they were royalty. But the talisman was taken away—"

"By the Sky Master, and given to the triplets instead, entrusting these wise and respected sisters. We understand how difficult that was," Dhruv finishes carefully, looking as if he's treading on thin ice.

"Difficult?" Jujhar scoffs. "The Sky Master *betrayed* her own kind in hopes the talisman would be preserved and safeguarded by the sisters. Which it wasn't."

"And you've been mad at the royals ever since?" Amir guesses. "That's a long grudge," he mutters under his breath.

"My ancestors' *grudge* is just," Jujhar counters, glaring at

Dhruv. "Could you ever truly comprehend being separated from something that not only belonged to you—but was a part of you? Even when the talisman was no longer in danger, Retanian royalty kept it from us out of greed."

The prince's eyes harden, not with hatred but with hurt. A look I recognize. I've worn the same gaze several times as the princess of Abai, receiving stares from aunties in the palace halls. Dhruv and I share something in common, that's for certain—a life of royal responsibility, and all the pain that comes with it.

But this is clearly an old feud, and we're getting nowhere revisiting it. I switch tactics.

"We want to keep the talismans safe," I say. "Professor Neel knew that and told us to come to you for help. And to give you this warning." I show him the slip of paper.

"*The Sky will darken if the feather is not protected*," Jujhar recites. His eyes burn sharply into the note. "This can't be."

"It's like we said," Amir adds gently. "The talismans *are* in danger. And your old professor led us to you for a reason. Maybe he thought your magic could help us?"

Jujhar shakes his head, still clutching the note in his hand. "Currentspinners today don't have the same level of magic as those of the Old Age. My ancestors were once able to move the land itself. They *created* this haven, the Island Market, for currentspinners. Our wind powers keep the islands afloat and close together, our own tropical oasis. Now, I can barely toss a few books around. It's the same with all magics. I mean, imagine seeing a flametalker today. It's almost impossible."

"But . . . we have," I say.

Dhruv and Jujhar both look askance at me. Their silence propels me to explain how we met flametalkers at the Glass Temple. Those who protected both their magic and the secrets of the Temple and knew a way to connect directly with the spirit of the Fire Master.

"You know much more about magic than I realized." Jujhar rubs his chin. He looks down once more at the note in his hand, face pale, and seems to come to a decision. "Prince Dhruv has likely already told you this, but . . . I am the keeper of the Sky Master's talisman."

I nearly choke. "You *have* the talisman?"

Jujhar's eyes snap toward Dhruv's. "You never told them?"

Dhruv gazes down at his feet. "It was not my secret to tell."

"I thought the triplet queens had it. Or their descendants. . . ," I query Dhruv with a raised brow.

"My mother wanted to see the talisman returned properly and peacefully," Dhruv says. "Which is why, ever since, we've maintained a good relationship, no?"

"Good?" Jujhar scoffs. "It took *centuries* for Retanian royalty to return what was rightfully ours." His eyes turn to meet mine. "Professor Neel worried this day might come. Said he knew a woman who was so interested in magic she'd kill for it. But that was years ago."

I nod. "A woman named Amara is searching for *all* the

talismans. She'll be after you next if she has not already found the other talismans. We want to stop her." I relay my story as quickly as I can. Jujhar's shoulders droop farther and farther as I speak.

"So will you take us to the talisman?" I say when I'm finished.

"I'm not going to let you take it just on your word," Jujhar says boldly. "If I'm going to entrust you with the single most important item I have, I want something in return."

I let out a breath. An exchange, then. "I'm listening."

"Wait," Dhruv cuts in. I glance at him curiously. "I know currentspinners have long been at odds with us royals—"

"*At odds* is a nice way to put it," mumbles Jujhar.

"*However*," Dhruv continues, "I'd like us to put that in the past, if you'd let us."

Jujhar huffs. "My family isn't all that good at trusting others after what happened."

"You are correct, Jujhar," Dhruv says, peeling his gaze away. "My ancestors were wrong to keep the talisman from its rightful family. And we have taken too long to apologize and atone for it. You have my word that I will personally see to it that my mother, and myself after her reign, care for the currentspinners' needs, and that we build a stronger relationship moving forward. The princess of Abai needs this talisman for an important mission. Are we in agreement?"

"Promises aren't enough," Jujhar inserts gruffly, though I can tell from his softening brows that he's listening to the prince.

Dhruv nods. "That's why I'd like to offer more. A guarantee that currentspinner needs will never be forgotten again. The position of adviser to the throne is yours, if you agree to it."

I nearly gasp, stifling it at the last moment. That is no simple promise—in Abai, advisers are rare and chosen with extreme care. To offer such a position is an enormous sign of respect, and the influence Jujhar would have is enormous.

"Will you help us?" Dhruv asks, extending a hand.

Jujhar is silent, his eyes on Dhruv's hand, and I hold my breath. *Please be enough*, I urge.

"You need to protect all the talismans. Which means you're involving me in some kind of end-of-the-world plot?" At first, I think he's going to back out, but instead, he forms a small smile, showing off two endearing dimples, and grasps Dhruv's hand warmly. "I'm up for it. Literally. I keep the vault high up. And I accept your offer."

As soon as he's finished speaking, it's like we've been tossed into a sandstorm: the wind rushes us from behind, and I find myself stumbling forward. Swiftly, Dhruv grips my left arm, while Amir clasps the other. Dhruv's and Amir's eyes find one another, oddly tense.

But I don't have time to say anything, because Jujhar snaps his fingers, and the wind picks up and we all rise a foot above the floor. I don't have time to gasp as our feet are thrust forward like a phantom's, floating through the once-still air.

"That's one way to get around," Amir jokes to Jujhar, though his voice quavers, neither of us having seen this magic before in our entire lives.

"We don't keep the talisman close to the ground, but to the sky," Jujhar explains.

Dhruv lets go of my arm, shooting another indiscernible look at Amir before he walks off, following Jujhar, his feet still hovering above the ground. Carefully, I mimic his tapping movements. Amir follows suit, his hand slipping from mine. As I walk, it's like I've stepped into the softest slippers. Like the air is silk and cotton, wrapping warmly around my toes. I lift my feet as though I'm walking on a staircase, and push away to ascend to the higher shelves.

"*Whoa*," Amir says. He taps his sandals in midair, but he still hovers, amazed.

"Back here," Jujhar says, leading us to the highest shelf. He reaches a vault and twists the lock in an intricate combination.

I lean in, watching the vault click open, and the invisible cushion beneath me suddenly vanishes.

A gasp escapes my throat and gravity seizes me once more. Blood races in my head as I tumble down. The floor rushes up to meet me, and I hold my arms out over my head, bracing for impact.

Instead, a firm hand grips my arm, halting my sudden fall. When I glance up, I find Prince Dhruv, hovering above me. With both hands, he lifts me, and we land somewhat more gently on the floor together.

"You saved me," I murmur, shaking, as my feet touch the floor, and I grip Dhruv's hands tightly, as if letting go will cast me back into the air.

"Anytime, Princess," Dhruv says, squeezing my palms. But instead of the joker I first met, his face portrays a soft, knowing smile. One I've come to enjoy.

Every nerve in my body lights like a flame, even after the prince pulls away.

"What *was* that?" I ask, craning my neck to see Jujhar floating down to us, Amir beside him. "Why did we suddenly drop?"

Then I see Jujhar's face, and I know something is wrong. He's pale, his eyes frantic as he lands gently next to us, and his hands clasp around something I can't see.

"I'm sorry," he says, voice guttural. "I lost control when I opened the vault. It's—the talisman, it's—"

With a startling rush of horror, I realize what he's about to say.

"Gone," I whisper. Jujhar nods, jaw clenched tight as though he can't bear to say the word.

"What do you mean?" Dhruv says.

Jujhar holds aloft his trembling hands. "I mean the talisman—a feather from the first skyhawk—*is not there.* I mean it was stolen. The only thing in the vault was . . . this."

He opens his palms, and my vision fills with red as rose petals fall to the ground.

I stand at the hull of the boat, at a loss for words.

How could Amara beat us here? I wonder, staring out at the floating islands disappearing into the distance as we head back toward mainland Retan. Our mission failed, miserably. I feel like I'm leaving the Island Market with less in my pocket than what I came with.

I want to forget about everything that just happened, but I cannot. A talisman, gone. Likely in Amara's hands. How, I am not yet certain.

"You know," a voice says, coming to my side, "there is a clear difference between you and Ria."

I glance to my left, heart warming at the sight of Amir. My cheeks burn as he gazes down at me. This is the closest we've stood together in days, and finally, there's no one around. Even Dhruv is busy on the other side of the boat, poring over a book he borrowed from Jujhar.

"And what's that?" I say, trying not to let my voice quaver.

Amir brushes aside a lock of my hair, resting his fingers against the shell of my ear. "You're starting to sprout worry lines."

My eyes widen, but from the way he's chuckling I know his words to be nothing more than a jest. I relax against him, letting my arm press against his.

"In hindsight," Amir says, more serious now as he turns toward the water and plants his hands on the boat rail, "at least we were able to make amends between Jujhar and Prince Dhruv."

"At least," I echo. "But now Amara has yet another talisman for her plan. We don't have much time left." A few more weeks and the full Blood Moon will be here.

"But she doesn't have all of them," Amir insists. "We haven't lost yet, Rani. *And*," he adds with a grin, "once we've beaten her, we can come back here and actually enjoy it. Maybe even try that mallet ball sport that the prince was talking about." Amir's eyes sparkle. Despite what just happened at the Island Market, he seems genuinely excited by what lies ahead. He's been through so much, spent nights alone shivering in cold alleyways while I've napped in silken beds, and yet he's the most optimistic person I know.

I gaze up at him, remembering all that he's shown me these past two moons that I never thought I could uncover about myself. There's so much I love about Amir: his sense of adventure, his kind heart, his princely yet rugged features. I want to melt against him and hold him tight, forget about everything, about Mother's stern warning.

But no matter how much I want him, I can't help but wonder if I'm holding him back. From the life he's always envisioned for himself—an adventurer, exploring lands and cultures only read about in books.

I don't want to think of what else he might want. *Who* else he might want.

"What's wrong?" he says, wrapping a hand around my shoulder.

"Nothing," I answer vaguely.

Amir dips a brow. "You aren't still thinking about Jujhar, are you?"

I shake my head. "No."

"Professor Neel? Or . . . Prefect Padma?" A slight note of teasing creeps into his voice. "You . . . didn't seem to like her much."

"It's not them. It's . . . *us*." I bite my lower lip. "It sounds ridiculous, but my mind keeps coming back to the same thought. What if you never met me? If you were still a thief, and escaped Abai and the Ruthless Raja?" His eyes darken at the moniker he once used against my father. "Would you have been better off? What if you could have had everything you originally wanted, and I've changed all that?"

"That's a lot of ifs," Amir cuts in. "Thieves don't dwell on the past; we look to the future."

"And?" I press, my gaze roaming his face, wanting, *needing* to know. "What do you see in your future?"

Amir turns his torso toward mine so we're pressed nearly against each other. He cradles my cheek in one of his palms. "You. I see you in my future."

Body flushing and tingling against his, I ache for more of his touch. "What do you see in yours?" he asks, voice soft.

"I . . ." I trail off, imagining a thousand different scenarios. The safe choices, the risky ones. I don't know why, but Prince Dhruv's soft smile fills my head, the feel of his hands squeezing mine after I nearly plummeted in Jujhar's study. Finally, I mutter, "I don't know how I can have what I want."

I don't know how I can have you.

Amir's gaze turns hot. It dawns on me that his answer was simple, easy. And here I am, hesitating over what I want despite him standing right in front of me.

Amir bites the inside of his cheek, as if he isn't sure if he should speak his next thought aloud. "You know, there have been lots of . . . *rumors* about you circling through the Retanian palaces lately."

"Rumors?" I say, pulling back.

Amir pales. "Raja's beard," he curses. "I shouldn't have said anything. Just ignore that—"

"Tell me," I say, too fast. "What rumors?" I'm used to rumors spreading about me back home, but I had hoped things would be different here.

"It's nothing, Rani—"

"Tell me." My voice is authoritative, one I don't normally use with Amir, and suddenly he looks at me like I'm not his friend but his ruler. Like he sees a bit of the Ruthless Raja within me. "Please," I add softly.

"It's about you and . . ." He sighs, running a hand through his hair. "Prince Dhruv. They think he sees something in you, and you in him."

I want to scoff, play off the rumors. But they're only untrue to an extent. A small part of me knows how easy it would be with Prince Dhruv, how *expected*. How pleased my mother would feel. And perhaps how happy *I* might be, too, if the way I feel around him is any indication.

"He's a reasonable man, if that's what you mean," I offer, cautious.

"Reasonable?" Amir chuckles, but it lacks any humor. "Be serious, Rani. Is it true?"

I attempt to formulate an answer, but my brain twists in knots. "I think I just . . . need some time to myself."

Amir stiffens but steps away, offering me my privacy. The space beside me is cold, empty, where I wish he was still. After everything that's happened today, fatigue and confusion wash over me. My head and my heart are in a stalemate, and I don't know how to settle this battle once and for all.

17

Ria

Irfan's lips thin as he gazes out the carriage window. It's late afternoon, the sun already sitting low on the horizon, and it's been a few days since our discovery in the woods. Since I've even *spoken* to Irfan. He uttered only a few words of greeting when he called me to the carriage, and since then I've been sitting in this Masters-forsaken carriage for who-knows-how-long, off to who-knows-where.

Rani *did* tell me the ex-soldier is the private type, one to hold back two secrets and only reveal one. I trust him because Rani does, but seeing him now, in the kingdom that's brought him so much grief, I wonder what he's really doing in the North.

Shima coils up next to me, watching Irfan with curious, slitted eyes.

The ssssoldier is nervous, she says, her blue-green scales ruffling as a breeze winds through the carriage. *Look at the way he keeps glancing out the window.*

I guess snake instincts are just as real as thief instincts, because mine are saying the same thing. Irfan's eyes keep shifting outside, peering through the curtained velvet flaps. I want to ask him why, but in minutes the carriage comes to a grinding halt and we disembark.

In front of a dilapidated house.

"Welcome home," Irfan says, almost to himself.

"This . . . is your home?" Shingles are loose and lying on dead grass, protected from the snow by the surrounding frosted pine trees. Underneath cracked windows, shards of glass litter the ground, a sign of intrusion.

"Was," Irfan corrects coldly. Shima's tongue flickers at my side, as if to sense if anything dark awaits us. From the cool look on her face, she's found nothing.

"Mind if I ask why you brought me here?" Irfan's still staring up at the house, and when I peer closely, I think I see tears filling his eyes. But he blinks them back just as fast, and his expression zippers into obscurity once more, a silvered soldier to the bone.

"Because of the bandits who tore through here." He juts his chin at the house, and I shudder. Bandits might've gotten me, too, back in Abai, if Amir hadn't found me on the streets.

Sorrow crosses Irfan's face, mixed with a darkness—anger. One I recognize. It's a face I wore while homeless, an orphan. The face that hid who I truly was underneath.

Seems like you two aren't so different, Shima says to me.

Still. Irfan didn't really answer my question as to why I'm here.

But looking at his drawn face, I see an opportunity to finally understand the man behind the mask.

"Do you blame the king for how your life turned out?" I broach. "Rani told me about the child-soldier training camps."

"Started by King Rohit's great-grandfather, and eventually abolished by King Rohit himself, after much pressure from his citizens—and daughter," he clarifies. "King Rohit may have reversed many children's fates, but there were many, like myself, who were not so lucky. The truth is, for many years, I did blame King Rohit. I couldn't forgive him or the blind eye he turned to those suffering." He shivers. "But being in Amratstan now . . . I see how much has changed. I see children roaming freely in the capital. I see how the royals' decisions are creating a better world; how my home country is freer than it ever was before."

I approach Irfan and place a hand on his shoulder, hoping my warmth will comfort him. "You have helped do the same, even if it wasn't here. I never thanked you for all you did for so many people in Abai. Amir's sister included. He's my best friend, you know."

Irfan laughs. "I know. And I believed Rani was you for *weeks*."

"Guilty," I laugh, raising a hand.

His silver eyes reach mine. "I always knew there was something off. I recognized her eventually, you know. Rani. She was a different sort of princess. She kept to herself."

It's true. For so many years, I never heard any news about the Snake Princess. I believed the rumors—the royals were half snake, killed people in the Snake Pit. Even now, I still get surprised when

I look in the mirror and see the snake birthmark on my arm, a reminder of who I am. The family I would have known, if not for the prophecy—of the *sisters of the snake.*

The prophecy claimed I would become too powerful. I think of the cobra within me, of losing control last week, and wonder— was it so wrong?

I shake myself. We *proved* the prophecy untrue. We chose our own fates.

I have to hold on to that hope.

"We shouldn't dwell on the past," Irfan says, pulling me from my thoughts. "*However*, there is something from my past that I've been meaning to speak with you about. I haven't stopped thinking over what Amara did to those snowbirds. About how she's willing to do anything to get what she wants . . . the talismans."

A shudder runs through me. "What's that got to do with your past?"

Irfan's lips straighten into a line. "Let me show you."

The inside of Irfan's house is even worse than the exterior. More glass glitters from the floor, dusty shards reflecting me until I'm split into a thousand pieces. Deeper in, I find small hints of what once was Irfan's family. A fallen-over portrait of a boy and his parents. A broken vase holding withered tulips. Dirt climbing up windowsills, tucked into corners of wood.

"It's this way," Irfan says now, leading me and Shima into a separate room that looks like a study. Also combed through, clearly, by the bandits. Irfan avoids looking at the wreckage, instead heading for an armoire in the corner. He braces against it and pushes it aside slowly, revealing a hidden latch in the floor underneath it. He lifts the trapdoor and bends to retrieve something from it, and I see him pull a small locked crate from the hole. I drift closer as he spins a dial to input a safety code and it clicks open. He pulls one drawer out, inspecting it before reaching in and holding out a small glittering object.

"What is this?"

"Look closer."

I follow his direction. When he turns the object over, I see it is a ring carved with an insignia that jolts me. The insignia of a snake.

I take hold of the ring, a spark lighting against my skin. The ring is reaching out to me, tugging on my magic so insistently, I answer its call.

My eyes close as magic, dark and cold, floods my veins. I'm seeing a memory—cloaked figures raiding this home, trashing everything within, one of them dropping their ring on the floor. A boy enters once the bandits are all gone, tears flooding his features as he picks up the ring.

I gasp, pulling out of the memory. *Irfan.*

"I've heard tales of the bandits who raided my home. I believe they're back in Amratstan," Irfan says, his gaze faraway. He hasn't noticed what happened to me—the way I was sucked into a memory from touching this simple snake ring.

"Who were they? The bandits?" I say, quivering, as I hand back the ring.

"I don't know, honestly." Irfan tugs something else out of the hidden drawer he opens using a code—a book. "When I was young, I'd only vaguely heard about this particular group of bandits—a cult of some sort—because of my parents. They had a close friend who wanted them to join the group. Apparently, they had been growing in numbers back then, because the Hundred-Year Truce was going to end in just over a decade's time, and they believed it might signal their leader's return, whoever that was. But their calling card, so to speak, was their snake rings and snake-shaped burn marks."

I think of the creepy man outside the tavern, bowing toward me. Could that man have been part of this group? Why would they still be on the rise, after Rani and I stopped Kaama and Abai from entering another hundred-year war?

"Did your parents . . . join?"

Irfan shakes his head. "No. So their friend turned on them. Probably told members from the group to raid our house—kill my parents, even—because of their lack of allegiance . . . and to learn more about what was in this book."

He flips it open, revealing a faint drawing of a sword, and an excerpt on the Tide Master's talisman.

"They were obsessed with the legends surrounding it. They thought the talisman was tied to the Snake Master himself."

"The Snake Master? What do you mean?" I say.

Irfan bites his lower lip. "It's all in this book. I've thought about coming back for it for years. But I became a soldier in Abai. And then I met . . ."

"Sanya?"

Irfan's eyes soften. "You could say that."

Sssomeone's yearning, Shima hisses. *I saw it in you, once, Ria. I still do.*

"Quiet, Shima," I tell her. I don't need to be thinking about what happened between me and Saeed on the hunt, not to mention I haven't uttered more than a few words to him since then.

I should be a relationship counselor, Shima sighs. *I'd make a fortune.*

"So, the talisman . . . ," I say, ignoring her quip.

"Right." Irfan places the book on a wooden table. Inside, the pages look fragile, worn, and he cycles through them. "My parents always used to recite this to me—a legend about the Tide Master's talisman." He points at a few messy, hand-scrawled lines.

The Snake River connects two kingdoms and two Masters. While its banks only touch Amratstan and Pania, its origins are more sinister, leading to the Great Deceiver himself, the Snake Master. Some say the river was once the home of this Master, hence the name, and that upon the destruction of Pania, only those of the Snake Master's or Tide Master's descent can locate the lost relics of the Tide Master. Under its eerie waters, the Tide Master's sword talisman awaits the hand of those who can wield it.

A chill colder than the Amratstanian snow settles over me. *The Snake River.* When I looked into it that first night in Amratstan, I saw that strange vision within its waters. The question is . . . why could *I* see that?

Irfan continues, "Naturally, the Snake River was searched for the sword, but to no avail. But that doesn't mean it can't be found. While there are no descendants—supposedly—of the Tide Master left, only one other Master had a connection to this river: the Snake Master. My parents thought that a descendant of the Snake Master might be able to find the Tide Master's sword in its waters."

I take in his words. "You think *I* can find it?"

"Do you have a secret triplet in Amratstan that I don't know about?"

I bite my tongue. Before I can say anything, the horses neigh from outside the house. The driver is getting impatient.

"We should get back," I say, scooping up the book. But Irfan lays a gentle hand on top of mine, stopping me.

"I . . . didn't tell you everything about my parents." He chews the inside of his cheek. "They did join the bandits for some time before they learned they were evil people and tried to back out. We were going to run, pack up and leave. We all might have been safe, if not for . . . *me.* One day, I spoke to a man I didn't know. The leader of the group. I told them where my parents were—at home. When I came back, it was in shambles. My parents were dead . . . because of my actions. What if I'd never spoken to that man? What if . . ."

"Don't." I place my other hand on top of his. "Don't do that to yourself. I've asked *what if* a million times about the death of my caretaker. It still never brought her back."

"Then how did you move on?" Irfan glances up, and I'm surprised to see him blinking back tears.

"It's not about moving on. It's about living in their memory. It took me a long time to figure that out."

Irfan nods, wiping his shirt against his eyes. "I want to bury the book."

I glance at the yard, where the sky darkens overhead. "Outside, then."

Upturned soil glimmers beneath us in Irfan's garden. Irfan drops his spade and settles the book deep into the earth. I help him cover it up, letting the wet soil clump against my hands. Irfan doesn't bother to wipe away his tears now, letting them drip into the soil. I clasp his hand in mine, twining our dirt-stained hands into one, and he lets out a small laugh.

"I'm not one for crying," Irfan sniffles. To see him in so much pain, it makes every loss I've felt return with a blaze, like a raw wound that has yet to heal. But they *can* be healed—I've learned as much.

"Yours tears honor those who have passed," I tell him. "Your family will always be with you."

"I know. I've found a new family, too."

When we're done, Irfan touches his forehead against the soil and murmurs something in a lilting tongue. An old Amratstanian saying, which he translates with a voice both rough and gentle:

"I seize the days I am with you, and I allow the night to keep you."

He rises from his crouch, then offers a hand. "Thank you, Princess Ria."

"Anytime, Irfan." As I stand, I catch sight of the moon, nearly half full, a crimson specter hidden behind a few clouds.

As the clouds move, the moon bathes us in red. We're running out of time.

Back at the palace, anxious nerves flutter through me as I stare out Zoya's window at the Snake River. That memory of the bandits— I saw that for a reason. Some connection to my snake magic.

I want to confide in Saeed about the discoveries Irfan and I made, but I don't know if he even wants to speak with me after what I kept from him. Or if I want to admit to him how much my power is growing. What if that's the answer behind why I let all those snakes loose, why I could see that memory in the ring?

I'm already frightened of my own power. I don't want Saeed to be scared of me, too. And each day that passes makes me more certain that I have no one to help me control it. Not even Shima.

I won't just wait for a dream to come while I sleep. I'll call one to me.

I pull on my cloak, ignoring how it smells faintly of Saeed, and hurry outside to the river below. I reach a narrow point in the

Snake River as the sky deepens to a bruised purple, shivering as a light snowfall begins. The red gleam of the moon gives the dark waters of the Snake River a bloody tinge, and with the snow falling gently from above, the whole scene feels like a dream turned nightmare.

But that's what I'm here for. I close my eyes.

I imagine that mysterious voice, the one that draws me closer each day. I think of how badly I wanted to open that door, like the voice's desires were my own.

When I open my eyes, the reddish moon illuminates my reflection in the river. Except I don't quite look like myself. My eyes are a deep emerald green, my lips fuller, my face smaller. This isn't me, nor is it Rani. Yet her name comes to me all the same.

"Raya. The Key."

The voice. As soon as it speaks, it pulls me in. *The Key.* I've heard that term before—in the prophecy from the Fountain of Fortunes. *And the Key of a Master shall set souls free.*

The voice continues, alluring:

"A servant to offer their Master's blood. A follower to find the missing Key. A Key to bring back the Eternal Night."

Whoever this Raya is, she flicks a smile at me, tugging me closer, wrapping her magic around me. *Snake magic.* I'm not immune, and with a gasp I crash straight into a vision.

I'm inside the Snake River. Schools of fish dart away from writhing snakes, which slink around in the murky shadows. A girl paces below the water, seemingly having no problem breathing.

When I see her emerald eyes, I realize this must be Raya, the girl I saw in my reflection.

"*Father*," Raya says urgently to a man meditating on the river-bed. "*They're here.*"

"*Who?*" the man asks without opening his eyes. I startle. That voice—it sounds just like . . .

"*Them. Darshin's descendants . . . and Ashneer's. Diya's are coming, too. This doesn't seem like a friendly visit.*"

"*I fear not the other Masters, nor their children,*" the man responds. His face shimmers like a fish's scales underwater: an odd, uncanny sight that sends fear coursing through me. He is part snake, his nose slitted, the lower half of his body a lurking snake's tail.

"*Then what do we do?*"

"*They cannot come down here, Raya. I won't let them harm you or Ruhanya. There's been enough of that.*"

He opens his eyes, releasing himself from his pose. His eyes are a startling red, and I realize, with horror, who this is. My ancestor. The Snake Master.

But what I don't expect is the way he cradles Raya's face with care as he promises to protect her. His *daughter*.

Another girl approaches from the surface, plunging straight down through the water and landing on her feet. She's an exact copy of Raya.

Her twin.

"*Father—*"

Before she can finish her warning, a spark of lightning flashes through the water. A storm brews overhead as if the river's surface is its own sky. Like a sudden monsoon, the waves crash angrily, whipping me back into the sharp shoals. But I don't feel anything, even as I watch Raya scrape against those same rocks. Instead of red blood, gilded liquid escapes her arms, and her twin swims for her, checking her injury.

A beam of red light narrowly misses the other girl. It's fire, plunging toward the riverbed with unnatural speed, unharmed by the water. The whole scene sets aflame. The shoals begin to shake, crashing down from the sudden rumbling earthquake. Weeds dart out, alive, wrapping around the girls' ankles. I reach out to free them, but the Snake Master is faster, moving with ferocity. It's clear this isn't normal—it's magic. A magical *attack* on the Snake Master and his home. The riverbed cracks in half, and a cough chokes me as debris fills the water and clouds my vision.

As the twins rush for the surface, I follow them, partly blinded by the light of the moon piercing the water. The flames are still there, but I don't feel their heat as I swim up—

I lift my head and gasp, blinking water out of my eyes. The moon is still a glimmer of red. I'm back at the Snake River with no one near, cold air rushing into my lungs, released from the vision. Somehow, I had plunged my head under the surface. How long was I underwater? Was I breathing? It doesn't matter. I saw something bigger than I thought. The Snake Master. He was attacked, and so was his daughter Raya. *Both* daughters. Twin daughters.

Everything I've discovered catches up to me with the night's fierce chill, making me shiver all over. I wipe my face with my fur-trimmed cloak and rush away from the river. I swear I see a figure watching from an overhead balcony, wearing a thick cloak like mine. *Saeed*, I think, but I ignore him and hurtle back to the safety of the Amratstanian palace, where I hope my dreams will not haunt me.

Or the voice I now recognize. The one that beckons to me almost every night.

The voice that may belong to my most infamous ancestor.

The Great Deceiver. The Snake Master.

18

Rani

The Sky Master's talisman is still missing.

Since our trip to the Island Market a few days ago, I've spent nearly every waking moment searching for any hint of where it may have gone, studying whatever I can about the talisman. So far I've had few results. I can only imagine what will happen if it is truly in Amara's hands right now, along with the rest of the talismans. Never mind how she got the talisman in the first place. A spy, perhaps? I drop my head onto the mango wood desk in the study chambers. Will Amara unleash her soul magic soon, once she gets all the talismans? Perhaps set free the souls of the dead? How does she plan to destroy Kaama?

"Princess? Are you awake?"

"Hmm?" I startle in my seat when I notice who awaits me at the door. *Dhruv.* He's standing with his hands behind him, back stick-straight, a sly smile sneaking onto his face. "You know you don't have to spend all morning in the study room, correct?"

"I wanted to learn more about the talismans. Where we could find the others." Now that Amara has the Sky Master's. I wonder how far Ria has come in her journey, which talismans she may—or may not—have found. "We haven't gotten any closer to learning what could destroy the stone, either, or what lies in that secret locked chamber." Amir has tried his best to pick the lock, but to no avail.

"Which is why I think we need to step back."

"Why?" My vision is still blurry. "We should press onward—"

Dhruv's footsteps silence me. As he moves closer, I take note of the golden threads that line his kurta, and how well the outfit suits him. He bends down to meet my eyes. "A professor once told me that to step back is to take a look at the bigger picture. If we focus too much on one detail, we might miss the whole thing."

My cheeks heat at the way he gazes at me so intently. I hate how right he is.

"Then what do you suggest?"

"Breakfast," Dhruv says, winking. "And a change of scenery." He offers a hand, palm up. "Will you join me?"

The royal carriage grinds to a halt along a shrubbed path. The sand and stone surrounding the Academy and the three palaces have given way to a line of neem trees that now thicken into a forest. After freshening up and sharing a meal with Dhruv, we left in the carriage, our destination unknown—to *me*. I didn't even tell Amir where I was going. I told myself he won't mind figuring out more about the hidden chamber and the talismans while we're gone, but the truth is, I can't face him after everything I've said. Or *haven't* said.

Now, away from the bustle of the capital, the constant chattering I've grown used to has dulled, replaced by the ruffling of swaying trees and cooing birdsong.

Sparrows soar past me as I exit the carriage. A small dirt path forms a break between the trees, and Dhruv gestures toward it.

"Dhruv, I might have pretended to be a commoner, but the truth is, I'm not a fan of"—I wave my hands at the ground— "*dirt.*"

"I assure you, this isn't a jungle trek. It's . . . a surprise."

"Oh?" A pleasant warmth steals over me. Most of the surprises I've had lately haven't been pleasant ones. Despite myself, I'm looking forward to finding out what this one is.

Indeed, it seems Dhruv enjoys surprises. When I haven't been obsessing over the stolen talisman or the chamber, I've spent what little free time I've had being pulled away by Dhruv on little adventures. We visited his favorite spot at the Academy; tastetested Siva's new treats; even played a game of mallet ball, a sport involving a flat wooden stick and several wooden balls.

I would be lying if I said I wasn't trying to avoid someone else, too. But after my conversation with Amir, I don't know how to address all the questions—and emotions—circling through me.

With a resigned sigh, I enter the forest, swatting aside overgrown tree branches and kicking aside dead leaves. Fallen leaves are a normal sight even in early winter, but this amount seems excessive. Perhaps it's a sign—that the poisoned Blood Moon truly is decaying the Retanian landscape, and the rest of the world, faster than we thought.

I lift a branch out of my view, and there in the distance sits a small sanctuary. A cliff faces us, water spilling gently over the sides in a bolt of silver. A dull roar fills the air as the water splashes down into the shimmering pool below. A waterfall! My mouth gapes in awe. If Amir were here, he'd certainly be saying *Raja's beard*. But a princess can't be caught cursing, much less by a prince.

"This way." Dhruv pulls me along the bank, leading me to a set of stepping-stones that connect to the other side of the water. I swallow hard, watching Dhruv as he begins his trek, keeping both hands extended on either side of him for balance. Halfway across, he turns around. "Coming?"

I shake my head. "I'll fall."

"It's shallow. Narrow, too."

"Then I would get my cloak wet." I wrap the reddish-brown Academy cloak around me, and Dhruv bites his lip as if to keep himself from laughing. I decided to wear it on our journey, thinking it would help me blend in, hiding the ostentatious sari I wear beneath. But in the middle of nowhere, it makes me feel a bit foolish.

Dhruv teeters on the rocks as he turns and skips over a few stones, landing in front of me. He offers a hand, bowing. "Princess Rani, may I have the utmost fortune of taking you to the hidden gem of Retan, the sparkling waterfall of Jhanswa City? I promise I will lead you carefully over the rocks, and if you fall, I will do the same."

I laugh, placing my hand in his. "Indeed."

Prince Dhruv leads the way, helping me from stone to stone. "A bit to your right—yes, you've got it," he says as I release his hand and balance on my own. I laugh as I hop onto the next rock. The feeling of the stone under my sandals, slippery and uneven, is so unlike the smooth palace grounds in Retan or even Abai. I finish crossing, taking Dhruv's hand at the end, and he helps me back onto solid ground.

With the two of us standing there, Dhruv glances down at our intertwined hands, and I follow suit. I'm reminded of a few days ago when he saved me from falling. He'd been the one to release me, but this time, he hasn't let go.

I flush as I pull away. We're so close to the waterfall, the sound of the water roars over my thoughts.

"Follow me!" Dhruv calls over the din. From this angle, we can move behind the waterfall itself, and when we're there, the sound completely changes, like we're in our own bubble. A sheet of water spills ahead of us, spraying flecks of mist our way. It's refreshing. Exciting, even.

"I've never seen a waterfall," I admit.

"This is one of Retan's most secluded places. I come here to think."

"And what are you thinking of now?"

Dhruv leans against the rock wall behind him. "My upcoming examinations. Mother wants me to do well. To prove to the kingdom that I can be their leader someday."

"I know how you feel," I say, thinking of my time with Tutor and Saeed. "But I wasn't such a good student." My gaze flickers up to his. "What *did* happen between you and Professor Neel? He said you were avoiding him."

Dhruv smirks, but his eyes hold no mirth. "I stopped going to his classes. I told you before, about how the students think that I have everything figured out because I'm royal. But that only adds more pressure. The students . . . they all stare at me. I hear them whispering behind my back. *He's a royal. Probably bought his way into the university.* I haven't been to class in a few moons. Mother has no clue."

"But . . . I thought you loved the attention." I think of the way he waved at everyone at the party, or the gaggle of students who'd stared at him at the so-called reading circle.

"Not when people expect you to be the best," he says, "yet secretly think you're not worthy."

The way his voice cracks sends angry heat coursing through me. "They have no right to say that. You are worthy, Prince Dhruv." I approach him, coming to his side, my arm brushing against his.

Dhruv blushes. "I'm glad to hear that someone likes me for more than my looks. Outside of Ranjit-ji and Siva Auntie, of course."

I cannot help the little giggle that escapes my lips. *Curse my mouth.* Though what I said wasn't a lie. But he doesn't know the truth—my feelings for Amir. Even if, by being with him, I might be depriving my kingdom of a stronger alliance. And . . . does Amir even want that? I glance at Prince Dhruv. He, like me, is expected to marry someday, have heirs, and continue the traditions of the kingdom. He, like me, carries a burden on his shoulders—one I haven't been able to express to anyone outside of Ria.

I scramble through my thoughts. Once, I thought all I wanted was freedom from my home. But now that I have that, I crave freedom for my heart, too.

Dhruv interrupts my thoughts. "What's life in Abai like with your new sister?"

"You know?" I say, startled. "I hadn't thought word had made its way abroad yet."

"I *might* have heard Mother speaking with the palace keeper this morning. Mother loves those kind of tales."

"What tales?" I'm not sure if I want to draw closer to Dhruv or farther away as he chuckles warmly.

"Tales of found family. She actually wasn't born the queen. She was an illegitimate daughter."

My brows lift.

"When the former royal—my grandmother—passed with no marriage and no heir, supposedly, the throne was empty for five years. And then my mother, Meeta, was found at an orphanage. She was the spitting image of the previous queen. And while others badgered her about her status, most Retanians knew who she truly was. She was the heir no one knew existed."

"How did they know she was part of the royal bloodline?"

"Besides her face?" Dhruv says. "A few palace hands found proof written in my grandmother's journal, speaking of an heir born out of wedlock. They knew Meeta was the girl. Soon, my mother grew up, and she had me." He smiles genuinely. "The tale of you and your sister intrigued me. It reminded me much of Mother."

Strange, how Dhruv's family shares a story so similar to my own family's. A missing royal, lost, then found.

"Some people still don't believe Mother is the true heir of Retan, even after all these years. There are groups who wish to see the monarchy end." Dhruv shrugs. "But let's not discuss that right now. I brought you here to cheer you up. And I think this will do just the trick." He pulls out a pair of gloves. "They're sky-magicked. Jujhar gave them to me before we left his study."

"What do they do?"

Dhruv hides a smile. He pulls on one glove and hands me the other, and the moment the glove reaches my fingertips, it disappears.

"It's . . . invisible."

"And so are we. Look down, Princess Rani."

Quizzically, I do. My skin shimmers with a strange silver light. Are we truly invisible to the naked eye? I can still see Dhruv—perhaps because I am wearing one of the gloves?

A second later, I notice my feet are no longer on the ground—we're floating, just like in Jujhar's library.

"Oh!" I cry, falling forward. My hands land on Dhruv's

shoulders and I clutch them fiercely as he chuckles. "You could have warned me."

"But that wouldn't have been so fun."

"I don't like heights."

"Perhaps because you've never seen the beautiful view." He takes my hand and we float to the front of the waterfall, lifting higher, higher. I cling to him as we rise close to the top, staring out at the Retanian landscape. My breath catches.

"*This* is what I came to show you. So we could spend some time alone together."

"A-alone?" I say, glancing up at him.

He nods. "I don't mean to be so forward, Rani, but I enjoy spending time with you. You are quite the puzzle to figure out, you know. Sometimes you act like a true princess. Other times like a common villager. I don't mean to say one is more preferred than the other. Only that you have a duality to you. A riddle to be solved, to be unlocked, like the Three Blessed Sisters' chamber."

My skin flushes from his compliment. "All we're missing is the key."

"The key to the chamber?" Dhruv begins, gaze intent on mine. "Or the key to something else?"

My heart flips in my chest. I avoid his crisp gaze to look out at the three palaces jutting out like strong tamarind trees in the distance, glittering in the dewy light. Something about their shape seems familiar. And as if I am a flame to a wick, the answer comes to me.

I point at the three palaces. "They form the shape of a triangle. Like the sisters' symbol, the sun with a triangle inside."

"Indeed," Dhruv offers, but he looks confused. "And?"

"So what if that has to do with this mysterious *key* we're looking for? The key should be shaped like a triangle, if that keyhole has given us any indication, but even Amir can't deduce how the lock works. What if it's not a lock at all? What if it's something to do with the Three Blessed Sisters' research and study of magic?"

"That's what we hope to find within the chamber," Dhruv responds, still befuddled.

"Three sides of the triangle . . . and perhaps three magics to open the door. You don't need a key—you need magic!" I think of the magic I felt when I pressed my hand to the door, the way it surged through me. Magic *must* be the solution to revealing the chamber.

"The queens *did* value all magic equally," Dhruv says, a grin stealing over his face. "And it would be an incredible safeguard, a surefire way to keep people out of the chamber unless they had consensus—unless they worked together. Nice deduction, Princess Rani."

"Why thank you, Prince Dhruv," I say, giving his hand a squeeze.

"We need three magics, then. My snake magic, Jujhar's sky magic, and perhaps . . ."

"Professor Neel's relic of the Fire Master?" Dhruv asks. "It's not direct magic, but if it came from the Fire Master's volcanoes . . ."

"Brilliant!" I say, excitement racing through me. Could this be it? Our way into the chamber at last?

"We'll send word for Jujhar and Professor Neel as soon as we get back," Dhruv says eagerly, returning us to the ground, his hand still lingering in mine.

"We'll be one step closer to learning how to destroy the Bloodstone and stopping Amara."

"Then you'll be leaving Retan soon," Dhruv says with a note of sorrow. I don't nod.

His words entomb me with a question I haven't dared ask myself until this moment. With all that I now know about Dhruv, with the connection that we share—will I truly want to leave him behind?

Can I?

At the Gold Palace, Ranjit leads us inside. We change into appropriate attire for the dining hall and arrive there within a bell, where Queen Meeta laces her fingers together at the table.

"A way into the Three Blessed Sisters' chamber that no one has been able to open in centuries?"

Dhruv nods. "This time will be different. I feel it."

I explain my trips to meet Professor Neel and Jujhar, with Dhruv's help. The missing talisman. The queen raises a brow at her son.

"*You* went to the Island Market? We haven't been there in years, beta."

Dhruv's cheeks redden. "Mother, this *Amara* situation is life or death. The Sky Master's talisman is in dangerous hands." He says Amara's name without fear but rather with disdain. "And my presence in the Island Market will only help us connect with the currentspinners, something we should have done long ago. We have a duty to our people."

"And you'll do your duty to finish that plate of food," Queen Meeta says, eyeing Dhruv's untouched first course. Even I've been too nervous to eat. But knowing I'll have the queen's, Dhruv's, and Amir's help in the coming days settles my stomach.

I dip the aloo tikki into a bright-green chutney and take a bite. Though the potatoes were fried, there is no oily residue in my mouth. Instead, spices and soft peas linger on my tongue.

"Am I wrong in noticing there is something going on between you two?" Queen Meeta says.

I nearly choke. My hands freeze mid-wipe on my silk napkin. The rumors about me and Prince Dhruv have found their way to the queen herself, then.

"We . . . work well together," I admit, turning my gaze to the prince. He's hyper-focused on the food in front of him and gives nothing away.

"Is that all?" Queen Meeta continues.

Dhruv's cheeks look red now. "Mother, Princess Rani is here for a bigger reason. Our countries are at stake. The Blood Moon is swiftly approaching." He eyes a dead plant in the corner of the room, its wilted leaves sagging where I only just saw them standing upright this morning.

Queen Meeta nods, dropping the subject with a twinkle in her eye that suggests she's indulging us. "Indeed. We have had strong ties with Abai for a long time. But I sense a shift in our political state with yours."

"How so?" I ask.

"Your father nearly went to war with the Kaamans. He welcomed it. While we are glad no blood was spilled on the battlefield, there still hasn't been any certainty of what will happen between these kingdoms."

The queen pauses, seeming to weigh her words carefully. "And yet, here you are. The very same raja's daughter, working day and night to achieve peace between our kingdoms."

"Not only ours. A treaty will be renewed between Abai and Kaama—I'm certain of it. At the upcoming peace summit, it will be signed." I inject as much authority into my voice as possible.

"I see your determination, Princess Rani," Queen Meeta says. "And indeed, I have received word the summit will be held the night of the Blood Moon."

I nod. "We need to stop Amara from collecting all the talismans before that night—or find a way to destroy the Bloodstone before she can use it. If she succeeds, she means to turn herself into the Soul Master and destroy Kaama and everyone in it." I haven't yet told Queen Meeta that last part, too afraid of her reaction.

Queen Meeta raises her brows. "Sands above. Your mission *is* of utmost importance. My son will help you at every available moment he can." Her eyes dance as she speaks, the insinuation on her tongue ringing too clear.

"I plan to," Dhruv promises, gently placing his hand over mine.

I try to smile, but my lips shake and my heart quavers. As the servers bring in the second course, I catch the slightest movement by the door. Someone is standing there behind the servers, and as I look over, a gasp locks in my throat.

Amir. Staring at Dhruv's hand over mine. I pull away, but it only makes me look guiltier.

Amir's face flushes pink.

Before I can speak, he bolts from his spot, leaving the dining room entrance. I stand abruptly, tossing my napkin aside.

"If you'll excuse me," I tell the queen. I don't mean to be rude, but right now I can't wait for her permission to leave. I ignore the servers' puzzled stares as I rush for the exit and find Amir's frame turning the corner of the Gold Palace's halls.

"Wait!" I call out, hurrying to catch up to him. I veer right, into the nearest corridor, to find Amir mere steps away from the main exit. I only manage to catch up to him when we are both outside, the starry night sky now twinkling overhead.

"Amir," I breathe, clamping a hand to his shoulder. "I haven't seen you—"

"All day," he fills in. "I'm aware."

I lower my hand to my side. "Back there, that was nothing. Just Dhruv trying to comfort me."

His face goes stony. "He's been trying to *comfort* you the entire time we've been here. Which, by the way, hasn't been that long."

"That's not fair. I swear it's not what it looks like."

"Then what is it?" His brows frown, matching his lips. "You've spent lots of time with Dhruv lately. And today, you go off with him on some adventure I have no clue about."

"It was a surprise—"

"I get it," he says. "The other day, on the boat, when I brought up those rumors . . . I really thought they were just idle gossip. But they're true. Everyone's talking about you being in love. And I don't exactly fit the description of a pristine prince, so it's pretty clear who they're all talking about."

"I don't care what description you fit," I tell him. "And *love*? Dhruv and I just met!"

"You seem pretty cozy for just meeting," Amir states, looking back at the palace. "I'll bet he'll be here any minute to check up on you."

I expect the words to feel as harsh as a slap, but instead, they're soulless, quiet. Like Amir doesn't want to believe them—and neither do I.

"We don't know each other that well," I repeat. But my throat turns thick with unspoken words, remembering the moments I've shared with Dhruv these past few days. The way I've connected to Dhruv, one royal to another, both of us facing a world with a thousand pressures and questions in our futures.

Why is my heart so tangled up? Amir should know what I feel for him is boundless, even if Dhruv has been a comfort. *I* should know what I feel.

Amir shrugs. "Maybe you should give him a chance." He steps back, eyes hardening. "It's not like you told your parents about me, anyway."

"I thought you weren't bothered by that," I whisper too harshly. I reach out to him, but he shrinks away.

"I wasn't. Until now, when you don't seem to mind showing affection for someone else." Amir kicks at the ground. "We're here on a mission. At least I am. Are you?"

I do not have time to utter an answer before he's gone.

19

Ria

The boat sways unsteadily beneath my feet.

It's the day after my excursion with Irfan, and now we're standing on King Rohit's double-floored vessel on the Snake River. Crags of rock jut out from the mountain rising high as a tower before me, and icebergs float lazily across the deep-blue waters. Next to me, Aditi watches the river with wide eyes. She's joined us on this boat ride, along with King Rohit himself, Princess Zoya, Saeed, Irfan, and me. Even Shima is perched on the railing of the vessel, watching the lake with keen eyes.

The vision from yesterday returns to me. My face, with those green eyes. Me, reflected as a girl named Raya. The fire attack on the Snake River. Now, as we sail over it, my snake magic hums in my veins. Though I'm still full of questions, I know one thing is true: my snake magic *is* responding to this river. I can only hope that we will find the Tide Master's sword in the Snake River, as well. I told the rest of the group what Irfan and I had discovered last night, knowing they would want to join this trip.

Aditi comes to my side. "Don't worry, we'll catch Mistress Amara soon. Even if I'm not exactly looking forward to it."

"You aren't her servant anymore," I remind her. I cup her chin in my hand and bend so our eyes meet. "And I promise, she'll never hurt you again. You've grown a lot, you know, Aditi."

"I'm not any taller," she remarks.

I laugh. "I meant as a person. What you went through, losing Mama Anita, and then everything with Amara." I bring my hands to her palms, flipping them over. The scars are still there. Whip marks.

"Mistress Amara wasn't a nice person," she admits.

"She was more than *not nice*," I say. "She hurt you. She hurt Saeed, too."

Aditi looks up at me, eyes curious. "Is Master Saeed angry at you, miss? I haven't seen you two together since your hunt. I . . . heard about the snowbirds."

Raja's beard. I wanted to keep that a secret from Aditi's precious ears, at least, but it turns out people gossip in the Winter Palace just as much as they do back home.

I sigh, my eyes trailing upward before they catch on Saeed. I hadn't realized he was standing on the deck, peering over at me. I pull my glance away, though I can still feel his eyes on me. Aditi's right—we've barely spoken more than a few words since the hunt. Not to mention what he might've seen me doing by the Snake River last night, if he was indeed the one watching from that balcony.

"May I speak with you, Ria?" a voice comes from my right.

Zoya. Aditi nods respectfully and leaves me alone with the princess.

Zoya faces the water. "I wanted to ask you how you're feeling. The discovery of those snowbirds was rather rattling."

"Honestly, I was pretty scared. But I think Saeed is the one most scarred by it all," I admit.

Understanding dawns on Zoya's features. "You truly believe his mother was the one to do that to those snowbirds?" When I nod, she blows out a breath. "To be honest, everything that's happened to you and your sister sounds like it came out of a storybook rather than real life."

"I love a good story," I remark.

"Me too," Zoya says, a rare smile spreading across her lips. "Have you heard the tale of the old Amratstanian queen Laila the Great? She was one of the most powerful stonebringers to exist. In her reign, she moved the White Mountains so that the people wouldn't be so far from the palace. It was she who created our kingdom's maxim: *May the mountains move you.* Our people are strong believers in the Masters in the skies," she continues. "The people who forged our kingdom turned the very rocks into mountains—stonebringers. Others who helped to found Amratstan used wind to sweep snow from the clouds—currentspinners."

I nod, remembering Mama Anita's stories. The thought of her tucking me into bed at the Vadi Orphanage relaxes me, especially after the strange horrors I've seen over the last few days.

"So we pray to not only Amran but to our Masters," Zoya

explains. "The Sky Master and Earth Master were close, according to legend." She gazes at me sidelong, grinning. "You like to dig into history, don't you, Ria? Rani wasn't much the same. You two really are different."

I think of Rani, how far away she is. A pang of wistfulness fills me. Even though we only just met two moons ago, she's a part of me I never want to see go away.

Still, I remember the scared look on my own sister's face when I lost control of those snakes. Was she afraid of me? I never told her the truth. I've never really admitted it to myself, either. That I *liked* the feeling of all that power in my veins, the cobra lurking in my belly. The call that I'm realizing now comes from the voice of my ancestor.

Not a second later, I feel my snake magic pull at my attention, almost as if something has snagged against it. Unable to stop myself, I jerk over the side of the boat to see something glimmering below the water, a ray of silver among the waves. I follow it as we drift past, squinting to try to make it out. It looks long and sharp, like a talwar. But even through the water, I can spot something etched into the ebony handle. A wave.

Is that . . . the Tide Master's symbol?

"Do you see that?" I ask Zoya breathlessly, pointing over the railing.

"See what?" She looks down, searching the water, but she only shakes her head.

"You can't see it?" I point directly at the shining silver sword. "It looks like a sword. What if that's the Tide Master's talisman? It's got a marking on it, like the Memory Master's and Snake Master's talismans do." Something about this sword calls to me, tugging at the magic in my blood. Somehow, I know its truth.

"All I see is water," Zoya says, frowning.

I'm reminded of Irfan's words yesterday. That maybe only someone with snake magic, on the Snake River, could find the Tide Master's sword. Am I really the only one who can see it while it's underwater? Is that why I feel its call?

An uneasy feeling creeps up the back of my neck. My gaze flits upward, catching on a rock on the shoreline not far in the distance. My breath catches in my throat.

"Amara," I whisper.

Because she's standing there, surrounded by icebergs and crags of rock. Her mehendi-dyed hair flares in a rage of red. I shudder as I spot others hiding in the rocks next to her, each of them wearing a jade-colored cloak and holding out their arms to the sky.

Something hits the bottom of the boat, and the vessel sways. I clutch on to the railing, eyes locking with Zoya's in fear.

Thump, goes the vessel's golden starboard. *Thump. Thump.*

My blood surges in my veins. I look back out at the crags of rock, but Amara and the others are gone.

We race to find King Rohit on the other side of the boat. He has unsheathed twin swords from his scabbards, Saeed tight on his heels. I halt midstride, feet frozen to the planks beneath me as the ship sways ominously again. A shadow crosses the deck, drowning us in darkness. Aditi's face pales. I follow her gaze up, up, up—

Into the eyes of a black snake the size of the ship. And in its mouth, the sword I saw in the river, balanced precariously between its fangs.

"Sea sapni," Saeed gasps from beside me now, face blanching as the snake bares its bloody fangs at us. The snake magic simmering in my veins heats to a boil. Shima hisses at the black snake in response, her scales flashing a myriad of colors, and I feel her fear just as deeply as if it were my own.

"Saeed," I say. "That's the Tide Master's sword."

Saeed's eyes lock with mine. "How do you know?"

"I just do," I snap, too harshly.

Saeed looks slightly taken aback before saying, "Ria, you need to move below deck. And take Aditi with you."

I want to tell him that thieves don't hide—they act—but as the snake reels down, red eyes blazing into mine, I stumble backward. Its mouth arches open wider, deadly and large enough to swallow a slew of people whole. I eye the sword in its mouth, framed by wickedly sharp fangs poised to kill. Before it can reach us, Zoya and Aditi pull me to the staircase that leads below deck, and Irfan ushers us to a cabin at the bottom of the boat.

Leaving King Rohit and Saeed on the deck.

"We have to help them," I say once we're below, explaining how I saw the Tide Master's sword. I'm shaking and shivering, the magic within me flaring. *Control it*, I tell myself. *Control the snake.*

But one look at Shima, down here below the deck with me, is enough for me to doubt. My magic is strong—but strong enough to control a twenty-foot-long snake?

Thump. I clutch Aditi against me as the entire ship shakes.

"Sea sapni shouldn't exist this far north." Zoya visibly trembles as she clutches her fur cloak tighter around her sari. Her face is made of shadows, the flickering candlelight in this cramped cabin offering little reprieve from the darkness.

"Maybe it has to do with Amara. I saw her on the shoreline. She's close." Just like I saw her that day in the palace during our dinner. She's always been closer than we imagined—I just didn't want it to be true.

Everyone is silent. I shut my eyes, unable to rid myself of the fear for Saeed and King Rohit up there, alone.

How could Amara have done this? How did she even know we were going to be here?

Irfan breathes heavily, clutching his bow and arrow as if that might defeat the sea sapni alone. And with the way he's standing in front of us, feet planted like the last line of defense—I think he might expect to.

Another blow against the ship makes my stomach churn. I grasp on to Aditi, feeling her shivering—no, *shaking*—beneath my fingers. I tuck her close to me as the undulations rippling through the boat fade. My worst fears manifest in my mind. *We're all going to drown in the cold water, the last thing we ever see—*

Out on the streets of Abai, my biggest worry was getting

something to eat for me and Amir. Never had we planned to face giant snakes—especially not ones that live in *water*.

"Do any of us have a plan?" Zoya interjects, voice high. "My father is up there fighting a giant *snake*. If we don't help, we'll all become snake food!"

"Snake food?" I mutter. My eyes connect with Shima's, and a thought threads through me. I think this princess just gave me an idea. And a damn good one at that.

"I have a plan," I say suddenly, forcibly wiping away every worry, every misshapen thought. I have to act. It's what I did best on Abai's streets, and it's exactly what I'll do now.

When I tell the group my thoughts, they look at me like I've grown a third eye. "Do you have a better idea?" I say.

No one speaks.

"I thought so." I turn to Shima now. "Do you think you can do it?"

A moment later, my blood warms, as if Shima is curling around me. My gaze against Shima's becomes fiery, meeting each other with equal strength. The rope in my mind that attaches us glows like an ember.

Yesss, Princess Ria.

"Good," I say. "Zoya, Aditi, stay here." I hear their protests, but I don't stay to listen, exiting the cabin with Irfan and rising to the deck with Shima close behind. But when I ascend, there's no giant snake in sight. King Rohit and Saeed twist in place, weapons at the ready with nowhere to aim them.

"Where is it? Can you still speak to it?" I ask Shima. Step one of our plan. Shima nods, closing her eyes as if reaching out to the sea sapni. *It'sssss hiding*, Shima says after a beat. *It wants to sssssspeak with you.*

"Me?" I squeak out, watching Shima's scales turn a deep red, almost black. The color of fear.

At least the first part of our plan—Shima speaking directly to the snake—worked. "But where'd it go?"

As if in answer, the ship lurches. My hands grasp on to the nearest railing, and Irfan grunts beside me as he steadies me. Saeed reaches my right side, looking nauseated before his eyes widen. He's gazing down into the water.

"I think I found it," he whispers.

I'm afraid to look down, but I do. Its red eyes are the first thing I see lurking below the water. Teasing us, ready to pounce like a tiger.

"You think you can control this thing? Get the sword?" Saeed whispers, hands tightening on a talwar—one from King Rohit's matching set.

"You told me something about the Tide Master's sword. That it has the power to cut through almost any element. Is that true?"

"I suppose we'll find out."

Irfan's silver eyes flare with fear. He turns his gaze to King Rohit, who looks frozen in place as he peers down at the snake.

"Irfan," I say, turning to him, "prepare yourself. I'm going to lure the snake up. When it's here, wait for my signal and shoot."

He nods dutifully and moves steps behind me. Can't say no to a princess, I guess. Or maybe I sound more confident than I feel.

I face the bow of the ship, and Shima joins me. Together, we stare out at the river, and I call upon my magic.

"Come here," I command the snake, threading conviction into my voice. Shima joins me, using her voice to lure the snake near.

Clossserrrr, she says. *Closssserrrr.*

I feel something shift, making the boat lift slightly and then drop down, crashing against the waves. I slide backward, but Saeed's there to catch me, holding me steady. I barely register his arms wrapped around my waist as a shadow eclipses the boat again. Scales rise, glimmering in the sunlight. A hiss comes from the snake, now towering over me with curious red eyes.

I pull away from Saeed and reach the bow again. I've spoken to Shima with only my mind—I can do it with this snake, too. *What do you want?* I ask the snake, stalling. A hand behind my back, I gesture Irfan forward, hoping the snake doesn't notice him.

Skies, this plan better work. I glance to my right, spying King Rohit, who looks pale as his ivory linens, but readies his weapon regardless.

I turn back to the snake. "Is it food you want?" I ask, eyeing the sword. Its eyes flash with hunger. I was right. A snake can never resist a fresh meal—I've felt Shima's hunger in my bones more than once.

The sea snake comes closer, its body thudding down onto the deck. I stumble back as it moves toward me, beads of water slipping from its scales and landing in heaping droplets on the floor.

I raise an arm, ready to signal Irfan to shoot, when Shima says something.

Wait. The snake has a message for you.

"A message?" I say, lowering my arm. "Why are you out here, all alone, in the middle of a river? Did someone send you here?"

We sssea snakes do not like land, it tells me. *But we obey two Masters. And the one speaking to us now is he of stories and untruths, and he wants something. For his host to be free . . . so he too can be free.* They *are the ones who sent me.*

"Host?" I ask.

His plot stirs . . . , the snake continues.

"Who?" I choke out. "What host? Whose plot?"

The large snake before me rumbles something akin to a laugh. *He has called to you, snakespeaker. You know who my Master is.*

Ice floods me. My fingers turn numb. The memory of that voice pounds through my skull. *I can teach you so much. Come . . .*

"That—that can't be—"

No. I'm flustered now, and that's no way to control and distract this snake. I can feel it slipping from my grasp. I'm no Great Snakespeaker. Maybe I'll never be great at all.

You will, Shima confirms by my side, but I still don't feel an ounce of the confidence I should.

The sea snake's voice pierces my mind again. *Come, my children. . . .*

Before I can squeak anything out, a slew of small snakes slip up and onto the ship deck. Several slither over to Saeed, and I shout out as they slink past his guard and pin him to the railing. More slide around his ankles, squeezing.

"No!" I shout when I see they're doing the same to Irfan and King Rohit, whose silver eyes bulge as snakes wrap around their throats. "Please," I cry to the large snake before me, "don't—"

But it only draws closer, until there's barely any space between us, and I feel its hot breath on my face—

"Keep it still," Irfan calls out, having cut the snake from around his throat. I dig into my snake magic, not caring how unwieldy it is. It's powerful. I *need* it to be powerful.

"Obey me!" I cry out. Blood rushes through my veins, but that's not what makes me heat from the inside out. It's the magic, coursing through me like lightning. I grasp on to it with my mind and tug, *hard*, before staring down the sapni. "Obey me!"

My tongue tastes like copper, like blood. *Obey me*, I chant in my mind, over and over. The snake finally falls under my spell, turning completely still.

My heart hammers in my throat. I stare at the snake's glassy eyes, wondering if it truly worked. The snake doesn't attack, instead staring at me like a stray dog.

But as soon as relief floods through me, that connection shatters. The snake magic swirling inside me shrivels, fleeing my veins until they feel empty as a dried-up river.

You are not my Master, cries the sapni before it rears back and strikes, fangs aimed right for me. I leap aside just as the snake's giant fang hits the floorboards, breaking through the deck. It lets out an annoyed hiss, eyes swiveling to look for me as it tries to pull itself away from the floorboard. It's stuck.

Irfan lets an arrow loose. It lands cleanly at its target, spearing the snake through the left eye.

The snake shrieks, and in that instant I reach into its mouth and grasp the Tide Master's sword. I whip out my arm and cut through its trapped fang so cleanly, the tooth breaks in two. The snake wrenches back from the deck, leaving part of its fang stuck in the wood. Its pain hums through my veins as if it's my own, turning me numb. I watch as the snake thrashes against the sky, a beast of the sea writhing like trapped prey, a mouse in a lion's den.

And locks its angry eyes on mine. Fang and eye dripping blood, the snake isn't done with me yet.

"Raja's beard," I curse, just as a voice rends the air. The snake turns its head.

"Stay away from Princess Ria!"

I whirl. "Aditi?"

Not just Aditi. I see her with hands bound behind her back, the bruise on her head a clear sign of a scuffle. A hooded, cloaked man grips her shoulders behind her, his nails red with blood, like they've been rabidly chewed down. He's wearing a black mask, molded against his face and stopping just short of his mouth. His cloak matches the others' who were standing next to Amara.

The same cloak as the servant I saw with Amara, spilling his blood into the Snake River.

The Black Viper. Here, in the flesh.

Irfan's silver eyes darken with rage as he eyes the man. He must recognize the snake markings on his hands—markings like those of the bandits who raided his home.

Irfan whirls his bow and arrow toward the man.

"Let her go," I tell the Black Viper with as much conviction as I can muster, unsure if Irfan will shoot. The snake remains hovering over the boat, ready to strike—but some unknown force keeps it at bay.

There's something about the tilt of the cloaked man's head, the playful smirk on his lips, that I recognize.

"Let's see what your magic can do, Ria. You are the Key, after all."

Key? I think of the fountain's prophecy. *The Key of a Master shall set souls free.*

I am the Key? To what? It's absurd. And yet I've been having dreams of a door. Of a key.

As the hooded man tightens his grip on Aditi, she whimpers. The snake mark on his hand flares, almost like it's burning his skin. Without thinking, I lunge forward and grab him by the hand, my palm pressing against his snake mark.

"Agh!" the man cries, reeling. Aditi ducks away. The man's back hits the railing, but I'm not done with him yet. I grab him again, pressing my palm and my magic more firmly to the mark now. His screams echo across the boat, but I don't care. There's something I relish about this—the feeling of my magic sinking into him like a knife.

He hurt Aditi. He deserves this. I twist the knife of magic and fall deeper, deeper . . .

A high peal of laughter rips me away from my magic. I pant from the exertion and release him with a gasp. The Black Viper crumples to the floor, heaving. No . . . *laughing.* He glances up, a smirk reaching his lips.

"You are certainly the one we have been looking for." The Black Viper grins. "With you, the Key, our Master shall be a god."

"What Master?" I demand, a thousand questions raging inside me. "Amara? The woman you're working for is no Master yet."

But the man laughs again, shocking me out of my rage. A maniacal grin splits his face as he looks toward me and holds his palms up, showing the scarred serpent there in full.

"Amara?" he asks, almost crazed. "I do not serve Amara, or any of this earth, child."

"Then who? And *who are you?*" I spit.

"It's not who I am, but where I came from. . . ." The man's voice deepens. "Akshya and Hitesh."

"What did you say?" Irfan demands, his hands tightening on his bow as he lunges forward.

I whirl around to push Irfan back, and in my distraction feel more than see the man shove past me and grab Aditi by the collar. I lunge for her, but the man only pulls out a dagger and brings it to Aditi's throat.

My breaths halt.

"You want this girl back?" he says, voice gravelly as his eyes rise to the snake. "Give me the sword."

If I do, I'll only be helping Amara get one step closer to her goals—becoming the Soul Master and destroying Kaama. But I can't let Aditi be taken. I won't.

I glance backward at Irfan, signaling him. He knows what to do; I can see it from the look in his eyes. Grasping the sword firmly, I turn back to the cloaked man. I gaze intently at Aditi as I slide the Tide Master's sword across the deck. Just as the man is about to bend down to grab it, Aditi rears her leg back and kicks him with so much force, the man buckles.

"Now!" I shout to Irfan.

A sharp whizz blows past my ear, and too fast, I see it all happening: Irfan's arrow loosed, shooting right for the man's heart.

But the man drops, desperate fingers reaching the sword. The arrow is just about to pierce his shoulder as he disappears with the talisman, leaving nothing but a plume of black smoke in his wake.

"W-what—" I begin, whirling to find Irfan gawking. But the next moment, his eyes harden, burdened with sorrow and loss and revenge. I don't need to be a mindwielder to understand that look. That man was one of the bandits who hurt his family, split them apart, and left them for dead. And now they've all escaped again.

But there's no time to linger—not when I see what Aditi's doing, facing the large sea snake head-on. It's poised as if it wanted to strike at us while we were distracted. But Aditi splays her hands out in front of her, palms facing the snake, and for some reason, the sea sapni seems trapped, as though it's hit an invisible wall.

"Aditi!" I cry, rushing toward her. Light exudes from her palms, bright blue as the ocean, and the snake shrieks in response.

The smaller snakes' thoughts pound through me, flood my veins like the very water we glide over.

We only obey two Masters.

The Snake Master and the Tide Master.

All the snakes begin to slip off the boat. I have no clue how this is happening, but there's no time to halt Aditi's progress. Once powerful and hungry, the large snake now coils and shrinks back, whipping its hooded head. As Aditi holds her hands aloft, the snake crashes into the river, a vortex of water whirling up from where it lands.

The connection between me and the sea sapni snaps in two, and the pain melts away. But the boat rocks from the impact of the snake's fall, and we tumble back as the bow tilts toward the sky. Saeed grabs me just in time, his other hand clutching the railing. I hang on to Saeed for dear life as the boat splashes back down, rocking back and forth like a pendulum until it settles.

My mind is spinning by the time everything ends. I find myself in Saeed's arms, cradled against him. His chest rises and falls quickly—too quickly. I press a hand against his chest and look him in the eyes.

"We— We're okay," I tell him.

"We are?" Saeed's eyes shutter. "Are you sure this isn't death, Princess?"

"I'm pretty sure we'd be inside a snake's belly if this was death." Still, Saeed doesn't laugh. We both know what just happened—

giving up the Tide Master's sword in exchange for Aditi's life. And what that means: Amara has gained another talisman.

As for how Aditi got that snake to leave . . . I glance back at her, watching her stare at her hands, as if that blue light was imagined.

"I think that's the last time I go on a boat," Irfan says from nearby. He hangs on to the railing, looking sick. But King Rohit is still in the corner of the boat, far away from us, staring into the water with terrified eyes. I move to where he stands, staring into the pool beneath, the water rippling like he's thrown a stone. Something stirs along the surface—red hair like flames.

Amara.

I withhold a gasp as she dives deeper into the river. All I see now is her tendrils of hair as she swims away, slipping from our grasp once again.

Sahil

Where the Snake River was once my sanctuary, it now burns alive. Even my memories of it are set aflame, singed to ash as bitter as the air coating my lungs, my chest, and the empty space where my heart should be. If you were here, brother, perhaps you could have shielded my daughters with your magic, or twisted the Masters' souls into ones of understanding and compassion. Something I now lose with every passing day.

Time blurs after it all ends, after we escape the water with nothing but the clothes on our backs, but the fire-singed memory remains. The harsh gale stretching the water open like a wound—my daughters, Raya and Ruhanya, barely escaping the next blast that licked the water's surface. I knew too quickly what this was. A warning. What I didn't understand was what my fellow Masters were warning me about. I was no danger to them, and still they hated me with every fiber of their being.

I didn't need a reason why. I needed to run.

"Raya, Ruhanya," I tell my daughters at our destination. Near

the center of our continent, closer to the snakespeakers Amran formed with his own hands after my First Descendants, I feel much more at peace. The water was never our home, that much I now understand.

We need our own home. A place secluded and sealed with our magic. A protector.

Every day, I meditate over this spot. Part grass, part desert, the earth does not respond to my call, but the more I focus, the more I feel my magic threading into the ground, becoming one with it. Soon, with patience and the fortitude of my magic, we will have a home.

Days later, as I lay my hands on the earth and feel it rumble just slightly, as if curious about the magic within me, a young girl approaches to greet me, her eyes lingering on mine.

"Is that you, Preethi?"

The girl's face, once chubby and small, begins to shift into an older landscape. Her eyebrows become thick and full. Her round nose elongates, and her lips thin, wrinkling into a frown.

No longer a girl but a Master. Preethi can affect the minds of others, even their memories, but she doesn't often use magic to change people's perception of her face—unless she doesn't want to be seen.

"Sahil," Preethi says, carrying a bundle of fabric. "I should have known you'd see it was me."

I simply shrug. Preethi, unlike my other kin, speaks my name with respect instead of fear.

"I heard what happened."

"The whole world has," I snap. "It seems hatred has taken root everywhere."

Guilt overtakes her features. "I haven't been fair to you, Sahil.

And while I've never hurt you or your daughters, I'm afraid I've done something worse."

"What's that?" I ask, still focused on the magic pulsing through my blood and into the ground, twining with every fabric of life, every stitch, every molecule.

"I've withheld the truth. The reason our fellow Masters despise you."

"All but you and our lost brother, it seems."

Preethi nods solemnly. "You deserve to learn the truth."

"I don't want to hear it. I'm busy, sister."

"But, Sahil—"

A piercing whoop of joy comes from nearby. Both Preethi and I twist toward the sound. Raya and Ruhanya are staring at a crack in the dry earth. My sister and I join them, watching as Raya wipes a bead of sweat from her brow.

"It took a while," Ruhanya says, "but we discovered how to begin building our home." She points at a crack in the shape of a circle. Blood, gleaming golden, sparkles in the center.

"Ruhanya, you shouldn't—"

"She didn't. I did." Raya reveals her cut hand. "Father, you said yourself that my blood, that my magic, is stronger than you've ever seen. If I just use a bit every day—"

"Use?" I boom. "You're not going to bleed yourself dry."

"I won't," Raya shoots back. Sometimes I forget how much like me she is. Her emotions and instinct drive her magic, unlike Ruhanya's, whose power is more refined and practical. She can call snakes with ease, study their venoms in an academic sense. My two daughters, truly encompassing the breadth of my powers; truly each one of a kind.

"Sahil, you must let your daughters loose sometimes. Children need time to learn and coax their power." Preethi wears a kind, knowing smile. I hate when she's right. Even though my daughters are on the verge of fourteen summers of age, I sometimes forget that they are, in fact, still children. I rely on them too much.

"Fine. But I will be monitoring your progress," I tell Raya. As I take her hand, her blood smears onto my skin, her magic connecting with mine. Something strings taut between us, a tether that ties father to daughter, Master to magic. This—this is indeed a magic like I've never seen before. It surges and beats beneath her skin, like its own living thing.

"I came here to offer you this." Preethi hands each girl fabric—two matching purple saris. Ruhanya gasps in delight, and from beneath her cloak three snakes yip giddily, matching her enthusiasm as their scales change colors.

For a brief moment, I let that joy in, too.

Preethi pulls me aside, her smile falling. "Have you seen them? Those magicless beings who devote themselves to you? They call themselves the Serpent's Tongue."

An intriguing name. While Amran created snakespeakers, there are others, those born without magic, who wish to be like us. I suppose I cannot blame them for wanting the magic rooted deep in my blood.

"The other Masters say your followers are an army. That soon, you'll retaliate."

"If they want a fight, they'll have to look elsewhere," I tell Preethi, though the idea of revenge is sweet as a fresh mango on my tongue. "They're no followers. Not yet."

"What does that mean?"

"That I'm focused on this. Our home. Surely you understand me?"

"Of course," Preethi says, her magic aura pulsing comfortably against mine. Snake magic and memory magic go hand in hand. I sometimes wonder if that is why Preethi has been so kind to me all my life, even as I came into the world last of the Masters, aside from you, brother.

"You're thinking about him. Manav," my sister says, your name swept onto the wind, foreign and familiar all at once.

"I should learn to mask my emotions," I tell Preethi with a grumble. "But yes. I think of him often. And I feel the Soul Master's magic is still alive . . . in Raya."

"Does she know?" Preethi asks, amazed.

"I believe she senses it. While she hasn't wielded any newfound powers yet, I assume it's only a matter of time."

"Her magic could rival that of any Master's," Preethi says with a sneaky smile. "She is destined for great things. I don't need to see the future to know that."

As Preethi leaves, I turn back to my daughters, watching as their magic spins and dances along the ground and the very snakes beneath them, as the night steals the last rays of light from the sky.

The Memory Master is correct. Raya is destined for great things.

But greatness always requires sacrifice.

20

Rani

The three palaces are full of riddles, but the greatest riddle of all is Amir.

Some days he speaks to me, others he doesn't. It's like we're a ball of yarn, unspooling and fraying and falling and tangling. A thread of tension turns into a knot by today, when Amir and I can hardly glance at each other without remembering our unfinished conversation.

I feel even emptier when I remember the stolen talisman. The one Amara likely has in her possession. We might all soon pay a deadly price for letting her take it.

Knowing our time is short, Dhruv sent word for Jujhar to travel to the palace on his skyhawk, Sahara. He also visited Professor Neel, who remained skeptical of our plan but promised to visit tomorrow after his class, when Jujhar is scheduled to arrive.

Abai's sun, I pray this works.

As we await their arrival, I spend some quiet time alone

exploring Retan's three palaces. While the Blue Palace is comforting and familiar, I bump too often into Amir, unsure what to say, and scurry off like a scared servant. I don't quite know what to tell him yet—not when my heart hasn't settled, either.

Instead, I head for the Saffron Palace. The arched entrance is made of red sandstone bricks, leading to the beautifully decorated towers. The orange-reddish bricks look weathered and strong all the same, like whoever built the Saffron Palace wanted it to stand tall for the rest of time. Turrets spiral into the air, laced with hand-painted globes of fire, symbolizing Retan's link to the Fire Master's descendants, flametalkers who helped build the queendom even though they weren't royalty themselves.

Inside, windows like honeycombs scatter light, speckling the sunset along the floor. The entire entrance hall is bathed in orange, the walls painted with sweet orange blossoms. Two sets of stairs flank the building, connecting to a hallway above us. Though this palace is much shorter than the other two, it makes up for it with ornamentation. Three chandeliers, each carrying an endless number of candles, look like balls of ocher fire.

Near the main hall, I discover Prince Dhruv on an ornate bench, poring over a book. However he doesn't look altogether moved by it, his eyes slowly drooping, and mouth hanging open in fatigue as he reads.

"Is that the great Prince Dhruv *drooling?*" I say playfully.

My voice jolts him from his stupor. Embarrassed, he shuts the book, checking for saliva. I'd almost feel bad for teasing—if he hadn't tricked me immediately upon meeting me.

"Princess Rani. Sorry, I haven't been sleeping much lately."

"It's not a problem. I was kidding about the drool. How are your examinations?" I ask.

Dhruv smooths a thumb over his book. "Not terrible. But that isn't entirely what's been keeping me awake."

"Right. The talisman," I add quietly.

Dhruv nods.

I can see the topic is weighing him down, so I switch subjects. "You haven't properly shown me around the Saffron Palace yet. I must say, this one seems the most extravagant of them all." Even though this palace is the shortest of the three, it is also the widest, boasting endless mazelike corridors.

"Ah, then I've been neglectful! Let me show you the best part." Dhruv sticks his arm out, and I wrap mine around his smoothly as he leads me to a greenhouse in a secluded sector of the palace.

"I find myself coming here often; it's quiet and not too far for a moonlit stroll. Did you know Retan's first royal detective built this very greenhouse as a spot dedicated solely to thinking? And gorgeous greenery, of course."

"A royal detective?" I wonder. "Like a scholar?"

"They were a scholar, yes. *Someone* had to start thinking about that sealed chamber and the queens' mysterious deaths. Retan is full of many mysteries. But it looks like you're the first to crack the case."

"I hope," I add, stepping into the greenhouse ahead of Dhruv. I glance around the sunlit room, full of plants of all sizes.

"Queen Sunita studied these very plants, and the ways in which the Retanian microbiome functions as mostly a desert plain with little greenery," Dhruv explains. "She cataloged every plant native to Retan."

"Sounds tiresome," I say, smoothing a finger over a nearby dahlia. While dahlias are typically native to Amratstan's cooler climate, they cannot survive in extreme cold. Which makes harvesting them a rare affair—and pricing them an expensive one. Saeed gave me a dahlia on my sixteenth birthday, a symbol of our blossoming love.

Love was so simple then.

As I head deeper inside, heat presses against me from all sides, as sweltering as the Abai sun. As though I've entered a pocket of the southern jungles, palm fronds tickle my cheeks, and I reach out to touch the blooming flowers.

"I would offer you one," Dhruv says, "but Mother would kill me. She keeps this place pristine, and allows no one except the gardeners in here. Not even me. But considering she's away at the Gold Palace . . ."

I laugh and drop my hand. "You don't need to give me anything."

Dhruv comes up behind me and leans against a rock at the base of a miniature waterfall. I'm reminded of the day Dhruv took me to his little hideout.

He bites his lip. There's something on his face—like a secret caught among the stars, thick with wonder. I remember his words that day. *I don't mean to be so forward, Rani, but I enjoy spending time with you.* My whole body flushes. I cannot deny that I like the way Dhruv opens up to me, the buds of a blooming friendship, just like these flowers.

Dhruv pulls his necklace out from where it was tucked into his kurta. "In Retan, every royal visits the Lalkian Caves to receive a firestone. There are many uses for it, but some also believe that it glows when you're near someone you love."

"Has it?" I ask thickly, his words trickling through me. "Has it glowed?"

Dhruv shakes his head, but I swear I see a small sparkle from the stone—or perhaps it's just a trick of the light.

He abandons the rock and leads me deeper into the greenhouse, stopping at a lonesome tree with bright-green leaves. "Maybe I'm like this tree. Maybe I'll always be rooted in one spot, alone."

I step closer to him, pretending to examine the tree. "I used to feel the same way. But when I switched places with Ria, I discovered more. Who I truly was. Who I could be."

Dhruv turns to me, his arm brushing mine. I think of Amir's warmth; Dhruv's coolness. Amir's honest inelegance; Dhruv's perfect polish. Two opposites. My heart twists, caught between two people, two lives, two paths.

"And who can you be?"

"I . . . could be the queen. I could change people's lives for the better. And my sister . . ." I trail off, thinking of Ria. Will she want to reign with me? Is that even possible, to be sister queens in Abai, like the Three Blessed Sisters? There's a striking nature to Ria, a boldness. She is fire to my ice. Yet queendom feels so far away. What's happening now with Amara, with the missing Sky Master's talisman, looms over me.

Dhruv must notice my silence, for he leads me away from the tree and back toward the greenhouse's entrance. "You've had a lot of changes in your life recently."

I pause, watching his back as he continues down the path. "And you?"

He spins. "What about me, Princess Rani?"

"Do you ever wish for change?"

He shrugs. "I've been one person my whole life. The prince. But if you don't mind me confiding in you, Rani . . . sometimes I wish I were just a normal student. Maybe I truly am treated differently from other pupils, and I just haven't noticed."

"You're smart, Dhruv. You have to give yourself credit sometimes." Without hesitation, I stride toward him and grasp his shoulder. "And be kind to yourself, too."

His eyes settle on mine like warm honey. He takes my hand off his shoulder and drags my palm to his lips, pressing a gentle kiss against it. *Abai's sun.* The greenhouse grows a hundred times hotter, and my body instinctively steps closer. Half of me wonders what *could* be. Dhruv understands what it's like to feel alone, isolated, the way I felt in the Abaian palace for years. Some might call us a perfect match—a prince and a princess, each sharing the same struggles, weights, futures.

Dhruv, a prince . . . or a partner?

I'm beginning to confuse the two myself.

Dhruv looks like he's about to speak more on the subject, then changes his mind. "How is your sister? Did you write her a letter?"

"No," I respond, realizing I haven't had the chance to write to her. With every new development in Retan, it completely fell from my mind.

Absentmindedly, I lean down and grasp the anklet I gave Ria before we left. A parting present.

Or perhaps more. Shima *had* imbued the anklet with snake magic—her idea. I gently unclasp the anklet and hold it in the air, admiring the single snake charm attached in the middle. But as I peer closer, I notice something else—two smaller charms beside the snake made of pure gold. A snowflake and a burning flame.

Were those there before?

Shima taught me that objects can bring us closer together. As twins, Ria and I share an innate bond, a link between our minds that can transfer words and thoughts—if we're close enough, and typically with Shima's help. But we've never tried such a thing so far from each other. Now, we're kingdoms apart—but we've still got our twin connection . . . and our anklets.

With Ria wearing the matching anklet, threaded with the bonds of our magic, it might be worth a try.

A princess never falters. Today, I will not break that vow.

"Could I . . . have a moment alone?" I ask Dhruv.

Ever courteous, he nods and waits by the greenhouse entrance. I settle at the base of the nearest tree and lay the anklet gently on my lap. I envision my magic as a chest of drawers as always, except now, I pull on two magics of a sort—mine and Ria's. My fingers loop through the gold, magic blending with metal, until I feel heat and ice colliding, a thread of magic, like an unbreakable rope, forming in my mind and arching into the distance.

A bond. My connection to my sister.

With my eyes closed, it feels as though I am in a dream, eyes roaming beneath the surface of a new world. I see Ria and many familiar faces—Saeed, Aditi, and even Princess Zoya, a childhood friend—disembarking from a boat. Under them, a river from many childhood excursions with Zoya comes to life. *The Snake River.*

When I glance down, I see that I am in the river, gently bobbing in the water. Except I feel none of it.

Ria? I ask. My voice is hoarse and nearly silent. Despite this, my sister turns around. Am I truly here? Can she see me? This feels nothing like the mind link we called upon when we were posing as each other, but perhaps we can still speak?

I hear her mumble something to Aditi as if through water, and the servant girl nods and scurries into the Winter Palace while Ria paces along the bank. And though I'm not sure I am truly here, I feel a cold rush of wind steal my breath as snowflakes descend from fluffy clouds.

"Ria?" I call, this time hearing my voice. It's distant, even to my ears, but Ria spins toward the river, her eyes searching for me fruitlessly.

"Am I dreaming again?" She touches her forehead as if to check for a fever. I try to wade through the water, but the tide pulls me back. *Your anklet, Ria!* I try to say, but the coursing river swallows my words.

Finally, after glancing left and right once more, my sister reaches down and plucks off her anklet. "Why is this so hot?" she asks herself, and when she glances up, she spooks herself into nearly dropping the gift.

"Rani! You're—you're—"

"I'm here," I tell her, grinning with the rush of success. "I made a mind link!"

"But this . . ." Ria carefully inches into the water, letting the waves lap at her feet. "You're made of water."

I glance down at my hands for the first time. I can see through them, and as I wiggle my fingers, I see that I am indeed more water than skin, more river than girl.

I don't even have a moment to be spellbound, because I can already feel my magic running thin, the bond heavily pulling at my energy. This distance is nothing we've ever been able to accomplish before, and it's not easy. "Ria, I came here to check in on you. Are you okay?" I regard her with worry. She doesn't look like she's been sleeping, and she clutches her cloak to herself as though she'd fall apart if she let go.

Ria wrings her hands, ignoring my question. "Don't worry

about me. I'm sure you've been busy in Retan?"

My sister shivers in the cold air. I wish I could reach out to her, if only to give an inkling of warmth, but the river holds me in its clutches. "Yes. Hunting down a centuries-old mystery can be quite time consuming."

Ria's jaw drops.

We exchange stories like offerings to the Masters in the Old Age, each astounded by what we've seen and discovered. I reveal what we learned from Scholar Neel about the talismans and am shocked to find that Amara had taken the Tide Master's talisman from right under Ria's nose. It makes my news about the Sky Master's talisman even worse. We both fall silent when we realize Amara only needs two more talismans—the Earth Master's map and the Fire Master's compass —to unlock the lifeblood of Amran from the stone.

"This . . . is a lot to process." I let out a deep breath. But I can tell there's even more to her story that she hasn't let come to light. Something like darkness and despair clouds her eyes. "I know I asked once, but I can't help being the older sister sometimes. Are you absolutely *certain* you're okay?"

Ria finally drops her hands. "Something's been bothering me since we got off the boat." She describes the man who attacked Aditi, bearing a strange mark of a snake on his hands.

"What do you think it means?" my sister asks.

"That snake symbol hasn't been spotted in centuries, at least. The Snake Master had fanatics for many years," I explain, remembering what Father taught me as a child, a story passed down from snakespeaker to snakespeaker. "Mostly harmless, those who wanted to align themselves with the ruling snakespeakers. But not all. The Serpent's Tongue—that's what they call themselves—were the only group to mark themselves with snakes, and they were . . . ruthless. Are you certain you saw that snake mark?"

Ria nods, shivering. "It was just one man. Maybe I was seeing things. But . . ."

I raise a brow.

"There was something off about him, the way he looked at me. It was greater than respect—almost like . . . reverence."

"The Serpent's Tongue worshipped the Snake Master during his time before and after the Great Masters' Battle. Before he disappeared, he bestowed a bit of power upon these fanatics—and tethered them to their Master through an ancient form of snake magic. If they truly are active again . . ." I pause, the last part ringing in silence.

"It's probably nothing," Ria says. "Besides, we have bigger problems on our hands."

It seems like far more than *nothing*. But she's right, we don't have the time to dive into yet another mystery. And looking at my sister's wan face, I just want to comfort her.

"We'll stop Amara and her foul plans, I swear it," I assure her. But she only nods, seemingly unconvinced.

"We're close to discovering how to destroy the Bloodstone," I continue. "The answer *must* lie in the sealed chamber. As soon as the scholar and currentspinner arrive at the Blue Palace, I shall put my plan into action."

"Which *will* succeed," Ria says, reaching a hand out. "Rani, I . . ." She trails off, her expression dark with some emotion I can't read.

"Yes?" I nudge gently. Something about her tone makes me think that she's been waiting to say this for a while now.

But she just looks down at our hands, at the pressure I can't feel.

"Nothing. I'm sorry, I'm just worrying." She looks up at me, suddenly determined. "We'll get through this."

I don't attempt to decode what's lurking in her words. Instead, I try my hardest to grasp her hands in mine. For a moment, I feel her, her magic, steady and true, flooding through her where mine is already faltering from strain. She's not the same girl who messed up her magic at the ceremony in Abai. She's someone else. Someone stronger.

Before I can say another word, I feel my body begin to fade, and a tide washes over me, swallowing me whole and breaking the mind link entirely.

"They said you'd be here," comes Jujhar's gruff voice the following day. Dhruv, Amir, and I turn on our heels to face him. We're standing before the sealed chamber, where we've been waiting with Queen Meeta for the currentspinner's arrival.

"Jujhar. You came."

"It was a quick trip, considering." Jujhar's skyhawk, Sahara, chirps obediently from his shoulder. "But I'll be honest, I'm worried we might be too late to find my family's talisman. What if we never retrieve it?"

"We will," Queen Meeta promises Jujhar boldly. "And I might add, it is a pleasure to meet our future adviser. Dhruv told me all about you. It's been a long time since we royals have spoken to currentspinners. We shall value your perspective greatly."

"My apologies for not having arrived yet to fill in the adviser position, Queen Meeta," says Jujhar in a sober tone I haven't heard from him before. Up close, I notice he's trimmed his beard and mustache, looking far more regal than a man who owns a dingy tavern. "I've been looking for someone to take over my establishment while I'm away. I can't give up the tavern entirely—after all, it's on the land my ancestors built. To be honest, I'm more used to the company of my books, but this adviser position is an opportunity I can't pass up." Those dimples make a flashing appearance. "My family would be proud."

"Indeed, they would," Queen Meeta agrees.

A different voice chimes, "I brought what you asked for!" I glance over at the arriving Professor Neel, who holds up his trunk. "Oh, Jujhar. What a pleasant surprise!"

"Professor," Jujhar says with a smile that I'm almost shocked to see. Who knew Jujhar could be pleasant? "I wish it was under better circumstances."

Professor Neel tuts. "Shall we begin?"

I nod, facing the door as I explain my theory. "I've been think-ing. No key could fit this lock, but what if it was a metaphorical key? Something that represented the triplet queens' beliefs? Which is why I believe, as there are three sides to a triangle, it may take three magics of sorts to unlock the door. A way to represent their belief that all magics were equal." I press a hand to the door. A buzz whirrs through my fingertips and up my arm, confirming my suspicions. There is magic at work here. Or rather, a mecha-nism that recognizes magic.

"Feel it," I tell Jujhar. He copies me, resting his large hand on the framework. Jujhar withholds a gasp, and I smile with relief. So not only my magic responds to this door.

"Three sides of the triangle, and three magics to unlock the chamber." I nod at the trunk. Professor Neel produces the magma rock and brushes some of its ash onto his fingers, covering them in soot.

"From my time as a scholar, I theorized about magic, relics, and their connection to the sisters. But I didn't think opening this door possible. I suppose we'll find out, won't we?" He manages a nervous laugh, but the hall of the Blue Palace remains quiet with tension. Finally, he presses his hand to the door, the third magic—the Fire Master's, contained in the magma rock—locking into place.

Nothing.

I press my hand firmly against the door, willing it to open. But though I still feel the energy behind the door, nothing happens. I push harder, but it feels as if the door is waiting—almost like something is missing. Jujhar sighs, shaking his head.

"I suppose we're wrong."

"Jujhar—" I begin.

"If I may," Professor Neel cuts in, "perhaps we need to look for a different solution."

"Such as?" Dhruv wonders.

"Something besides magic," Amir offers. It's the most he's said aloud this whole time. We turn to him, puzzled but intrigued.

"Think of it this way. The queens said knowledge is the greatest magic of all, right? Which means they must have thought people without magic and people *with* magic were equal."

"The queens spoke of their reverence for magic and non-magic users often," Queen Meeta confirms.

"Yeah. So let's say Rani's theory is right. *Partly.* If you have three people with magic, then you need the opposite. Three people without magic." He gestures at himself, Dhruv, and Queen Meeta. "That makes an equal balance."

Finally, Amir looks up, wearing a small but powerful smile. I return it, feeling both a warm rush of affection for his cleverness and berating myself for not thinking of it sooner.

"I think it's worth a shot," Dhruv states. He steps next to me and places a hand on the door.

"It's a good idea, and a strong safeguard." Queen Meeta places her hand on the door. Amir steps forward and does the same. For a second, nothing happens, and I brace myself for another disappointment.

And then the floor shivers, a purr that echoes into a deep rumble. A creaking sound emits from the stone as it pushes inward, forming a rectangular doorway. Softly, I push on the stone as it grates against the floor, and we simultaneously heave the door open.

"Incredible," Professor Neel says in wonder. "This chamber hasn't been opened in a thousand years!"

As if to prove it, a cloud of dust follows, and the professor falls into a coughing fit. I peek through the door. A cobweb draping overhead makes me wary, but Jujhar swats it away, intrigued by the staircase winding deep into the darkness below.

"How safe do you think that thing is?"

"Dunno. What's important is my plan worked, didn't it?" Amir asks, huffing with pride. I allow myself a smile, not caring that we haven't spoken properly in days.

"I'll go first."

Wait, I want to say as Amir begins his descent, but he moves forward steadily, pausing at every creak. I clench my fists all the while, finally letting go when Amir makes it down safely.

As the rest of us descend toward the underground, a draft tickles my ankles, and when we reach the bottom of the steps, four sconces on the wall light up. They are balls of flames—like the fireglobes in the Island Market—hovering in the darkness. The thrill of witnessing such ancient magic crawls up my spine. The room we land in is narrow—a corridor, more like. Plucking up whatever courage I have left, I push to the front of the group and march through the corridor, delving deeper and deeper underground.

At least fifty steps in, the corridor gives way to a larger clearing: a circular chamber bricked with reddish stone, with two other narrow doorways that are covered in rubble and ash.

The chamber is a dark, shadowy thing, but more sconces with flames light up as if sensing our presence. All around us, I spot writings in the Retanian language of the Old Age. It's similar enough that it's legible, if not easily read. Still, a few names leap out at me: Preethi. Ashneer. Mandeep. Darshin. Diya. Sahil.

The names of the Masters of Magic.

"This chamber must be beneath the three palaces," Dhruv says, speaking with the delight of a child who's just filched a sweet treat.

I scan the writing on the walls. More stories, likely written by Queen Saira. Is this the secret the Three Blessed Sisters were hiding? I see nothing about the Bloodstone, and my hopes deflate.

"How are we supposed to find our answers?" I ask, gazing around. "It could take hours to read all this and find what we seek."

"I don't have much personal experience with magic, Princess Rani," Queen Meeta says, "but we've come this far. Perhaps you must look to your own magic to help you in times like these."

She's right. But how? What would Ria do? She would want us to keep going, to not give up. To try and to keep trying. It took incredible courage for her to live as an orphan, a thief, and eventually, a princess. I could use even an ounce of her bravery now.

I dig into my snake magic, imagining it like a chest of drawers, with four subsets I can call and pull at my will. I open all of them, letting my magic fill me entirely, and I feel a tug toward something in the corner of the chamber. My feet lead me instead of my mind. I flit toward a symbol engraved on the ground, that familiar triangle, calling to the magic in my veins. *Come*, it says. *Find me.*

Entranced, I bend down and press on it. The floor quakes, and the symbol disappears in a whirl of dust like quicksand. What's left is a golden object that I pick up with trembling fingers.

"What's that?" Amir says.

"It looks like a sundial," Dhruv observes from behind me.

Indeed, it does. Dhruv and Amir sweep to my sides as we all inspect the sundial. Its gold exterior glimmers in the overhead light.

I shiver as I find the word *Manav* inscribed on the bottom. Who made this? Somehow, this object felt like it was calling my name, like it *wanted* me to find it.

The same way the sisters' symbol appeared in the magma rock. They *wanted* me here. This chamber has been calling to me from the moment I arrived—a sign that this is where my answers lie. I know it.

"Could it be . . . ?" Professor Neel rubs at his balding head. "*Manav* was the legendary name of the Soul Master. Is this . . . ?"

He points at a piece of stone in the center of the sundial, dark as night. As soon as I touch it, the dial begins to glow, light zipping around the engravings until it's formed a complete circle.

This is magic, but it's a magic unlike anything I've ever felt.

I squeeze the sundial in my palm. That tingling feeling returns, this time in my toes. Something deep within me sparks to life, like a snake writhing in my belly. As soon as the tingling disappears, the chamber begins to shake.

"Duck!" I cry, throwing my hands over my head. The rest of the group follows, Professor Neel muttering a prayer to Amran. But no rocks fall from the ceiling, only ash, sprinkling us with soot.

"There they are," a voice proclaims.

"Well, *finally*. I was getting restless."

I startle back, soot shivering off my form. The voices don't belong to any of us.

Three plumes of smoke escape the ground. I cannot believe my eyes when I see them forming into ghostly shapes of queens past and present.

The Three Blessed Sisters.

21

Ria

On the night of Princess Zoya's birthday, the Winter Palace ballroom is already buzzing. I'm dressed in a beautiful black lehenga beaded with beige pearls, the darkness of my clothing eerily echoing my grim thoughts.

It's been a day since the attack on the boat, and everyone's still reeling, unsure how Amara succeeded once again.

But Amara isn't the only one on my mind. Even with Rani right in front of me through the mind link, I still couldn't tell her what was on my mind. My dreams have abated, but I can't forget that mysterious voice that I've been hearing—or the way it echoed the Snake Master's in Raya's memory.

The sea serpent and the hooded man's words echo in my mind.

I do not serve Amara.

There's only one other person they would serve. But even as my thoughts spin closer I shut them down, unwilling to believe it.

Had that man really been a member of this Serpent's Tongue, a follower of the Snake Master? After a millennium of silence?

Don't forget about me, a voice rattles inside my brain. Though Shima is back in my bedchamber, I've noticed that with my growing powers and experience, I can hear her from farther distances.

You really do get star treatment, you know that? I tell Shima through my head. Yet her snark doesn't make my heart lift like it normally does.

Because we gave up the very talisman Amara wants. *The Tide Master's sword.* We had it in our grasp, and if we don't move fast and find the other talismans, then we've already lost.

Golds and blues cover every surface of the ballroom, the Amratstanian crest's colors. The floor itself is made of ice and covered in floral rugs to keep people from slipping, though no Amratstanian native seems to have a problem with that. Looking around, I estimate this whole ballroom is twice as large as Abai's throne room. Palace staff weave around guests, offering silver platters of bite-sized foods. Little puffs of dough filled with savoury spiced creams; mini pakoras, the fried besan and potato a heavenly treat; and mounds and mounds of chutneys.

Not to mention the towering diya, a lamp bigger than any I've ever seen, next to where King Rohit and Princess Zoya greet guests. I catch sight of the physician Veer standing next to them. I approach him.

"I haven't thanked you for the tonic you sent me." I haven't felt a whisper of Amara's presence in the last few days, and if the tonic's helping, then Veer's the one to thank.

"Of course, Princess Ria!" He grins widely, revealing slightly yellowed teeth, and presses his gloved hands together. "It is such an honor to aid a snakespeaker."

"And it would be *my* honor to dance with you."

I whirl. Saeed is all suited up, dressed in a midnight-black kurta pajama threaded with gold, and the small hoop in his ear winks under the candlelight as he offers me a shy smile.

As Saeed gazes at me, heat blooms in my cheeks, like a fire that won't burn out. He doesn't wait for me to answer, instead extending an arm and saying, "Shall we?"

I grasp his palm firmly. We fit right in on the dance floor, already bustling with people stepping to the beat of a tabla. It feels good, forgetting about everything, enjoying the moment. Saeed takes a hand and spins me—once, twice, the third making me land right in his arms, my back to his chest. He rocks me from side to side there, his breath hot on the back of my neck.

"Are you tinkering with our engagement dance?" I ask him teasingly.

"Why only perform a dance once?" He spins me so I can face him, chest-to-chest. "Besides, our dance was *good*."

"Oh, you mean when I nearly slipped?"

"When I caught you."

It's so strange to think of that time as *simpler*. I was pretending to be Rani, deceiving everyone around me. Dancing in Saeed's arms, not knowing who I was or what my future would hold.

And here I am now, a thousand questions still thundering

through me. "Saeed, why've you been avoiding me—*us*—these past few days?"

"It seemed like you were avoiding *me*."

"I never meant to. I thought you didn't want to speak to me. You have to know that, Saeed."

"Even tutors can be oblivious to these things. But you're right. I didn't want to speak to anyone about my mother, so I've been spending a lot of time alone in the library. Reading about the White Mountains and the Earth Master's talisman, books written in an old Amratstanian tongue."

"You never told me you could read in other languages."

"My father was a learned man, supposedly. I've always strived to emulate him. It made my mother happy." Saeed looks into the distance as if he can see the memory of his father there. "He attended university at an early age in Kaama before joining their army of Warriors. Old Amratstanian tongues were thought to be the primal language of the North, before our continental common tongue was instated three centuries ago."

"You really are a good tutor," I say with a grin.

The music slows and the light seems to dim around us. "I never apologized," Saeed says, "about how I acted the day we found the snowbirds. I didn't want to believe that my mother could do that. Have such dangerous power."

Dangerous power. Even if he doesn't know it, I'm brought back to my own dangerous magic, my inability to control it. Would my power scare Saeed, too? As it has so many others?

He twists his torso closer to mine, and questions spark through me. I know how my power feels, how lethal it could be if I let it.

Powerful. Cunning. Deceptive.

I've always been prone to deception. It's kept me alive. Yet somehow being *myself* for the first time in an unknown territory is even more terrifying than pretending to be Rani.

"You don't have to apologize," I say, my voice thick with all that's unsaid. "I should have told you about what I saw sooner. I just didn't want to hurt you further."

Saeed's eyes darken. "Ria," he says softly. "It's not you hurting me. My mother's decisions are her own—I would never blame you for her choices. I hope we can be honest with each other."

We've slowed in our dance, and I take the opportunity to lean my head against his chest. Saeed's easy admissions make me want to be honest with him. But it's always been harder on my end.

"Do you think we'll find her?" I wonder aloud. "Your mother— she could be anywhere." I look up at him, and it looks like his hazel eyes are piercing into my soul. I only met him moons ago but I swear it's felt like a lifetime, everything we've been through together.

"Do you still think I'm a stuck-up tutor?" he asks.

"No. What does that have to do with anything?"

"It shows that attitudes can change," he explains. "And when we hope, we prosper." He waggles his brows. "I studied philosophy, too."

"What *don't* you know?" I grin up at him.

"The distance of our continent from other land masses," he says, perfectly scientific.

I laugh. "You taught me a lot as a tutor—I guess I can forgive you for that oversight."

Gently, he reaches forward and brushes my cheek with his thumb. "You were a good student."

My stomach swirls, a storm of confusion and desire. I want him to lean in—I want him to step away. Instead, I press a hand to his chest. "The other night when I was sitting by the Snake River . . . why were you watching me from the balcony?"

"Balcony?" Saeed says. "I was never on any balcony."

"Then who—"

A burst of applause snakes through the room. I nearly jump, mind whirring, as I turn to find Zoya about to light the diya. As she lights the lamp, her chunni flutters through the air like a puff of cold winter wind, her eyes finding mine.

Zoya and King Rohit have kept to themselves since the incident on the boat—I'm pretty sure they're both scarred after seeing a twenty-foot-long snake. She cocks her head toward the corridor next to the ballroom, as if asking, *Meet me there?* I frown. It must be important for her to leave her guests like this.

I nod, reluctantly say goodbye to Saeed, and exit the ballroom. In the corridor, I pass a server who offers me a delicate dessert, and I can't help but grab one. Flavors erupt in my mouth—toasted coconut and pistachio. Small bites of candied fennel seeds fill my mouth, as refreshing as the Amratstanian air.

Mid-bite, the air chills, and something falls from the ceiling—
snow?

"Do not be alarmed," Zoya says as she approaches me. I take
her in: her hair falls down to her waist like a waterfall, sleekly
parted down the middle; her bangles look as cold as ice; and her
lehenga is crisscrossed with silver jewels, matching her short blouse
that leaves her midriff bare. "The palace was enchanted by both
a currentspinner and a tidesweeper. The tidesweeper drew rain
down from the sky and the currentspinner sent a blast of chilly air,
making the rain turn into snow."

I stare up at the ceiling. It looks like wispy, magical clouds have
formed in the air.

A stunning sight indeed.

I'm startled by the sound of Shima in my mind. She slithers
toward me from my right, letting her tongue flicker out to taste
the snow. *Sweet, isn't it?*

"I thought you preferred rats," I tell her. "And what're you doing
out of the chamber?" Luckily, the corridor we stand in is empty.

There aren't many rats to be found here, Shima admits, ignoring me.

Zoya says, "Princess Ria, I wanted to speak with you about
something. I saw you outside the day you were sitting by the Snake
River. I wanted to know what you were doing out there all alone
at night."

Zoya was the one watching me? She never attempted to speak
with me about this on the boat ride over that very same river

yesterday. Then again, maybe she didn't know how to bring it up. "I didn't realize that was you on the balcony."

Zoya only bends a brow, confused. "No, I wasn't on any balcony. I just meant—seeing you there got me thinking a lot. Rani and I used to play on its banks all the time, right where you were standing—I remember following the river up to the Ivory Tree my mother loved so much. It was a fun place for kids, before her passing." She presses her hand to the wall, her eyes filling with tears, before she takes a deep breath and continues, "My mother would read me stories about the Earth Master's talisman there, in the woods by the Ivory Tree. . . . Ria, I think there might be something important about the Earth Master's talisman that we've been missing."

"Like what?" I say, heart beating. "Does it have to do with this Ivory Tree?"

Zoya looks contemplative. "The tree . . . I'd nearly forgotten about it. I couldn't bear to return after my mother passed. She never wanted to leave that place, especially toward the end. Even Physician Veer had to go out there to take care of her."

"Did someone call for me?"

I nearly jump, startled for the second time in one night. "Oh. Veer, we were just—"

"Talking about how you took care of Mother," Zoya says, eyes far away. I can tell her mind is working fast, though I don't know why.

Veer approaches us. How did he know we were here? He has a

habit of turning up just when he's needed.

"She truly was a wonder. Always telling the most amazing stories—especially about the Earth Master's talisman. If only it had never gone missing." The physician bows his head out of respect.

Zoya's eyes light up. "Mother passed not long after your family's last visit. Afterward I erased that Ivory Tree for so long from my memory. Erased anything to do with my mother or with the Earth Master's talisman."

Veer plants a gloved hand on Zoya's shoulder. "It is normal to forget such things after traumatic events. I taught you that, didn't I?"

"You also taught me the talisman might still be out there. And I'm thinking you might be right, Physician Veer."

"What're you saying?" My gaze volleys between the two of them.

I can tell they're both thinking the same thing, because Zoya says, "Veer, can you escort us to the woods? We won't be long. I need to return to the party soon—but this can't wait."

The physician nods. Before I can utter a question, Zoya grabs a cloak off a nearby rack and tosses it my way.

The woods are dark at this time of night, even with the burning candlelit lantern. Shadowy branches rise like nightmarish monsters, and the knee-high snow isn't helping our trek through the darkness.

"How—much—farther?" I ask, breath puffing in the frigid air.

I can't believe it, but I'm starting to miss Abai's relentless heat. Not to mention its lack of mountains.

We sssnakes aren't equipped for such weather, Shima agrees, shivering as she slithers at my side. She flashes wildly—a bright yellow for curiosity, a deep maroon, a bright green—

"It should be close," Veer says, startling me with his oddly low-pitched voice. A fur-trimmed cloak covers his face, protecting him from the cold.

Zoya holds the lantern higher. "Wait. Do you see that?"

I squint into the darkness. All I can see are the trees, the reddish light of the half moon, and . . .

Three shadowy figures approaching us.

"Zoya . . . ," I begin. My thief instincts kick in, telling me to flee, but back in Abai, there would be no snow, no heavy cloak to weigh me down. I'd be light on my feet, evading my captor.

"Stay back!" Zoya cries. She shoves the lantern forward, illuminating the shadows' faces.

"Raja's beard," I curse. "Irfan, you scared us!"

As he steps into the light, Irfan raises two hands in surrender. Neeta and Neesa exchange shy glances with one another. "Apologies," one of the twins says. "We didn't mean to frighten you. Or your companion." She gestures at the hooded physician, blending in with the night.

"We left the palace this morning in search of any other bandits like the man from the boat," Irfan explains. "It's alarming that they were able to come so close as to surprise us on the Snake River. We thought there might be more."

"And you thought the woods would be a good shortcut?" I retort.

"Ria, we think we found the culprit."

Something about his tone sends a shiver down my spine. "What are you talking about?"

Irfan's silver eyes pin against mine. "I mean, we think we know who that man was. The names he mentioned, Akshya and Hitesh—they were close friends of my parents. The ones who betrayed them. He's—"

Before Irfan can finish, Veer interrupts, pointing into the distance with a sharp shout. "Princess, look!"

Zoya gasps, following his lead. "Blazing mountains!"

I bring my gaze to where she's looking. Highlighted by the lantern is a tree quadruple the size of any other out in these woods—one we *definitely* didn't see during our hunt. Its bark is white as the snow beneath it but peeling in some areas, and its sturdy branches quiver in the Amratstanian wind.

"There it is," Zoya whispers, feet drawing near as if hypnotized.

With tentative footsteps, Veer leads us toward the tree. Zoya circles the tree once and then, almost frenzied, drops and begins digging away at the roots. I hold my breath, afraid to interrupt this moment in the slightest: something about it feels like puzzle pieces clicking together. Finally, Zoya lifts something up to the moonlight, covered in snow but miraculously unharmed.

A map.

She turns to Veer, tears shining in her eyes. "You were right."

"The Earth Master's talisman," confirms Veer. My heart stops as I spot an emblem imprinted on the map in the shape of a mountain. His eyes widen at the sight of Zoya's hands, red and raw from digging in the snow. "Here, Princess—give me the map, and I'll give you my gloves. You shouldn't hurt your hands further."

As the map touches Veer's gloved hands, something within me shifts. Shima's voice enters my head in warning. *Ria . . . I smell something odd on this man.*

Blood.

I turn to Shima in alarm before hearing Veer's odd chuckle. Irfan stiffens from behind me, squinting deeply at the physician he hasn't met. I hear him nock his arrow just as Veer releases his hood, turning back his head until he's gazing at me with darkened eyes.

"A servant to offer their Master's blood. A follower to find the missing Key. A Key to bring back the Eternal Night."

I've heard that before—on the banks of the Snake River. Zoya gazes at Veer in horror as he drops his gloves from his fingers. In a flash, he stands and practically flies across the snow, grabbing me by the clasp of my cloak with too-tight fingers.

"Let go of me!" I cry, my eyes flying up to Veer's as I try to pull away. A gust of wind blows by us all just as Irfan fires, and the arrow zooms past and lands in the tree bark, trembling.

I gasp as I take in Veer's face, the shadows lining his eyes, his dishevelled hair. Those gloved hands, now bare . . .

To cover up his reddened nails. To cover up the sign of the snake imprinted on his hands. I shudder as I think of his nails digging into Aditi back on the boat, covered in blood.

"You're the Black Viper," I whisper so only he can hear me. He nods, his yellowing teeth bared in an unhinged smile.

"Of course. I'm surprised you didn't realize earlier . . . when I was watching you from the balcony."

"That was you," I breathe. "You were talking to Amara about me—about needing a girl."

"Don't be so vain, Ria," the Black Viper grits out. "I needed *Zoya* to hand me the map. And now I've done it."

"Unhand Princess Ria at once, Veer!" Zoya cries, anger replacing the horror in her face.

At Veer's name, Irfan slings another arrow into his bow, rage clouding his features, but Veer draws me even closer to him and Irfan hesitates. I raise a hand. "Wait!"

But Irfan's eyes look wild. "*This* is the man I was talking about. I learned of him from Neeta and Neesa. We uncovered the truth—he's one of *them*. From the group of bandits!"

I stare at Irfan with wide eyes. He lowers a brow as I nod imperceptibly, hoping he'll catch on. *Let your captor think he's in control, then strike.* A tactic I learned from Amir and used often if merchants ever caught us thieving.

Looks like his teachings are useful here, too.

Veer laughs, guttural and mocking, his lips spreading into a thin smile. "It is as I told you on the boat. You are the answer to everything, Ria. In time, you will come around. And now that I have the missing talisman . . ." His voice grows deeper, and I finally recognize it as the one I heard on the boat.

"No! Give that back!" Zoya yells, reaching for the map, and Neeta and Neesa spring forward to help. But Veer yanks me away from the twin Sentinels' grasp, holding on to me bruisingly tight.

"Release her, *now*!" Irfan demands, holding his bow at the ready even as his voice trembles with fury. Neeta and Neesa mirror him, standing firm across from us.

"She must not be harmed!" Veer says. The arm of his cloak slips as I try to jerk myself out of his grasp, and I flinch at the sight of his chipped nails.

"A nasty habit," Veer says with a slow smile. "The gloves were necessary, in case anyone saw *this*." The snake mark on his hand flares with bright-golden light.

"My Master is calling. And we always answer."

Not a second later, Veer tightens his grip on my arm and the woods melt away.

The unending darkness pricks me, like a tingle at the back of my neck whenever I was close to getting caught during a theft. I felt the same thing when I first met Rani—when I was caught by her in her own closet. Like someone is watching. Or waiting.

I lift myself up onto my elbows, feeling the ground spin beneath me. Snow. And the scent of blood.

"What's going on?" I mutter. I crack open my eyes fully. To the left of me roars the Snake River, a little ways away from the Winter Palace, and to the right—

A chill spreads through me as my eyes lock on a cloaked figure. Shima, who traveled—transported?—with me hisses in reproach, though she looks fatigued, as if the trip cost her some of her energy.

My tongue freezes in place. As the figure inches closer, and red hair spills free of their cloak, my nightmares come to life.

"You're here."

"Indeed I am." Amara's shoulders shake as she laughs. I make out more cloaked figures behind her, including Veer. "And so is the rest of the Serpent's Tongue, thanks to their connection to our Master."

The *rest* of the Serpent's Tongue. Veer isn't alone; Rani was right. This fanatical group is active once more, but I didn't want to believe it.

I don't have long to contemplate this, because when Amara bends over me, I'm shocked to find a woman I hardly recognize. Almost all of her face is jarringly scaled over, both nostrils turned to slits. Her hair looks brittle and worn, and when she speaks, her voice is as enticing and haunting as a snake's rattle. Her mouth opens in a smile, revealing startling white teeth, two protruding out like fangs.

I turn away, unable to bear looking into her face, and find the cloaked figures stepping forward, each holding glowing objects in their palms.

"Are those . . . ?" I whisper.

"The talismans?" Amara says, moving back while sneering at Shima. "Indeed they are. For so long, I did not know many of their locations. Or even what they were. But I learned in time, with my Master's help. And you, dear Ria, couldn't even begin to stop us. Do you even know why we've been seeking the talismans?"

She sees me startle at the pronoun and smiles, revealing again her sharp teeth. "Yes, *we*. Surely by now you know my Master. How his mind is so deeply connected to yours. . . ."

I do. I've felt his call deep in my bones, haunting and familiar at once. But I won't admit it aloud.

Amara's laugh is like the growl of a tiger. "*Ria*. Your power is incredible. Even stronger than Rani's." In the darkness, I see her eyes flash. "It was so kind of you to retrieve the Tide Master's sword from the sea sapni for us. And of course, we were still missing the Earth Master's talisman. Luckily, Veer has been a great help. His parents were devoted acolytes of the Snake Master. They were in league with many others in the Serpent's Tongue. They even tried recruiting their friends . . . and punished those who didn't join them."

Punished. My stomach drops, roiling with anger and nausea all at once at the reminder of the raid on Irfan's home.

"The whole time, you knew where the Earth Master's talisman was?"

Veer's voice is oily. "I'd had a hunch. But I needed Princess Zoya's help, for this talisman may only be passed to a mortal for their possession if it is *given*, not taken, from a descendant of the Earth Master. I reminded Zoya for years that her trauma may have blinded her to her own memories. Without realizing the importance of the talisman at the mere age of eight, she, with your sister as the unwitting accomplice, hid the talisman in the woods. It seems both had completely forgotten about the ordeal. Children's memories do puzzle me."

I stumble back. So I was right. I knew my father wasn't a thief. He never took the talisman . . . because Zoya and Rani did. A small prank that spiraled out of control.

"Wait," I begin. "You said all you had left was the Earth Master's talisman? But what about—"

"The Fire Master's talisman?" Amara finishes for me. "Don't worry, dear Ria, we've thought of everything. Quite a few members of the Serpent's Tongue tried to get past the sandtiger and . . ." She grimaces. "*Failed.* It is with great sorrow that their bodies will forever remain at the gates of the Glass Temple, but their hearts were committed to the mission."

"To *steal* the compass?" I spit. I know enough about the talisman from Rani's trip to the temple. Getting past the tiger should have been impossible.

"Indeed," Amara says. "But the sandtiger was easy to distract when faced with the might of my Master's companions. You know these jungles—full of snakes, willing to do our bidding."

A bloody grin creeps over her face before she continues, "Eventually, we were able to get one member past the sandtiger in all the chaos and retrieve the compass. He barely made it back alive."

My blazing thoughts are put to rest when Amara produces

something red and glowing from within her cloak. I swear I hear the beat of an aching heart.

The Bloodstone.

I rush forward, ready to grab it in a blur of rage.

"Stop!" I cry. But something snatches my chin, forcing me still. Amara's hand, nails digging into my cheeks. I'm thrown back to being in the Abai palace, the whip-sting of Amara's hand striking me across the face.

"With each of the talismans together," Amara says, her breath feathering my cheeks, "and the Bloodstone I already hold, I will finally have the power I seek. The ultimate reward for my patience.

"All I must do now is put the talismans together and unlock the lifeblood of Amran to retrieve the power I was promised. I can finally make my wish."

"And then?" I say, voice shaking. "You'll turn into the Soul Master and destroy Kaama. You'll become every bit as bad as the people who hurt you. Who hurt *him*."

I know I've hit a raw point. Amara snarls, "Once I retrieve my husband's ashes and reap his soul, no other Kaamans matter."

She grabs me by the hair and shoves my face toward the Snake River. In its waters, I see my eyes turn green, just as they had the night I came here. The night Veer was watching me.

"Do you see the power I hold? The power we *both* hold?"

I blink my green eyes, watching my face shift into Raya's. But Amara's not talking about my power, or Raya's. In the next moment, Amara's face changes in the water, rippling until her eyes burn red and blood drips from her lips. Just like in my dreams.

"*Ria, my descendant, my daughter,*" comes a voice from within her, but it's not her own. I can't even form words as I realize this is no dream. He's here.

"*It's time we officially met.*"

22

Rani

I blink back my disbelief as a kind voice says, "You may all rise. You've found us."

"Queen Saira," I breathe.

"Queen Sunita," Amir says.

"Queen Sampada," Dhruv finishes.

The queens' feet touch the ground with a gentle thud.

Magic such as this is wondrous and strange, tingling at the snake magic in my bones. Queen Meeta and Dhruv press their hands to their hearts in a sacred greeting, each gaping in awe at the presence of their ancient ancestors before them, the founders of their kingdom. While the queens' faces are identical, a deep brown with the same crooked, almost sneaky, smile, they wear different strands of flowers in their braided hair, matching the colors of their respective palaces. Night-blue lilies for Sampada, marigolds for Sunita, and yellow-gold roses for Saira. Their dress is that of ancient Retanians, something I've only seen in paintings and textbooks. They sport simple brocade skirts embellished with silver thread, and a thick trim border on the bottom portrays a stitched story: saints speaking to the Masters and poring over books, magic-wielders of the Old Age controlling flame and tide, and villagers on horseback wearing Academy cloaks. Their heads are fitted with matching gilded crowns, embedded with firestones from the Lalkian Caves.

"You are all the first to discover how to enter the chamber. We are impressed," says the first queen. "I am Rani Sampada."

"The eldest," says the middle queen. "Also the one known for helping build the Academy itself. But knowledge isn't everything. What about creation? What about stories, poetry?" The woman flips her braid behind her with a sigh.

"You must be Queen Saira," I say. "My name is Princess Rani of Abai."

"I am Prince Dhruv of Retan," Dhruv introduces himself as well. "And this is my mother, Queen Meeta. This is such an honor. But . . . *how* is this possible?"

"You're an inquisitive one, Dhruv. Must have some of Queen Sampada's genes."

"He has *all* of our genes," the third one corrects. "I'm Queen Sunita. I helped build the Saffron Palace. We built this chamber as a safeguard, in hopes that anyone who wanted to find our greatest secret would come and reveal us."

"It is a bit drab down here," Queen Saira quips. "We could have picked a spot with better lighting."

"*Lighting* doesn't matter right now." Queen Sampada sighs. "Our ghostly forms cannot last long. This is a magic only made possible by a relic nearly a thousand years old." She points her chin at the sundial clutched in my fingers.

At this, Professor Neel can't seem to contain himself. "My queens, I must ask—the relic you speak of. It has the name *Manav* written on it. In my studies, I've only ever heard this as the name of the Soul Master. Is it—could you tell me—"

"Indeed." Queen Sampada seems to take pity on the professor's fumbling, nodding at him. "The sundial is a relic left behind by the Soul Master himself, before he was Unmade."

"Why was he Unmade?" Amir asks.

"A long story," Queen Sampada says. "But is this why you called us? To learn the secrets of a long-vanished Master?"

Mind whirling with questions, I say resolutely, "No, Queen Sampada. Or, not entirely," I amend. "We're here to ask you about the Bloodstone. We know you studied it, and . . . we want to destroy it. Someone very dangerous is currently in possession of it, and we believe she'll use it to become a new Soul Master."

I expect the queens to find that preposterous. After all, everyone else has. But they only look solemn, any joking forgotten.

"Then I suppose I should further explain that the sundial allows us to appear before you today, even in just this ghostly form. It was not just a relic of the Soul Master. It was made from his very body. A body that he did not possess for long," Queen Sampada says.

The six of us remain starkly silent.

"He lived a short life, the Soul Master, and a few of his bones remain in that sundial with the ability to keep souls within. We passed *our* souls into this relic so that we could awaken, should anyone ever need us in the future. And it seems the time has come."

I gape, mind bursting at the seams.

"Amran came to fear the Soul Master encroached too much on his own powers, those over death and life," Queen Saira says. "And so Amran chose to Unmake him. The Snake Master, who was the Soul Master's only true companion, begged Amran to spare his brother. But Amran would not be denied, and the Soul Master faded from this world."

"What does this all have to do with the Bloodstone?" Amir wonders.

"Everything."

The sisters speak the word in unison, their voices melding into one. For a shocking few seconds, silence. Then the walls of the tunnel begin to shake. But it's different from before. This isn't some supernatural phenomenon; it feels like an earthquake, a tremor passing as fiercely as an autumn wind.

My breaths turn shallow, and I shield myself again. Rocks fall from the ceiling, sliding right through the sisters' forms. They glance upward, unbothered as the tremor finishes. None of us is scathed, but fear plants itself deeply into my bones all the same. Something in my magic spikes, flares, flashing hot like a warning. I feel a deep pull from within me, like a call from magic to magic. I've felt my magic before, but not like this—not like a pull to somewhere else . . . *from* somewhere else? What is happening? Why am I feeling this?

"What was that?" Prince Dhruv asks.

"We should hurry," Queen Meeta says. "Blessed Sisters, my ancestors, would you please continue?"

Queen Saira nods. "The Soul Master's Unmaking set in motion a chain of events that led to the creation of the Bloodstone itself. It is not so easily destroyed. To have even a chance of succeeding, you will need to understand its origins, and possess a weapon powerful enough to counter it."

Amir speaks up. "A weapon?"

"In the Malwan Pass," one of the sisters answers. "As the birthplace of the Fire Master, its volcanic fires are magical. Strong enough to destroy something as dangerous as the Bloodstone."

"Hold on—a *volcano*?" Amir asks breathlessly.

"Multiple volcanoes." I glance at Dhruv. "The Malwan Pass was once used as a trading route between Abai and Retan. But we don't have the Bloodstone—we can't take it to the Pass."

"There is another way to destroy the stone," Queen Sampada reveals. "You see, the Malwan Pass isn't simply a location. It's a trial, a test of the mind. Endure it, and the Pass will present you with the object you seek from its fiery depths. You will receive something strong enough to destroy this Bloodstone. When you get to the path, move forward and go left at the fork. In the cave, one of you must face this trial. Only the person who passes the trial can wield the object the Pass presents to you."

A trial? I shiver. It is up to Ria or me to destroy the Bloodstone. Our magic, combined, took down Amara once. But to face this task on my own—will I be strong enough?

"If I might ask . . ." Amir gulps. "If you knew how to destroy the stone, why didn't you?"

My mind darts back to what I learned about the sisters. They all died mysteriously, all on the same day. . . .

"You did try," I realize. "Didn't you? You attempted to pass the trial and . . ."

Failed. The word won't leave my mouth, as dry as the brittle air outside Jhanswa City.

Queen Sunita nods, answering for all of them. "We were foolish—unprepared and overconfident. Thankfully, we left this charmed relic here as a safeguard to inhabit our ghostly forms should we have failed."

How can we possibly surpass a trial not even the triplet queens could best . . . together?

"We can do it," Amir says boldly. "We must. Which means we need to leave for the Malwan Pass as soon as possible."

Amir turns to leave, waiting for me to join. But I'm glued to the spot. I look at Dhruv and Queen Meeta, both eyeing me. Do they believe I can succeed? Or is this all folly?

"Thank you, Your Majesties," I tell them. "I promise you I won't fail."

And I promise it to myself, too.

"Wait, Princess Rani," Queen Sunita says, adjusting the bindi at her forehead, "you are a descendant of the Snake Master. You carry his blood in your veins."

"I don't carry his deception," I say, perhaps a little too firmly.

"We never assumed so." Queen Sampada tilts her head. "But as we said earlier, to destroy the Bloodstone, you must also understand its origins. Your ancestor was not always a deceiver. Would you like to know the true story?"

My mouth goes dry. "You can tell me about the Snake Master?"

Queen Sampada's head tilts. "There is much more to the story. When we were younglings, barely your age, we spoke to the Memory Master often. It was she who taught us of the Snake Master's deception, during the Great Masters' Battle. She who entrusted us to find the stone and destroy it."

I gasp. "You've spoken *to the Memory Master* about the stone?"

Queen Sunita nods. "The Memory Master saw our futures within us during a pilgrimage she took across Retan. We weren't yet queens when she told us what she foresaw—us finding the stone and destroying it. Preventing a future where the stone was manipulated."

"A future with Amara," I say under my breath. "But the Memory Master's prediction didn't come about—the stone wasn't destroyed."

"Not all futures do." Queen Saira gazes at me. "For one decision, one path, can change the course of destiny."

I know that much is true—I was able to change the fortune

the Memory Master gave my parents, the one about me and Ria becoming foes. My sister and I changed that fortune—together.

"But the Memory Master offered us a memory only we could share," adds Queen Sampada.

"Yes," I say before she can even finish. "Yes. I want to know more. Could you tell me?"

"I will do much better than that," Queen Sampada says. "I will show you. All of you." The touch of Queen Sampada's fingers feels cold against my forehead. A tunnel opens up in my mind, transporting me deep into darkness.

When it clears, I am standing in a strange landscape—barren fields of burnt grass, a gray sky like the calm before a storm. Before me sits a man bent on his knees, hands in supplication. The veins in his hands look shot with black.

"H-hello?" I ask. But someone passes right through my body, walking toward the man. Neither of them seems to hear me. Somehow, the queens have sent me back into a dream—a memory, though not of mine.

With bated breath, I step toward the man on the ground, and when he looks up I swear he's staring at me.

With eyes like blood, spilling slow, laborious tears.

He moves his gaze away from me. "Raya, we must go again. The Snake Pit is not complete."

I spin to see a girl. Young, not yet my age. Her green eyes are dim and tired, and something about her seems drained.

"Father—" starts the girl, barely able to raise her frail-looking arms. But she doesn't finish her sentence, instead nodding at the man. I nearly trip backward when I finally realize who she's looking at.

"The Snake Master?" I whisper to myself. Is this truly him? The man who is my ancestor, the Great Deceiver whose serpent magic sings through my veins?

A flicker of a memory returns to me—the Fire Master, telling me a hidden truth in the Glass Temple. The Snake Master was no deceiver at first. What changed him?

The Snake Master stands, cloak swishing in the wind, and slinks toward the hole in the earth—what I realize is the beginnings of the Snake Pit.

The girl follows, and in a practiced, almost ritualistic manner, she presses her hand to her father's chest. She uses a knife to cut her skin, and I startle when I see the gilded color of her blood. This girl isn't just the Snake Master's daughter—she is his First Descendant. But she is not the only one.

There is another girl, identical to this Raya, who stands at the edge of the Pit as well. She looks healthier than her twin, but there is something frustrated and desperate in her gaze. As I watch, she follows Raya's lead, pouring blood into the Pit—except when her blood hits the soil, it merely fizzles away, repelled.

Again and again, they repeat this step. The Snake Pit glows from the power of their blood, as magic unfurls and coils like the very snakes that begin to sink into the Pit. I watch as the Snake Pit takes on a life of its own, rippling and shifting, wielding the very power drawn out from Raya's veins, manipulated into being by the Snake Master himself.

Time blurs. Days, or perhaps weeks, later, Raya and the girl I learn is named Ruhanya lie on the earth, starved. They—as with all First Descendants—shouldn't need anything but water to survive, but they look . . . emptied.

The Snake Master gazes into the Pit and then moves, using nothing but a hand to signal the continuation of the ritual.

"But, Father—" Raya begins.

"This is what I want," the Snake Master interjects. "A home of earth, a place of peace." An almost feral look enters his eyes. Hunger—I've seen it before, in Father's eyes, when he was manipulated by Amara. But this is different. This isn't a desire for power . . . it's a deep, personal ache. In his eyes, a memory takes flight. I see his home being burned. I see the other Masters and their descendants taunting him. In a blink, the memory vanishes, and his eyes become hardened.

"The closer we dig to the core of the earth, the more my power grows. And while I don't know the reason, I do know that I feel a pull toward it. Your magic, too, will refill. We must keep going."

The Snake Master smoothly slides over the edge of the Pit and, against gravity, enters the Snake Pit at an angle, using nothing but his snake's tail to guide him down. I peer, somewhat horrified, over the edge, squinting to look inside. I let out a piercing scream when I realize I've gone a step too far, and plummet over the edge.

I'm falling, falling, falling.

My heartbeat roars in my ears. A hundred questions run through my mind.

And I land in a new landscape.

I'm sprawled out in a dark hole. A small fire lights the stone walls, glimmering mica schist, a sea of black. Snakes writhe along the walls like worms, blood smudged along their scales like crimson ink. I stare up at the hole above me, a cutout of a beautiful, cloudless night sky. This must be a different day.

Next to me, a voice catches my attention.

"She's freezing, Father," says Ruhanya, her cheeks full compared to the girl clutched in her arms. They wear matching purple saris, but the second girl looks dazed, pale and shivering. *Raya*.

"The fire was supposed to help. It *will* help." Shivering, the Snake Master pulls off his own cloak and offers it to his daughter, but her lips are already blue.

"We've gone too far. We need to undo this," Ruhanya says. The gems embedded in the stone walls around us glimmer in agreement. I can practically taste the snake magic, coppery and tinged with blood, that fills every inch of the Snake Pit.

"This latest step cannot be undone." The Snake Master rises, more determined now. "The Pit now has no physical borders. It exists in a space and time of its own. We will never be harmed."

"Unless we harm ourselves," Ruhanya spits, rising. "Look at her. She's *dying*, Father!"

"She is merely tired. Just as I said, we—"

"Your desires will end up with *both* your daughters dead. Your descendants from Amran will only remember you as a killer!"

"Stop," Raya coughs out, using all her strength to rise. Ruhanya gasps, helping her sister to her feet. Her whole body looks cold as ice. "Let us finish this."

"Raya—" starts her sister. I feel a sharp ache inside me, like Raya is my own twin.

"Sister, I'll only get better once we've completed this," Raya reasons, but there's something heavy in her voice, like heartache. She offers a shaking hand to her father.

"Please," she says. It takes moments for him to follow through. He retrieves his knife and cuts her palm, but this time the blood moves sluggishly, like time has slowed. With each drop that hits the ground, the coppery smell in the air burns, swelters, and grows. The magic within Raya is enough to call a thousand snakes.

Like Ria's, I realize.

Almost instantly, Raya cries out. Her sister and father rush forward as she crumples to the ground and lies flat on her back, gasping for air.

Ruhanya falls to her knees beside Raya and cups her sister's face, but Raya's mouth is frozen in a howling scream, as though that final cut had ripped something from her. From her toes up, her body begins to turn gray and harden, ensconced in stone, until she is nothing but a statue.

Magic flees her body in a curl of smoke. Gold particles fill the air like a dusting of stars. I can sense this magic in my bones.

Soul magic. It feels like the precipice of death, of dark matter and nightmares that cling like a second skin. But why would that kind of magic exist in Raya?

A roar rips out of the Snake Master as he bends down, examining her hands, her body, and the odd, glowing red center of her stone chest, beating like a heart.

"Raya," the Snake Master urges, grasping her almost menacingly, as if this is a game. But Raya doesn't stir.

"She sacrificed herself, Father," Ruhanya cries into her hands. "She's *gone*. Gone because of you."

"No. Because of *them*." The Snake Master shivers fiercely. I, too, shiver as I step closer to the Snake Master, taking in the weathered lines creeping on to his face, the crow's feet by his eyes. He's tired, wanting, craving.

He takes the stone from Raya's chest, which glows with red light. I gasp, for I would recognize that stone anywhere.

The Bloodstone.

But the story went that it came from Amran. Unless . . .

The Bloodstone was a magical vestige of Raya. Of her *heart*, turned into a gem as bright and magical as the ones in this very Pit. The Snake Pit always held more than snakes. It also houses magical gems that carry the souls of those who've died in the Pit. Tutor taught me that.

Which means that Raya's death, with the intertwined snake and soul magic inside her, is the reason why all these soul gems exist.

The dirt at the bottom of the Pit writhes, and hundreds of bloody snakes overtake Raya's form, slipping over her and dragging her into the earth itself. Ruhanya cries and clings to Raya's hand, ordering the snakes away, but it's not enough.

Raya is the Pit's first victim.

The Snake Master screams, the sound etched with pain, sorrow, and revenge as he clings to what was once Raya's heart. The noise pierces me, moves me to tears. *This* is the man everyone fears. The man, the monster, the Master pushed to the brink.

He holds out the stone as it projects light, making the snakes cower away. But there's nothing left of Raya. He sweeps the light across the Pit, forcing the snakes to bend to his will. Raya's heart still holds some of her magic. *Persuasion*, that of a snakespeaker. And the untold power of the Soul Master.

Overcome, the Snake Master plunges the stone toward his chest, and it fractures into a hundred pieces and hovers over his skin, slowly being absorbed piece by piece, until the stone is a part of him. His chest explodes with red light. I cover my eyes with my hands until the light dissipates . . . until I am no more.

Until I am no longer Princess Rani.

I grin, for I am the Snake Master.

When I look down, I am his skin and bones. I am renewed. I am . . . *different*. I hear something beating in my chest. *Boom-boom. Boom-boom.* It rattles and soothes me at the same time. I feel it in the tips of my fingers. Blood roars in my ears.

How odd it is to have a heart. *Her* heart.

I promise to avenge her, even as Ruhanya promises to abandon me.

I travel to the Snake River and stop when I see a figure across the waters. My sister, the Memory Master. I call her to me, and the waves respond, dragging her across the water like she is weightless. Preethi joins me, eyes darkened.

I waste no time with trivialities. "You said she was destined for great things." My voice chokes before I can say her name.

"Greatness, for many, comes with death." My sister's face is solemn but pained.

"So you knew. You *saw* how she would die, and yet you left my daughter with nothing but a useless parting gift."

"A sari is more than a gift; it is a memory. Every piece of fabric is a piece of us. And while I saw your daughter's destiny, I knew not her fate. That lies with you."

"I didn't cause her death," I say, voice shaking with fury even as the words feel untrue. "*They* did. You know, don't you? Why the other Masters despise me? It's because I was given two children instead of one. It's because Amran gave me more than them."

"No, brother. They hate you because of your past." The tattoo on her wrist—a bright purple eye—flares with light. The Memory Master's face, usually glowing, dims like a harbinger of darkness. "You know of the Eternal Night, don't you?"

I nod. Many feeble humans believe it. And others, too, those who are . . . *believers* in me, for whatever reason.

"Your followers believe they are one with you, born in a world that you bred."

"I bred?" I ask, not quite understanding. "I was the last Master

Amran created. How could I have bred this world?"

Preethi dodges my question. "They burn their hands with the symbol of a snake. A symbol of devotion."

"Devotion I never asked for," I say, although I am intrigued.

My sister's voice reveals the truth. Every word makes me sink deeper and deeper into the ground, until it feels like the river is swallowing me whole.

The world was not brought to life by Amran, but by his first and only companion—a snake. But as the snake made the world, its heart, too, poisoned it, bringing about a Blood Moon and a night that seemed to never end. . . .

"I was the snake? The cause of the Eternal Night?" I breathe when she is finished. The Eternal Night—the night when the Blood Moon was fully present, and poison took root in the world. The night when Amran created the four elemental Masters to rid the world of the poison.

My poison.

My chest, always empty, always heartless . . . because of *this*?

Preethi nods somberly. "Yes, brother. You were Amran's companion at the dawn of time. But that isn't all. Our other brothers and sisters were created—to clean up the mess you left behind, as they put it. I was made fifth, to erase the memory of the next Master . . . you."

"Amran lied." My gaze hardens. "He never told me I was made at the beginning of time, his companion, his—"

"He wanted to make you a Master, Sahil. My initial purpose

was to erase your memories of these sins. To help you start life anew, even as your heart remained the core of this world. Amran hoped I wouldn't have to use my power to alter any more memories, so I didn't. He hoped our brethren would accept you."

"Accept," I laugh without mirth. Only one Master has ever truly accepted me, outside of Preethi. My brother Manav, the Soul Master, Unmade because others viewed him as much too powerful. For every time he brought life, death soon followed, as the energy of one must always be transferred to another.

"There is one more thing. A prophecy. For you."

I dig my brows lower, waiting. I want her to press on, but she looks as if she isn't sure if she should tell me the truth.

"Please," I say, tears rising to my eyes. "Raya is dead. Tell me, what future could I possibly have?"

Finally, Preethi concedes. "The prophecy spoke of those who call themselves the Serpent's Tongue. In the far future, their descendants' desires to help you will remain. But your wishes cannot be accomplished—not without the Key."

"Key?" I wonder.

"A girl. She will be of your blood, a snakespeaker whose power will be the strongest you've seen. In the future, you and the Serpent's Tongue will need her to pursue your wish . . . of returning the world to its origins. It will be impossible without her power." She pauses. "Brother, I tell you this to prepare you, to warn you against these coming evils. To give you a reason to take a different path."

Her hand lands on my chest, bruised by the stone. "I feel Amran's lifeblood within this Bloodstone, and the remnants of the Soul Master. And something else . . . Raya. Her spirit. Her *heart*."

"It was hers. But it became something else." I draw it out of my chest and stare down at the thing Raya once called a heart. The Bloodstone beats in my palm, calling to me, begging me to make a wish. . . .

A wish I shall get.

A memory mists over me. Raya, making wishes on stars with Manav. But stars are just souls of the sky. And it is time for me to harness this stone's soul magic, with its ability to grant wishes, for myself.

"Sahil, promise me you will remember my warning. The destruction it could cause. I know who you are. The others will come to see you, too—as I do."

"I promise," I tell Preethi, leaving the river.

I've never kept a promise in my life.

I hold out the Bloodstone. In time, I will learn a charm to protect the stone, ensuring only someone of my blood can find it. No one shall intercept my path or that of my descendants. Never again.

A wave of light projects from its depths. Its power sings in my veins. It calls to me, telling me . . .

The Masters blame you for the poisoned world. They think you a Great Deceiver.

Then deceive I shall.

They are the ones who burned my home, who tore me down. *They* are the ones who pushed Raya to the brink. They are responsible for her death. If I can't turn them to stone as well, then I'll find another way to hurt them.

Months pass as I learn to harness the stone's power. Once I have protected the stone for my lineage, I bend it like clay, and will each Master to suffer as I battle them at the Snake River. Their attacks pebble and harden my skin, and then—they are gone.

And I am a shell.

I shiver as I slip back into my first form—until I am scales and slippery skin, a shining weapon of darkness.

Until all I know are the walls of the Snake Pit, the hiss of the snakes, and the beat of Raya's dead heart.

23

Ria

The Serpent's Tongue chants my name as I'm swallowed by ever-consuming thoughts of the Snake Master.

"Ria, the Key. Ria, the Key."

My magic ignites, and my eyes close instinctively. The world falls away as stinging light burns my eyes. My gaze moves up, up, up . . . to meet his.

Red eyes. Scaly skin.

"Ria . . ." he calls. I stalk forward to meet him.

Like a sudden wind, all breath leaves my lungs. What's worse is the feeling inside me, like light and dark battling for air. For it is only the two of us now.

I'm standing in a dark room, no longer next to the Snake River. All I can make out is his hooded face, the black cloak swirling around his body, a hundred vipers thrashing around him on the floor.

"Welcome, Ria."

I falter back. "Where—"

"*The Snake Pit was beginning to suffocate me. Hundreds of years will do that to a weakened Master. I thought a change of location was in order.*"

I feel faint. I remember the first time I heard his voice, rising like steam from the Snake Pit. He's no longer in the Pit—he must have escaped . . . but the only person to have escaped the Pit is—

Amara.

"*I found a human vessel that could hold me. I'm too weak to have a body of my own . . . for now,*" the Snake Master says. "*This is a mindscape, like the one you built with Rani. Here, away from reality, I am free to have my own form. I thought it was time we met, face-to-face. It is always a delight to see my kin.*"

I step back, almost tripping over the hem of my cloak. He's right—this isn't one of my dreams anymore. Were they ever really dreams in the first place? Or just a different plane of reality?

Beneath his hood, his lips spread into a sinister smile. In the candlelight hovering over us, I notice something strange: a silvery thread that connects me to *him*. It shivers and waves, but when I try to touch it, it snaps into place like a strong cord.

"If I'm your kin, is that why I'm a . . . Key?" I ask aloud for the first time. I think of the chant Veer—the Black Viper—recited. "But for what? Why *me*? Why not Rani?"

"*Dear Ria,*" the Snake Master tuts, "*your parents knew the power you could possess. They tossed you into the streets because of it.*"

"They didn't toss me," I retort, but something cold licks my spine. They *did* give me up because of my potential power. A power I've learned is growing, changing—evolving. A power I've hungered for, a power that has clamored within me like a fire barely kept at bay.

"That doesn't answer my question."

The Snake Master frowns. The snakes bare their fangs, tongues slipping in and out of their mouths as they leap at me. In fear, I hold a hand out and swat them away, imagining them leaving my sight. With a swipe of my hand my magic casts them aside. They all spring to the left and buckle to the ground like they've hit an invisible wall.

I stare at my hands, watching them shake as the snakes cower and slip away, returning beneath the Snake Master's cloak.

"Your power is immense. Almost as immense as mine. Though it is . . . unwieldy."

Unwieldy. A memory surfaces: the night I set all those snakes loose on the palace guests. Then later, the sea sapni ripped free of my control no matter how hard I clutched it.

My power defies expectation.

"Your power is a gift. But it also needs to be controlled. Wielded." My mother, Queen Maneet's words.

The Snake Master holds out a hand that's oddly pale. *"I can teach you to control your power. Let me help you, Raya."*

"Raya?" I echo. A shudder passes through me. "That's not my name."

"Correct. But when you gazed into the Snake River, you saw

Raya's eyes. You saw her memories. Do you know why? Because I wanted you to see them."

He stops to fix me with an intense gaze, darkening as his story continues. *"The other Masters, as you've seen, have always cast a shadow over me. I am not like them. In many ways. Amran gave me two First Descendants—twins—but there was always one who was stronger. One who possessed untold power. There have been no twins born in my line since, not for a thousand years . . . until eighteen years ago. Even from my place in the Pit, I felt my connection to you. You are special, like Raya was."*

I shake my head. "I don't understand. So what if I'm powerful?"

"Back on the boat," he says, *"I saw the way you maimed the Black Viper. You could have stopped, but you didn't. Raya was like that. She was not afraid of her emotions nor her power. She let her anger fuel her."*

I recall how I felt when I pressed my hand against Veer's snake mark. Like I was starving, and this power was feeding me.

The Snake Master bends his hooded head to the thread binding us together. *"You can see the thread connecting us. That is how I knew, even after what happened to Raya, she was never truly gone, that she would one day return . . . for a piece of her was reborn into you."*

My breath catches in my throat as his mouth sets in a grim line. The cord between us offers a phantom memory, a moment of immeasurable pain: the Snake Master watching helplessly as his brother Manav, the Soul Master, was Unmade and his fragments scattered across the earth. One piece lodging into Raya, surfacing only as she sacrificed herself to the Snake Pit. Her heart turning to stone . . .

The Bloodstone, I realize with a gasp, as her screams pierce my ears.

I've heard them before. My first night at the Winter Palace, when Veer woke me from my nightmare. But I didn't realize I'd been hearing *her*.

The final memory offers me a shimmering image of the Creator, speaking the Snake Master's true name. My ancestor. The Great Deceiver.

Once simply known as Sahil.

The Snake Master cants his head sideways. *"Don't you feel something different inside you, Ria? Ever since I left the Pit, my current of magic has run stronger, like it was when Raya was alive. It seems you now hold the core of this power. Let me help you, and we can grow our magic as one.*

"Together, dear Ria, you and I can accomplish great things. A reshaping of the world anew. Together, you and I can bring about the Eternal Night."

"The Eternal Night," I say, head pounding, Raya's screams still echoing in my ears. "What is that?"

He does not answer me with words. Instead, the mindscape disappears and we're standing in a world of red. The Blood Moon, full and inescapable, hovers above a dry desert, a barren, destroyed world. I try to swallow my gasp of terror, but don't know if I succeed. My fingers itch to shield my eyes from the utter *wrongness* of the world in front of me.

With a snap of his fingers, that world melts away and we're back in darkness.

"The world as it was first born," I realize through numbed lips. "The poisoned world."

"I was born as the world's first snake before I became a Master," he tells me, *"Amran's first and truest companion. And yet I never knew until the Memory Master unearthed the truth for me. Like how your parents kept the truth of your birth from you."*

Thoughts rush through my skull. I don't know how to grasp any of this. His voice, sweet and syrupy. The return of this Eternal Night. Is that why the Blood Moon is coming?

There's so much I don't understand, but I don't get the chance to ask. A blizzard-like wind whips my hair across my face, and when I swipe it aside, the Snake Master is gone. The scene before me melts away, and I'm back to staring at the Snake River. In my reflection, my eyes have returned to their normal dark color. *Not Raya's.* But the moment I think of it, I sense that cobra slithering within me. I can't deny it—I know what this cobra is that I've been feeling.

It's a piece of Raya. The daughter of the Snake Master, reborn in me.

I start at the sound of voices. I turn to find the Serpent's Tongue staring at something—the Bloodstone, glowing in Amara's palm like burning starlight.

"No!" I cry, rushing toward her, but Amara—the Snake Master—only flings me back with a wave of her hand. I land face-first in the snow, Shima weakly curling around my fallen arm for comfort.

My head spinning in a nauseous whirl, my body aching like I've been beaten, I can only watch in horror as Amara twitches her hands toward those around her. One by one, the members of the Serpent's Tongue peel off their hoods, their grins slashes of red in the consuming darkness.

"Offer the talismans."

The followers obey. Each of them places one talisman on the ground until they form a circle. The compass for the Fire Master, what looks like an ancient bird's feather for the Sky Master, the scepter for the Snake Master, the sword for the Tide Master, and the map for the Earth Master. Finally, Amara takes off her cuffs and drops them onto the snow. The circle completed, she plants the stone on the slushy dirt in the center.

"*Rise*," the Snake Master tells her. And she does.

The talismans begin to glow at Amara's feet, and I watch as rivulets of gold rush out of them and latch onto the Bloodstone. Amara sighs, like a cloud exhaling the first rain of summer. The golden blood cascades over the Bloodstone until it looks bright as the sun.

The stone begins to shake and shimmer, rising into the air. The fiery blood within it—the lifeblood of Amran—turns a burnt-orange hue. And when she moves to clutch it in the air, thrust it into her grasp, I can feel the warmth exuding from it. The Creator's blood, like the heat of a thousand fires.

"Once I make my wish," Amara says, grinning, "all I will need is my husband's ashes to bring him back to life. And then my destruction of Kaama can begin."

Her final words are wispy as smoke, acrid as fire.

"Make me the Soul Master."

Within seconds, the ground shakes. I watch Amara rise into the air, clouds gathering overhead. She glows like that burning starlight of the Bloodstone, but for a different reason. She screams as her veins turn from deep blue to red to black.

Not a scream of triumph. One of complete anguish.

And I realize the truth. She isn't becoming the Soul Master at all.

Instead . . . a different Master is rising.

Amara shrieks again, dropping the Bloodstone to the ground. A fever fills her eyes as a snake slithers out of her mouth and onto the snowy grounds. It grows and lengthens until it reshapes itself into the man in my mindscape. Into my ancestor, the Great Deceiver.

The Snake Master sneers, retrieving the Bloodstone from the ground and rising into the air. *Thank you for being an obedient host, Amara. It seems your wish failed while I have succeeded. These six talismans have finally given me the strength to stand alone. And to possess all the talismans is to possess the power of our Creator . . . of Amran.*

Within the next instant, Amara screeches with dismay, her face bulging with veins that make her look less human, more monster.

Somehow, without the Snake Master within her anymore, she's . . . withering. Like she's been bled dry.

With a thrust of her hand, she flings a knife out from the folds of her cloak and presses it against Veer's neck. "*You* told me this would work," she rattles out, eyes bloodshot. Her formerly devoted acolytes step back, frightened, as they watch Amara's wrath unfold. As her fingers shake and her grip tightens, digging steel into flesh.

"I promised no such thing," Veer manages in a garbled breath, a slick smile rising on one side of his face. "Long live the Snake Master."

The others bow in reverence, their heads touching the snow as they turn from Amara to the Great Deceiver. *"Long live the Snake Master!"*

At those words, a serpentine twist writhes in my belly, and the pounding in my head reaches a crescendo. I gaze down at the Snake River and away from the chanting in front of me, watching my face morph between Ria and Raya.

Veer obeys the Snake Master. . . .

Veer tried to hurt Aditi. . . .

Veer made the capital believe he was a palace physician, hurting them instead of healing. . . .

In the river, I see my eyes flash green. They're Raya's eyes.

They're *mine.*

I lift myself up and hiss with a voice as alluring as a snake's rattle.

"*Stop,*" I tell Amara, snake magic resonating through my bones. Her grip slackens on the knife.

"Don't you see I've been betrayed?" she spits at me, fighting against my magic, her eyes still trained on Veer. "This isn't your fight, girl. Stay out of it while I get my revenge."

I don't know what powers overcome me, but I speed in a flash toward Amara, one hand forcing the knife out of her grip. She stumbles back, eyes widening on mine.

"*G-green,*" she whispers, staring at me as if I were a feral animal, her index finger trembling as she points at my newly flashing eyes.

"*How fortuitous,*" says the Snake Master, watching us from above like a god from the heavens. I suppose he is. Biding his time in the Snake Pit; using Amara's body to retrieve the talismans. So why do I get the feeling that his business here is unfinished?

"What do you want?" I ask the Snake Master, my eyes locked on Veer's. I bring the tip of Amara's knife to his throat, watching it draw blood, but Veer only grins.

"*Isn't it obvious, Ria? I've snuck into your dreams . . . I've seen your life . . . the pity others take on you when they see your uncontrolled powers—no, the fear . . .*"

"Stop," I demand, my hand shaking. "Stop, or I'll kill him."

"*Kill* me?" Veer sneers. "You don't have the strength," he spits out between gritted teeth. "No one has the strength to match my Master's."

My blood boils. "He's not your Master!" I force my hand to

stop shaking, pressing deeper into the Black Viper's skin, then repeat my statement to the Snake Master. "I swear I'll do it."

"You think I care for the Black Viper?" the Snake Master tuts. *"He's nothing more than a tool."*

Veer's eyes finally widen. "M-Master, I've been loyal to you. I brought you what you sought, even when you possessed a new form—"

"My form shall not matter any longer. And as for you, I have no use."

That cobra rises up inside of me, its fangs snapping with desire. There's no pain, only pleasure.

And thirst.

"P-please," Veer begs with spittle on his lips, his bravado utterly vanished. I hate the way he begs. Hate the things he's done, the lies he's spewed. Hate the lies I *believed*.

I no longer want to simply control my unruly magic. I want to use it. Embrace it.

"That's it," the Snake Master tells me. *"Let go of that anger. Let go, Ria."*

I drop the knife but keep my arm raised. Veer expels a sigh of relief.

But the cobra within me has me on strings. Shima responds to my emotion, my unspoken demand, and she slithers forward. Hissing fills my ears as snakes emerge from the riverbed in droves.

The world around me goes silent, save the furious beat of my heart. I taste blood on my tongue, feel Shima's unstoppable hunger—and watch as Veer's expression widens into shock as she lunges with the other snakes. He tries to escape but can only scream as the snakes wrap around his ankles, his legs, and Shima sinks her fangs into Veer's throat. His legs give out as he collapses into the snow. The snow beneath him reddens, and his once-bright eyes turn dull, lifeless.

I drop my arm. Cold, cold air shivers around me, and a piercing pain stabs my forehead. I fall to my knees and gasp.

What have I done?

"I wasn't sure you'd go through with it." The Snake Master chuckles. He turns, about to disappear in a black plume of smoke before he halts, gazing at me.

"My offer remains, Ria. I will be seeing you soon."

I blink, and he is gone, leaving nothing but a faint swirl of smoke behind.

There's no time to process where the Snake Master went. I can barely process what my hands did—what *I* did. I stare at my palms, the blood speckling my fingers. I turn them into fists. I killed Veer. I brought him to justice.

I hurl in the snow.

Everything after that happens so quickly, I can barely keep track. The Snake Master's followers disappear into clouds of smoke, leaving Amara where she stands. Amara, staring at Veer's still form, falls to her knees next to me, her face consumed by veins of black as she shudders uncontrollably.

She's weak. Barely alive. And now . . .

"My son," she mutters, almost to herself, before bringing her dark eyes up to mine. "I need my son." Her body shivers, and she looks so small and delicate in this moment, like she could be carried away wherever the wind takes her. She shuts her eyes as her skin glows with iridescent light, as if being consumed from the inside out.

I can barely wrap my head around what's happening. She reaches out to me, her eyes pleading as she croaks, "*Saeed.*"

I shudder, jerking away as Amara's body slumps toward the ground and her skin begins to pull away, turning to fragments of dust rising into the air. When her eyes meet mine, they hold none of the bloodlust or anger of moments ago, just pain, and I see myself within her. When I would sleep alone on the streets, so hungry I could barely utter a word, afraid this night would be my last. Everything changed for me; hope blossomed into my life, and I accepted a path I didn't think I'd get the chance to have. But Amara doesn't have a choice. She's dying, right before my eyes, and—

Saeed. I need to find him. I need to—

Crack.

I peel myself up from the ground, which I realize, with a start, is still tremoring. Horrified, I whirl to find the tents surrounding the Winter Palace, not far from where I am now, are alight and aflame, sending billowing smoke and the acrid smell of fire to the skies.

I rush back to Shima and check that she's all right before

stumbling through the haze of smoke toward the Winter Palace. I can't bear to look behind me, as Amara's body fragments further. I have to find Saeed.

When I'm close to the palace, screams rise. Glass shatters. Mud squelches beneath my feet as I finally make it inside, trembling as I try to push my overtaxed body to move—and find pandemonium. People flee as all the candles are extinguished as though by a sudden wind. In the ballroom, guests are scrambling. Snowbirds have flown inside through broken glass windows, and they swoop down, slashing at the guests' heads like they're vermin. One flies straight for King Rohit, and I quickly push him aside. The bird slams right into the throne, then falls into the seat, motionless.

"What's happening?!" the raja cries out. The bird opens its eyes. They're red. I hadn't noticed before, but bite marks cover its neck.

"No." I swallow a gasp. The birds—we found them in the White Mountains. *Dead.* Or presumably so. What if they weren't dead after all? The birds' eyes eerily remind me of another's. The Snake Master's.

And the bite marks—what if they were *poisoned* with his venom?

"What has he done?" I whisper to myself, before remembering I have done no better. I gaze down at my hands, seeing them swim out of focus. I swear, for a moment, that they are painted with blood.

More cries from outside startle me from my haze. Where is Aditi, Saeed? I assure the raja is okay before sprinting out of the party, headed straight for the exit.

At the threshold of the palace, I spot Saeed clutching his arm. The fabric of his kurta has been slashed, exposing his brown skin reddening with a line of blood.

"Saeed!"

His eyes find mine and he rushes over, grabbing hold of me before I can even feel the cold Amratstanian air. "Stay inside, Ria. I don't want the snowbirds attacking you, too."

Is that how he got that wound? "But your—" The words stick in my throat. But Saeed *has* to know.

"Your mother," I say finally. "She's here, by the Snake River. She—" My voice is so shaky, tears are filling my eyes, and I know I'm rambling so much that Saeed has to cup my cheeks to calm me.

"She what?" Saeed says, voice urgent.

"She used—the talismans, the Bloodstone. She thought she could become the Soul Master, but she didn't, and now the Sn—" I stop myself short.

"What is it, Ria?" Saeed gazes at me in confusion and growing alarm, unable to understand my rambling.

"Fire!" someone cries. I turn, yanking Saeed with me as we rush into the cold. There's no time to explain to him what just happened. Smoke chokes my lungs as people throw buckets of water onto the flames.

Flames the Snake Master and his followers must have created as a distraction from what happened at the Snake River.

"Get inside, everyone!" I see Irfan ahead of us, calling out to the hordes of people crowding at the entrance. "Stay where it's safe!" He must've come back to the palace after I was transported.

But there's no time to stop. I ignore Irfan and rush through the grounds, Saeed hot on my heels. The cool air is mixed with the scent of bitter ash, drifting all around me like dark snowflakes.

"Where are we going?" he huffs behind me. Around us, the fire continues to spread. While the snow has done a good job of keeping the fire at bay, the tents are easily flammable.

I don't stop until we're at the Snake River.

"Mother!" Saeed cries, falling to his knees beside her and reaching for her. But just before he can, Amara grabs on to his wrist.

"My son," she whispers, raising a hand to caress his cheek but lacking the strength.

Saeed chokes back a sob. "Mother—what happened—"

Amara shakes her head. Closes her eyes. "It was *him*," she shudders out. She points a crooked finger to the side, where the Snake Master had disappeared. Saeed glances at the river, where Veer's body lies bent on the ground, his wound still bleeding him dry.

"V-Veer?" he gasps. "What did he do? What happened to him?"

Amara shakes her head. "Let go, Saeed. I can hear your father. His voice is calling me. . . ."

"No," Saeed croaks out, trying desperately to cling on to his mother, but his fingers slip through her, as though sifting through sand. "Stay here. Don't leave—"

"I must," she says. And with a final, chilling exhalation, her body sheds to nothing but ash and dust in a sea of snow.

Amara

There is no sensation quite like pain. She knows this. It pulses inside her like a second heart, then flutters in her chest, spiraling into numbness. Yet the feeling pales in the face of his betrayal.

He tricked her. He used her.

His name takes a moment to come back to her, forgotten like those first moments upon waking from a dream. *Sahil*, the Snake Master. The man who'd rescued her—

No, she had rescued *him*. So why did his betrayal leave her gasping for breath, leave her in a pool of ashes and dreams deferred?

From somewhere afar, a bird crows. A burning sun sears the sky. She can feel her body on the ground, heavy as a sack of rice. Not ashes, then.

Where am I?

She tries to lift her leg. An arm. A finger. Nothing obeys except her head, which yields to one side as her eyes crack open to find an ocean of roses. Stretches of red petals reach up to touch her fingers, greeting her, lifting her up and pointing toward the threshold of a strange, glowing doorway.

A door . . . to where?

A deep ache swells across her body. She feels . . . *empty* without the Snake Master's presence. As though she had given too much when allowing him room. Like she'll never be whole again. But she never needed the Snake Master to be whole, did she? She only needed Kumal. And her son.

Dear Masters, will I ever see them again? she asks the sky.

Had Death opened a door for her? And had she willingly entered? The sheer shock of the realization feels like a jolt of lightning. She will never see Saeed again. She won't harness the power of the cuffs. But she will also never again feel the pain of her father's whip on her palms.

She wonders, briefly, if power is pain, or if pain is power. Without pain, she never would have found the Bloodstone. Without pain, she never would have felt the cuts along her arms that healed into scars. The cuts in her heart that never closed.

"Close your eyes, Amara."

She fights against the voice before realizing it's Kumal's. A voice full of pain and loss, love and remembrance. A voice that once sang Kaaman lullabies to her son, soothing him to sleep.

Go past the wall, the snow that falls
In Kaama we dream of peace for all
Go past the gate, we seal your fate
In Kaama we answer the call

"I won't," she tells the voice. *"I won't."*

The thousands of roses crowd around her, angered by her resistance. Petals blacken at her touch, as if a horrid rot has taken root in the soil. Too soon, the vines wrap around her wrists, throat.

"Close your eyes," he reminds her. For a brief moment, she continues to fight back, wrestling with the thorns. But it's no use.

So, against the searing sunlight, she listens. The roses swallow Amara whole, burying her in a garden of her own making.

24
Rani

"Rani? Rani, wake up!"

I cough. Hands grope my arms and lift me up. Stars fill my vision as I come to.

"Abai's sun," I whisper. "Was that a dream?"

"Nope," Amir says, clasping on to me with clammy hands. "I saw it all, too." He glances over at the triplet queens. "Please, oh mighty queens, never do that again. I think I'm going to be sick."

"Me too," Dhruv says from my right. Queen Meeta rises gently, but she rubs her head, face flushed.

"I'm afraid it was necessary. I trust you saw all you needed to?" Queen Sampada asks.

We nod. And shiver. But I'm certain none of them were possessed by the Snake Master the way I was. That felt like a power that belonged to me alone.

"Then you now see the truth." Queen Sunita's face hardens. "The Snake Master was born as a snake, not with malice in his heart, but poison. And when he was turned into a Master—"

"The other Masters feared his power. *Harmed* him. So he returned the favor." The words pour out of me, and I feel the Snake Master's rage and sorrow like it is my own, a monsoon of pain.

"After Raya's death, I sensed other magic in the air. Not magic like mine. *Soul* magic. And when she turned to stone and was consumed by the Pit, all that was left behind was . . ."

"The Bloodstone," Amir confirms numbly. "I thought that was supposed to be Amran's gift or something."

"In a way, it was," Queen Sampada responds, her tone heavy with sadness. "It was Amran's way of leaving something behind from Raya, for her sacrifice. For her loss of magic. That is why his blood runs through the stone. The Pit was complete after her death. It needed a victim."

I shiver, remembering the Snake Master's warring greed and grief. It was true, then. The Snake Master wasn't just the Great Deceiver. He was once a father as well. He once loved his daughters. But that love was soon replaced by wrath.

"Raya's death changed the world as we know it," Queen Saira says. "Though few know her tale. The Snake Master ensured as much, consumed with vengeance as he was after her death."

The phantom queens go silent.

"So the Snake Master took the stone for himself and used it for evil? To banish the Masters?" Amir asks.

"What do you believe?" Queen Sunita asks, head tilting at me with curiosity.

"I think the Snake Master wasn't just one thing, not simply good or evil," I say, my heart heavy with the weight of what I now know. "But regardless of his intentions, he *was* the reason for the Blood Moon—and this Eternal Night."

Professor Neel and Jujhar have to take a seat, reeling from this information, while the queens mutter between themselves urgently.

Queen Saira points upward. "I sense the moon is almost full. You do not have much time left."

A note of panic creeps into Amir's tone. "For the Blood Moon to return . . . it would have to come from the Snake Master, as it did the first time. Does that mean the Snake Master has returned, too? That's impossible, right?"

It should be. And yet . . . I recite the prophecy in my mind, thoughts churning like a roaring sea.

A missing heart to be restored . . .

"Of course," I whisper. "The first line of the prophecy." I look at Amir.

"A . . . missing heart?" he asks, nonplussed.

"*Raya,*" I tell him, feeling my own heart begin to thunder in my chest. "It has to be!"

"But how could her heart be restored?" Amir questions. "She's dead. What does any of that have to do with this Eternal Night?"

"I'm not sure," I say with uncertainty.

"The Eternal Night was a time of darkness and doom," Professor Neel notes. "We scholars know that much. It happened once . . . it could happen again." His voice turns grave.

Queen Meeta frowns. "Then we must make arrangements for the Malwan Pass immediately. Scholar Neel, thank you for your help. Queen Saira, Queen Sampada, Queen Sunita—we are in your debt, forever. Jujhar, would you draw a map for my son's companions to begin their travels to the Pass?"

Jujhar nods, but his eyes flicker to the queens nervously. "I—I thought the queens of old were betrayers, just like my ancestors believed. But the Sky Master had trusted you for a reason. I—"

"There is no need for apologies," Queen Sampada says with a kind smile, which quickly dims. "I believe it is time you leave. We cannot appear again, but our souls will continue to live here in this chamber, and we hope you will keep it open to all."

"We will," Dhruv says with a bow. "Always."

The following morning, the gardens of the Saffron Palace greet me like an ocean. Marigolds lap at my ankles, the roots sturdy because of stonebringer magic from the Old Age, but rotted leaves falling from beckoning tree branches pepper the air. A sign of the seeping poison, I remind myself. Only now do I know where this poison is coming from—not just the Blood Moon, but the possible return of the Snake Master himself.

Nearby, Jujhar mounts his skyhawk, Sahara, who has grown ten times her size than when we saw her in the tavern. He offers me his hand-drawn map, the ink now dried. "The journey won't be long," he assures, "if you keep to the path."

"Thank you," I tell him, watching as Amir helps to load the luggage, chatting easily with a few palace hands not far from the front-facing gardens.

Jujhar follows my eyes to Amir, and then says, "Good luck to both of you. I'm kinda glad you visited me. But please get that damned talisman back, will you?"

I match Jujhar's smile. "I promise."

Sahara's wings spread in a great span as she takes flight. I look back to Amir, unable to help myself, and then startle when I hear a voice come from beside me.

"Something is troubling you," Queen Meeta notes, coming fully to my side. "The boy . . . Amir?"

I glance up bashfully. "How did you know?"

"Queens have a sixth sense." She snickers. Warmth floods through me at her gentle teasing, so similar to Jas Auntie's that it makes me want to confide in her.

"Amir and I are so different. I think he's beginning to see who I really am. Who I'll always be. The princess of Abai."

"If I might give some advice," Queen Meeta begins, stepping closer to me. Birds chirp overhead, peering in on our conversation. "Love is not simply a task to be completed. It is something we discover within ourselves and others, like pieces of a quilt to be stitched together. We do not need to be the same as others to match.

"You must listen to both your head and your heart. My marriage to my husband was made with my head, not my heart . . .

and wasn't made to last. He left for a quiet life in Retan's most remote villages."

"I had no idea," I murmur. "I'm sorry."

"It was more of a . . . mutual understanding," Queen Meeta answers, eyes darkening. "It happened many years ago, during Dhruv's rebellious phase."

"Dhruv had a *rebellious* phase?" I scoff. Poised, princely Dhruv? Mischievous, sure. But *rebellious*? He was Professor Neel's favorite, likely one of the smartest students at the Academy, and he wasn't terrible at sharing his feelings, either. He was, in so many ways, perfect.

"Oh, yes. He was much like his father. He went horseback riding without permission *far* too often and would participate in Retan's deadliest competitions. It was like he wanted to test his mettle. He spent time with a few of the currentspinners of the Island Market trying to learn a magic that couldn't be learned by an ordinary boy. He sneered at his duties and wore simple clothes to the most elegant functions."

That I can imagine. But a rebellious Dhruv is still too strange, despite his liking for pranks. I can't imagine him doing anything to damage his reputation—or his family's.

"What changed him?"

"Part of me thinks he changed when his father left. Part of me thinks that he became more aware of the expectations placed upon him as the prince."

I knew that all too well, having been raised under the raja's rule.

Queen Meeta rests a hand on my arm, looking queenly as ever. "Look at me, going on. I will stop pestering you about my son. Today is a big day. Retan will miss you both. *I* will miss you."

"You don't . . . despise me?" I wonder aloud. "For not knowing what I want?" In so many ways, I despise myself for it, for the muddled mess of emotions that I cannot decipher—and the people I've hurt in trying.

"Life isn't about knowing what you want. It's about finding what you need." Queen Meeta smiles, wrinkles forming around her eyes. "And you deserve more than just a few weeks with a queen and her son in a foreign kingdom to figure that out. You have your whole life ahead of you, Rani. Live it."

Her words bring tears to my eyes. "Thank you, Queen Meeta. For everything. You're just as wise as the Three Blessed Sisters."

"But not nearly as amusing," she says with a wink.

We leave for the Malwan Pass within the hour. Dhruv insisted on coming along. Of course, Queen Meeta approved his travels first and, along with Ranjit, wished both Amir and me the best of luck. It felt odd hugging the queen of another kingdom farewell, and somehow familiar all the same. She understands the weight of royalty. She understands *me* where it seems like even my mother cannot. I can only hope the queen feels the same—and that I've done Abai, and my parents, proud in my time here. That an alliance is in our future.

A carriage pulls us away from the Blue Palace. I turn around once more to survey the three palaces: Gold, Blue, Saffron. Saira, Sampada, Sunita. When I first arrived in Retan, I had no idea of the treasures I would find within these palaces. The secrets the sisters held.

Nor do I have any idea of what Ria has been up to since the boat attack. I wish there was a way to speak to Ria to figure out what's truly going on with Amara and the possible return of a Master.

I reach for my anklet once more. I connected with my sister once after we parted ways, but now more than ever, I desperately need to speak to her.

I keep the anklet in my palms, warming it with my magic the whole way to our first rest stop, a grand water well in a village called Nadi. Women hold barrels of water over their heads, moving elegantly through the streets with saris tucked and draped with hibiscus flowers. As Amir refills our waterskins, I stare at the water pooled beneath us, rippling my reflection back at me. A fragmented version of myself.

But as I move my mouth to speak, my reflection speaks first.

"It worked!" my sister bellows. Her face ripples in the well, clear as glass. Amir nearly drops his waterskin.

"Raja's beard—is that Ria?" he nearly screeches.

I grab the waterskin before he can drop it. "Yes. Twins have power beyond magic. They have a connection. *We* have a connection."

I smile down at my sister; I expect her to offer a sneaky one back, but instead see only a quivering smile and red-rimmed eyes.

"I didn't call upon the mind link—how did you show up?" I ask her.

"I used the anklet just as you did the last time," Ria tells me, voice uneven. "You didn't answer for the first few attempts. But now—"

"I'm here," I say, relieved. No wonder my anklet was warm. It wasn't my magic—it was hers, calling to me. We just needed a vessel to communicate.

"Do you have news? You go first—" I laugh as we speak at the same time. But Ria pinches her mouth closed, like she is about to deliver a terrible story and can't bear to tell it.

So I offer my story first. "We're headed to the Malwan Pass in Retan, bordering Abai. We believe there is a trial set there by the Fire Master. We can obtain what we need to destroy the Bloodstone."

"You found all that out from the scholars?" Ria asks.

"Not exactly." I glance at Amir as he says, "Three triplet queens kinda helped us out. They were dead, though. For centuries. Reviving them was some tough work."

My sister gapes. Amir tells her about how we learned to unseal the closed chamber the queens built beneath the palaces.

"We felt a strange rumbling yesterday. Did Amara use the talismans? Has she become the Soul Master?"

"Not exactly." Ria fiddles with her hair nervously. "She made her wish with all the talismans present. But . . . it didn't grant her wish. Instead, it set something within her free. Our infamous ancestor." She doesn't offer a name.

I parse through her words. *She must mean . . . the Snake Master.*

Nausea overcomes me, and I cling on to the well. So Amir was right.

"I know this is a lot to process, Rani, but I saw him firsthand. I . . . *spoke* to him. The—"

"Snake Master," I shudder out. "The sister queens showed me a memory of his. It was . . . enlightening. When he used the power of the Bloodstone against the other Masters, he was left only a shadow of his former self. He must've disappeared into the Snake Pit, all those years ago." The power of the stone was enough to leave any mortal deathly ill—like Queen Amrita, our ancestor who hid the stone in the Var River, knowing its dangers.

I'm more terrified than I am relieved that Amir was right about his Snake Master theory.

Ria speaks up. "Shima told me something after Amara disappeared into the Snake Pit: that someone was biding their time in the Pit. She couldn't say his name; she was bound to her Master's secret."

"How did you learn this?"

"I . . . I spoke to the Snake Master. He took over Amara's body when she fell inside the Snake Pit. He was too weak to escape on his own, so he made her think she was in control, getting the talismans for her own gain."

Ria pauses, her mouth set in a grim line. "But instead, he used the talismans to strengthen himself. He turned it all against her so he could have his own body again."

I try to process all this new information about the Snake Master, my mind a maelstrom of thoughts—how he existed *within* Amara. Yet it looks like Ria is holding something back. But before I can ask, Amir pipes up beside me.

"The prophecy said the Key of a Master would set *souls* free." Amir bites his lip. "She could still find a way to get what she wants, and become the Soul Master to free her husband."

"Unless that line wasn't about her," Ria says, almost beneath her breath. "I think the Key is something else. Not a physical thing but . . . a person."

"Ria . . ." I touch the water, trying to feel her as I do the rippling well. "Is there something you're not telling me?"

Her lips quiver. "It's Amara," she says quietly. "After the Snake Master betrayed her, he took all the talismans, along with the Bloodstone, and disappeared. After he was gone, Amara became weak. Like a part of herself was lost. . . ."

Ria trails off, her eyes not meeting mine.

I shake my head in shock. *The Snake Master has the Bloodstone back.* "What happened then? Where is she?"

"She . . ." I swear I see tears fill her eyes. "She's not . . . a problem anymore. When the Snake Master left her, she—she faded."

"Faded?" I ask. "Like . . ."

"Died," Ria confirms softly.

Amir and I lock gazes. None of this feels real.

"She broke apart into ashes, like she couldn't hold herself together anymore." Ria takes a deep, shaky breath. "We have to focus on the bigger enemy and find the Snake Master."

"What do you think he wants?" Amir asks.

"An Eternal Night. He asked me to . . . no, he *told* me himself that's what he wanted. He has all the talismans now. That's what he was using Amara for—to gain the power of Amran, and then create an Eternal Night: the endless darkness the world was born in."

I nod, remembering everything I learned from the Snake Master's memory. "We have to stop him before the Eternal Night can happen. And we need to meet. Once I face my trial at the Malwan Pass, we will have a weapon to destroy the Bloodstone. But we'll need to confront him to stop him. And we don't know where he'll be."

"We'll figure it out," Ria says, her gaze suddenly determined.

Another thought strikes me. "Father is in Kaama right now, for the peace treaty. We can make our way and meet there—and warn him of what's to come."

Warn him of the Snake Master. The one who deceived Amara. And our true enemy all along.

Ria starts to speak, as if finally about to tell me what I can feel her holding back, but her words are garbled. "Wait!" I cry. I reach out for my sister, hands grasping the water. It slips right through my fingers.

"Rani—soon—" Ria says.

Where my sister once was, all I see are the dim, broken pieces of a reflected sky.

25

Ria

I stare at the burn marks in the snow.

Amara, here at the palace. Amara, gone. And Veer . . .

I will my hands to stop shivering, for the blood to leave my forever-stained hands.

What's done cannot be undone.

Shima stares at me now, coiled up. *Still thinking about last night, are we?*

"How can I not?" I shudder. "Amara was *right here*. And the Snake Master . . ."

It was a panic to put out the fires and get everyone returned to their bedrooms, but even then, most people didn't feel safe enough, and fled the palace grounds instead. After the chaos was over, I sat with Zoya and Irfan, explaining everything that happened after I was transported to the Snake River and came face-to-face with Amara.

Almost everything. I couldn't speak of my discussion with the Snake Master. And how Raya took over . . . how I shared her hunger, her thirst, and killed—

Was it me who killed Veer, or Raya? A piece of her has always resided within me. A piece that has always been connected to the Snake Master. And I can't deny how good embracing that magic felt—despite the horrid action that came with it.

As soon as Amara died, only her ashes remained. Saeed gathered as much into his shirt as possible and carried them back to the palace. Still distraught, he later joined the conversation, needing to know what happened—needing closure. My sole explanation to the group was that Veer had killed her, a member of the Serpent's Tongue who'd taken revenge on Amara for attempting to be a Master. I explained the viciousness of the Serpent's Tongue, how they used and tricked Amara and took the talismans for themselves. I couldn't bring myself to say what happened to Veer—or who he was truly working for.

If only they knew the truth.

Riddled with guilt, I knocked on Saeed's door after he left the conversation with Irfan and Zoya, but he refused to answer. I haven't seen him since. I could have spoken up. I could have told him about the circumstances of his mother's death—how the Snake Master had weakened his mother. But I failed to follow through in that moment, and now I don't know if I can. He'd been through far too much in the past day. Too much to be told his mother died a pawn in a Master's game.

Shima's snake scales bloom a lilac shade, then flush with a deeper mauve. The color of confusion, I've learned. It still catches me off guard, the way she can read my emotions.

Footsteps sound from behind. I pale when I catch sight of King Rohit in a sling, Zoya holding on to him on his good side.

"Amratstan isn't safe anymore," I say, forgoing a greeting. This morning, I confirmed a plan with Irfan for our departure to Kaama. I see him now, walking slightly behind the Amratstan royals. He's carrying some of our luggage, with Neeta and Neesa not far behind with the rest.

"We must head to Kaama to warn King Jeevan and King Natesh of what happened here last night," says Irfan, nodding to the king. "Who knows if they might attack again." His hands are heavily scratched. He defended so many people from the snow-birds last night, but he seems steadier than ever. I realize that after everything he's discovered upon returning to this kingdom, he's finally discovered who he truly is. Not a soldier, not a follower. A leader.

"We have about a fortnight until the moon is at its peak. The Serpent's Tongue is a real threat."

You have no idea how much. No one knows the whole truth of what happened last night—about what happened to Veer, about the offer the Snake Master made.

"Saeed and Aditi are all packed and ready to go," Irfan announces. Just then, I catch sight of Aditi at the front entrance, waving at me timidly.

"I want to help, too," Zoya declares, voice firm but eyes pleading.

"You're coming?" I'm stunned. What happened last night, the danger we all faced—and everyone is still willing to help? My heart thumps, grateful. I'm not that thief girl on the streets anymore. I have friends I can rely on. *Family.* Just as the positive thought comes to mind, Saeed appears in the entranceway. His face is emotionless, stoic, and a hush spreads through everyone gathered.

"I want to spread my mother's ashes," he declares. Silence beats thick in the air. These are the first words he's spoken to us today. His eyes are red-rimmed, but his voice is steady. "My family's Kaaman estate, where I lived as a baby. It is on the way to the palace. I must stop there."

No one dares argue. They can see the pain in Saeed's eyes. They've all felt loss, too.

Zoya's eyes volley between us. "Neeta and Neesa shall join us, too. We'll ride our water buffalos."

A pang of sorrow hits me when I think of how I hadn't had the guts to tell Rani the truth this morning. I can't bear the thought of how she'd look at me. Maybe next time I'll tell her everything.

It will all be better when I see her again in person, even if I was just getting used to this place. I didn't think I'd be so sad to leave Amratstan, even with this skies-damned cold.

"Before you leave," King Rohit says as Zoya and Irfan get the luggage loaded, "I have a story to share with you." Before I can question him, he continues, "The Amratstan of centuries past was not the same as it is today. Our kingdom began with currentspinner magic and stonebringer magic working in tandem—sky and rock, and a dual monarchy with it, all working in perfect harmony. But after a time, there grew a divide between people of these magics."

King Rohit licks his lips. "Some claimed the stonebringers had stolen the Sky Master's talisman, a claim that incited many battles to come. Others that the currentspinners were behind the rift. They blamed each other when they should have been listening." The raja gazes directly at me. In his eyes I see an apology for the way he's ignored our warnings about Amara. How he, and his kingdom, were the ones hurt in the end.

King Rohit continues, "If we divide further, we will never find hope. Amratstan is whole now, no longer divided—but it was a truth Amratstan learned through much pain."

"Sounds familiar," I say, thinking of my father, the raja, trying to make amends with Kaama's king, Jeevan.

"I haven't thought of that piece of history in years," he says. "To some, magic is a fable of its own."

I grimace. "I used to think magic wasn't real, either. I didn't even know about the talismans until two moons ago."

"Then you have aged much in these two moons," he says. "And even in the midst of new revelations, you figured out the truth of Amara coming here. I respect your courage on this mission, and your openness. We should all be glad to possess the same. And I am sorry for the rift between your father and me. May we grow and prosper." He presses three fingers to his forehead, and I do the same.

"We will get your family's talisman back," I tell him.

"The talisman," he says, "is not as important as my daughter's life. Whatever you plan, please keep her safe." His eyes shine with tears. I've never seen this side of him, and it makes me respond in kind, tears springing to my eyes.

"I promise."

I hope I can keep that vow. Already we face a greater threat than we ever could have anticipated. That skies-damned prophecy tricked us. We thought it was speaking of Amara and her wish to become the Soul Master, but in fact, it was prophesying the Snake Master's return. Me, as his Key. And the end of days.

As the Blood Moon approaches, he'll only become more powerful. And whatever the Snake Master's greater plan is in the end, we've only gotten a taste of it.

Turns out traveling by water buffalo can be a real pain in the arse.

I glance over at Saeed perched atop his own steed. He still hasn't spoken a word since our departure from the Winter Palace except instructions on how to get to the estate, his mother's ashes safely stowed in his pack. Meanwhile, I'm holding on to the reins for dear life and muttering under my breath like I'm mad.

Maybe I am.

A full day's travel, and we're now in the wilds of Amratstan, inching toward Kaama's western border. I shiver under my fur cloak—Saeed's gift to me. It still smells like him. A touch of sandalwood, a hint of syrupy sweets. But something about it turns sour when the cobra within me rises—the piece of Raya I haven't been able to talk about with anyone else, especially not Saeed. Not after what happened to his mother at the hands of the Snake Master. Not after what I *did*. If he knew what lies within me, what would he think? If he knew that I was capable of—of— I can barely think the word to myself. *Murder*, I tell myself firmly. *That's what it is. You can't call it anything else.*

I look back at Saeed, feeling my heart ache. He knows nothing of the Snake Master's return. Would I lose him if he knew how similar I am to my ancestor? My feelings are . . . *complex*, to say the least.

The Snake Master has been planting memories in my head. The thought should scare me, but it doesn't. Despite what he did, despite everything . . . he understands my magic in a way no one else has. And ever since his escape from the Snake Pit, my magic has only grown stronger.

My offer remains, Ria. I will be seeing you soon.

We camp in a snowy clearing that night. Thankfully, Neeta and Neesa have brought tents, and setting them up is a welcome distraction from my buzzing thoughts, the cloudy skies, the cracked earth.

"I'll gather firewood with the twins," Zoya says. I perk up before realizing she's talking about Neeta and Neesa. A drop of sadness hits my belly; even though I still don't know everything about being a twin—or even a sister for that matter—I wish Rani could be here with us as we move toward Kaama. Maybe she could help me with whatever's going on inside me.

No, I realize with a start. *Only the Snake Master knows my power.*

When Zoya and the twin Sentinels are gone, I finish setting up one of the tents with Irfan. His deep-silver eyes tell me he's hiding something—it's a gut instinct we thieves have. I don't want to directly ask him what's on his mind, but . . .

"Are you sad we're leaving Amratstan?" I think of how he brought me to his old house, ground to shambles by the Serpent's Tongue. Pieces of all of us lie in Amratstan now, whether our pasts or our present.

Irfan knots the base of one of the tent's poles and locks it into the grass beneath a pile of snow. "Sad?" He knocks the pole into place. "Honestly, I have no idea. It's not home anymore. Not really."

"Don't you feel a tie to your country?"

"Didn't you want to escape your home country, not that long ago?"

"You got me there," I admit. "But then I found my family." As soon as I say the words, I wince. Not everyone has a family to go home to, and Irfan is one of them.

Irfan doesn't speak, confirming my thoughts.

At his silence, I say, "There's still Sanya." Wistfulness fills his gaze and his cheeks flush. I quirk a smile. I know *that* isn't from the cold.

"Sanya seems like a great person," I say. "I haven't gotten to know her well, but Amir is my best friend." *Amir.* I nearly choke on his name. I miss the way he laughs, the way his smile tips too far on one side, the way he would cheer me up without fail when we were alone on the streets.

"Sanya's too busy to think about things like love."

It's too easy to see what she means to him from the way he says her name, like a bird singing its song. Even Shima caught on, when we were at Irfan's old house.

"She's with Jas back at the Foothills," he says now, shaking his head. "And I'm doing my duty here. When I return to Abai, we'll see where I belong."

"Maybe it's not *where*," I say. "Who means the most to you in this world?"

His eyes soften against mine. I already know the answer.

"Sanya," he whispers. "And Jas Auntie." He quirks his lips. "Even Amir and Rani."

"*And who means the most to you?*" a voice says in my ear.

I turn, but no one's there. A chill sweeps over me. I don't know how, but I know it's him, the hiss of his voice too distinctive, luring me closer.

My sister, I answer to him in my mind, but that isn't the image filling my head. Instead, it's Raya, gazing at her father one final time before turning to stone in the Snake Pit.

Later that night, I sit in front of a partially frozen lake just outside camp with Aditi. Saeed didn't eat dinner with us. The bloody moon is a reminder of what's to come, a globe of fire in the sky.

"You wanted to meet?" I ask her.

She nods. "We didn't have much time to spend together in Amratstan. And ever since what happened on the boat . . ."

I think of the way the sea sapni reeled back at the light exuding from Aditi's palms. With everything that's happened since Zoya's birthday, I haven't had time to think much about it. Guilt knots within me at Aditi's troubled expression. This has obviously been bothering her, and I've been too wrapped up in my own troubles to notice.

"The magic I used," she says slowly, "I've been feeling it more and more since that day. I feel a pull whenever I'm near water. And being surrounded by all those sea snakes, there was something humming in my veins."

"You mean . . . the magic of the Tide Master?"

Aditi nods imperceptibly. She dips a hand into the water. "I've been afraid to test it out since then. I don't know what will happen. Maybe I'll cause a monsoon," she jokes, though I can hear the nerves threaded through her voice.

Too stunned to laugh, I mull over the facts in my head. Aditi and I attended the Vadi Orphanage, a place to keep children with magic. To suppress their powers. We knew that she likely had untapped powers, but I never expected them to manifest so quickly.

"Well, I'm no expert at magic, but Shima taught me a lot while I was pretending to be Rani. You have to let your emotions guide you. They'll help open up your abilities." I point at her hands. She presses a finger to the water, concentrating. Nothing happens.

"I don't think I can suddenly learn how to do magic so fast, miss," Aditi says meekly.

"It doesn't have to be perfect," I say, wrapping an arm around Aditi and giving her a squeeze. "You just need to try."

Aditi brushes her fingers over the water, and I sense a shiver passing through her. "What's wrong?"

"Nothing," she replies. "It's just . . . why has my magic come out now? Why not before, when we were on the boat to Amrat-stan? Or any other time in my life?"

"They tried to suppress our magic," I remind her. *They*. The headmaster of the orphanage. And my own father. "I didn't recognize mine until I met Shima. Maybe yours just needed that push, as well, and you found it with the sea sapni. And now, it is finally ready to be released. So just let it happen."

Aditi smiles at that, dunking her hands in the water again so they're palms-up, and little bubbles form above the tips of her fingers. She gapes. "I did it!"

I clap. "You'll be able to do bigger things with practice."

"Can we keep this between us?" Aditi asks. "I'm still figuring out this magic for myself. I don't want everyone else questioning what powers I have, even if they saw what I did on the boat. It feels like a secret."

She's right; it is a secret. But magic is like that—something you want to hold close. Before I met Shima, I never realized how much I was missing: the feel of magic in my bones, my connection to both Shima and Rani.

My connection to the Snake Master.

"Of course," I say, shaking myself from my dark thoughts. "And who knows—maybe one day we'll be able to do our magic *together*."

"You think that's possible?"

"I was able to connect to my sister from hundreds of miles away," I tell her. "Anything's possible. Maybe we could conjure something in the water—something that connects the both of us."

Aditi's eyes sparkle. "Like a portrait of Mama Anita."

My throat tightens, but I nod all the same. Closing her eyes and concentrating, she sweeps her hand again over the water, which bubbles and froths. When the bubbles quickly disappear, Aditi tries to sweep her hand over the water again, but nothing happens.

"Think of something that brings out your strongest emotions," I tell her. When I opened the Pit for the first time on my own, Shima had made me think of Mama Anita. My heart had snapped in two—with frustration, with grief powerful enough to force the Pit open.

"Mistress Amara," Aditi mutters to herself, her eyes still closed, freezing as she realizes what she has said. A tumult of grief and rage is bottled within her, the whip marks still staining her palms. Scars that will never truly fade.

"No. Think of Mama when she was alive," I say gently. "The best magic is derived from emotions of love, not anger."

"I'll try," Aditi promises with a small nod, her delicate frame straightening. I take her hand in mine, channeling my snake magic.

I don't know how, but it feels like the Snake Master is right there at the back of my mind, guiding me, aiding me. It's easier than ever to feel and direct my magic properly. I squeeze Aditi's hand, imagining the water rippling, turning to glass. Our magic fuses together, light and dark, sweet and smoky. I keep going, keep digging, until—

Until I see Mama Anita within the water.

Aditi leaps for joy, but too fast the image of Mama Anita is swept away, replaced by the rippling reflection of the growing red moon that jolts us both back to reality. We have so little time left before the full Blood Moon arrives—a harbinger of the Eternal Night, the world as it was originally formed.

The world that the Snake Master wants me to help create.

An offer he gave me that I cannot, *will not*, accept. But I can't lie to myself—after living in the orphanage and alone on the streets, it feels good to be wanted. Even if it's by the Snake Master.

Or is that Raya's thinking?

"Lynx?" Aditi says, pointing at the water. Her finger shivers, and it takes me a moment to realize why.

Because it's not just the moon's reflection—the water is beginning to turn red. As red as the Snake River in my dreams. I recall Amara spilling her blood—no, the *Snake Master's* blood—in the river the night before the ceremony. With Veer's help, she must have been instigating the return of the Blood Moon.

Aditi and I stand, peering over the water. What's going on? The ground beneath my feet turns dry and cracked. Weeds at an unnatural angle, like death is imminent.

If the Eternal Night really is coming back . . .

With you, the Key, our Master shall be a god, I remember Veer saying.

All he needs is me.

The trees loom over me, vines like snakes hanging from centuries-old banyan trees. My hands turn cold as a snake's scales, and I feel my magic respond to my fear.

That's when I hear the hisses.

The vines that hang from the banyan trees slip and slide, moving on their own. I squint into the darkness as they move toward me. . . .

Not vines, I realize. *Snakes.*

Aditi screams, and I grab on to her and pull her close. I remember the way I'd brought the snakes from the terrarium to the Western Courtyard, that day at the palace. Now, somehow, I'm making snakes *come alive.*

Power floods through me, and my veins heat, blazing with a thousand fires.

"*Bring us to our Master . . .* ," the snakes hiss as one. I stumble backward, pulling Aditi with me, watching as the snakes grow in number, each of them slipping and sliding over one another as their beady black eyes fuse with mine.

"Stop!" I cry, and when I lash my hands out in front of me, splaying my palms, the snakes stop as if frozen. Gasping for breath, I yell, "Leave!"

It takes a few seconds for my eyes to adjust to the darkness. And soon, I see it—the snakes are hardening, turning brown as the earth beneath them. Their bodies wither away, slithering back toward the banyan trees they came from, becoming vines once more, swaying in the breeze.

I fall to my knees from all the power I've used, from the hissing filling my ears, from the tears streaking my face. When I look up into Aditi's eyes, I find a too-familiar fear in her gaze.

She's afraid of me. Of my power.

There's always been this darkness inside me. From thieving out on the streets, to the snakes that followed me as I walked home from the orphanage. I didn't know it then, but I know now.

This power could destroy me.

But this power is mine.

Sahil

Where the world ends, darkness shall begin.

Flecks of ash float with snow in the sky. From where I sit at the peak of Mount Davra, I can sense the woman, Amara, past the doorway of death. Her scent still fills my nostrils—wilted roses and cardamom. And . . . something permanent as a scar and scalding as hot tea.

Burnt and broken dreams.

Amara was the perfect host. After all, I needed to inhabit someone who possessed a strong form of magic, like the Memory Master's talisman; someone who could hold my magic, my thoughts, and my memories without fail. A feeble human would have simply shriveled and died with a Master living within them. But Amara possessed deep power. Her aims were the same as my own. Destruction. Revenge.

She served her purpose. How delicious it is now, to finally be freed of a mortal body—to feel the pads of my own fingertips, my feet touching the soil of tilled earth for the first time in a millennium.

Before me lie the six talismans so obediently given to me. With the right amount of focus and pressure, they obey my command, and shrink until they are small enough to look like charms. I attach them to the chain on my neck, feeling their power like a buzz of swarming insects. Immediately, my body reacts in kind, and my mind opens up, filled with possibilities. My vision grows sharper, so I can practically see over the horizon.

A mortal in possession of all the talismans is like a bird trapped in a cage. There is no granting mere mortals such power. It would consume them utterly. But a Master . . .

"Excuse me, O Mighty Snake Master," interrupts a man. I turn from my position, finding that the fellow is nearly out of breath from the climb. When he lowers his hood, I see he's just a boy. Verging on manhood, but a boy nonetheless. He wears a hooded cloak, and his palms are stamped with snake marks. A child of the Serpent's Tongue.

"You may approach."

The boy rubs his knuckles. "F-forgive me—"

"Speak, boy," I snap.

"I wish to tell you that the girl is headed for Kaama. We've spotted her leaving the Amratstanian palace. Her powers are growing ever stronger."

"Good," I tell him. "I've felt the change, too. But we cannot rush this. She must come to us of her own accord."

"Yes, O Mighty Snake Master."

I beckon him forward. "Come closer. Let me see your eyes."

Slowly, he inches forward. Fear-flecked, as I assumed.

"Hold no fear of me, young one. I wish only for respect, and I will share the same with you."

"Did you share the same with the Black Viper?" The boy jerks back almost immediately after speaking, and I can tell he didn't mean to speak his mind. I can't help the laugh that tumbles out of my mouth.

"Veer's death served a purpose greater than his life. The girl has proven her devotion, not only to us—but to herself. But you needn't worry, young one. So long as you serve me, you will be rewarded. I trust that you and your guardians have kept the Bloodstone safe?"

The boy nods, vigorously this time.

"No Master can stand against me, and no mortal will, either," I assure the boy. "I will tell you of how I banished all the Masters, even the final one who stood against me. Listen to my story, and then you will not need to fear."

Clouds gathered overhead as I approached the final living Master with sluggish footsteps. Her wiry hair, usually soft as clouds and hanging down to her waist, clung to her sweaty face and neck. The symbol of the skies blazed on her limbs like armbands, four swirls signifying the four winds. Today, however, I felt no wind from the north, south, east, or west. Today, there was only stillness.

A peace I hadn't felt in a long time.

"Please," Mandeep begged. "You're weak, brother. Look how using Raya's heart has changed you. She would never have wanted—"

"Don't you dare speak for my daughter." Her words thundered between my ears. Yes, my cheeks were sallow and my breaths labored.

Using the Bloodstone had indeed changed me. But it was a welcome change, a needed change.

A new beginning.

Rage settled like a stone on the Sky Master's shoulders. She summoned the winds, flaring out her hands, but in her exhaustion the effort was almost laughable, and I barely had to bat away her attempt at stalling me.

Next to the Snake River, this moment was almost poetic. My old home. I had already used the Bloodstone to dispense with the other four Masters, banishing them to the skies from this very spot. Now I faced my final adversary.

"I'm your sister. Like Preethi."

Mandeep's words made me pause. Preethi was my sister once. But the day she'd told me the truth, everything changed. I was never born as a Master. I was never meant to have brethren. I was a companion to a god, meant for greater things, and now, I too would ascend to that level.

"She kept my memories to herself," I said, feeling rage stir in me once more. "Do you know how I felt all my life? Under the torment of you and my other 'brethren'? My chest hollow? My skin always too tight, the air always too thick? I was born a snake. So a snake I shall be."

"No—" the Sky Master started. "You cannot kill us. Our spirits shall always remain."

I held out the stone in response, watching its red glow bathe the Snake River in blood.

I watched as my wish took hold on the last Master, and the wind carried her away, breaking her piece by piece until she was but dust.

Behind me, low murmurings assaulted the air. Windless, the world was. But as I turned, the cloaks of my followers swirled around their ankles, like rabid dogs awaiting a meal. It was time these mortals had a leader.

"Follow."

26

Rani

The stars of the Jhanswa Valleys are nothing short of brilliant.

I gently brush my fingers along the starscope before me like I'm petting my snake familiar. It's perched over the edge of a giant piece of sandstone, overlooking the desert dunes. The moon, a shade of light red, casts an eerie light over the desert below. The sands shift, looking like granules of fine cherry powder.

After a long day of travel, Dhruv, Amir, and I found a small tavern to stay in, and lumbered into sleep. I hated that my dreams were mostly nightmares—images of the Snake Master reborn, the Eternal Night sweeping over the world, or Ria finally confronting me to tell me what's wrong, only for her lips to dissolve to ash and my dreams with them. I confided in Dhruv about these dreams, and even told him of the Snake Master's ambitions upon his release from Amara.

Now, the following night, we've paused at a rest stop at this sandstone landmark, where thick crowds of people flit below, admiring the magic-crafted hills and stonebringer-forged statues. I move to gaze into the starstope again when a voice speaks from behind me.

"The starscope was invented by Queen Sunita herself, you know. She loved nature, but she also loved wondering about the worlds beyond our own."

I turn. There Dhruv stands, bag slung over his shoulder, wearing a lazy smile. My heart skips. "Hence the star-shaped trees," I conclude, pointing at the few carved trees peppering the desert landscape, before turning to peer through the starscope. Small flickering dots of light float across my vision. "Firebugs again?" I think of the last time I saw them, back in the restricted library. *They'll lead you where you need to go.*

Dhruv approaches me, his arm brushing against my side, and I cough to hide my nerves.

"Sands above," Dhruv says, pointing up at the sky. "That's the Memory Master constellation: Preethi's Star."

"There's a constellation named after her?" I ask, staring up. If I tilt my head, I think I see the outline of a face, eyes, a slim nose. It reminds me of when Amir pointed out the crown constellation while we sat in the Forest of Hearts. The constellation he was named after—*Amir. Prince.*

For many nights, I've tossed and turned in bed, unable to stop thinking about my and Dhruv's shared connections, shared hardships. The thread tethering us together, the ease with which we spend time with each other. Prince and princess.

But Amir doesn't need a crown to be royalty in my eyes. In many ways, he's a prince in his own right.

"Some say you can only see the constellation on auspicious evenings," Dhruv tells me. "Even more auspicious is that we're on the very path of her pilgrimage, the one she took long before the Snake Master's deceit." He points at a sandstone building not far in the distance. "There's a shrine there for the Memory Master. She was revered here in Retan, too, not just in Kaama where her descendants created their own kingdom."

"I never knew she was so well admired here," I breathe. "Or that she even took a pilgrimage." I think of how little I know of all the Masters. *You remind me of the Snake Master*, the Fire Master had told me. *He had goodness inside him once.*

Had he been talking about the Snake Master before Raya's death? I shiver, still unable to fully piece together the never-ending puzzle of my ancestor's life. His legacy.

A firebug drifts close to Dhruv, landing on his shoulder. I hold back a grin as he brings a hand to it, letting the bug drift onto his forefinger before bringing it close to his firestone necklace. I swear the necklace glows—either from the firebug, or . . .

My cheeks heat. *Some also believe that it glows when you're near someone you love.*

The firebugs in the library had led me straight to Dhruv, too. But what if my heart wants something—*someone*—different?

"It is as the Three Blessed Sisters believed," Dhruv says. "Knowledge can be just as great as magic. We brought the two together to find the chamber, didn't we?" He smiles, his eyes lit by the firebug.

"We did," I say, voice catching as Dhruv's eyes remain on mine. I'm reminded of the day at the waterfall, the peace I found with him.

Dhruv lets the firebug drift away, watching it in the distance. I catch myself studying his profile, the strength of his chin, the slight crook of his nose, a mix of powerful prince and rebellious boy.

"What?" the prince says softly, turning to me as if he senses my gaze. He takes my hand into his before lifting it to his face, dragging my thumb across his lower lip. "Am I drooling again?"

But he's not joking this time. His eyes are intent, smoldering. My thoughts are loud, a sandtiger's roar. *Dhruv. Amir. Dhruv. Amir.*

As he leans in, my palm heats, imprinted with the feel of Dhruv's lips. When he's a mere breath away, all I can see is that firestone at his neck, pulsing like a firebug's wings.

I pull back, too fast. Gasping in the humid air, I try to straighten my thoughts. Ignore Dhruv's all-consuming stare. He quickly glances away.

"I'm sorry," he breathes.

"Don't be. I just—" I start, flustered. "I must excuse myself."

Before Dhruv can say a word, I rush off. I skip down the sandstone steps two at a time, my heart kicking in my chest as I wade into the thick desert crowd.

Coldness sweeps over me. *What am I doing?* I know how I feel about Amir—I know how much I want to be with him.

And yet, an ache steals my breath. Being with Dhruv would be so *easy*. He would know what to say, what to do in front of even the snobbiest nobles. My parents would approve. And I would live my life without the worry that, one day, Amir will decide I'm not worth the scorn and the smirks he faces by my side.

And I would learn to exist without the passion and challenge that Amir brings to me every day. Without the love that inspired me to do the impossible.

I don't know how long I've been running when I finally stop for air. When I lift my eyes, the Memory Master's shrine is before me.

People filter out of the shrine as I enter, and within moments it's almost empty.

Almost. There is a boy here. When he turns, my heart stutters.

"Amir?"

In the dim light of the shrine, he no longer seems like a boy. Where Amir was once lanky, lean muscles now stretch the fabric of his shirt tight across his chest. I force my eyes back up.

"You scared me," I whisper. Oil lamps light the space around us, casting a glow across the relics in honor of the Memory Master. *Preethi*, I remember from the Snake Master's memory.

"I was just brushing up on my history," Amir states. "Apparently, a bustling city once existed here, before a great sandstorm tore through the outer villages. But this shrine remained intact, a symbol of the Memory Master's strength."

I draw in a breath. "Where did you learn all that from?"

"There was a plaque at the entrance." He winks.

I stifle a laugh, grateful for Amir's levity. I step closer to him, wanting to wrap my arms around him but knowing I shouldn't, not with my feelings so scattered. Still, Amir's gaze remains on mine, and mine on his, neither of us quite close enough to touch but feeling each other's heat.

"You . . . ," Amir begins, looking down while clearing his throat. "Were you with Dhruv?"

I blanch. Amir can see the answer on my face, and smacks a hand to his forehead. "Why did I say that? *Why* did I bring him up when—"

"When what?" I ask. When our eyes connect, my heart roars. Wishing, wanting, hoping.

"When . . . ," Amir begins before looking away. "When you've been spending so much time with him." He moves his gaze up halfway, to my lips. "Do you . . . like him?"

My lips burn in response, as if remembering both the warmth of Dhruv's lips hovering over mine, and Amir's lips during the Night of the Sisters.

At my silence, Amir fishes a coin from his pocket, fiddling with it. I reach over and brush the coin, fingers caressing his.

"Why don't you toss it and find out?" I say, removing my hand from his. "Kings, I like you; fools, I like Dhruv."

"You really like putting things up to chance?"

I smirk. "I think no matter how it lands, we're allowed to pick our fates."

Amir hides a grin. He flicks the coin with his thumb, and it lands back down on his hand. He smiles to himself, not looking away from me. We don't have to know which way it landed.

My heart tugs me toward him, but all my traitorous mind can remember is what nearly occurred moments ago with Dhruv.

What will happen when we return to Abai? Will Amir want to stay with me despite all I told him? Despite the uphill battle it might always be?

My heart's desires are a constellation of questions with no answers.

As my thoughts pound, Amir takes my hand, and I find comfort in the familiarity of it. He wraps his other arm around me, bending his head down so our foreheads are pressed together. Tears slide into my eyes and my lips ache as I reach up, caressing the stubble on his chin. With all the tumult in my heart, I haven't realized how much I've missed this. Missed *him*.

But a faint susurration from the front of the shrine makes me freeze. I turn, watching as the door blows open, revealing a woman with ghostly white hair and a pair of plum-colored eyes. A symbol on her wrist flares with light. An eye?

She tilts her head to the side, giving me a probing look. But somehow, fear does not enter my bones. She looks familiar.

She looks like—

"The Memory Master," I whisper. But how could that be? The Masters were all banished by the Snake Master. But somehow, my bones ring with truth. She shimmers like a mirage from the heavens above.

"Princess Rani of Abai. I have seen you many times over in my visions. In some, you are a savior to all. In others . . . you fall as your sister turns against you."

"I don't understand." My heart freezes in my chest. "Ria wouldn't turn on me."

The Memory Master dodges my comment. *"You seek the trial at the Malwan Pass,"* she says. *"I wish you Amran's luck on your journey, Rani. The Fire Master himself once controlled the fires of the volcano. He is the one who set the trial you must face."*

"You know what will happen during the trial?" Amir asks, shivering as he takes in the Memory Master, confusion crossing his features.

"Everyone's trial is different," the Memory Master—Preethi—reveals. *"But I did not come down to my shrine to warn you about that. Rather, there is something you must know. I know you saw that memory of the Snake Master,"* she whispers to me. *"He did not banish us like he thought. Sahil was my brother, once. I thought he deserved to know the truth of his life. Of his poison. But by that point he was beyond my reach. It only turned him more poisonous, more ravenous for power. His poison continues to grow."*

"The dying lands," I say, thinking of the withered flowers throughout Retan, the murky gray skies. All from the Snake Master's return. "The world is off-balance."

"And it will continue to be," reveals Preethi. *"For the Snake Master himself created the world with a poison that could never die. Unless . . ."*

"Unless?" I press.

The Memory Master thins her lips. *"To destroy the snake that created the world is to destroy that."*

She points at my hands, where I feel my snake magic thrumming through my veins. My mind rushes with a thousand questions.

"What does she mean?" Amir asks from behind me, arms crossed over his chest as if trying to suppress a shudder.

I turn back to the Memory Master. "Are you saying if we successfully destroy the Snake Master, my magic . . . will disappear?"

"The only way to end your feud with the Snake Master," she concludes, *"is to end the Snake Master himself. End your magic."*

End . . . *my* magic? Cold floods my veins. I think of my life as if it were Ria's, spent alone on the streets, thinking I have no magic. No Shima.

"Wait—" I say. But before I can move, the Memory Master begins to sparkle.

"You will know what to do, Rani," the Memory Master says. *"Your true destiny is yours to control."*

Then, with a swirl of the sands, she disappears.

27

Ria

The snakes won't leave my mind.

Last night, I dreamed of that bubbling red water, those vines coming alive. Slipping and slithering toward me until they wrapped around me and there was no beginning to Ria and no end to the snakes.

Like I was the Snake Master himself.

I haven't heard his voice in days, and even though the flames of tonight's hearth at our new camp pleasantly lick at the air, warming me from the outside in, there's still a coldness in my bones. An emptiness, going for so long without feeling his presence.

And Raya's.

That power washed through me like euphoria. Embracing the unruliness, the wildness, of my magic. My mother, Rani, Saeed, *everyone* wanted me to control myself—present myself to Abai like the princess they expected. But the truth is, I've never fit into a perfect box, and I don't know if I want to. Not after seeing how much I've evolved, how much I could still grow.

I bring my gaze upward. This far north, the night sky is incredible—and not like any sky I've ever seen. Blue-green light like puffs of smoke drift through the cloudless, starry sky above us.

"What *is* this?"

"The northern lights," Zoya explains, coming to sit at my side. "The phenomenon comes about in northern Amratstan once a year, around the time of the winter solstice."

"I've never seen anything like it." Back in Abai, even when I dreamed about leaving my birth kingdom and never looking back, I never imagined I'd see something as beautiful as *this*. My eyes tear up at the thought.

But Zoya looks up at the sky with a solemn face. The face of a princess torn from her duty. From the side, she shares many of her father's features—a sharp nose, stark silver eyes. I remember King Rohit's words to me, the last day we spent in Amratstan.

"Your father asked that I keep you safe, you know."

"I don't need protection," she says. But she laughs as she says it. I guess Princess Zoya is just as stubborn as me and Rani. Must be a princess thing. "I came on this journey because I want to help," she continues. "I've spent lots of time in my kingdom, and I know my way around it. We might be princesses of different kingdoms, but that doesn't mean we can't unite. After all, *we'll* be the rulers someday."

"Agreed," I say. As I stare at the green and blue lights spreading across the purpling backdrop of the sky, her last words trigger a thought—we *will* be the rulers. At least, Zoya will be. But that doesn't explain what will happen between me and Rani . . . which of us will take the throne.

A lump fills my throat.

Zoya crosses her arms over her fur cloak. She gazes at the smoke rising from the hearth, eyes softening. "I wanted to thank you, Princess Ria. For so long, I've been cooped up in the palace, I'm sure much like your sister once. To go on an adventure like this . . . even a daunting one . . . is something a princess should be willing to do for her people. My mother went on many adventures in her youth. I always wanted to be like her."

"I think you are," I say. "I always want to be like my caretaker, too. I lost her not long ago." I reach for her hand and squeeze, feeling her warmth entwine with mine.

She plants a hand over mine, a tear slipping from her cheek and falling to the ground. "Then let's remember them both."

But as she turns away, something miraculous happens. Where her teardrop fell in the snow, a small pink flower now rises to life.

"Come on," Zoya says, standing without noticing the flower, "I want to show you something else." She drags me away from the fire pit, from the tents where the twin Sentinels, Irfan, and Aditi sleep soundly.

And takes me to a shining silver lake covered in mist, where Saeed stands, smiling when he sees me.

But that smile is a mixture of joy and apprehension—does he want to talk about what happened to his mother?

"He wanted to meet you. *Privately.*" Zoya smiles shyly before turning away and heading back into the forest. I remove all thoughts of that strange flower that bloomed from her tear, gazing at the lake.

"You called me?" I begin.

Saeed nods. His eyes are no longer red-rimmed, but I still see grief around them, hovering like a shadow.

"I wanted to apologize for being so closed off the past few days. It's just . . . the way I behaved when my mother . . ." He shudders out a breath. "When my mother died. It was just so sudden, so unfair. I thought I would at least have the chance to speak with her, to try and convince her that—"

"Don't apologize, Saeed. Your mother didn't deserve any of that. Sometimes, the ones we love are taken from us too soon."

"And all we can do is treasure our memories of them," Saeed says, completing my thought. Although Saeed and I haven't always understood each other, we've endured hard times together. Now, with even more turmoil ahead, I wish I could forget everything we have yet to face, just so we could live hand in hand, heart in heart.

"Thank you for saying so, Ria," Saeed murmurs. "But I still want to apologize. My grief for my mother is no reflection on you. I'm sorry for the way I've treated you these past few days."

My throat closes up. I hate how easily he absolves me of guilt when he doesn't know the full truth of what happened.

"There's something else. Something I want to show you," Saeed reveals before I have a chance to respond.

"What is it?" I ask.

"It's not . . . physical." He sits on a rock by the lake and gestures for me to join him. I take my seat on the edge, apprehensive.

"You seem preoccupied," Saeed notices.

I clench my fists. This moment should be perfect. There's nothing between us but sparkling night air and the greenish-blue northern lights above us. But all I can think of is Amara's death—and everything that went horribly wrong.

"I suppose I shouldn't be one to talk. I mean, I'm preoccupied, too. I can still see my mother. In visions."

"Your . . . *mother?*" I ask. Why would she still be haunting Saeed's visions?

"I meant," he says, glancing down at my hands, perched on my lap, "that they haven't been visions of the future, but memories of the past. Memories of *her*."

My cheeks redden as a sharp wind knifes past. "What have you seen?"

He bites his lower lip, and I catch myself staring. "I want to show you. If you'll let me."

"You want to transfer a vision to me? Is that even possible?"

"We've made our snake magic and memory magic work in tandem in the past, haven't we?"

"Yeah, by—" I cut myself short. *By kissing.* Well, almost. I find myself wishing to hear Shima's snarky voice in my ears, some biting remark to make me snap back to the present, though I know she's fast asleep. "You know," I add quietly.

"I think I know a different way," he says, leaning close to me. "May I?" He slips his hands around my palms, cradling them. I swear his touch could light a fire from how much it makes my blood spark.

"And how, exactly, does this work?" I say, keeping a lightness to my tone. If I say anything else, I think my breaths might run short.

"Just watch." As he cups my hands together, silver light wisps out from between our intertwined fingers, his magical aura pressing against mine. He opens our hands so our palms are facing the sky. Like the bright northern lights above, a new light display is at work: one made from Saeed's own memory magic.

In the silver wisps, a scene grows to life. I see everything he wants to show me—

His mother, cradling him as a babe. His mother, stewing together a meal fragranced with clove and cardamom. His mother, reaching out for him, whispering a promise into his ear.

"I will always protect you."

When Saeed lets go of my hands, the scene washes away. The silver wisps float into the air, disappearing into the colorful light of the sky.

"That's what I wanted to show you," he says. I shiver, thinking of Amara as I've never known her. As a woman Saeed has known, held on to, for his whole life. She looked nothing like the maniacal woman that fell into the Snake Pit. She had a past, once. A life of her own.

Before she lost it.

"That was a beautiful memory," I say.

"I wanted to share it with you," Saeed murmurs, glancing down. "I sometimes feel as if I'm the only one who will remember her that way. And I don't want her to be remembered for the wrongs she did."

"She won't be," I tell him fiercely. I'm reminded of the love the Snake Master held in his eyes when he spoke to Raya and Ruhanya, before everything went wrong. The home, the safety, he had so desperately wanted to give them. Before the Great Deceiver was born.

I wish, too, that there was more the world would remember of him. Maybe we wouldn't be in this situation now.

"The world won't remember her as the villain, Saeed. I promise."

Saeed's gaze flickers up to mine.

After the snowbird incident, it feels like Saeed and I have been dancing around the topic of me and him. And after what happened to his mother, it didn't feel right to bring it up. That day in the snow feels like it belonged to another lifetime. The feel of him pressed against me that day now seems almost as if I imagined it.

I'm very good at the art of avoiding.

"You know," he whispers, "some say when you see the northern lights for the first time, it's the perfect night to make a wish."

I arch a brow. "You think I believe that so easily? I was a thief, after all. And thieves don't rely on wishes. We rely on our hands and our eyes. Our senses."

He bites back a smile. "You caught me there," he says. "Still. I want to make a wish."

I'm hit with a memory of being alone with Amir on the streets of Abai, sleeping in alleyways like curled-up cats, dreaming of a life up here in Amratstan, or down south in Retan. I guess I got part of my wish—traveling to an unknown place, a wish in my pocket, and hope as bright as the starlit sky.

"What will you wish for?" I ask him.

"Isn't it obvious?" he says, looking to the sky. His proud, strong nose is illuminated, followed by his deep-hazel eyes. "Shall we wish together, Princess Ria? Or are you afraid of having your thief card revoked?"

I playfully elbow him. "Fine. I'll make a wish." I nod, and we tilt our heads together. "One," I say.

"Two," he follows.

"Three," we both say.

I wish for us to return safely home, for the peace treaty to be signed with Kaama. I wish for the Snake Master to end his hopes for destruction.

And, despite the distance between us, despite all the things I can't bring myself to tell Saeed, I wish for something else. Something I don't have the courage to say aloud.

A future with Saeed accepting me, Ria instead of Rani, wholly and completely. Magic and thievery all.

Saeed grasps on to my hand once we've both made our wishes. "Ria, I know you're never supposed to speak a wish aloud, but right now I want to." There's a hunger in his eyes I haven't seen before, a yearning, a wanting.

The scent of Saeed's soap tugs on my senses—a heady, musky scent. His breath puffs into the air as he arches toward me, our lips inches away. My core heats, every inch of me burning, aching.

"I know," I say as I lean in. I want to kiss him as myself, Ria, a girl who was once nameless and now carries the weight of a new history, a new dawn.

My lips soften beneath the first touch of his mouth, and it's like the fire banked within us both for so long roars to the front. He parts my lips with his tongue, and my fingers find purchase in his curls. Not a second later, he brings a hand to my leg and I move to straddle him, wrap my legs around his torso so my back faces the lake. Our kisses grow deeper, and I bring my hands down under his cloak, grasping at the seashell buttons on his kurta. My fingers brush the skin underneath, the planes of his chest. My thoughts grow heady, consumed with heat and ice, everything opposite melding together into one.

"I missed this," he says against my lips when we break away for air. "While I was gone from the Abaian palace . . . I never stopped thinking about you." He returns his lips to mine for another kiss—one I don't want to break away from.

I never stopped thinking about you. Me. Ria. But what version of me? The one Mother and Rani see, or the one who killed a man in cold blood?

He means me, every inch of me he's gotten to know.

I just don't know how much longer I'll be that same Ria.

Saeed softly snores next to me that night. I opted to sleep in his tent, so as not to wake Aditi or Shima, but it seems sleep won't come for me. As I shiver under my thick fur blankets, I don't wish the nightmares away. Not tonight. After Saeed confided in me, I finally know who I have to confide in.

I channel my snake magic, dig into it, the way Shima has taught me all this time. I feel my snake familiar, fast asleep. I sense the camp—still, silent, all sleeping.

I won't be afraid any longer.

I press a kiss to Saeed's forehead and creep out of the tent, heading for the ghostly lake.

I sit by the water and close my eyes, pressing my fingers into the snow beneath me. I unfurl each element of snake magic, each lesson I've learned, until that mindscape fills my every thought.

"*Come, daughter of snakes . . .*" I hear him say.

"Welcome me, Snake Master."

There's a tug from within me, that cobra rising. When I open my eyes to that dark mindscape where we first met, I know I've done it.

"*Ria,*" he says from behind me. I turn. "*I must admit, I am surprised you came so quickly.*" His black cloak swishes around him and I watch those tiny snakes slip and slide around him, hissing as they call for me.

"Tonight is a night of surprises," I tell him, thinking of my kiss with Saeed. I approach him, keeping my gaze steady as my heart thumps in my chest. I see that cord between us, taut as a high-strung bow. A symbol of his connection to the piece of Raya within me.

"*Indeed it is*," he says, lowering his hood. For the first time, I see his face, the scales covering flesh. I see an inkling of myself, my power, my bloodline.

"Will you help me with my powers?" I ask. His words have been haunting me for days.

The Snake Master smiles at me. "*Yes, Ria. I spoke true. I am the only one who can help you with your powers.*"

"And what would you get out of it?" I challenge. Part of me knows the answer. Knows what he wants.

The Snake Master tents his scaly fingers. "*Your magic must be harnessed. The Blood Moon swiftly approaches, and you are the Key to the Eternal Night's return.*"

"Tell me what will happen," I say, "if the Eternal Night returns."

"*A new world*," he says vaguely. "*If we work together . . . you cannot imagine the world we could create and rule. A world that we shall shape. I saw that desire in you, Ria. I know you feel it, too.*"

Part of me—the old Ria—wants to disagree. But the present Ria can't. I feel it, my connection to him, ringing in my bones. That cobra rising within me. Have I always had this connection to the Snake Master? I was a thief. Am still a thief, in so many ways. A deceiver in my own right.

Despite the Snake Master having deceived Amara, I can't pull back. I need to strengthen my magic, *embrace* it, the way a flower embraces the sun and the moon embraces the tide.

I extend a hand, not daring to move my eyes from his.

"I accept your offer."

PART THREE

A Shattering of Storms

28

Rani

Rolling waves against a black sky. Volcanoes dark as shadows in the night. Like behemoths, sleeping giants waiting to awaken.

We've arrived at the Malwan Pass.

After three more days of rest and travel, the horses pause at a narrow dirt road covered in volcanic ash. The Pass is a straight path, volcanoes towering on either side of us, leading directly to Abai's southernmost border. Home feels so far and close at the same time, within reach yet miles away.

"We made it," I breathe. I dismount the horse after Amir slides off. He's still not used to riding, I can tell, despite all the time we've spent together on horseback. A thief never truly learns to get off his feet, I suppose.

The entire way here, my mind couldn't escape the Memory Master's warning. Each night since, I've dreamed of a hundred different paths my future could take. Could my magic really disappear? Is the Blood Moon prophecy destined to come true, or can we change it like we did the prophecy about our birth?

And what did she mean that in her visions she saw Ria turning against me? Was she speaking of the old prophecy—the one we thwarted?

Or a new one?

I won't let that happen. My sister is not just my blood; she is my other half, the piece I've been missing my whole life. I wouldn't dream of a world without her—or a world where we were pitted against each other.

Almost against my will, I remember the night we tried reopening the Snake Pit. Ria's mind seemed elsewhere. Her magic felt like it was working *against* me instead of with me.

"This way," Dhruv says, pointing at the trail. In the darkness, it's hard to make him out, but then I feel his cool hand softly grasping mine and leading me forward. My shoulder brushes against his as he tugs me ahead, and I don't dare think about what almost happened a few days ago. Not that Dhruv or I have spoken about it, instead always dancing around the subject.

Our footfall is the only sound as we meander on the path, Amir way behind. Wind whistles past us, kicking up dirt and debris from the once-active volcanoes. These aren't normal volcanoes—they're *magical* ones. Ones the sisters knew would help me destroy the Bloodstone.

If I pass my trial.

Once I pass it, I correct myself. We continue on until we reach the forked path, just as the queens foretold.

A forked path—a place where fates veer.

Dhruv or Amir; princess or thief. It seems my life lately has been full of decisions.

I will have to make one now.

Dhruv lets go of my hand and speaks low so Amir cannot hear. "I've been afraid of getting close to you, Rani. Afraid of *this*." He gently clasps the glowing firestone at his throat.

Me too, I answer silently. I hate the way Dhruv's eyebrows curve with despair. The way he speaks with something between regret and longing.

"Do you believe in destiny, Rani? Ever since my father left, I've been afraid. Afraid I'm destined to become like him and abandon my family. Abandon the ones I love."

Is *that* why Dhruv had a rebellious phase—and a tortured heart?

I press a finger to his lips, shushing him. "Dhruv, no matter what happens . . . you're not bound to your destiny. You'll become a great king."

"And you a great queen," he says against my finger. He leans in, placing the smallest kiss beside my lips. "Oh," I say when he moves back. My lips tingle and warm.

"Good luck, Rani."

Dhruv retreats, but I'm rooted to the ground.

I shake myself. I need to focus on what's ahead of me, now.

I take the left path, as the triplet queens instructed, and it leads me to a cave glittering with stones. Rubies and gems that are not too different from the bloodred ruby we once hunted for.

Before I can enter the cave, I hear something behind me. A rustle. I shriek before turning.

"Oh!" Mortified, I realize that it's only Amir, his hair tousled and shirt stretched thin, arms dangling at his sides like he doesn't know what to do with them.

"I . . . came to wish you good luck," Amir begins, planting a hand on the back of his neck. "I know you're a bit scared—"

"Scared?" I raise an imperious brow. "Princesses don't get scared." Though I speak playfully, a part of me wills the statement to be true. Fear has no place in a trial.

"It's okay to have fear, Rani," Amir says, taking my hands, his own sizzling warm unlike Dhruv's. "No one is perfect. Not even me," he adds with a cheeky grin.

I chuckle, releasing his hands and wrapping my arms around him in a hug. I plant my head against his chest and breathe out slowly. "It's true. I . . . I guess I am scared." The sisters didn't tell me what this trial would entail—just that it would test me in ways I never imagined.

"If we didn't have fear, we would never have met," Amir says simply.

I pull back. "What do you mean?"

"If I wasn't afraid of letting down my sister, I wouldn't have left her and found Ria. Wouldn't have found *you*," he corrects. "And if you weren't afraid of staying in your old life—afraid of never fulfilling your tutor's old wish—you wouldn't have found me." His voice breaks.

"I thank the stars I found you, Amir," I whisper. "You've always been there for me."

"Hey, you were there for me, too. You helped me reconnect with Sanya and Jas. You helped me remember what believing in something meant." He swipes aside one of the locks of hair that have fallen from my braid and tucks it behind my ear. His fingers linger there for a moment before sliding down to my neck, wrapping around the back of it, and pulling me closer.

I hover there for a moment, our lips breaths apart, before he smiles and plants a kiss on my forehead. "Good luck."

Two kisses in the span of minutes.

"I'll need it," I breathe, neither of us pulling back. After a few beats pass, I finally give in and hug Amir once more, my closest confidant in this whole world, and remember every instance we shared together.

I don't want to lose you, I think.

When we pull apart, he leaves with a parting glance. I square my shoulders and face the cave once more.

As soon as I enter, the stones on the walls begin to glow one by one, forming a line. A path—a direction.

I follow the glowing stones. The path leads me to a cavern with a lone pedestal in the center. The lights of the stones illuminate an object on the pedestal. At first, it looks like a stone, but as I move closer, the object glows. An orb of light, with rippling smoke floating in and around it. I reach out, feeling a cool sensation prickle my fingers as I grasp the orb. Then, with a sudden invisible tug, I feel myself slipping into the orb itself, and falling into a world of white.

Whispers attack me from all angles, jibes as sharp as knives. *"She is here . . . the Snake Princess."*

I turn, searching for the source of the sound. But the whispers come from invisible forms.

"We should introduce ourselves—"

"—the girl must be tired from traveling—"

"—we haven't had a visitor in centuries—"

"Can someone please explain what is going on?" I interrupt.

"Welcome to the Malwan Pass," a voice says. *"We are desert dwellers, invisible to the human eye. We were born from the fires of these volcanoes, made by the Fire Master's very touch."*

"Our bodies are shapeless," comes another voice. *"We have no company but each other . . . until now. You are here to seek out the Fire Master's trial, then?"*

"I—" I gather my thoughts. Never have I heard of invisible desert dwellers. If the sisters hadn't pointed me here, I would have already left the cave, certain this was some kind of trick.

"This is no trick, my girl."

"How did you—" I pause. So, desert dwellers with mind-reading powers, too. I suppose I've seen stranger magic before.

"To answer your question, yes," I say, breathing deeply. "I'm here for my trial."

"Then a trial you shall have."

A sudden wind sweeps away the darkness. Red light glows beneath me, a pulsing heartbeat. I turn in place before realizing I'm standing on a small platform made of obsidian, just large enough to fit my feet. I wobble, careful not to fall. My stomach drops when I see how high up I am.

Standing over an ocean of lava.

Standing atop a *volcano*.

My heart sinks to my feet. I cover my mouth with a hand. This is not real—this is a trial.

I lower myself and hang on to the pedestal with both hands. "What do I have to do?" I ask shakily.

"Face your fears and find the truth. Ice shall dismantle; fire shall liberate. Solve the riddle, and you shall receive the thing you seek."

My brain fizzles with questions. "What is the riddle? What will I have to face?"

The desert dweller doesn't answer. But it doesn't have to. Because before me, rising from the fires of the lava, is the most fearsome creature I have ever seen.

The creature bares its teeth, sharp as fangs. The fires illuminate fur black as night, a wet snout raised into the air. A howl rips from its throat, so loud it shakes me to my bones. Its eyes are reddish orange, the lava below us reflected in them like flames from a hearth.

In seconds, the creature pounces at me like a wolf. I barely have time to register the leap before I'm moving. I wobble on the platform, looking down to find another one nearby, and I leap over as the creature attacks. It skims my arm, claws raking my skin. "*Ugh!*" I scream, landing on my knees on the next platform, my shoulder vibrating with pain. The creature crashes into the rock behind me and snarls.

I shiver despite the lava around me. This heat is scorching, like a hot day in Anari Square rather than the pleasant warmth of Amir's touch.

Amir. I wish he were here with me now.

Before I can think of him for long, I notice the silence behind me. Something keeps me glued to the floor, so I spin my torso.

The creature is gone.

In its place are a thousand tiny black particles, swirling into the shape of a funnel.

My hair whips around my face, and the chunni once clinging to my shoulder flies off, sucked into the vortex of dust. I close my eyes, bracing myself against the wind and grasping desperately at whatever I can find on this rocky platform.

"Rani!" someone yells.

I turn. It can't be. "Amir?"

Dust swirls on a nearby platform, and a figure appears in the shroud. The dust falls, revealing him.

Amir.

Somehow, some way, it's true. Amir is in my trial. I rise to my feet. "How—what—?"

"I don't know," Amir says, though it sounds more like a yell. He leaps to my platform and then clutches my arm, but the vortex makes me stumble. He pulls me back, away from the vortex—

Until we're both falling.

Until we're plunging toward the lava.

Until the cave disappears, and I'm lying on top of Amir, crashing to the floor with a grunt. My bones shake. I cough out a cloud of dust.

"Where . . . are we?" I croak, pulling myself up off Amir's chest. We're standing in a dark desert, the creature gone, only a circle of dust swirling on the sand before us.

I hold the side of my head. Did I imagine the wolflike creature and the vortex? Or was that the first part of my trial . . . somehow summoning Amir?

Queen Sampada told me that the trial would test the mind. She was right. But the scrapes and bruises already littering my arms let me know that trial will have consequences beyond my mind alone.

"I dunno—" Amir's voice catches in his throat. He turns to me. "I was waiting outside the cave. Somehow, I felt you were in danger. Like you were calling me. And . . . I ended up in your trial."

I swallow thickly. I had been thinking of his name. Thinking of him.

Then the particles of dust begin to move in front of us, this time taking the shape of . . .

. . . a rising serpent. Exactly like the birthmark that formed when Ria and I connected our arms, the first day we met.

"*Sisters of the snake,*" I whisper, remembering the prophecy of me and my twin.

The cobra, now a ghostly-looking shadow, darts at us with its fangs bared. It crashes into the sand between Amir and me as we split ways and plunge to the ground. Hissing with fury, the ghostly snake rears its head at us.

That's when I notice something strange. Like a limb, the snake is *growing* something off the side of its head, taking the shape of another. The creature now bears two heads, two sets of fangs, and four menacing, beady red eyes, all attached to one shadow body.

"Run. Now." Amir stumbles toward me, but I catch him by the arm.

"No!" I shout. "This is a trial. We can't run . . . we have to face it. Or else we'll—"

End up like the Three Blessed Sisters.

I feel the daunting stares of the snake on me.

Control it, Rani, I think, but its vicious red eyes and dripping fangs root me in place with terror.

"I can do this," I mutter to myself.

"You need to do it fast," Amir pants. He's tense, poised to run.

"I know." But as the snake slinks closer, looming like a shadow even against the night sky, I feel my snake magic slip away from me, writhing like Shima when I first held her. Our connection wasn't always easy. In fact, the first time I met her, her fangs drenched in blood from a fresh kill, I ran screaming.

I hold a hand out, like I'm keeping that writhing snake in place. My magic *must* listen to me.

I do not want to hurt you, I tell the creature. Its eyes flash with recognition. It slinks closer, and Amir moves to brace me, his presence steady by my side.

Listen to me, I say, rifling through the many drawers of my snake magic, pushing every ounce of it I possess toward the monstrous snake. *Listen to me and stop this.*

The snake halts and, before my eyes, begins to grow smaller.

Was this it? Have I faced my fears, passed my trial?

I hold my ground as the snake shrinks, its body separating until it forms twin serpents that I recognize.

"Shima!" I cry. The two snakes are an identical copy of her, both eerily ghostlike beneath the moon. I drop to the ground, trying to touch them, but my hand passes right through their silky snakeskins.

One of us is not like the other, says the first snake. *One of us is true, the other false. You must use your mind to find out which is which.*

And then you must kill one of us, the second says.

"What?" I shout. "I can't—" I gulp as the two Shimas begin to look more and more real, their eyes piercing and lined with rose, their scales fluttering between green and blue.

Choose wisely, the first snake warns.

Your choice will affect your snake companion in reality, the second hisses.

They both look steadily at me, identical down to their very last scale.

I can't get this wrong. I *can't* kill Shima.

"Tell me the first thing you ever said to me when I was eight summers old," I demand.

They answer as one: *Excuse me, but do you know where I can find a spare rat around here?*

I huff. I know I won't have long to keep questioning them, so instead I shut my eyes and focus on coming up with something better. Stronger.

Shima, help me, I tell her. The real Shima will hear me. She *must* hear me.

Control your past, she says to me, her ever-familiar voice jolting through me. *To command your future.*

Control. I've never had much of that. I was always losing track of Shima, letting my magic slip loose, even getting jarring headaches after sharing a short conversation with her. Every moment I've spent with her flashes through me. Anger when she ripped my lehengas apart. Annoyance when she first commented on my relationship with Saeed. Love when my parents showed me none of the sort.

I cannot lose her now.

I've used my snake magic to convince others to do things, to *believe* me when I spoke. I've used it to command snakes to do my bidding. But now, I must snag on to something new. My eyes shutter closed. I visualize the magic I need, coaxing it out like a snake to its prey.

When I open my eyes, the world looks different. Like I'm looking through a snake's eyes. Everything is tinged a shade of green. The tether I always feel with Shima comes forth, sliding in the air and coming to life. I see my magic at work, coiling and spiraling right to both snakes.

An idea sparks inside me. Only one Shima can truly feel my magic; only one Shima will share my bond.

As I draw closer to the snake on my right, I notice something wrong with the tether between us. It's sparkling, but beneath the light, the thread is breaking. I speak again to Shima telepathically.

Shima, if you hear this, I miss you.

The thread breaks further.

I was once afraid of you.

The bond gets looser.

During our Bonding Ceremony, I felt like I would die. Like the pain would split me bone from skin. But you kept me together. You kept us together. I've always feared my magic, and the truth is, I never grasped it quite the way Ria has. In fact, it scared me how quickly she learned to possess snake magic.

Go on, the right snake shudders out. The bond is so close to snapping, I could pull it like a rope. But truth will outwit strength in this trial.

I've learned not to be afraid. My parents gave Ria up out of fear. They traded her life away in cowardice, unwilling to try to change the future they saw. There's nothing I can do to change her past. But I accept her. I accept my parents. I accept my magic, no matter how inferior it may seem. And . . .

I take a deep breath, the words I've doubted for so long ready to be freed. Words spurred on by all my conversations with Prince Dhruv.

I'm ready to be queen. I'm ready to one day take the throne of the Great Snakespeaker and care for my people.

The thread finally snaps, breaking from the snake. It crumples to the ground in a heap.

Congratulationssss, says the left snake.

"Thank Amran," I say, tears welling in my eyes as I lean down and gather the snake in my arms. The green film coating the world washes away as my snake magic slinks back into its drawers.

Shima feels real now, solid as the sands, and I let her coil around my wrist. Familiar, warm, and true. I shut my eyes, relishing in her touch.

The desert dwellers' words ring through my mind. *Face your fears and find the truth.*

And I found Shima.

When I open my eyes, my snake familiar is gone, but her warmth lingers.

The sand whirls around me like a second vortex.

"We have to move!" Amir says, pulling me back. The sand stings my eyes as we rush away, away, and into the nearest thing nearby.

A small, dilapidated stone hut.

We slam our way inside, shutting the door behind us as the sand crashes against the doorframe.

I hold my breath. *One. Two . . .*

And open my eyes when I hear Amir let out a noise of recognition.

Tears rush to Amir's eyes as he takes in the house we stand in, the little moonlight pouring in. The timepiece lying on a forlorn couch, identical to Amir's.

A shiver trails down my spine.

"Amir . . . ," I begin. "Is this . . . ?"

"My old home," he says, letting go of the doorknob and heading deeper into the room. "Yes." He glances at the timepiece, then pulls the same one from beneath his shirt. "This . . . isn't possible."

I approach him and bend down. "We're in a trial. Maybe it is," I say.

Control your past to command your future.

"You mean, we're in the . . ."

"Past?" I finish, just as two figures appear on the sofa. One of them, a woman, cradles a baby in her arms.

"What should we name him?" the woman says, looking into her lover's eyes.

"Amir," the man says swiftly, brushing the baby's bundle of hair back. "For he will one day be a prince."

Amir chokes on his words beside me. "Is that . . . ?"

I nod, unable to speak. The father leans down, pressing a kiss to the baby's forehead, while the baby fusses. Finally, the child calms down.

"When he is older, I shall give him this." The father lifts the timepiece from the couch with sparkling eyes.

"This is incredible," I whisper. I turn to Amir, but suddenly, his face has gone cold.

"I want to leave," Amir clips, then turns on his heel and heads for the door.

"Why?" I ask. He twists the knob, but the door won't budge. When I turn back, his parents are gone. The room dims as two mirrors take their place. One is ornately framed with gilded flourishes. Embellished snakes with golden eyes peer over the mirror frame. The other mirror is much plainer, though it still boasts a silver border and the symbol of an eye on top. The Memory Master's eye.

Amir steps forward. In each mirror, a new reflection greets him. The gilded mirror reflects a man with Amir's face but a princely stature, a laurel-leaf crown fitted to his head and extravagant clothes wrapping around his form. He looks calm, cool, something assured in his expression that's scarily like Prince Dhruv's. I step into view of the mirror, but my reflection goes further, placing a kiss on Amir's cheek and wrapping my arms around him from behind.

Amir reaches out, but his hand ripples against the mirror like it's silver water.

"This is another trial. *Your* trial," I realize. I faced the snakes head-on, *controlled* them, and found the real Shima. I confessed everything I felt about my heritage, becoming queen, and my renewed relationship with snake magic. Now, it's Amir's turn to seek the truth. *His* truth.

In the other mirror, Amir roams countries living a thief's life, barely keeping out of trouble. Barely getting by with the bruises on his skin and the hunger in his belly.

Who he would've been, had he never met Ria or me.

"*Choose carefully,*" comes a voice of the desert dwellers. "*Tell us your wish and it will be yours.*"

"That's easy," Amir says, even as I notice him working his jaw.

He reaches for the gilded mirror again, but this time, the snakes around the mirror's frame come alive and slither up his arm, over his legs, and around his neck. They don't stop the onslaught, wrapping tightly around his skin and cutting off circulation so he's clasping at his throat for air.

"Stop!" I shout. Amir collapses to the ground, air stuck in his throat. I try to rip the snakes off him, control them with my magic, but I've suddenly lost that spark. Fury overtakes me as I look up. "He never made his choice! You told him to tell you— and he never did!"

"*His actions spoke loudly enough,*" the dweller responds.

"Give him another chance. Please," I beg. My fingers scrabble uselessly against the golden snakes wrapped around his throat. I watch as Amir's face blanches, as life bleeds out of him. Just like it bled out of Raya. Out of the Three Blessed Sisters. *Not him*, I think desperately.

"*What do you propose?*"

"A trial is supposed to be fair. He never gave his answer," I insist, voice hoarse. "Let him try again. Make it harder if you must."

"*Harder,*" the voice mimics, intrigued. "*If you wish it to be so. . . .*"

Suddenly, the snakes slink away. Amir gasps for air. I cry as I cradle him in my arms, shock coursing through me at what almost happened. When I finally wipe my tears away, the hut is gone. We're back in the desert, but the two mirrors remain. Amir struggles to his feet.

"Harder?" he coughs. "I almost died, Rani."

While I know it's in jest, and I'm elated to see Amir is partly all right, I can't help but shiver at his words.

What have I done?

"*This is your last chance,*" the dwellers warn. "*Enter your new trial. Pick your poison . . . or we shall poison you.*"

29

Ria

I kneel before the Snake Master, bowing my head.

"*You will be a good student,*" he purrs, planting a hand atop my ahead, and I feel a strange buzz go through me, like a flash of lightning and the hiss of snakes. The serpent blood in my veins ignites, and the cobra slinking in my belly writhes with pleasure.

I rise.

It's been one day since I accepted the Snake Master's offer. One day of travel, of camping in the cold Amratstanian woods, only to have awoken in the middle of the night and tapped into my power, entering this strange mindscape to train with my ancestor.

Talk about an unlikely alliance.

There's no other choice, I remind myself. I have to learn. I have to know how I can wield my magic.

The cobra within me grins. Raya. Does part of me enjoy this, being with him? I can finally revel in the darkness simmering in my veins, embrace my magic.

"*I am glad you returned here tonight, dear Ria,*" he tells me. "*Not many would have had the courage to face me. I am sure you've heard the stories of me, your ancestor? The Great Deceiver?*"

"You have quite the reputation."

"*I do,*" he says. "*But do you know why I was given the moniker?*"

I think of what I saw the night of Zoya's birthday, when I slipped into the mindscape and met the Snake Master for the first time. "I saw your memories."

"*My home was burned. My daughter, dead. I was born with no heart; I gave it to the world, and I was reviled for it.*" With a swoop of his hand, his snakes flee from his cloak and rush to the edges of this dark space, squealing. I hear a crunch—feel them satiate themselves. I smell the rats all too well.

It's a good thing Shima's asleep.

He leads me deeper through the dark room to a lit fire. Everything feels like a dream—this entire world—but I know it isn't one. It's the strength of my magic, my connection to the Master himself.

I won't ignore him any longer.

He called me the Key, and if my magic, dark and strange and wondrous, is true, then that means I'm also the only one who has a connection to him deep enough to . . .

Help him bring back the Eternal Night, an insidious voice within me says.

He drops his cloak, and I see him for what he truly is.

A snake.

The lower half of his body is nothing but a snake's tail drenched in blood. The top half of him looks human—as human as a Master can appear.

"Here, a place of my own creation, I can show you what I have always been. Never truly a snake and never truly a Master, but something in between."

I force myself to look away from his snake tail. "Why?"

"You have seen, haven't you, Ria?" he says, red eyes piercing mine.

I did. "Tell me more. About the Eternal Night."

He leans down so his face is lit by the fire. *"I shall. But only because your magic is like no other snakespeaker's I've ever seen, in all my years in the Pit."*

"You . . . watched me?" I shudder. Did he see me when I first practiced opening the Pit with Shima? Sensed me when I switched places with Rani? Yes . . . I'd heard his voice before. He was speaking to me through the Pit, his hiding place.

He chuckles darkly. *"Many others in my line have been powerful, too. I thought they would be the Key. But you—you are something else. The cord between us is proof enough."*

"I've only just discovered my magic," I say.

The Snake Master licks his lips. *"And yet, your power is extraordinary. Power is a delicious thing. Don't you agree, Ria?"*

"Power can taste rotten, too."

The Snake Master looks pleased. *"Even rotten things find a way to thrive. It is why my poison spread so widely across the earth. It was never intentional, not at first. My brethren should have known that.*

But once I saw the way they regarded me, like I was a monster . . . well, I suppose we're all a little monstrous, aren't we?"

I think about the power fluttering through me, the dark feelings that claimed me the moment I touched Veer's snake mark back on the boat. *I saw the way you maimed the Black Viper,* the Snake Master had told me afterward. *You could have stopped, but you didn't.*

Because it felt good, hurting Veer. It felt good to be in control. *And when I killed him . . .*

I shudder, removing the thought. *"Only your power equals mine,"* the Snake Master continues. *"I knew I would be weak when leaving Amara's body. I needed the six talismans to release myself, and with them, attain a power only Amran has held."* His whole body seems to glow, brighter than a Master's, brighter than a god's. *"The world sees me as one thing, a Master of deceit. Perhaps I am. When one only hears cruel stories of themselves, they can easily become those stories. Yet I am more still. I am snake, I am Master. We exist in multitudes. And so do you, dear Ria."*

His words ring true in my bones. "I'm a thief. And a princess. Both."

I'd thought the same thing just weeks ago, when Rani and I came together after our little showdown with Amara. But now, after weeks of being separated from Rani, after weeks of fueling the dark magic in my veins . . . am I still the same Ria I left back at the Abaian palace?

Can I be more? Should I be?

"That's right," he says, coaxing me to speak.

"I'm not just one thing," I continue. "The world saw me as a thief, scorned me as a street vagrant . . . Now I want them to see me as their ruler."

"*We can both be more than we are,*" he says, slithering closer until he's nearly towering over me. "*Soon, I shall use the Bloodstone, the gift born from Raya, to finally offer myself my own heart. The world can keep the poisoned, mangled heart they so scorned. And I shall give them what they deserve: an Eternal Night that will give way to an eternal dawn.*"

"A new world," I say, thinking of his words earlier.

He tents his fingers. "*I made the world, didn't I? It is only fitting that I reset it. Now that I possess all the talismans, I hold the power of Amran, which will help me achieve the impossible. When I am strongest on the night of the Blood Moon, I shall unleash my godlike power and attempt something never before seen. I will open a door to the Eternal Night. And you, dear Ria, are the Key to that door.*"

I remember all those dreams of wanting to open a door—wanting so badly, but always failing to see what was on the other side. Was it always going to come to this? Was I always meant to fulfill this destiny?

That's when the Snake Master grins. "*I shall bring forth a new Eternal Night. I shall change the course of history. Call it a second chance, if you will,*" he says. "*It is what Raya would have wanted. A world I wanted her to see.*"

Me. Raya. One and the same.

"*But it is not Raya I need now. All I need, dear Ria, is you.*" He illuminates the cord between us, and I notice that it's thicker now, like rope.

He must see the startled look on my face because the Snake Master rumbles a laugh.

"Can't you see? We are the same. Each of us a rattlesnake wishing to be a cobra. So be it. Become the cobra within you. Believe in it, my apprentice."

I let my trembling hands fold in toward me, snapping at the cobra within me to rise. It does, hissing at me, craving more power.

"Keep going."

This time, I welcome the cobra. I tell it to fuse with me until we are one. I imagine that door in my mind turning to flames. But instead of the image of a door, I see me and Rani, rising like twin fires, our snake magic bright and burning. I rise higher than Rani, watching that crown sit on my head instead of hers. Next to me doesn't sit my twin sister . . . but the Snake Master.

I open my eyes. The Snake Master, pleased, approaches me. He lifts my palm and brushes his fingers over it. My skin burns as my palm sears, hot as a flame. But there's no discomfort. If anything, this heat is everything I've relished in life—the opposite of Rani's ice. I'm not on fire. I *am* fire.

When the Snake Master pulls away, I see what he's done.

There, imprinted on my palm, is the image of a snake.

Night after night, we continue like this—me practicing how to open the door, unlocking the power buried within me. Now, two nights before we reach Kaama, I'm still not asleep. I lie on my pallet, my body frozen while thinking of all the practice I've had with the Snake Master . . . the secrets I've withheld from Saeed. Training with the Master who betrayed and murdered Saeed's mother in cold blood.

But as long as I have the Snake Master on my side, as long as I practice my magic, I'll only grow stronger. And I'll need that magical strength the night the Blood Moon arrives. I'm sure that once I meet Rani in Kaama, she'll form a plan to take down the Snake Master and stop the Eternal Night. Stop our ancestor's reign . . .

A reign I could be part of . . .

Saeed stirs next to me, his chest heavily rising and falling. He's in such a deep sleep, I don't want to disturb him, but I angle my body upward and gently shake his arm.

"Saeed," I whisper. "Saeed, wake up."

"Hmm?" He rolls over toward me, careful not to put pressure on the arm that was hurt during the snowbird attack. His eyelids are heavy from drowsiness, but once he sees the concern on my face, he sits up on his elbow. "*What'swrongRia?*" His words slur together.

"I've been having more nightmares," I lie, wishing to get *something* about my training with the Snake Master off my chest. I hate how much I've been hiding from Saeed.

"Of my mother?" He dips a brow. "But she's—"

I shake my head. "Someone else."

He blinks the sleep out of his eyes and sits up farther. "Who?"

He sounds sober now, his voice hoarse from sleep, and suddenly that makes my body tingle all over, with the way his drowsy eyes look down at me beneath thick, dewy lashes.

Maybe I shouldn't have brought this up at all. I clutch at the quilted blanket. "You don't know how badly I want to tell you, but . . ."

Saeed wipes his sleep-crusted eyes and presses a hand to my forehead, as if expecting a fever. "Are you sure you're getting enough sleep, Ria? These past few days you've seemed a little out of it."

"I'm fine," I snap. My voice comes out in a growl I don't expect, and Saeed notices.

A rumble comes from within me—the rumble of the cobra. Pleased. Satiated.

"I meant," I continue, "these nightmares have been showing me something. What if there was someone different who had been involved in your mother's death?"

"You mean besides Veer?" His mind is working fast. I can practically sense his questions. *What happened to him that day at the Snake River?*

"Maybe," I mumble vaguely. I look down, my stomach falling to my feet. I want to tell him so badly the truth of what happened that night. The blood on my hands.

But he only tilts my chin up and says, "Forget about him, Ria." Saeed plants one of my hands against his bare chest and wraps his own around it. The hand with the snake mark. Luckily, I've been good at hiding it. Even now, I can barely think of what that mark means as I feel his heart thump steadily like the beat of a tabla, unlike the backflips of my own.

"I don't want to think any more about him or what happened that night than I should. You've done enough for me already. Helping me discover the truth about my mother . . . helping me set her free." His throat tightens.

I try to lighten the mood. "What can I say? A thief has good senses."

He laughs. "You and your sister might be opposites, but I see similarities within you both, too. Boldness." He raises my hand and plants a kiss against my knuckles. "Courage."

"I had to have courage on the streets," I tell him. "Though looking back on it, I think it was cowardice, trying to run away instead of facing my destiny head-on."

And to think, I was going to run off after meeting Rani— going to take her money and precious jewels and leave, as soon as I discovered the secret of my birth.

"Whatever you're thinking about," he tells me, releasing my hand and cupping my cheeks, bringing my gaze up to his, "just promise me it's nothing dangerous."

Dangerous. Meeting the Snake Master has been much more than that.

"I think I might have a different definition of *dangerous*."

His laugh echoes in my bones, but he asks again. "Promise me."

"I promise," I whisper. He leans in for a kiss. He tastes like fresh flower blossoms and candied almonds. He tastes like the moment between beginnings and endings.

But he pulls back too soon, gazing at me with curiosity. His aura pulses around me, memory magic and snake magic calling to one another like a snake's rattle.

"Something wrong?" I say, sensing that cobra within me rising, my magic tugging at my veins. His magic is a predawn sky, mine a moonless night.

For a split second, he hesitates, brows frowning in concern. I forcibly push down the cobra, the darkness of my magic, until my veins are empty.

Finally, Saeed shakes his head, eyes drowsy with lust once more. "Nothing at all," he says, voice low and sultry.

I tuck my body over his as he kisses me again, more hungrily this time, fusing my lips against his until every thought disappears. No snakes, no magic, no Masters. Just me and Saeed.

But I have to meet the Snake Master again.

I pull away for a second, hesitating, my breats hot against his. He gazes at me, a question in his eyes. With a hand, he drags his searing fingers beneath my tunic, brushing them against the bare skin of my back. I nod infinitesimally.

I ignore the snake magic whispering in my bones as I press Saeed down onto the pallet beneath us.

The Snake Master can wait.

30

Rani

Pick your poison . . . or we shall poison you.

The mirrors suddenly expand and combine into one. The new mirror rushes forward, until we fall through its silver sheen and into a new world. I recognize it as the Gold Palace's gardens, where Amir first handed me a flower that crumbled to ash. I watch as we part ways and I leave with Queen Meeta. I watch as Amir stumbles around, lost, until he ends up in front of his own mirror in the Blue Palace. He tosses off the jewelry Dhruv gave him to wear, rips off the clothes that made him look more suited to the palace. He covers his face with his hands.

Next to me, Amir stiffens. "I don't want to see this again."

But we do. We watch as days pass, as he pores over his outfits, rehearses lines in that very mirror, reads books about Retan that he secretly stowed away on the trip here. As he gazes longingly at me while I play mallet ball with Prince Dhruv, or leave in a carriage for the waterfall.

And then, a new version of Amir appears, holding flowers

and donning a confident smile. I watch as we return to Abai, as Mother and Father give him that same lavish laurel crown that he wore in the gilded mirror, as we become one.

But as time passes, Amir sickens. Sickens with worry, with regret. He covers his emotions with badges of honor, hardening himself until he becomes as stoic as a Chart.

Is this our future? What does this mean? Will Amir be unhappy in this future with me?

No. This cannot be the only path the dwellers have for him. After all, our futures are ours to decide.

"Not in this trial," the dwellers confirm. I hate how easily they can read my thoughts. Those are reserved for me alone—and for Shima. I clutch Amir's hand tightly. At the very least, I won't let him go through this alone.

Now, time slips backward and shows Amir on the streets of Abai, but on the fateful day he would have crossed paths with Ria, he chooses a detour for Kakur, a southern Abaian city, instead, following a man's broken promise of food and shelter. With Ria never having met Amir, he walks right into a trap—a thief now thieved. With nothing and no one, he stumbles aimlessly through Abai, attempting to steal enough money for a boat ride away from this world. Instead, he falls prey to hunger and starvation, to loneliness and misery, all eating at his bones and mind.

"Pick your poison," the desert dwellers repeat. *"Pick your path."*

"This is—disturbing," Amir chokes out. A life of death, or a life of suffering? Neither option ends in happiness. Neither is fair.

But Amir's life has never been fair.

"Time is running out. . . ."

The palace walls slip away. Back in the desert, the mirror faces us, hauntingly reflecting us, in this present moment, right back. We're both on our knees, at the will of the desert dwellers.

At the will of the trial.

If Amir chooses wrong, this—*us*—will be over. This isn't simply about making a choice. It's about defining who we are. Who Amir wants to be. And with one wrong slip, one wrong word, we'll both be dead.

Then, Amir's words, caressing my ears: "I can't pass this. I can't choose, Rani."

My breath catches as the whispers of the dwellers become deafening as an elephant's stomp.

"That is not an option. If you wish to die, the lavas of the Malwan Pass will not hesitate to consume you."

Amir stares defiantly at the invisible creatures. "So? Kill me then. Let me die. Or better yet—let me stay here. Forever. But let Rani go."

"Amir?" I cry in shock, and even the dwellers can't withhold their gasps.

"No one has ever given up on the Fire Master's trial. Are you sure this is what you want?"

"Yes," Amir says without hesitation. "But you have to promise to let Rani go and give her what she seeks. A way to destroy the Bloodstone."

"Amir, no—"

"Rani, let me do this." His eyes harden on mine. Like he can't even bear his own words.

"She will be free . . . once you've faced the volcanoes."

Gulping, he turns away, staring back at the mirror. "Good. I'd like to see myself in the mirror one more time. As a prince, with Rani. *Please.*"

There's no bitterness in his voice. No despair. Only a gentle break, bringing forward the truth. The very real, very terrifying possibility that Amir might not actually pass the trial. That he would choose to fail to let me be free.

"This isn't right, Amir," I tell him. My thoughts consume me. How I wish I'd never pushed Amir away. How I wish we could have been together despite all my silly, complicated feelings for Dhruv. How I wish I could spend my final moments in this world, in this trial, with *him*. Amir Bhatt.

My flower.

In the mirror, Amir's face appears, princely and practiced. Slowly, he reaches toward this version of himself, letting the mirror ripple as his hand reaches out and then through the mirror itself. With a prayer to Amran, Amir reaches for the crown and pulls it off his head, drawing it out. The boy in the mirror doesn't budge as Amir—*my* Amir—looks down at the crown in his hands, at the delicate golden leaves.

His fingers tighten around it, to the point where the edges begin to cut into his fingers.

"Amir, please—" I start, but with a sudden motion Amir draws back his hand and throws the crown at his own reflection. Instead of passing through the mirror and at Prince Amir, it cracks the glass, every corner and jagged edge of the crown breaking and splintering the mirror until it shatters at his feet.

The sand whirls, taking us away from the scene. We crash onto the ground, and when I look up, breathing heavily, I see we are surrounded by glimmering stones.

We're back in the cave.

I raise myself from the ground. "Amir—you're alive."

"Are you sure?" he asks, staring at his hands.

"How did you know that would work?" I ask him, too full of wonder that he's here, that we're *both* here, when I almost lost him.

The boy I truly love.

"I didn't. I was prepared to stay here, Rani, if it meant you'd be free. I could do something worthwhile, something important. My whole time in Retan, I've been holding you back. Holding you back from being your real self . . . with Dhruv."

"That's not true," I whisper. "Amir, when we met, you gave me adventure, courage—a love I never could have even imagined I could possess. And now, all I can give you in return is a life of scorn from elitist nobles and endless responsibilities. I was afraid I was holding *you* back. I was afraid you could never want this life with me. That you'd trade away every awful glance to be back with Ria on the streets again."

Amir shakes his head, standing. "I would trade nothing to be away from you, Rani. I had no idea you felt that way."

The truth is, I didn't know what I felt until this exact moment. I've been afraid of other people's thoughts—of myself, of Amir— for so long that I haven't been able to be myself with him the way I've always wanted to.

"You know what I realized?" Amir asks, pulling me from my thoughts. "This trial battles with your mind. It shows you futures that don't yet exist. It lets you travel through a mirror of magic. But *we* are still the ones in control of our futures. And I wasn't about to let some all-seeing mirror tell me I couldn't be with you. So I took the sharpest thing I could find from within the trial and used it. The mirror bent to my will." He gulps. "At least I hope it did. Is the trial over? Or are we . . ." He reaches out for me, as if to reassure himself I'm really there.

I'm not going anywhere.

"I don't know," I tell him, clutching his arms tightly. "But I never want to see you hurt again. Not because of me."

A small smile tugs at Amir's lips. "When we first met, every-thing about you was confusing. Your precious clothes, your jewelry, even your smile. It wasn't Ria's. But I didn't understand why."

My heart thumps.

"When I truly learned who you were, and I saw how much you cared for the people you were meant to stand for—and for Jas, Irfan, and my sister, I understood just fine. You're the princess. But you're so much more."

He angles his torso toward me. "I don't want to lose you, Rani," he whispers. "But I was prepared to let you go. To be free."

His words make my heart swell with adoration. I watch the curve of his lips, the quirk of his brows, the scar lining his features— each a story all on its own.

"Don't leave," I tell him.

"I won't." Amir's voice lilts at the end, barely hanging above a whisper. "I didn't cross the continent to leave you alone."

Never alone again, I think, almost dizzy with happiness and relief. Unable to stop myself, I push myself onto my toes and into his arms, crashing my lips against his clumsily, desperate to hold him close.

Amir wraps his arms around my waist and lifts me closer, kissing me so deeply I feel breathless, the shock of heat between us brightly burning. I feel his own giddy joy in the press of his lips, as he pulls away from me just enough to lift me up and twirl me around. I never want this moment to end.

We're alive. We're alive, and our future is ours to decide.

I press a hand to his chest, remembering. "The desert dwellers spoke to me at the start of the trial. They told me to solve a riddle."

"Riddle?" Amir echoes, setting me on my feet but still holding me close.

"*Ice shall dismantle; fire shall liberate. Solve the riddle, and you shall receive the thing you seek*," I recite. "Ice represents my past— *our* pasts—and fire my future. The Fire Master wanted me to see how I could face my past . . . and find our future."

"*Our* future?" Amir echoes, eyes crinkling at the corners. My heart leaps in my chest just as another voice says, "*Then you are wise, Princess.*"

I look up. Something floats from the top of the cave and into my now-open palms. It's a blade with a bejeweled hilt, the rubies as red as the Bloodstone itself. I slip off the gilded scabbard. The blade is curved, inscribed with letters from the Old Age. Half my face is reflected in the steel, in the ancient, beautiful symbols of the old tongue. I can make out most of what it says: *Forged in fire, I shall not bend or break.*

"A knife?" Amir says.

"*It is your gift from the Fire Master,*" the voice says. "*The thing you seek. Use it wisely.*"

The weapon to destroy the Bloodstone. And much like it, I will neither break nor bend until our mission is fulfilled.

I hold Amir's hand as we leave, because I know now that I never want to let go.

The horses kick up plumes of dirt as we forge our path to the Kaaman palace. I ride with Amir, Dhruv on another steed. One last stop before we warn Father, stop the Snake Master, and destroy the Bloodstone.

One final destination until this is all over.

The paper and ink I bought hours ago to write a letter for my father weigh heavily in my bag—until I find a courier with a Kaaman seal. With the extra coin I give her, my warning and note

of impending arrival should reach Father soon. But still, we ride like the sun might never rise again. Not with the Snake Master preparing for something as disastrous and world-shattering as the Eternal Night.

Days of travel carry us inexorably onward, and I keep close to Amir most of the time, neither of us wanting to be far from the other after our trial. But one night after we've set up camp underneath a dark, starry sky, I find Dhruv by a stream, skipping rocks. I inhale shakily and approach him. We've been courteous to one another, but drifting apart since the trial. I haven't had the courage to tell him about Amir.

But I must find that courage now.

"Dhruv?" I say when I come up to his side. I pick up a rock and twirl it between my fingers. "You never told me you knew how to skip rocks."

"My specialty," he jokes. "It's all in the wrist." He flings another rock, and it skips ahead, leaving three perfect ripples in the stream.

"I'm sorry," I tell him at last, casting the rock into the water only to watch it sink. "I haven't exactly been open with you, Dhruv. I want to fix that."

Dhruv casts a sidelong glance at me before picking up another rock from the sand and dirt beneath us. He throws it onto the water, watching it skip forth into the red-and-orange sunset.

"I know," he says.

"You do?"

He nods. Once the rock is out of sight, he turns to me, shoving his hands into his pockets, and suddenly he looks the way he did when we first met. Not a prince, but a boy. Not a royal with the weight of a kingdom on his shoulders, just someone who likes to joke and have fun. That's the Dhruv I've gotten to know. The one I don't want to stop being friends with.

"You can speak with me about anything," Dhruv says finally. "A prince is open with his people. And with fellow royalty." He offers me a mock bow and I giggle.

A rush of thoughts enters my head. "What I want to speak with you about . . . is my trial."

He raises a brow. "What about it?" I've only told him the basic tribulations. The creature, the snakes. But not this.

"My trial was a test of my past and future, and Amir's future," I explain. "And it was when I had to truly acknowledge my future that I realized what was wrong."

"Wrong?" he echoes.

I nod. "I realized the truth of what I want my future to be. I don't want to stay in Retan; I want to be in Abai."

In my head, I add, *I want to be with Amir.*

"Oh," he says finally. "Part of me knew this was coming," he adds, laughing lightly, though my stomach knots at his words.

"I think I did, too." I look steadily at him, a pang of regret in my belly—but only for hurting him, not for the life he could offer me.

Dhruv smirks, though there is something bittersweet in his smile, too. "Well, I do know one thing for certain." He's standing straight now, every inch a prince, as he looks at me with a soft gaze. "You and Amir. Fast friends, I once thought. But there's more, isn't there?"

"Is it that obvious?" I whisper, though there is no humor in my tone.

"He looks at you like you're stars in the night sky," Dhruv says simply. "And you, him. I know that look. I've had it before myself."

I look down, thinking of what Amir and I saw during my trial. "My trial illuminated the truth. I realized what I wanted my future to become." I exhale. "I know this could work. But it's not about if it *can*. It's about if it *should*."

He steps closer, and I'm surprised to find him smiling. "What should be . . . I think I understand. I've lived in fear for so long, Rani. Afraid I would become like my father. I don't want to live in fear of the future, or in fear of what people think of me. I'm sure you understand."

I gaze up at him, thinking of what his own future could be. A prince with a partner at his side—with someone he trusts fully, with someone he loves.

"You showed me something, Dhruv," I tell him. "You showed me a new world. You showed me new customs and traditions and people. And you helped me open my heart when I thought I had to keep it closed. I hope you will keep your heart open, too, without fear or judgment."

Dhruv picks up another rock and skips it across the water. "I could never wrong you for what your heart tells you. And keep it open," he adds, "for you never know who you might let in."

I smile, finally letting loose a laugh. "You really are a prince, Dhruv. One who will take great care of his people. I know it."

"And you, too, Princess Rani," he says. He bows deeply. "Or should I say, Abai's future queen?"

I bite my lip. "You could say that." My heart warms, growing in my chest, telling me that I don't need to hide who I am, or change, or compromise, for anyone.

I shall tell Mother the truth. I shall tell her everything.

I can be myself. And so can Amir. Together.

It doesn't matter if it's not easy, or what others will think. The future is ours to create. And we're going to shape it exactly how we want.

"Before we rest for the night, I have a question about the Fire Master's knife," Dhruv says, pointing to the scabbard at my waist. "If it's powerful enough to destroy a stone, then I hope it's powerful enough to destroy this." Dhruv pulls his firestone necklace over his head.

"You want me . . . to destroy it? But, Dhruv—"

"I don't want to be constantly reminded of love," he tells me, and for once, a raw, anguished pain etches across his face. "Of . . . of what I'm missing. It's easier to just forget than to hold on." He blinks. "Isn't it?"

"No, it's not." I grasp his hand, and the firestone within it, then place it carefully back over his head. "I noticed how often it glowed around me. But there are many types of love; it wasn't simply romance, it was admiration. As I admire you. The firestone was brighter in the presence of Ranjit, of your mother, of Siva Auntie. You don't need it to show you your path, or who you're supposed to love, because you already know, Dhruv. Keep your necklace. Keep that love inside you."

"I . . ." Dhruv smiles to himself. "Thank you, Rani. And I pray to Amran that this works." He gestures at the knife and leaves me by the stream.

I, too, utter a prayer. I've passed the trial, but I have an even greater one ahead. There is little time left until I must use this knife. Until I must destroy the stone, the Snake Master . . . and my magic.

31

Ria

When we arrive at Kaama, I'm surprised to find the rumors are true.

Fruit really does bloom year-round here—even in the dead of winter. Pink fruit—pomegranates, Saeed tells me—hang like blushing jewels from tree branches as we pass through a garden limned with frost. It's nighttime, the sky peppered with starlight, but the fruit is . . . *glowing*.

"They look magical," I tell Saeed. Memories of last night flash back to me at his warm gaze; I ended up falling asleep in Saeed's arms instead of visiting the Snake Master, and all day I've felt a strange absence in my bones. But I don't dwell on it, because we've finally made it past the border.

We're in Abai's once-enemy kingdom.

I remember thinking I'd never step foot here. I remember thinking Abai would be at war with Kaama, and I'd be somewhere far, far away from it all.

Seems like fate still led me here.

"Maybe they are magical." Saeed lifts a brow, leading us toward his father's old estate, which isn't far from the border. Thank goodness, because riding those water buffalos wasn't comfortable, to put it lightly. Now that we're in Kaama, we've left the water buffalos behind at an old stable, where they'll be well fed, and are now traveling the rest of the way on foot. Neeta and Neesa left us at the border, due to return to their duties at the Amratstanian palace. Thankfully, they trust Irfan and the rest of us to keep their princess safe. But I'm not sure she's the one truly in danger.

"We're not far," Saeed tells me as we begin to shiver from the nighttime air. Though Kaama doesn't feel quite as cold as Amrat-stan, it's definitely chillier than Abai would be this time of year. The frost and peppered snow on the ground can prove it. "Just another hour out." I can tell Saeed is healthier than he's been in weeks. Though he clings to his mother's ashes, speaks to her nightly from beneath the stars, the dark circles under his eyes have faded, and color has returned to his cheeks. Maybe with relief now that we've arrived. At the estate, our one planned stop on the way to the palace, he can finally set her free.

I spend my time walking side by side with Aditi at the back of the group, she practicing her magic secretly anytime we pass by frozen ponds or lakes, trying to see what she can do. One time she makes a ripple in the pond; another, she casts a loop of ice from the pond and right into her hand. It seems her wariness of me from that night next to the lake has melted, and we spend our time giggling to avoid thinking of what will pass the night of the Blood Moon.

It shall be a new dawn for you too, Ria, a voice tells me from deep within. But it is not my own.

The estate looks like a miniature palace against the night sky.

Turrets rise from left to right, and windows shaped like domes act as eyes peering out into the world. I shiver at the brown-bricked stone, the dilapidated appearance of the exterior.

"No one's been here in years," Saeed says, staring up at it.

"You read my mind," I say, also staring up at the house as I approach his side. "Do you remember it?"

"Only Mother's stories," he answers darkly. "She always told me where we lived, how we lived. We only needed each other."

A knot twists in my stomach at the thought of his mother. Saeed's voice sounds thick, strained. I interlock my fingers with his, steadying his gaze with mine. His eyes darken. He shutters them, like he's fighting off an oncoming headache. Or preparing for the task ahead. I press a hand to his temple, wishing I could soothe the pain.

We step inside, Irfan, Zoya, and Aditi following more slowly.

The interior of the house is gray and gloomy—and so cold even a ghost would shudder. If I say something, I'm sure it'll echo throughout the whole place. I approach Saeed, who's now standing by the mantel above the fireplace in a separate area for living quarters. The room is spacious, almost as large as Rani's chambers, but instead of bright royal purples, the floor is covered in dried rose petals and dust, cobwebs and dirt.

"After Father died, Mother left his ashes in Kaama," he says to no one in particular, "where he was born, instead of keeping the ashes with her. She wanted to begin a new life in Abai. But instead, she was only plagued by the thoughts of their past life together."

The room chills with silence.

"This painting," Saeed says, turning toward the fireplace. I move to stand next to him, catching sight of the portrait on the mantel. "Mother commissioned it for her wedding to Father. There was no party, because neither of their families approved of their marriage. So they held one in private. A room full of roses, Mother always told me." He gulps. "It's why, when I proposed to Rani, I laid out a whole room of roses for her."

Remembering his past relationship with Rani makes my heart twist with a thousand emotions.

"Then we'll honor your mother however we can," I tell him.

Saeed turns back to the portrait of his mother and father, both of them young and rosy-cheeked, flushing from first love. I wonder if I see a little bit of myself in Amara's face—the youthful glow, the promise of a grand future.

I wonder how it went so wrong.

Saeed finds a lever hidden behind the portrait. As he turns it, a slim opening pops up from the mantel, revealing a small urn.

His father's ashes.

"We'll spread her ashes in the garden next to his."

I plant a hand on his shoulder. "And finally set them free."

The moon's glow outside is telling, a red orb of misfortune.

Only Saeed and I are outside in the cold, letting the remainder of our group rest for the night before we continue our trek to the palace tomorrow morning. Saeed spreads out his father's ashes first, and finally, after a deep breath, reaches into his pack for his mother's. I press a hand to his arm, comforting words on my tongue, but only nod instead. I give him a small smile. One to offer him strength.

We need light if we're ever to defeat the dark.

He spreads his mother's ashes, focused on the task at hand. Tears prickle my eyes. Amara may have done many terrible things, but she was still Saeed's mother. What if it had been someone close to me who had been possessed by the Snake Master? Aditi, perhaps? I shudder. I think of every moment I've spent with Aditi: poring over books, connecting over Mama Anita. I think of every moment I've spent with Saeed: discovering the truth of my past, finding a love I didn't know could exist in my once lonely life.

Saeed clings to my hand, lowering his head in a prayer. He presses his head to the ground, and so do I. Offering our final respects.

Wind whispers past my ear, and I look up. Petals float through the air, then gather on the ground like fallen leaves skittering on the grass. But the petals aren't dried, they're fresh. And this garden is dead—so where did these petals come from? My hand tightens on Saeed's, and he makes a noise of confusion.

"Ria, what is it—?"

That's when I know he sees it, too.

A funnel of rose petals rises from the ground, each gathering to form the shape of a human, draped in a sari and glowing with an eerie light. A ghostly figure, a woman made of flowers and starlight.

Amara.

"I'm here, my child," she suddenly speaks, her petal eyes and lips gentle and fluttering with the wind. Behind her, a glowing door forms in the air.

"H-how are you here?" Saeed wonders, tears spilling down his cheeks.

"Because I am not fully gone," she says. "As you spread my ashes, I gained enough strength to step into the world of the living, if only for a moment."

"I don't understand," Saeed says, shivering as cold wind nips at both of our skin.

"I may have crossed the gates of death, but I am not dead. Not yet." Amara bends down so she's eye level with her son, and Saeed gasps as she plants a hand on his cheek, the soft rose petals brushing his skin. "Son . . . there is something you must do for me." She leans in close to his ear and says, "You must let me rejoin this world."

"Rejoin?" I can't help it; the words spill out of me, and Amara whips her head around to the spot where I sit. Her dark eyes rest on mine, and for a moment, I expect that familiar confusion to fill her face the way it had when she saw what I did to Veer. But instead, she appears weakened, and she speaks with her heart and not the consuming revenge that burned inside her for so very long.

"You haven't told him, have you," Amara says, turning back to her son. "About that night. About the Black Viper. About . . ."

I stay rooted to my spot, not daring to look over at Saeed even as I feel his probing eyes.

"So he knows nothing of what happened at the Snake River? Of my turmoil, my betrayal? Of what you did that night, or what your ancestor *offered* you?" Amara's voice rises. The petals flutter, like a skittish horse.

Afraid she might lash out.

I shake my head, unable to meet Saeed's or Amara's gazes.

"Ria?" Saeed says, his hand meeting mine, the touch of his fingers like flames against cold skin. "What is my mother talking about? What offer?"

Out with it, Ria, I force myself. I shudder in a deep breath and say, "V-Veer."

"The palace physician," he recalls. "From Amratstan? The one who you said killed my mother."

I nod. "He's not the one who hurt your mother. She grew weak . . . because something—*someone*—had been living inside her ever since she escaped the Snake Pit. It was . . . my ancestor. The Great Deceiver."

Saeed's eyes sharpen with realization. "That's impossible. Mother, tell me the truth."

"He needed a body, a place to escape the Pit he's called home for centuries," I explain, the story falling off my tongue too easily now that I've finally released it. "He worked with Amara to gather the talismans, but only for his own gain. For his chance at reclaiming a body and the followers who obey him."

"The Serpent's Tongue," Saeed registers, voice weak. He stares at his mother—at the glowing vision of her, who nods along, mouth set in a firm line as I reveal the truth.

"You mean to say my mother was taken over by the *Snake Master*? That he clung to her like a parasite?" He glances at his mother in disbelief.

"I had control of my body," Amara tells her son. "I just didn't realize how weak I would be once he finally left. It felt like he'd drawn on my essence to escape, but never fully broke away completely. I still feel connected to him. Like I can't be severed from him."

I hate how I feel the same way.

"But if you defeat him . . ." Amara collects her thoughts, staring up at the bloody moon. "Then perhaps I can rejoin this world. Perhaps I'll be free, Saeed. Free of him. Free to live again with you."

"Mother—" Saeed begins.

"Believe me, son. Believe *her*."

With that, the wind picks up again, breaking Amara into

remnants of ash and roses, each petal sweeping away with the wind. I watch as they travel through the shimmering open door in front of us, which then magically seals itself shut, cutting off the golden glow from this endless night.

A doorway . . . to death?

One petal remains on the ground within Saeed's reach. He caresses it in his hand silently.

Saeed doesn't move his torso to face me. I don't know how much time passes in silence, until I can't bear it a moment longer.

"I'm sorry I didn't tell you sooner, Saeed. I didn't know how. I know how this sounds—"

"It sounds unfathomable," he interrupts me. "You kept this secret from me? A Master, your ancestor, killing my mother—*using* her in some kind of game?" Hurt leaks into his voice. Our conversation many nights ago tugs at my thoughts. All he wanted was for his mother to be seen as she was before all this—before her thirst for revenge. Now Amara would be seen as the woman who had hosted and been tricked by a deceptive Master.

"I wouldn't lie to you, Saeed," I whisper, cheeks heating.

Saeed only runs a hand through his curls. "No, you wouldn't. But you would hide a secret or two. There's something else you're not telling me, isn't there, Ria?" When I don't respond, realization dawns on his face. "My mother said *he* made you an offer."

"Y-yes," I say, wanting to run from this conversation. I can't bring myself to meet his eyes. "The Snake Master . . . wants to help me control my powers."

"And you told him no," Saeed says, brow furrowed. At my silence, he nudges again. "You told him no . . . right, Ria?"

"He's the only one who can teach me to control it," I whisper, but even to my ears I sound unconvinced.

"The Snake Master deceived my mother. He is the reason she's *dead*," Saeed begins incredulously, anger threading through his every word. "And you planned to *make a deal with him* all along?"

"Saeed, I—" But he doesn't let me finish.

"Your magic . . . I felt it. Not just today, but over our time together recently. It felt like a dark rush of power, a craving that could never be satiated. I've never felt snake magic like that before."

He goes silent, expecting an answer. What am I supposed to say? *Oh, apologies. The Master who took over your mother is training me now. He believes I'm the Key to his plans.*

Saeed wouldn't understand. Doesn't understand.

"Are you training with him?" Saeed whispers. I don't speak. After a beat of silence, he furrows his brows deeper. I can tell he's trying to hide his expression, the turn of his mouth wrinkling with disgust, but I know him too well.

"So what if I am? I'm the Snake Master's descendant. I have a special connection to him. *I'm* special," I emphasize. "Maybe that's why my power is growing. Maybe that means I'm destined for something greater."

"I'm sure my mother has spoken those same words. We all think we're destined for greatness. But you—" He shakes his head. "Just because a prophecy said that you were destined for darkness doesn't mean you actually are. You're not like *him*, Ria."

I once thought the same thing. "Maybe I am." I finally turn my palm up, showing him the snake burn for the first time. The tie that irrevocably tethers me to the Snake Master. I was once scared of snakes. Once ashamed of my unwieldy magic. But I'm not scared anymore.

He offers me nothing but a startled stare. I've never seen Saeed look at me this way. Like he doesn't know me.

Or maybe he's just starting to.

32

Rani

Compared to Retan, Kaama is downright freezing. I wonder how Ria has withstood those Amratstanian winters. Luckily, we purchased winter cloaks in western Kaama with Dhruv's coin, and after five days' travel by horse and boat through Abai's southern cities, which Amir skillfully *arranged* for, we've reached the Kaaman palace.

The palace is a giant fortress of gray and purple stone, a place of protection and stability. Understandably so—a hundred years ago, Kaama had been embroiled in a centuries-long war.

Lapis lazuli forms a ring around the enclosure, like it's some kind of magical protection spell. This gate looms much higher than the one in Abai—no climbing over this one. It's wrought iron and dark as night, tipped in black ink. Beyond the gate, the deep-purple door leading into the palace has been hand painted with gold, sweeping flourishes making the shape of an eye.

Warriors in purple robes carrying silver-ribboned spears flank the grand stone walkway to the entrance, where my father and the king of Kaama await us. Father must have received my note in time, because he wears a look of equal worry and relief.

King Jeevan of Kaama offers a welcome in the continental tongue. I bow with my palms pressed together, and Amir follows a bit too late, transfixed by the sight before him—by two kings, once ready for war, standing side by side. No treaty has been signed yet, but I hope this is a good omen for Abai's and Kaama's future.

Father draws me into a sudden hug. I laugh in surprise, unused to him being so demonstrative but happy to be in his arms again, until he speaks in a careful, shaking voice:

"I received your letter. The Snake Master is truly alive?"

I nod, feeling my smile ebb away as I speak. "He hopes to bring about an Eternal Night. A return of the world he created." Pretense won't help anything, and the truth escapes me like a secret kept close to my chest for too long.

"He is our ancestor, Rani," Father says soothingly, sweeping my hair back. "He won't hurt us."

"But he'll hurt *them*." I look at the Kaaman king and his Warriors. At Amir and Prince Dhruv.

How can I keep all of them safe?

"I see," Father says, and I can tell the gravity of the situation has been weighing on him more than he'd like to admit.

"Perhaps this is a conversation better conducted over a cup of chai?" King Jeevan snaps his fingers, and two guards pull open the doors to the palace, inviting us in. I startle, almost having forgotten the others around us as I spoke with my father.

As Prince Dhruv heads inside with my father, I turn to Amir. From days of travel, he looks more tired than usual. But all the same, he gently laces his hand with mine, comforting me as we step over the threshold.

After settling into our guest rooms, I join Father, King Jeevan, and his council. The room is spacious enough to hold at least a hundred people, though there are few people gathered here now. This must be where the peace summit will be held in just one night's time. The room is already aglow with Kaama's signature purple, banners streaming from the ceiling and portraits of the ever-glowing eye of Preethi staring down at me.

I try not to mull over the Memory Master's words, her *warning*, to me as I take my seat.

Prince Dhruv and Amir are already settled in. I watch as Dhruv takes a careful sip of his tea. King Jeevan clears his throat and says, "Prince Dhruv of Retan, I am honored to welcome you to Kaama. There is much we Kaamans can learn from Retan, including your ways of pacifism. Where did that all begin?"

"Truthfully?" Dhruv asks, setting down his cup. He glances at the door, where two royal guards robed in armor befitting a Warrior watch for passersby. "We have always been a land of peace. It began with the Three Blessed Sisters, the first rulers of our queendom."

"They were highly educated," Father agrees with a knowing

smile. "Daughter, what did you learn from the scholars in Retan? Were they willing to speak about the Bloodstone?"

"Yes. And . . . more," I say, thinking of what we learned of the Snake Master's past, his descent into vengeance. "But even more pressing is our freed ancestor. I do not know where the Snake Master is any longer; Ria didn't have the chance to tell me. Speaking of Ria, is there any word of her arrival?"

"Your sister and her companions should be here any moment. We recently received her message; Amara's death came as quite a shock." Father turns his head gravely toward Jeevan. Unease settles in the room. The king of Kaama must know that Father was once manipulated by Amara, and the tragic consequences that could have unfolded if her plan had succeeded.

"Amara is no longer the enemy," I state. "But our ancestor . . ."

"The Snake Master is a foe I never could have imagined we would face in our lifetime," King Jeevan says gravely. "We must stop him."

"With my magic and Rani's," Father promises. But I shake my head.

"The Snake Master possesses all the talismans. Our magic alone won't be enough. We need more." *We need Ria.*

Father says, "Then we require a response. An army, should the Snake Master appear with his own." The Serpent's Tongue. The thought of an army of them sends ice down my spine.

"We'll prepare the troops," King Jeevan says, standing. "The Warriors must be warned and directed appropriately. Canceling the peace summit will cause drastic uproar. We must maintain a semblance of calm for our visitors."

"The Charts that accompanied me can help, as well," Father offers, nodding toward King Jeevan.

I glance at Father, and the two look to be in agreement.

"A Master cannot be dealt with simply by force." Dhruv breaks the silence with the tone of a prince. "But the Snake Master could be weak. He's spent centuries trying to recover, and he's only just returned to his own body and begun to heal. Weapons could maim him, but we'd need something powerful."

"I might have a solution. We still keep most of our artillery from centuries' past. Our cannons and war elephants will be prepared," assures King Jeevan.

I droop my shoulders and lean against the tall gilded back of the chair. "Now we wait."

Come nightfall, hundreds of troops are lined up like toy figures in the courtyards, sharpening their spears and talwars. I watch from my guest room as a sea of purple marches across the grounds, launching into their training. Some fight in hand-to-hand combat; others carefully fill the cannons with spiked iron balls.

"You okay?" Amir asks from behind me. I start and press a hand to my chest.

"Amir," I breathe. "We should really stop startling each other."

"Point taken," he replies with a half smile. "But you didn't answer my question."

"I think so." My voice wavers.

"We have the knife," he tells me. "We'll destroy the Blood-stone. We'll stop the Snake Master."

"That's what I'm afraid of."

Silence echoes throughout the room. I gently press my head into the crook of his shoulder. He rubs my back in a gentle, calming movement, then kisses my forehead.

"You're afraid of losing your magic," Amir confirms. We haven't spoken of it since the Memory Master appeared at her shrine. "But you're more than your magic, Rani. You always have been. It wasn't magic that pulled me to you."

I glance up at Amir, feeling a moment of stillness, of peace, in his eyes. Like the calm before a storm.

I press a kiss to his lips so firmly that we almost fall over. Amir laughs against my mouth. I want to bottle this moment forever.

But movement from outside catches our attention. A group approaches the entrance walkway, dressed in heavy cloaks. I would recognize Irfan's bow and quiver anywhere. And just behind him—

My sister!

I half yank Amir from the room and down to the entry hall. I see Ria enter first, dropping her hood. Aditi peers out from behind her, taking in the fortress that is the Kaaman palace.

"Rani!" Ria finds me and rushes to meet me halfway. We slip our arms around each other in a fierce embrace. I feel so many things at once: relief, love, and warmth.

She pulls away and hugs Amir. I take Irfan's hand in greeting and turn to find a girl I didn't expect, with striking features and long, silky black hair.

"Princess Zoya—"

"Princess Rani—"

We both crash into a hug, spinning in circles. Once my fiercest friend, it's been years since I saw her last. Zoya looks so much like her mother now. At least from what I remember during my last visit to Amratstan—her mother passed shortly after.

After we exchange pleasantries, Zoya's voice lowers. "Do you remember that map we buried? It was the Earth Master's talisman."

"What map?" I ask. But a faint memory chips at the back of my mind, like an icicle slowly melting away. Both of us, giggling as we ran through the snow, alight with mischief and glee at what we had snuck away from our fathers. "We hid something. . . ."

"Together," Zoya finishes.

Ria smiles at us, but it's a sad one, heavy with secrets. I know what I must do. I pull her into another comforting embrace. "Come now, sister. I've warned King Jeevan and Father about the Snake Master. We're doing everything we can to prepare."

My sister pulls back, pitching her voice to a whisper. "Let's hope it's enough."

"Tell me what happened the night the Snake Master appeared. Everything that you weren't able to say earlier," I urge Ria later, hugging a cup of chai to my chest in the early hours of morning. It seems neither of us can sleep now that we've finally reunited.

Ria works her lower lip. "Something terrible."

"Amara?" I prod, moving closer to my sister. "Tell me the truth, Ria. I can tell when something is wrong. Did the Snake Master . . . do something to her?"

"You could say that," Ria says. Finally, she turns to me, her expression stoic, before revealing, "After the Snake Master betrayed her, Amara became weak. She faded . . . and then came back. *Partly.*"

Before I can ask a single question, Ria relays the entire story bit by bit. By the end of it, I have a hand covering my mouth. "Amara's . . . a spirit who can return to our world if we defeat the Snake Master?"

Ria shrugs, still curling in on herself like there's more she should say. "So she believes. But to go up against the Snake Master, we'll need more than just our magic."

"We have Saeed," I reason. "He has memory magic. Perhaps to defeat the Snake Master, we'll need descendants from *all* Masters. Zoya's a descendant of the Earth Master."

Ria perks up. "Aditi's a descendant of the Tide Master."

My eyes bulge. Ria hides a shy smile. "Her powers were suppressed at the Vadi Orphanage," she explains. "Would be nice if we knew a currentspinner or a flametalker," she jokes, only to see my answering expression and pause.

I lift a brow, and she reflects me.

"But we do." I grab my pack in the corner of the room and set to work immediately on crafting a message to Jujhar at the Island Market and Taran, leader of the flametalkers back at the Glass Temple. "With Jujhar's skyhawk, perhaps they could all get here fast enough."

Ria raises her brows even higher now. "But what do we do when we face him? Sure, I've been training—"

"Training?" I ask in surprise. I'd always had to drag Ria with me to practice our magic.

Ria bites her lip.

"What's wrong?" I peer deeply at her—she's hiding something. I know my own sister. And I know I'm right when Shima slithers into the room, speaking to both of us with her snake's hiss.

She'sss been practicing.

Ria sticks her tongue out at our snake familiar.

"Practicing what?" I say.

"My magic," Ria relents. "With . . . the Snake Master." Slowly, she lifts a palm, where a snake burn lies.

It takes a few moments for the words, for the image, to register. "But that's—"

"Impossible?" Ria finishes, laughing spitefully. "My magic is great, Rani. Uncontrollable sometimes, yes, but only because it's so powerful. He's the only one who can help me." As Ria reveals to me the truth of her magic, the truth of the Key, I fumble for words.

I shake my head. "So then what?" I say, my voice snappier than

I wish it to be. "You've been practicing with our enemy? Who we're *trying to* stop? How? *Why?*"

"I need his help, Rani!" Ria's voice rises, and she throws up her arms. "You wouldn't understand."

"Only because you won't talk to me!" I say, stung. "What am I not understanding? What could you *possibly* need from the Master trying to *destroy our world?*"

"I killed someone!" The words seem to rip themselves from Ria's chest, leaving her breathing harshly as she spins around to turn her back to me. I hear her take another breath, shaky with some unnamed emotion, as I stare at her in shock.

I open my mouth to speak, but nothing comes out. Silence hangs in the air between us with an almost tangible weight.

Killed . . .

"I killed someone," Ria continues. "With my powers. I couldn't stop them. Or me, I guess." At this, she finally turns to look at me over her shoulder. Her eyes shine with the telltale gleam of tears, but her mouth is set in an uncompromising line. "And I knew you wouldn't understand. So I went to someone who would."

She turns to face me fully, and some of her bravado seems to fade.

"You can't even say anything," Ria says, her voice breaking.

I don't know *what* to say. I want to comfort, want to question. My mind spins, but when I begin to speak, only one thing escapes.

"Who . . . ?"

Ria snorts, but there's no laughter in it. "It was Veer. The Black

Viper, the one who had been helping Ama—the Snake Master. He was there when the Snake Master returned. And he was taunting me, and he had already hurt Aditi, and I didn't want—" At this, her voice breaks again and she goes silent, biting her lip as tears begin to fall in earnest.

My heart wrenches in my chest, and I instinctively reach toward my sister and grasp her hands gently. She startles and looks up at me, and I squeeze her hands in mine.

The truth is, the strength of Ria's magic *does* scare me. I've never felt—or known—magic on her level before, not even our father's. Hearing all of this, my mind pulls inexorably toward the Memory Master's prophecy, that one of us would kill the other.

What Ria's power is now capable of, and all it could become, terrifies me. But looking at my sister now, I can see the truth in her eyes: it scares her, too.

And if I know anything, it's that my sister and I are stronger together. I won't let my sister's fear push her toward a terrible decision. And I won't let any prophecy dictate our fate.

"You're not the first to lose control, Ria," I begin haltingly, remembering my own near miss with Saeed, when a rogue dream almost ended with Shima poisoning him. "That doesn't make you a killer. It doesn't define who *you* truly are. Snake magic feeds off our emotions, our fear and pain. You did the best you could in an impossible situation, when you were hurt and scared."

Ria's eyes well up once more, and I pull her into my arms fully. I wrap her up as tightly as I can, and feel her hold me close in return as her tears soak into my shoulder.

"We *will* figure this out, Ria," I tell her, shoving every ounce of determination and surety I have into my words. "We'll work on your magic, and we'll find a way to help you control it. You don't need the Snake Master for that. We only need each other."

"But the prophecy said, *And the Key of a Master shall set souls free*," Ria says, her voice thick with emotion as she pulls away from me. "What if it's about me—the Key—and my magic setting free this Eternal Night? What if I'm meant to do that?"

I clutch Ria's hands and feel that fierce power sweep through me—through us. I've never felt her power like this . . . like a mountain rising to meet the sky.

I pull out my knife, a gift from the Fire Master's trial. We both look at it, an acknowledgment of what lies ahead. The blade shines, and when I touch it, it feels as hot as an iron. Only this can destroy the stone. Only this can shatter its power.

"Remember, Ria, we have done this before. Prophecies and visions do not determine our fate. *We* do. And I know you won't choose the Eternal Night." I pause, letting my words of comfort sink into her. "We cannot forget our plan."

"Which is?"

I take a deep breath. "Destroy the Snake Master for good."

Ria looks taken aback and unsure, her eyes red-rimmed.

"The Memory Master told me that if we destroy him," I explain, "we'll stop the poison that's spreading across the world. But at a great cost."

"Of what?" Ria says.

No longer able to keep this secret within me, I tell my sister the truth.

In just one more night, when the clock strikes midnight, the Blood Moon will be full. And our final fight against the Snake Master will begin.

The night might end in blood, but it will not end without a new dawn.

33

Ria

The night the full moon arrives, the world drowns in crimson.

Every inch of the Kaaman palace gardens are trimmed and hedged to perfection, the thorny white roses clumped together in bushes curling away from the red light. The Blood Moon has arrived, and everyone in Kaama has taken notice. Mothers sweep their children indoors. Others lay their heads down in prayer, hoping that tonight, Amran will give them peace instead of war.

I'm afraid we're getting the latter.

The Eternal Night might come true.

A group of ambassadors from all over the kingdom, all dressed in distinct shades of purple and black, peruse the gardens with sharp eyes. I glance down at my simple garb. A lavender salwar and black pajami, fitting right in with the nobles swarming the palace for tonight's peace summit. Rani wears an identical suit, except her chunni loops over her shoulder and has been tied at the opposite waist. A trick I've used many times to keep it out of my way when I'm running. I'm surprised she's picked up on it.

Everyone else in our group, now knowing the truth about the Snake Master's return, also blends in. Saeed cuts a striking figure, having swept his hair back. He hasn't spoken a word to me since we left the estate nor shown me so much as a cold glance. I'd rather he display *some* emotion than none at all. But I suppose I brought that on myself.

Irfan has trimmed his beard, silver eyes sparkling in the moonlight. Meanwhile, Shima keeps a diligent eye out for the Snake Master.

Guards stand militant outside; to most, they look like protection for the kings as the peace summit prepares to begin, when in truth, I know their purpose. They are ready, along with Charts. I wonder if they will be enough.

I stare up at the night sky, sending a prayer upward. I'll need whoever's up there on my side tonight.

King Natesh, the raja of Abai and my newly discovered father, joins me at my guest chamber balcony minutes later. We stare out at the sky, drowned in red.

I can't help but see the full Blood Moon as an omen that everything will go wrong. And maybe that's how things are supposed to be.

No. I force myself to turn to the raja, who mirrors my movement. His gaze sharpens like an owl's.

"Walk with me, daughter."

I follow closely behind him with nervous hands. I'm still not quite over how beautiful and resilient the Kaaman palace is, like a mess of contradictions. On the outside, a place built for war—and within, a colossal castle that protects its residents and shows devotion to the Memory Master.

We escape down a flight of stairs and end up on the lower level. Purple curtains drape over the double-doored entrance, and paintings of the Memory Master's symbol have been inked in silver and gold on the domed ceiling.

That symbol sends a pang of hurt through me. After everything Rani told me last night about the Memory Master's foretelling, my stomach roils with unease. Snake magic is so new to me, yet so completely a part of me. I don't know if I'm ready to lose that part of myself.

The raja carefully plants a hand on my shoulder, as if to comfort me, and I lift my gaze to his.

"I know we haven't spent much time together," he says, "but I want to apologize again for all the wrong I've done you, and my kingdom. There is still much we need to discuss."

"The Vadi Orphanage," I say, thinking of the future project I've wanted to take on. If we fail tonight, who will help those children?

No, I think, shaking myself. *We won't fail.*

"Thank you." I nod to my father. I believe the raja and I can do good, one step after another. Healing takes time, after all.

"I have a gift for you." At those words, I raise a brow. He

reaches for a bejeweled talwar enfolded in his kurta and hands it to me with open palms. "This is an ancient sword, believed to have been made by one of the first ever snakespeakers. My father passed it on to me, and trusted that I would use it one day against the Kaamans." His gaze darkens. "I only hope now you can put it to a greater purpose."

My hand quivers as I take the sword from him, which is etched with golden serpents and set with fine jewels. It is heavier than expected, but as I curl my fingers around its hilt and hold the sword ready, it feels right.

I'm about to thank him again when, from the corner of my eye, Irfan approaches. He looks every inch a soldier, and even bows at the sight of my father. Despite their strained history, King Natesh responds in kind. "Irfan. You came."

"At your request," Irfan agrees. "What is it you wanted to tell me?"

I glance at my father in confusion as he fishes for a small badge from his breast pocket. He offers it to Irfan, hand outstretched, and I catch sight of the Abaian crest.

"I have an offer for you," King Natesh says. "Should you wish to accept, I would be grateful to have you as general of our cavalry of Charts."

A new Head Chart? I gape, remembering the last one, who had secretly helped Amara retrieve the Bloodstone, only to face his own grim demise. And now, the king of Abai is looking for a new one. . . .

None other than the silver-eyed soldier.

Irfan looks stunned. He's spent too long searching for a home, for a purpose. Will he accept? Is this what he's been looking for?

He reaches out, taking the badge with resolute eyes. "It would be an honor, Your Majesty. I have seen all you have done with the Charts these past weeks, and know I can now wholeheartedly serve alongside you."

My heart squeezes with relief, but before I can congratulate Irfan, Rani appears with Saeed, Aditi, Amir, and Prince Dhruv. A crease pulses between Rani's brows, her patience wearing thin. "Where are Jujhar and Taran? They should've been here hours ago by skyhawk."

That's when we hear it. Yelling, clashing. I rush to the back of the palace, glancing out at the widespread courtyard that goes on for leagues. A group of cloaked figures has gathered—the Serpent's Tongue. But how did they get past the guards? How could they appear like this, with no warning? It must be their gifted magic. With the Snake Master's return, they are stronger than ever before.

Rani and the rest of the group reach my heels, and I barely have time to cry for help when the onslaught begins.

In a flash, the Serpent's Tongue floods forth like a broken dam, falling against the Warriors stationed there. The sound of battle is nothing like I imagined. It's not just swords clashing and bodies falling. It's the very *real*, very earsplitting sounds of gasps and grunts, of freedom choked from throats, and victories yelled overhead. I watch as two men hurry through the din, arriving at the rear palace steps and trying to barter their way in. Rani's eyes light up. "Jujhar! Taran!"

"What's happening?" one of them says, the shorter of the two, with swirls of mehendi painted on his hands in the pattern of flames. *A flametalker.*

"The Serpent's Tongue is already here," Rani explains. Her eyes widen when she gazes up at the sky and points, whispering, "Look."

I turn.

Above the large open field dusted with snow, five figures float downward from the sky. Each of us, entranced, makes our way outside, mouths agape. Mountains rise not far in the distance, connecting to the rocky path that leads to the Kaaman palace.

I shudder as a cloud of snow settles over us, cast under a red glow by the Blood Moon.

"Who . . . are they?" Amir says.

We freeze at the sound of several voices in the frigid air, layered into one omnipotent tone.

"War has begun."

The voices boom, shake the very earth. They echo all around me, voices of the skies. Voices from within and without.

The five glowing figures hovering above the snow. Even from afar, I see their symbols. Sky, earth, fire, tide, and memory flare from their skin like they're made of light instead of blood and bone.

There is only one possible explanation. These are the Masters of Magic.

"Preethi," Rani whispers at the one with the symbol of an eye flaring on her wrist. She gazes at the ones with symbols of the Earth and Sky Masters. "Ashneer, Mandeep . . ."

"Darshin," Prince Dhruv continues for her, looking at the one embraced by flame. "Diya."

The last Master pins her gaze on us, symbols of waves covering her skin in glowing light. The Tide Master. Aditi gapes from next to me at the Master who shares the same magic as her.

The Masters look ethereal, heavenly, as they float closer to Rani and me at the front of the group. The one named Preethi gazes at me with a knowing smile. My mouth hangs open at the sight of the five ghostly figures.

"How—?" Rani begins, but one of the Masters answers for her.

"We were created by Amran to get rid of the snake's poison and the bloody moon," the Master says, a symbol of a mountainous rock emblazoned on his chest. The Earth Master, Ashneer. *"So on this night of the Blood Moon, when each Master is at their strongest, we are able to return."*

I gape, eyes trailing over each of their spirit-like bodies. All magics will be at play tonight.

"We are here to help the princesses of Abai," the Tide Master says. *"Descendants of the bringer of the Eternal Night. Daughters of the dawn."*

A man hovering beside her wears a small grin, his body like a chiseled stone wall cast aflame. Fire licks at his feet and hands, even the tips of his ears, but he doesn't seem to mind.

This must be the Fire Master, Darshin, his golden eyes looking down upon Rani with interest. *"We meet again, Princess Rani. I saw you find the Bloodstone at the place where kings forged pacts—the Var River."*

"And lost it," she says, shivering where she stands. I still cannot quite believe my eyes. They're all here, all the Masters except—

"Worry not. We are here to stop him."

My stomach knots from that simple phrase. Within me, the cobra awakens as if from a dreamlike sleep, incensed at the thought, its teeth craving blood. In my head, I imagine the Snake Master, away from the mindscape, away from his bindings; full, free, ready to rise to his full power.

Tonight, my choice will change everything.

Just as I think those words, the sky shatters with blinding green light. Rani gasps next to me, and behind me, the others look on with unbelieving eyes as a figure steps forth in front of the army of the Serpent's Tongue.

Crimson eyes meet mine, and the cobra within me answers in kind. *Father.*

Raya's father. My father.

The Snake Master has arrived.

34

Rani

The six Masters of Magic face each other for the first time in a millennium.

"Hello, my brethren," the Snake Master says, a vicious curl to his tone. *"How lovely it is to see all of you."*

"This is no easy greeting." The Sky Master grimaces, her eyes white as the snow enveloping the battlefield. She produces her hands, palm over palm, and a plume of smoky wind is released from them. The wind rises, rises, whipping my hair around with its strength, and we all look up as it forms into a funnel—

Headed straight for the Snake Master.

He rises into the air before the funnel of snow and smoke can hit him, and using his palms, thrusts forward a wind of his own, strong enough to move the tides. It raises the hairs on my arms, but perhaps that's only my senses telling me the Snake Master's powers are far deeper than we knew. The funnel dissipates into nothing.

The Memory Master's violet eyes darken. *"I'm afraid your prophecy is coming true, Sahil."* She glances at the sky. *"I can see your future. I can see your past. And I can see your downfall."*

"There will be no downfall," the Snake Master argues, hovering in the sky. *"Is that all you have? A funnel of stale air and a vision of a false future?"*

As he speaks, rock shoots into the air from beneath his feet, swirling impossibly like the stem of a flower to lock on to his ankle. The Earth Master grins as he shoots out both hands, pulling more earthen tendrils forth.

The Memory Master steps forward. Once gentle, Preethi's eyes flare with an anger that shocks me. The Snake Master's head snaps from side to side as the Memory Master's magic invades his mind. *"Stop this at once."*

"Give us back the talismans," the Tide Master growls.

Only then do I notice the chain glowing around the Snake Master's neck, with what looks like tiny charms—no, *talismans.* My lips part in shock. But where is the Bloodstone? I have the knife with me—but it will be useless without the stone present.

With a frustrated grunt, the rock shackles break off the Snake Master's wrist and ankles. *"You think your magic will work against me? I hold possession of all the talismans. I hold the power of Amran, and with my strength tonight, I will achieve my greatest wish."*

Just then, his gaze slithers to Ria. My skin freezes, and I fight the urge to shove her behind me, where he can't see. Why is he looking at my sister like that?

"But first . . ." the Snake Master says, grinning down at us. *"Would you like to see what the power of Amran can do? I can access far more than the magic of the talismans. I can retrieve even what was lost, do what my brother Manav was meant to do."*

Pulsing like an aura of darkness around him and as bitter as death, a swirling vortex appears. It grows, stretches until it is taller than the Snake Master himself. It beats, but not with life. For inside there is only death, and a hundred gray hands burst from the maelstrom. Gasps of horror echo around me.

This must be a darker side to soul magic—a place of souls damned and trapped. And now, the Snake Master has control of it. Ria wasn't lying—the Snake Master is truly stronger than we could have ever imagined.

"Soul leachers, I prefer to call them," the Snake Master says. *"This is the army Amara would have called upon had she become the Soul Master. Let me show you the power our brother Manav deservedly held. . . ."*

With a gesture from the Snake Master, the figures march out from the vortex, thudding into the snow as they head onto the battlefield. Their movements are slow and viscous, their bodies not used to the earth beneath their feet. Eyes lifeless, they twist their fingers, their nails gnarled and growing inward like talons. From their mouths drips white foam tinged with blood.

I watch in horror as the group of the dead arrive on the field and begin to make their way toward the palace, where the clashes and screams from the battle with the Serpent's Tongue rise. A cannon booms nearby, launching debris into the air.

I twist to the group behind me. "You need to help the Warriors against the undead and the Serpent's Tongue. Ria, Aditi, and I will handle things here." Jujhar and Taran agree, their magic launching into action, and Saeed and Dhruv quickly follow. I grab on to Amir's arm. "Be safe."

He leaves after offering me a firm gaze, Zoya not far behind him.

The Masters spring into action, swiftly heading for the battlefield to stop the undead from reaching the innocent. The Tide Master sends spirals of water at the undead army, but they merely shake off the icy liquid and trudge onward. The Earth Master grows vines from the ground, locking them in place. But the vines pop and break as they force their way forward. The Masters work in tandem, sending balls of fire and ice, tricking their minds and withering spirits. But the onslaught continues, the dead flooding from the vortex, until the Masters are completely surrounded and the army begins to slip past them to the palace. The Snake Master watches, pleased.

Everything moves sluggishly, my brain not comprehending that this is real. The soul leachers continue a relentless attack despite the Masters' efforts, reaching the palace and pulling souls from people's chests with their hands, sucking away their minds through their gaping mouths, lips cracked with blood. They're fearless, mindless. Marionettes in the Snake Master's show.

In this moment, as snow descends peacefully from the sky,

as the moon bleeds red, I know that this land, this *country*, and the Masters of Magic themselves don't stand a chance against the Snake Master. Not unless we do something.

"We have to end this—*together*," I tell Ria and Aditi. We join hands. Aditi's small hand cradles mine, and she glances up at Ria, a lynx and a mouse joining forces.

"Remember what we practiced?" Ria tells Aditi. "Feel the wave within you. Let it go."

We turn as one to face the Snake Master, and though he floats in the air, he is not out of our reach just yet. He's too busy commanding the onslaught, and harnessing the power of Amran, to worry about us. Perhaps that will be his first mistake.

Aditi nods, scrunching her nose in concentration. Droplets rise from the ground, swirling into a wave. It rises like a mythical being into the sky, then hovers over the Snake Master, about to drench him in water. He braces for the impact, but nearby, Jujhar jumps into view, and his gale spins the water into a funnel at the Master's feet, knocking him off balance.

Angered, the Snake Master clutches his necklace of talismans, and a *boom* rocks the skies, making the ground shudder and crack with earth and sky magic. The necklace must be where he accesses the power of the talismans. The power of a god.

For a blissful moment, the raging battle stops. People stare up as an unearthly glow spreads around the Master's form, and blue flames lick at his feet. He truly does possess a power not of this world.

And at his command, the battle resumes.

"Ria, Rani," Saeed says, panting for air as he finds us. All around us, war rages. Cannons boom, screams echo. The ground shakes as Kaaman war elephants descend from the north, covered with traditional Kaaman garments of purple and gold, their heads clad in plated armor. The elephants carry soldiers with bows and arrows and deadly spears tipped with snake venom—the Kaamans' last effort against the enemy. The scene would be awe-inducing if not for the splitting sensation of fear gripping me in a choke hold.

I cannot allow another person—or creature—to get hurt tonight.

Saeed utters in a panic, "Our army is dwindling. What should we do?"

"We need to attack the Snake Master to release his hold on the dead," Ria says, then looks to me. "As long as the dead keep coming, the Warriors have no chance." Aditi's brow furrows in worry, and Jujhar tries to make sense of the scene ahead of us, where Taran still fights with bright flames against the Serpent's Tongue.

"How?" I whisper, trembling at the scene on the battlefield ahead of us.

"We can use our magic *together*. We've done bigger things before," Ria reasons. "We need a way for our snake magic to be stronger than ever."

I agree. Now isn't the time to doubt. It's time to act.

We connect our hands in the air, facing each other. Our palms warm, creating heat, creating magic. I focus on my magic, feeling it connect with Ria's. Where mine is slow and steady, hers roars like a sandtiger, crashing into mine like fire and ice. Something explosive happens; a light exudes from our hands, bright enough to singe my sight. I close my eyes and feel a coolness at my ankles, slinking like a snake.

I remove my hands from Ria's, already knowing what's happened. "Shima," I breathe.

You called, and I answered, Shima says from below us. A pool of snakes follow behind her, from strong-headed cobras to lethal black mambas.

What mess are we in now?

"We need to attack the Snake Master and break his hold on the undead." Ria points at our ancestor, who sports a menacing smile. Luck is on his side, but not for long.

Together, Ria and I take each other's hands again and motion the snakes forth, led by Shima. They slither like a jade-black river, slinking through the parade of soldiers and right for the Snake Master. Under our command, they attack, forming a cage around the Master and blocking him from sight. A verdant burst of light breaks their formation, but Ria and I won't relent. With sweat dripping down my neck, I force the snakes to attack, which is much more difficult than ever before. It's hard for them to hurt their Master. But the Snake Master pays no mind to hurting them.

When I cannot hold it any longer, I let the snakes fall, my magic waning inside me every time the Snake Master is struck. I knew this would happen. But I won't let myself think of my magic dying.

Taran approaches to aid us, followed by Zoya behind him, her sword stained with blood. It's clear Zoya trained with the soldiers as a child, just as I remembered. She would look as graceful and elegant as ever, if not for the gleam of terror in her eyes.

We haven't won the battle yet, those eyes say.

Taran spins fireglobes from his palms with swift, even movements. They singe the Master's cloak, exposing his legs—or rather, snake's tail. Saeed's aura pulses against mine, and certainly the Snake Master's, twisting his mind until he feels a brutal, knifelike pain. Each of the descendants is helping us, fueling us, to stop the Snake Master. I sense the rightness of it in my bones. We can stop him, together.

Only Zoya is left.

"I can't—" she begins. I release my hold on Ria and slip the sword out of Zoya's grasp, then step back.

"You can. *You're* a descendant of the Earth Master. You might not have felt magic inside you your whole life, but it's there, burrowed in your veins. You just need to unleash it." Next to us, I see the others struggling to maintain their magic, and I know we're running out of time.

Zoya's mouth twists in panic. "I can't; I don't feel anything."

"Focus on your mother," I try. "She loved nature. She loved the woods."

Something sparks in Zoya. "The woods," she recalls, shutting her eyes. "The woods." She repeats those words over and over, and I'm amazed to see her visions come to life in a sudden and momentous surge. Breaking out of the ground, trees sprout, exact replicas of the ivory tree where Zoya and I hid the Earth Master's map. The Snake Master is now blocked on all sides by winding vines and thorny plants, growing over him like weeds.

"Will that hold him?" Ria asks, although her gaze is filled with wonder at Zoya. No one alive has seen earth magic like this.

Zoya stares at her hands, then hardens her gaze on the Snake Master. "I'll keep going if I must. But the Masters, Warriors, and Charts won't hold the dead, or the Serpent's Tongue, for long. I need to step back into battle."

As if summoned, we hear the garbled groans of the dead approach from behind. We spin to see a host of them headed our way, nearly upon us. I throw a desperate glance toward the earthen cage holding the Snake Master. We'll have to hope Zoya's magic works—we have another enemy upon us.

"No—we need you to keep hold of the cage. We'll handle them," I tell Zoya, gripping her sword. Having the same thought, Ria draws out her sword, and I recognize it as the same one Father once used.

One he's now passed on to his second daughter.

I nod at Saeed, and the group breaks. There's only a second for me to collect my breath before I swing the sword, remembering everything Irfan taught me about battle strategies. *Fighting is about instinct*, he told me. Fencing was always a talent of mine—but fighting in battle is something different altogether.

But instead of a soul leacher, the first person to approach me is a member of the Serpent's Tongue, appearing in a cloud of smoke. Immediately, he calls me a name I once despised. "Snake Princess," he says, revealing crooked teeth. "Your sister is much more valuable than you."

"We are equals," I tell him, trying to decipher the meaning of his words. A flicker of a memory reaches me; Ria, telling me she's the Key to the Snake Master's plans.

Still, the man pulls his sleeve back, revealing his palm. A thick, puckering scar cut into the shape of a snake lies on his hand, turning a terrible shade of red. He lunges for my exposed arm, and a burn sears my skin, hot as the Abai sun.

"*Agh,*" I grunt. With the hilt of my sword, I smash the man's forehead. He falls back, clutching his head with his still-burning hand, then screams in agony. Non-snakespeakers shouldn't possess this power, and from the dark lines escaping the man's eyes—inky black tears, I realize—this power is too much for his frail body.

He collapses to the ground, but the fight isn't over.

Flames lick the snow on either side of me—Taran's magic, combined with the Fire Master's. It contains a group of the Serpent's Tongue, but not enough. I nearly choke on the taste of ash and death in the air. My body is covered in wounds—knife-sharp cuts, burns from the Serpent's Tongue—that I feel each time I move. But I vow to forge ahead. Never before have I helped my people this way—by acting as one of them. By fighting with them side by side, steel by steel. Heart by beating heart.

I swear I'm numb by the time I find Saeed in my line of sight.

He's stumbling like he's been wounded, and a member of the undead reaches for him, ready to leach his soul—

"No!" I cry. I run for Saeed, feeling weightless despite the clouds of smoke and snow. I promised not to let anyone else get hurt. I promised myself, just last night before I fell asleep, that I would find a way to keep everyone safe. To keep a princess's honor.

I slash down the foul ghost of a man, and though he's barely fazed, I keep my sword level. I call every snake I can manage, my magic just about to burst, and within seconds, Shima and her legion of serpents appear at my side. Sweat breaks over my skin from the feat and the ghost's eyes widen. The snakes attack, lunging for him, as his skin peels back to reveal horrible gashes of sinew, of broken bone and torn muscle.

The snakes feed and feed and feed. Finally, I tear my gaze away.

I hold on to Saeed, who clutches his stomach. "Are you all right?"

"I'm not sure." He looks so aged in this moment, under the beaming red moonlight, but I still remember that boy I once loved. The boy I *thought* I loved. I realize our friendship is more important, and more powerful, than I ever acknowledged. I believed back then that I would do anything to save him. And at this moment, I still do.

I will save him, and save my people, no matter the cost.

"You're safe," I tell him, until I notice how pale his skin and lips have become. His eyes shutter closed as he expels a breath, and then his body collapses to the ground. I let Zoya's sword fall and drop to my knees beside him, clutching his shoulders as I try to help. His magic pulses against mine, familiar yet barely there. Something is wrong. His breath becomes a rattle, like a rotten seed in the husk of a dried fruit. Death looks as if it wants to take him into its clutches.

"Saeed?" I say feebly, using my hands to gently shake his head. A tear slips down his face. He's not responding. That's when I notice something beneath his vest. I carefully undo the buttons to find his shirt soaked with blood at the abdomen. A gash too deep to heal.

He was hurt even before I attempted to save him.

"No," I whisper in horror. Blood slips into the snow, forming a pool on the ground at his back. I stanch the flow immediately, ripping off a piece of my chunni to soak up the blood, but he still won't respond. I want to shake him awake, to make him remember who he is—a fighter, a dreamer. A boy who loved to the ends of the world.

I stare at Saeed, a tear frozen on his lashes, and press two fingers to his throat, praying for a pulse. Praying to feel his aura, his magic.

But instead, all I feel is ice, smoke, and death.

35

Ria

I raise the ancient talwar and mutter a prayer to my ancestors. Many have wielded it before. Now . . .

It's my turn to fight.

My sword sings as it whirls through the air, clashing against another's. A member of the Serpent's Tongue sneers at me when our weapons meet. Blood stains the gleaming silver of his blade, as red as the moon pulsing above.

"You are our Key," he reminds me. "You know what you must do."

I say nothing as I meet his sword once more, a deadly dance as we twirl through the sea of bodies. Purple-robed Kaaman Warriors; midnight-black Serpent's Tongue members; the undying soul leachers; and above us, the watchful gazes of the Masters, whose powers work to do the impossible and hold the dead at bay. But one is missing.

Where did the Snake Master go? The cocoon of earth he was

trapped in is no longer there. My stomach knots. He should be here. I need him to be—

In my distraction, the Serpent's Tongue member slips past my defense and his sword nearly slices my side. I sidestep him at the last moment and let my weapon reach his neck.

The acolyte only chuckles. "Will you do what you did to the Black Viper?" A dark smile overtakes his features. "Show me what you did that day. Show me why our Master chose *you*."

My hand shakes. I remember how good it felt to let Veer get what he deserved. I remember how the awful reality of what I had done hit me just afterward.

Raya. Ria. Raya. Ria.

Our names pulse in my mind until they melt into one. Until I swear I'm hearing my name being called from the skies. . . .

No. Not the skies. It's Rani, running toward me through the throng of bodies until she finally finds me with my sword aimed at the man's throat.

Her face is grim, and she barely spares a glance for the man across from me. "It's Saeed."

"What's wrong?" I ask, panic rising within me.

But my sister doesn't answer with words. She glances over at the member of the Serpent's Tongue and, after grabbing onto my sword, twirls, deftly parries, lunges, twists—until she pins the man to the ground and knocks him out cold with the hilt of the blade.

Huffing, she turns to me with a grave look in her eyes. "Come with me, Ria."

* * *

A body lies in the snow away from the battle. Curly hair. A soft yet sculpted face I would recognize anywhere.

Saeed.

At the sight of him, I rush in his direction. I fall to my knees in the snow, cold seeping into my bones, as I stare at his pale face. When I lean forward to touch him, he's as icy as the snow he rests in. I press my hand to his wrist, feeling for a pulse. Then I touch his neck, willing the warmth of my body to seep into his. But he merely shakes from the force, his head lolling to the side.

The truth of what's happened hits me.

Saeed is . . . dead. My breaths become harsh and fast until I'm light-headed.

No. No. NO.

Rage blinds me, setting me aflame. A sob unleashes from inside me, a broken dam of fury. "How did this happen?"

Denial strangles my throat, making my breaths quicken. Anger shakes my voice and tears spill down my cheeks. I'm shivering from Saeed lying on the ground with no breath, from conjuring all those snakes, from fighting against the Serpent's Tongue. Magic jitters inside me, threatening to erupt.

"It must have been a member of the Serpent's Tongue," Rani realizes, bending toward me as tears spill in rivulets down her face. I gaze at Saeed, noticing for the first time the pool of sticky blood, so dark it could be black beneath the red moon.

I ball my hands into fists. In this moment, I swear the snake coiled in my belly overtakes me. I swear my teeth elongate into fangs, ready to rip into flesh and blood and bone.

I swear I become a snake itself.

Rani watches me with horror in her gaze. "Ria . . ."

Images flash through my mind—the Eternal Night, the Snake Master at my side. If I had joined him, would this have happened? Could I have protected Saeed? But I don't let myself dwell for too long; I inhale deeply, forcing myself back into control, and let those images crack like shattered glass.

Not yet, Raya, I tell the cobra within. I loose a breath as my heart stutters to a slower pace. The feeling of those fangs retracts, and the writhing snake retreats at my command. I'm certain the serpent within me knows my plan. My *choice.*

My short time with Saeed flashes through my mind. Tears freeze on my face as I remember our first almost-kiss during our horseback riding. Then our more-than-a-kiss just a few nights ago. Then the day in the estate, where he told me I wasn't a harbinger of darkness just because of a prophecy. I didn't believe him.

We weren't supposed to end like this.

"There is no Soul Master to return him to life," a Master reveals from behind me. We turn to find her, the Memory Master, Preethi, her violet frame glowing. She looks with sorrow at Saeed, and I remember with a start that he's her descendant. *"He will soon join the others."*

"No," I say, my voice lethal. "I won't let him."

"Ria—" Rani begins, but I stop her with a hand, glancing at the sky. Where the Snake Master was once hovering, commanding his army, there is only air.

"Where is Sahil?" I demand of Preethi. The other Masters float down from the sky, looking weakened from using their powers against the Serpent's Tongue. "Where did he go?"

"He is your Master," the Fire Master says, his golden eyes aflame. *"You would know better than we."*

He's right. I close my eyes, feeling for the magic simmering in my veins, for the call of my Master. I ask Raya to guide me toward him, and within moments, an image is painted in my mind: the Snake Master, sitting in a lone cave. Our mindscape.

"Ria," Rani calls for me, and I snap out of that vision. The Masters stare down at me. I have only one thing to say.

"I know where the Snake Master is," I reveal. "And I know what has to happen."

I grab on to my sister's hand, instructing her to close her eyes. A pull, a tug, unfurls, like my magic folding in on itself. Rani's mind fuses with mine. And when I open my eyes, we're somewhere else entirely. A cave, with only a small hearth to light it.

Like the inside of the Snake Pit before Raya's death.

A mindscape, I tell Rani telepathically. *The place where I've been training with . . .*

The moment Rani's gaze lands on him, she gasps. Though she has seen him in the skies during battle, she hasn't seen him this close. But I am not stirred. I am immovable, unshakeable.

I am ready.

The heat of Rani's stare smothers me. She knows I've spent time with him, trained with him, but not more. I move closer toward where he sits before the fire, staring deeply into the flames as if in contemplation.

"Master," I greet him. I bow, and Rani hesitates before joining.

The Snake Master rises. A serpent's eyes, swollen lips, glistening scales covering his face. Rani loosens her stance, facing him fully for the first time.

"You have found me. I knew you would." His gaze pierces mine, then my sister's. *"Welcome, Rani,"* the Snake Master greets her. From behind him, Shima slithers forth. *"I called your familiar to join us. She seems very wise."*

Thank you, Massster. Shima bows her head, but I can feel the reluctance in her words. She had no choice but to arrive here.

As did I.

The Snake Master grins, his pallor brightening, his half-snake body lengthening. Behind him, I make out a group of cloaked figures—more of the Serpent's Tongue. One of them, just a boy, is holding the Bloodstone. Raya's heart.

"My new heart . . . ," the Snake Master begins.

I swear I can see, *feel*, the hole where his heart should be. Emptiness, coldness.

The cloaked figures come forward. *"Take your heart, Master, and with the Key you shall become the god of the Eternal Night. . . ."*

My heart thump-thump-thumps. I study the Snake Master with keen eyes, for he truly is our Master, and one I do not wish to let go of just yet. He's trained me for this exact moment. And I'd be lying if I said I wasn't an eager apprentice.

This is my fate. There are some things I cannot leave unful-filled, including my destiny.

Next to me, Rani looks like she wants to shake me, but it's too late for that.

It's time.

I bow on one knee and say, "Take me, Master. The cobra within me is risen, and I shall be your Key."

"Ria?" Rani gapes at me. "What are you doing? We're here to get the stone! To destroy it, and the Snake Ma—!"

But I do not turn to Rani as I say, "I'm sorry, Rani. This is the only way."

"Ria!" my sister yells again. "This is wrong! You saw what they did to Saeed—"

I filter out her words, instead bowing as if I were a servant to a Master.

No. A god.

The boy inches forward. Behind him, the Serpent's Tongue watch with a fervent gleam in their eyes as the child approaches his Master. He holds out the stone like a gift. There is no time for hes-itation as he plunges the Bloodstone into the Snake Master's chest. Our ancestor grunts from the sheer force of it, the power inching into his skin and bone. *Raya's* power. Shards of light explode from his body, blinding me for a moment, and a closed door appears before us. The keyhole shimmers with red light.

Could it be . . . ?

"May Raya's heart become yours, may the cobra rise, and may I open the door to the Eternal Night," I pray. I can feel all the magic I've practiced, all the darkness inside me, rise like a tower in the sky. Sweat slicks my brow, and I twist my hand as if holding a door handle. The door clicks open.

No longer glowing, the Snake Master smiles. With a sweep of his hand, the doorway flies open, revealing an endless, bloody sky.

"*Welcome, my daughters*," the Snake Master says, "*to the Eternal Night.*"

36

Rani

I black out. I don't know how I get from one place to the next. The following moment, I blink my eyes open, finding the world awash in red. The door behind us is sealed shut.

Scarlet sand peppers the ground beneath me. No. *Snow*, colored red. In the distance sit two fallen flags with the Memory Master's symbol.

The Kaaman palace is in ruins. A sunken world. But instead of a new world, it is the same one we came from. The battlefield. People running, screaming, as the entire world washes over in red. Trees flanking us have been set ablaze, like the moon can control both fire and tide.

It's all happening, right now. Because of my *sister*.

I pull myself up, calling out desperately to my twin. "Ria, what are you doing? Just because we share the same power as him doesn't mean we need to let him win." I inject my snake magic into my voice—spinning stories, truthful ones, to get what I desire. "Power does not need to make us delirious. We can change the way we use it—change the way we let our power affect us. This is *wrong*."

"*How so?*" the Snake Master says, eyes darkening, the stone dimming with them.

I shudder in a deep breath—and let it slither out. "We cannot shut out everyone around us," I say. "When you banished the Masters, you banished a piece of yourself. And soon enough, you'll be nothing. That's the consequence of the Bloodstone created in the Snake Pit." I train my gaze steadily against his. "Nothing in life comes without a consequence."

His gaze softens as he peers down on me. For a moment, he looks calm. Composed. Human. Then he speaks, and his voice is ice.

"*You remind me of her. Ruhanya. She abandoned me, too, when I needed her most.*"

"I am your dutiful apprentice, and my sister will soon follow," Ria interjects, glancing at me with hardened eyes. I can barely recognize her—recognize myself *within* her. "Please, Master, reward me. Honor us with Raya's and Ruhanya's presence."

"But they're—" I don't have time to complete the thought. *Dead.* With the whole of the world clasped in the Snake Master's palms, there is nothing, and no wish, he cannot fulfill.

The Snake Master tents his fingers, raises his chin. "*Of course, my dear daughter.*" Then his eyes flash and a snarl escapes his scaled lips. He touches the necklace of talismans at his throat, glowing with uncontrolled power. "*Come forth, my followers.*"

In the distance, a group of cloaked figures—the Serpent's Tongue—approach from the battlefield. As they get closer, I notice they're huddling around two people whose frames emit a golden light. The Serpent's Tongue parts, revealing . . .

"*My First Descendants, as you wished,*" the Snake Master says. "*Raya and Ruhanya.*"

I gape in awe at the shimmering visions of the Snake Master's First Descendants. If I look at Raya from a side angle, I can almost see Ria's face in hers.

"*I wish to undo my wrongs. Raya never deserved death. Show me that you, Ria, can be my First Descendant as we begin this new world. Face your sister for the final time.*"

Ria, too, looks shocked before she turns to me, eyes narrowed.

"Ria," I say, raising my hands. "This isn't you."

But Ria says nothing as the Snake Master hisses, "*You know what to do, Ria.*"

The sky darkens overhead. Before I can react, Ria lunges for me. I twist away, yelping, as the Serpent's Tongue's jeers fill the air. I am reminded of the Memory Master's prophecy of us, Ria and me, facing one another. *One of us would kill the other*, the prophecy had said. But no—we had changed our fortune. Reversed our fates.

Hadn't we?

But as I stare at the Ria ahead of me, I'm not sure if I am seeing my sister. I am seeing the girl in the Fountain of Fortunes, eyes hardened, our noses almost touching. I am seeing my reflection and my worst nightmare all at once.

"Ria," I breathe, reaching out for her, but she rears back as if burned. The snake mark on her palm glows.

The Snake Master chuckles. His tone is smoky, one of darkness rather than light.

"You two are cunning, like me. It is no wonder the Memory Master thought you both important enough to offer a prophecy."

"It wasn't just one prophecy we were offered," Ria says, still looking at me. "It was two."

I raise my brows at my sister, but she continues:

"A missing heart to be restored

A moon with tears as red as blood."

The Snake Master looks impressed. *"I take it you've figured out this prophecy, then?"*

Ria nods. "We have restored your missing heart, Master, beneath a moon with tears as red as blood."

"Indeed you have. And now, I must slake my thirst for a new world. A world that my brother Manav deserved to live in. A world that Raya deserved to live in. I'm doing this, in part, for them—for a future they never got to live. And to begin, I must fix the mistake I made when I lost Raya. I need her back. I need you, Ria, and you only. You know what you must do. You must destroy your sister, the way you would have if you had never been separated."

Is that true? If we weren't separated at birth, would Ria and I have grown up despising one another? Would we have grown apart, attacked one another in a fatal fight?

I won't let that happen. I won't let my sister be taken into the dark.

"This isn't what you saw in your vision, Ria!" I cry. "You don't need to be like our ancestor. We can change history. We already have!"

Ria blinks, unfazed.

Tears well in my eyes as I approach her cautiously, wrapping a hand around her cheek. This time, she does not flinch. But she doesn't offer me a look of sisterly love, either.

"If I'd never met you, Ria," I say, choking on my words, "I don't know who I would have been. But *you* changed me. Not anyone else. Not my journey into the jungles of Abai. *You.* You survived for years on the streets. You begged for scraps when I lounged in the richest palaces. I was selfish. Foolish. But looking at you, the life you've lived . . . I understand why you connect with our Master. Because he, like you, was lonely. Starving for a new life. I wouldn't blame you if you still hated royalty, or if you don't know where you belong. But just know that I'm where I belong. With you."

Ria stares at me, eyes reflecting mine. They turn glassy with remembrance, with love.

"I already knew all that, Rani," she says, her tone cold but her eyes almost teasing. And then, she offers me a gesture, one riddled with secrets. She crosses her fingers over her chest.

Anytime we need each other, here's how we'll know. My words, the day before we left the Abaian palace.

The realization dawns on me like a rising sun. I'm careful not to gape, to reveal anything to the Snake Master as Ria steps back from me, eyes dark as ever.

"We are no longer sisters," Ria says, turning to the Snake Master.

"*Good,*" he purrs. *"Now fulfill your destiny."*

Ria nods obediently. She lunges for the knife I earned during the Fire Master's trial, placed in a scabbard at my hip. She slips it into her hand and, in one smooth motion, aims the knife at my throat. This was the vision the Memory Master saw. Two sisters, foes at the end of it all.

No—not foes.

For Ria turns at the last moment, whipping the Fire Master's knife through the air. It cuts through the thick silence, turning over and over until it lands right where Ria aimed.

The Snake Master's chest.

For a moment, no one breathes. Even the Serpent's Tongue looks stunned, as if they cannot believe what has been done.

Then the Snake Master chuckles, blood pouring out of his lips. He stumbles forward, falling to his knees.

Ria grabs on to my hand, and I feel that snake magic between us bright as a thousand burning suns. Every memory I've shared with Ria flows through my veins. I sense the very half of her turning me whole, and realize the truth.

We are more than our connection to the Snake Master. Together, we are a brewing storm, a churning sky, and a restless sea. And we will stop at nothing to unleash this tempest and bring him to his knees.

I draw on everything I've learned with Saeed and Tutor. I draw on the power I felt during my trial, the power that led me to find the true Shima. I might not be as powerful as Ria, but I've had years of study leading to this moment. Years of bonding with Shima. Years of understanding snakes, fearing them, loving them. My connection with snakes isn't simple. It's as complex as a spider's web. And tonight, I will form that web, call upon the snakes, and ensnare the Snake Master in my trap.

Power flashes through me, turning me light-headed. With Ria at my side, it's so strong I could bowl over from it. But I won't make the same mistake I did last time, letting our power fuel us, letting the Pit come alive like a feral animal, claiming Amara as its own.

Snakes slip out from the cracks in the ground, reach us from every corner, until we are surrounded by them. By our companions.

When we unleash our magic, the snakes attack. But all too easily, the Snake Master pushes the snakes aside with his magic and yanks the knife from his chest.

"My dear Ria, I hoped it wouldn't come to this," the Snake Master sneers. *"What a foolish attempt to destroy the stone. Have you forgotten that you cannot harm someone who holds this ruby? You cannot hurt me, the most powerful of all Masters."*

"I thought so," Ria says, but she's grinning. Like she knew this would happen. "I might not be able to hurt a Master—but I can distract one."

37

Ria

It's time for my plan to take hold.

I knew I had to bring about the Eternal Night to gain the Snake Master's trust, but to make it believable, I couldn't tell my sister. And on this night, when the Snake Master's magic is at its peak, so is mine.

The Eternal Night isn't just for the Snake Master. It's for me. For Rani. For what we're about to do.

At the Kaaman palace, Rani revealed to me the truth of destroying the Snake Master. Our magic, gone for good. But I knew the Eternal Night would make our powers stronger. Possibly strong enough to survive the fallout. Tonight, we'll have to risk it all.

I pray our magic will be strong enough to outlast this. That *we* will both be strong enough to complete my plan.

The Snake Master taught me how to control snakes. It's time to control him.

"This is no distraction. You would attack me with my own weapon? I am their master. Not you."

"Snakes aren't possessions. They're companions," I say, inching ever closer to him. Rani follows suit, knowing I have something up my sleeve. I just need to keep talking—get within arm's reach, while he's still weak. . . .

"All the time I've spent with you has taught me something. Power is as precious as the ground beneath our feet, as dangerous as poison. And you've abused that power. I once felt sorry for you, but you simply wanted to use me. To use my rage and twist it into something to your benefit."

I pause and let the words wash over him before I continue, my voice as steely as my resolve. "But I'm not yours to control."

Rani and I call upon the snakes. They flood forth like undulating waves toward the Snake Master. Stronger this time. I embrace the Eternal Night, the poison of the moon, and let it feed me. I can be as dark and powerful as the Snake Master. *That* I'm good at.

The Snake Master staggers backward. A fierce wind floats by, and he coughs, eyes red with rage.

"You can't stop me that easily," he grits out.

The Snake Master sends spears of magic my way, in the shape of deadly snakes' fangs, but I stop them before they can pierce skin. When I send them back, they pummel the Snake Master and shatter to the ground, harmless.

"Bow to me, Ria, and I will let all of this go. I will keep you as my apprentice."

"No," I belt out, much closer now. So close to his First Descendants that we're nearly face-to-face, nose-to-nose. But as I speak, weakness spreads through me right from my heart. It feels like the Snake Master is siphoning the magic right out of me. Using me, just like he used me to bring this Eternal Night.

But *I* made that decision. I've turned on the Snake Master. And now, I have to follow through.

What I'm about to do is the biggest gamble I've ever made.

"Raya . . . ," I whisper. The Snake Master once inhabited Amara's body. Now, with his First Descendants present . . .

I grab on to Rani's hand. I channel my mind against hers, hoping our telepathic connection will strengthen—and when I feel our minds fuse, I know that Rani understands what to do.

On my count, I tell her. *One, two . . .*

Three.

We both leap forth, toward the visions of Raya and Ruhanya. The moment I feel their aura, it slips around me like the sea cradling a harbor. I focus my full attention on this—fusing my being with another's, melding what is within me and without. Raya's spirit fights back at first, and I dart a glance to my right. While I fuse into Raya's body, Rani becomes Ruhanya, eyes cast to the heavens as she bites back the pain. I turn back as the fusion begins. My bones crack, split; sinew tears and blood heats. I scream and yell into an abyss of nothingness until my body becomes whole and fully formed, a fleshed-out being.

I gaze down at my body. And then up at Rani's.

She looks like an echo of herself, and her eyes widen at the sight of me. "Is that you . . . Ria?" She reaches forward and touches my cheek. I nod, tears rising to my eyes.

My plan worked. We can harness the power of Raya and Ruhanya and end the Snake Master for good by doing what Raya did all those years ago. . . .

Rani knows my plan instantly, and she grins reassuringly at me. It's strange to see her face as Ruhanya's: her lips bigger, her nose narrower, her eyes wider. But somehow, I can still see an outline of her, the real her, underneath. The image reflected in her eyes—Raya—startles me, too. Gazing at my new body through my sister's eyes, I sense the snake in my belly growing stronger. My snake magic has never felt so strong, so stark, for I am the First Descendant herself. I no longer have just a piece of Raya; I have her full power.

And I'm going to use it to defeat the Snake Master.

"*Daughters?*" he says, leveling his gaze at us, full of confusion. We join hands and face him.

"I'm sorry, Father," I say, my voice melded with Raya's.

Rani and I both shoot our palms out at the ground, and in a whirl the bloody snow disappears, leaving only dry, cracked earth beneath. Veins form in the weathered ground from our simple command, from our sheer power, from the force of the Snake Master's First Descendants.

Crack.

"Fall," Rani says, spelling out our plan aloud. "Fall into the Pit."

A new Pit. *Our* Pit.

The Snake Master raises his arms, calling his magic forth, but our combined magics against him are strengthened, led by Raya's and Ruhanya's powerful snake magic intertwined with our own.

I shut my eyes and feel Rani's magic crackle like a hearth. Mine roars forth, and for the first time, I embrace my magic not because of my ancestor's wishes, but because of my own. My magic is an untamable beast, much like Raya's. And I taste hers with every beat of our hearts, copper and blood and something sweet—like a berry filled with poison. I allow that magic to deepen, to strengthen in tune with my sister's, and I open my eyes.

It's far too late for the Snake Master now.

The crack explodes, rocking the earth beneath us, and a hole forms, writhing like a snake as it grows deeper. The ground beneath the Snake Master's body gives way, and he reaches, instinctively, for his daughters. A cry for help glistens in his dark, hollow eyes. A plea escapes his lips, echoing in the distance of this endless night.

And in a moment that stretches like an hour, the Snake Master is swallowed whole.

The snakes flee with concern, following the Snake Master inside. Rani and I approach our new creation. Carefully, she collects the fallen knife from the Fire Master, the blade covered in blood, and returns it to the scabbard at her hip.

"Has it worked? Have we created a new Snake Pit?" Rani wonders.

A hand slams onto the top of the Pit, fingers sinking into the dirt, and my sister shrieks. The Snake Master pulls himself from its depths, blackened scales boiling on his skin. His slitted nostrils flare with anger. Rani and I fall back as the Snake Master rises once more.

He stands over us, wearing an ugly smirk. The Blood Moon shines behind him, bathing him in crimson light.

"I thought you were my daughters. I thought you were smarter than this."

"We are," Rani says, her voice shaking but resolved. "But we're also daughters of Amran. And you'll never be his equal." Rani turns her head to me. We've spoken with a mind link; we've transformed into the Snake Master's First Descendants; and now, so close to the Snake Master, I feel her aura as if it's my own. I won't lie; some of Rani's fear slips into my veins, too. But if I've learned anything over the past few moons, it's that fear ignites bravery.

Do you know what to do? I show her my desires, my future.

Rani nods. She leaps into action, distracting the Snake Master while I reach for his heart. Past his aura of magic, through his skin, feeling the very real parts of a Master. Blood, flesh, and bone.

Knocked off guard, he can only watch as I, his kin, pull the Bloodstone from his very chest. This shouldn't be possible—the Bloodstone cannot be forcibly taken without repercussions—but I'm not truly taking it. I'm getting it back, for Raya, *as* Raya. *Restoring* it to its rightful owner, just as the prophecy said.

It was never the Snake Master's heart to be restored—it was Raya's.

I stare down at the glittering ruby in my hands, listening to its faint heartbeat.

"*No!*" the Snake Master cries, reaching for me. But Rani and I are already prepared. My sister lunges for the hollow of the Snake Master's throat, gripping the necklace of talismans with one hand. With a force only gifted to the First Descendants, she tugs on the chain and breaks the necklace entirely, letting the charms—the talismans—cascade to the ground, powerless.

Powerless against the night.

Our Master no longer has me, the Key, on his side, nor does he have the magic to keep this Eternal Night alive. I watch behind him as the world changes, the red light searing behind him dimming into a soft pink. The sky cracks, chipping away like dry dirt and falling to the ground like feathers. The moon, too, slinks toward the ground, a red orb melting into the horizon.

The Snake Master presses a hand to his empty chest and stumbles back, gasping for air like he can't breathe. But then he glances up. I've never seen him look so honest. No rage, no revenge. Just . . . emptiness.

Rani and I meld our magic together. For once, my magic doesn't fight against hers. I think I know why. Because we've accepted each other. Everything about each other, the good and the bad. The dark and the light. Because we're sisters.

Sisterhood is its own kind of magic; not the kind passed down from a Master, but the kind that we build in each other. And tonight, it's time we used it.

We call the Pit to open wider, wider, until it reaches the Snake Master's tail. He slips inside inch by inch, using one hand to grasp on to the edge. But this isn't like with Amara. This isn't a misguided fall. This is intentional. A place to seal the Snake Master, his magic, and his being, without destroying him.

He will be the Pit's sacrifice, just as Raya was. Except this time, it won't be an accident.

He turned Amara into a puppet. He brought the world to its knees. It's time he faced the consequences.

"A new Pit," the Snake Master says, his voice almost dazed. He shakes his head. *"This is not how I imagined my future."*

"What did you think it would be?" I ask. In truth, I want to know. He's my ancestor, and there's no changing that.

"Eternal." The word hovers in the air, gently falls from the Snake Master's lips. Like a child discovering their name for the first time, or sweeping a finger over a blade of grass in an endless desert.

"Then eternal you shall be," Rani responds. Together, Rani and I hold out our hands.

We close the Pit, inch by inch, until it is nothing but soil and dust and nightmares come to an end—and the Snake Master, imprisoned forever under the earth. Not dead, not truly gone. I still feel my magic alight inside me, a sign of the pulse of life beating within him.

The members of the Serpent's Tongue glance at one another. Their Master is sealed away—their only hope thwarted.

They disappear in plumes of smoke.

It's over. Finally, it's all over.

I release my hold on Raya, letting the snake in my belly rest. I gaze at a small puddle of melted snow on the ground and watch as our reflections ripple and shift. Ruhanya, coalescing back into Rani; me, shaping back into Ria.

It doesn't hurt, Raya leaving. Not like it did when I pushed our auras together. I can feel a soft nudge of gratitude, light as the brush of fingers, before she pulls away completely.

As the Eternal Night shatters, the sky clears, returning to the stormy gray that hovers over the Kaaman palace's grounds. I blink, and with a dizzying shift we're back. The world has returned to normal, and on the battlefield there are only signs of wreckage and a ceased fight. The soul leachers disappear one by one back into the vortex, which seals closed in a blink. The Masters hover above us, their duties finished.

"Thank you," I whisper up to the sky—to both the Masters and Amran. The Masters nod back with sage smiles. Knowing the Snake Master can no longer harm them, they disappear into a plume of light. Perhaps to wander the earth again, now that they are free.

"There's just one thing left to do," Rani says, taking the Bloodstone in my hand.

"Not yet." I remember what Amara told me—that if we successfully severed the connection between her and the Snake Master, she would return. I still have a small piece of Raya within me—and with it, the elusive soul magic Amara desperately wished for.

"Ria . . . ," Rani begins. But I do not gaze at her as I hunt through the battlefield and land on the other side, where Saeed's body still lies. I can't even look at him, at the reality of him. It's like Amran hears my wishes, because something distracts me from spiraling into tears. A rectangle of golden light appears. It must be the doorway of death, ready to pull him in—

Or where someone is ready to step out.

A woman's figure exits the door, still carefully constructed of rose petals and starlight. I watch as that light explodes, as the roses flutter away on the breeze, leaving behind a very real, very alive body standing on the battlefield.

Her familiar, flaming red hair is the first thing I notice, followed by her smile. I recognize it all too well—the picture of release. "Amara," I whisper. Next to me, Rani stiffens.

"You have removed the connection between me and the Snake Master," Amara says, bowing her head. But as she moves her gaze downward, her eyes are caught on the lifeless body beneath her.

And a sob escapes her throat.

"Saeed?" Her voice is chipped like broken glass.

"He's . . . gone," Rani says, tears rising.

"No," Amara chokes out, echoing the word I thought over and over before our final battle with the Snake Master. She falls to her knees, pain exploding in her voice. "*No.* There must be a way to bring him back." She glances at both of us desperately. I don't know what to say. I had my one chance to speak to Mama Anita before letting her go for good. That wasn't the same as bringing her back.

Unless . . .

Amara must see something in my eyes. "Tell me!" she demands, desperation lacing her words.

Rani speaks. "When the Three Blessed Sisters offered me visions of the Snake Master's life, he explained why his brother Manav was Unmade. Something about his power of life also bringing about death. A transfer of energy. When one life disappears, another takes its place."

"Which means . . . a give-and-take. A soul for a soul," I conclude.

Can reviving the dead be accomplished with soul magic?

Snapping away my focus from Saeed, a shadow appears at the doorway of death. Amara spins to find a body stitching together from the ground up, every cell, every cauterized piece of flesh. The man is young, sporting the same curly hair and full lips as Saeed. But his eyes betray him, offering the longing sadness, a distinct lack of youth. A man who's spent years gone from this world.

"Kumal?" Amara's voice breaks gently. "It's you." Her whole body shivers as she stands, moving away from Saeed to take her husband into her arms before realizing he cannot step over into our world. With twisted fascination, I watch. Watch as she convulses with sobs of joy and grief and confusion all at once.

"I didn't see you inside the door," she admits to Kumal. "I did not truly belong, for I was not wholly beyond life, nor a true inhabitant of the doorway."

Rani and I try to process everything we're seeing. The scene reminds me of my parents rejoining with their lost memories of Ria. Of my twin. Our family became whole again.

I feel Amara's pain, burrowing deep inside me, the way the Snake Master's did the night I saw his memories.

Amara looks down at Saeed's lifeless body and back to her husband. She spins to face me.

"A transfer of energy," she demands. "You said it can be done. How?"

"You have a choice to make," I tell Amara. "This was your wish. To be the Master of Souls. You might not be a real Master, but you have the chance to bring your son back. In order for this to be accomplished, I would have to transfer your life for your son's using the small bit of Raya's soul magic housed within me."

Amara's eyes turn glassy at her son's name. She stands straight. One foot in life, the other in death. In the doorway of death, Kumal appears as sorrowful as a petalless rose.

"The world of the living isn't where you belong," Amara says softly to him. "Is it?"

"For our son to live, you must come with me, my rose," Kumal says. He fades back into the world of the dead, but the door is still open. Waiting.

Amara glances down at Saeed, and her body crumples. She leans her head toward her son. "Do it," she tells me, her voice filled with conviction and sorrow.

I approach Saeed, bending down toward him and injecting as

much of my soul magic—Raya's soul magic—into him as possible. Light fills the air, wispy as clouds.

"Please, Saeed . . . ," I whisper. "Return to us."

Amara adds, "I'm so sorry, my son. . . ."

Unending silence. My heart, thumping. My eyes closed, afraid of what might come next.

Then—a voice fills the silence. "I know, Mother."

Rani and I gasp. That voice is pure as honey and just as sweet.

The blinding light from my magic slowly disappears. I lift myself to my feet as Saeed's eyelids open infinitesimally. His clothes are drenched in snow and blood, his cheeks red. His eyes well up with tears.

"What happened to you." He says it not as a question but as a statement, clasping his mother's face in his hands. Her skin pales, turning the same shade as Saeed's.

"I'm fading," Amara says. "There is no greater love than sacrifice."

Saeed's voice breaks as he says, "No. Mother, please . . ."

"Let me do this, Saeed."

Tears slip out of Saeed's eyes as he forces back a sob. A spiral of a vision leaves his hands, threaded with violet light. From the threads Saeed has formed in the air, a memory surfaces. Him and his mother spending time in the Abai palace gardens. Saeed plucks a rose for her. In the memory, Amara's saddened face lifts with a spark of joy. "These were your father's favorite . . . and mine." The memory dissipates, leaving him and his mother clutching each other one last time.

Already fading from this world, Amara stands, shaking. Saeed's eyes follow her, as if he can't bear to look away as she approaches the doorway of death.

Amara steps back into the light, eyes holding on to her son before sliding briefly to me. "In life, we always have a choice. I hope I've made the right one."

The moment the doorway seals shut, it disappears in a gust of snowy wind.

Amara is gone.

I fall to my knees once more, tears filling my eyes as I throw my arms around Saeed. I don't know how much time passes, everything that's happened tonight barreling through us. All I know is that I need to hold on to who I have left in my life and never let go.

Moments later, Zoya, Dhruv, Amir, and the others all race up to us. They gaze down at Rani and me, peppering us with questions, but we have no time for explanations. Rani holds out the Bloodstone, and each of them stares at it with wide eyes.

After Rani places the stone on the ground, she takes out her knife. A sheen of the Snake Master's blood still gleams from the blade. "It's time," I tell my sister. I glance back at the group as they huddle around us, about to watch this event unfold.

Rani's grip on the knife wavers. I step forward and hold her hand, steadying it, both our grips heavy on the hilt. Rani won this from a trial in the Malwan Pass—now, it's time we use it.

"Together," Rani murmurs. So we plunge our hands down in

unison, watching as the knife breaks through the stone without resistance, fracturing it into a hundred tiny pieces. They spread like rose petals against the snow.

Zoya bends down and, using her earth magic, draws the pieces deep into the ground, burying them. I release a pent-up breath. We did it. We shattered this cursed stone. We saved our magic. And as the sky clears and my sister cries with joy, I realize we never needed the Snake Master. We only need each other.

Epilogue
Rani

Two Weeks Later

I knock on Amir's door twice. When no one answers, I poke my head through the gap and let myself in.

Amir's chambers are a veritable mess. I chuckle to myself as I stare at his unmade bedsheets. He asks the maids not to clean up after him. Running my hand over the bed frame, I see something twinkle from between the sheets.

I grasp Amir's timepiece between my fingers. The inlaid gold shines like the sun, beckoning to me like a songbird's call.

"Are we on time, Princess?" Amir says from behind me, and I nearly jump at his arrival.

"You scared me," I say, turning to him. *"Oh."*

My mouth drops at his formal attire—and his shorn hair, identical to the way it looked when I first met him.

"Figured I needed to look good for the official peace summit," he laughs. I blush. But his words are a reminder: tonight is a night of celebration, not war. Peace, not the past.

I have to remember that.

"Because the last one didn't go so well," I joke, though my voice is flat. I look down at my slippered feet—I'm nowhere near ready, unlike Amir.

"It didn't?" he says, tapping his chin and stepping closer to me. "Because if I recall correctly, you took down the Snake Master and saved the world. So I heard. *I* was off fighting an army of the undead."

I laugh, his teasing oddly soothing. "Then I suppose it did work out. The talismans are back where they belong," I explain. After the reign of the Eternal Night ended, the talismans transformed back into their regular states, and we offered them to their rightful magical descendants. Only Aditi refused her talisman— the Tide Master's sword—entrusting it instead to Professor Neel for safekeeping.

"You did the right thing," Amir says, approaching me and reaching out. He plants his hands on my upper arms, tugging me closer, and I rest my head against his chest.

Creating a new Snake Pit was no easy feat. My tether to my snake magic is still here, and so is Ria's. For now, we can breathe easy knowing our ancestor cannot cause more harm.

And with Amara gone, it's time to move forward.

"Here," Amir says, pulling me from my reverie. I lean back. In his hands, he holds the pearl hairpin he gave me over a moon ago. "I thought . . . you might want to wear it tonight?" He grins at me hopefully.

I smile. "A thousand jewels would never compare to this." I

reach up and kiss him on the cheek, savoring this moment, this small beat of time where nothing else exists except the two of us.

When I pull back, his cheeks are flushed.

"Guess I'll never get used to a princess kissing me," he laughs.

"Well, you should," I say. "Because I don't want you to leave. And neither does my mother."

"You spoke with Queen Maneet?"

I nod and perch on the edge of Amir's bed. As if answering my call, he sits by my side. Our legs press against each other, and neither of us pulls back.

"As soon as we got back from Kaama," I tell him, "I worked up the courage to tell Mother. She thought that my spending time in Retan might mean I would become closer to Prince Dhruv. But I told her things didn't work out between us . . . because I was in love with someone else."

Amir nearly chokes. "In love?" He raises his brows. "With . . . me?"

"No, with the prince of Kaama," I retort dryly.

"He *is* rumored to have good looks, huh?"

I elbow him. *"Amir."*

"I know, I know," Amir says. He leans in and whispers, "But the rumors are true, right?"

"Rumors be damned," I say simply. "I know who I'm in love with."

Amir's cheeks grow pink.

"Am I being too forward?" I wonder suddenly.

"N-no," he says, lowering his gaze and hiding a grin. "It's just . . . I've never experienced this with anyone before. Romance." He looks up at me. "To be honest, I didn't know if I'm doing any of it right."

"Love?" I ask him.

He nods.

"Does it scare you?"

He peers deeply into my eyes, searching them before smiling wistfully. "Nothing scares a thief."

"What about a prince?"

He perks a brow. "I'm no prince."

"You are to me," I admit. I thumb the hairpin. "To your parents, too. We both went through trials that day, you know. We couldn't have gotten the knife without it. It's because of you that we ever succeeded in destroying the Bloodstone."

Amir grins. "So I'm a prince, then? That prince of Kaama should watch out."

I laugh. "You are. I could have chosen a life with Prince Dhruv, yes. But that wasn't what my heart truly wanted."

Amir's gaze drops to my lips. "And what is it you truly want, Princess Rani?"

My answer is not one with words. I lean forward and press my lips against his. At the first touch, he looses a soft gasp, reaching forward with a hand and wrapping it around the back of my neck. I fold into his embrace, unable to let go—not wanting to let go.

But eventually Amir draws back. "In that case . . ."

He swiftly pulls something from behind him—a small box.

"What's this?" I ask. Before I can take the box from his grasp, he leans back.

"If I may . . . ," he says, a mischievous grin lighting his face. He snaps open the box and sets it on my lap.

Revealing a ring shaped like a lotus.

I gasp. No words leave my lips.

"It's a promise ring. I was going to wait, but y'know, now that you've admitted you're in *love* with me—"

"Oh, and you're not?" I counter playfully.

Amir's smile is like a thousand stars in the night sky. "I am. Thief's honor."

And just like that, every worry within me melts away. My heart leaps as he slips the ring onto my finger. This time, he is the one to lean forward and press a kiss onto my cheek.

"Guess I'll never get used to a thief kissing me," I say.

Our laughter echoes throughout the palace.

Ria

The peace summit is about to begin.

I stand at the front of the crowd in the throne room, perched next to my father. Opposite us sits King Jeevan and the rest of their councils. A treaty lies on the table before us, and nobles from all over Abai crane their necks to get a good look.

Unlike the celebration held here almost two moons ago, I'm on time, and Rani is the late one.

"Where is she?" I mutter to myself, just before I spot her. She rushes into the throne room, making it to my side. We're wearing matching outfits tonight—a request on our mother's part. My blouse is light green, my skirt a dusty pink. Rani's blouse is pink and her lehenga green—twins in opposite ways, down to our clothing styles.

Though I do notice one thing different about her.

Her cheeks—she's *blushing*.

"And where were *you*?" I whisper to her before the ceremony begins, the room abuzz as whispers vault through the air.

"With Amir," she admits, eyes trailing to where Amir has joined the crowd alongside Sanya and Jas, who both returned for the occasion. I turn back to Rani and notice the ring on her finger. My eyes widen.

"He did it!" I whisper-squeal. Rani widens her eyes, attempting to hush me, but I won't. I've been waiting to tease my sister about this for *days*.

Before she can speak, the crowd is brought to attention.

"Welcome, all," King Natesh says. "We hope the second time's the charm."

The crowd chortles.

". . . and we are grateful you are all here tonight, in Abai instead of Kaama as previously planned," my father continues, "to witness the declaration of peace between our lands." I clap with the rest of the crowd, and the kings each take a feather pen.

I hold my breath. This is it.

The moment war ends, and a new life begins.

I used to think the raja was a warmongering man. I used to think my life was worthless.

I won't think that anymore.

As the kings each sign the peace treaty, the crowd applauds. "May Kaama and Abai prosper!" they sing. And the true celebration begins.

The crowd cheers and parts, a happy chatter engulfing the room as some form lines to meet the two kings. Rani looks about ready to cry happily. But I'm betting it isn't all to do with the peace treaty. "Tell me *everything.*"

She pulls me out of the throne room and into a small alcove. "He said he was going to wait, but . . ."

"A thief can never wait," I tell her, winking. She laughs, and happiness like no other I've felt fills my heart. Tears spring to my eyes when I remember when I first met Amir, poor and riddled with sorrow. Just like I was.

We were both able to carve new paths for ourselves. New futures.

Ssspeaking of new futures, a voice says from below me.

I jump. "Shima!"

I catch sight of her blue-green scales coiled beneath me. This alcove really is her favorite place for small talk, apparently.

"What are you doing here?" Rani wonders, laughing.

Just trying to move things along, she says innocently, cocking her head toward the hallway.

Where Saeed stands. He lifts a tentative hand in a wave, and I wave back.

"Oh, so now who's blushing?" Rani says.

"I'm getting you back for saying that."

"Sure," Rani drawls, pushing me out of the alcove unrepentantly. I walk toward Saeed, who greets me with a bow.

"No need to be so formal," I say. But when he lifts himself up, his usually bright eyes look dark.

"There's something I want to show you, if you'll allow me."

Saeed has been like this for two weeks—his eyes, once full

of light, dampened. A side effect of the soul magic I used to save him, maybe, but also a marker of his grief. With his mother gone, I don't blame him. We've spoken about it, forgiven everything. It was ultimately Amara's choice.

Still, I have a feeling Saeed will never quite be the same.

"Follow me," he says crisply. He grabs a candlestick, the wick already lit, and leads me upstairs. We stop before a room no one has dared enter since we returned this past week, riding home with the two kings and spending nearly every waking moment preparing for tonight.

Amara's chambers.

"Are you sure you want to go inside?" I ask Saeed as he moves to open the door.

"I am," he tells me.

When we enter, I shudder. It looks no different from the last time I came in here with Saeed and Aditi and Shima. When we discovered Amara's secrets.

"I wanted to honor her in some way. If you'll join me."

"Of course," I say. He leads me to the back room, where that spiral staircase sits, and tentatively, we make our way up.

To Amara's shrine room.

Saeed sets down the candlestick and pulls a rose from his kurta vest. He places it on the floor, where a flurry of blackened roses and letters sit in a dome of melted candle wax.

"She's still here, you know." I grasp on to Saeed's hand, claiming its warmth and melding it with mine.

"I know." For the first time, I see tears fill Saeed's eyes. When one tear drops, I wipe it away with a hand. I don't move my palm from his cheek when he turns toward me. Where I once saw darkness in his eyes, I now see release. Freedom.

Free from a terrible past. Free from a terrible fate.

"They're together now, your parents," I say, voice wobbling. More tears spill—mine, this time. Despite everything Amara has done to us, Saeed will always keep a piece of her.

"I'm glad," Saeed says, turning his lips into my palm and kissing it. Heat spreads through me like a summer's sunset. But I feel something else, too. He hasn't fully recovered from what occurred on the battlefield.

His hands and face turn pale the way they did the moment he woke from death. I swear his body flickers like candlelight. "Saeed—"

"I almost died. I *did* die. But there was no way I could leave you. Not even in death."

"There was no way I could leave you, either," I whisper, squeezing his hand. "Are you sure you're well?"

He nods. "I'm recovering . . . but I don't know if I'll ever be fully myself. But I'm not afraid of that," Saeed clarifies firmly. "I feel . . . closer to you."

I think of the piece of Raya resting within me. She held a piece of soul magic in her, too.

Just another thing connecting me to Saeed.

I know this magic will never go away. And like the darkness

within both me and Saeed, I don't want it to. This is who we are now.

"Do you remember what I taught you about the bridge between Abai and Kaama?"

I nod. "I thought I taught *you* that."

He laughs. "Now that Kaama and Abai are finally working together, maybe that bridge will be built someday. People won't have to worry about who they love, or where their lover comes from."

My lips frown. "Like your mother."

"Two worlds," he agrees. And he's right. Amara was born from two countries, two worlds; now she rests in a liminal space between worlds, too.

Saeed pulls another rose from his vest.

"For your mother?" I say.

He shakes his head. "For you. I don't want to see roses and remember my mother's fate. I want to see roses and think of you."

I smile despite the tears still clinging to my face. "Thank you, Saeed." I reach up on my toes and plant my lips against his, warmth spreading through me like sunlight, melting with the darkness to create something new, bold, everlasting.

And when I pull back, I take the rose, thorns and all.

I meet Rani in my chambers later that night.

Moonlight shivers through the parted silk curtains, a gleaming white light instead of red.

"It's a sign," Rani says as we sit on the bench by the window. "We're past the prophecy now. We did it."

I take her hand in mine. "Together."

She smiles. "And did Saeed take you on a romantic moonlit walk?"

I shake my head. "He gave me this rose, actually." I pull it from my dresser and twirl it between my fingers. He's right. Roses no longer have to be a sign of Amara's wrath, of her vengeance. It was and will always be a symbol of her love for Kumal.

And now, a symbol of the budding relationship between me and Saeed.

"Well," Rani says, turning to the window. "There's a lot that's going to change now. Have you . . . thought about the future?"

"What about it?" I wonder.

Rani looks down. "You know. Being queen?"

My breath hitches. "Honestly, I was going to ask you the same thing."

Rani leans toward me like she's about to tell a secret. "When the time comes, I think we could both rule side by side, like the Three Blessed Sisters," she says. "What do you think?"

I grin. "I think we could make the perfect queens." Sure, the thought of ruling a kingdom still scares me—but I've faced so many fears these past few moons . . . I won't be afraid of being a queen. "As long as we always trust each other."

Rani smiles, reflecting. "I should have trusted you the night of the battle. Known you would never turn on me. You always have something up your sleeve, thief girl."

"And don't you ever forget it," I say with a wink, laughing before continuing. "It was a risk. But at least the other Masters are free now." I look out the window. "Where do you think they are?"

Rumor is, people have seen the Masters themselves walking on the earth, felt magic thrumming through the ground again.

But I know the rumor to be true, since the banishment of the Masters ended when we locked the Snake Master away, his hold over them finally released.

"Anywhere," Rani says, leaning back and glancing at the sky. "Someday, magic will be everywhere again, like it was in the Old Age."

The vision of it overtakes me. There's still so much out there— the futures we'll bring together for this kingdom. Though we didn't destroy the Snake Master for good, his banishment in the world of the Eternal Night, sealed off by our snake magic, has allowed our lands to heal from his poison. Already Retanians have been sharing messages with us, telling us of how they're seeing an improvement in their crops. Already we've seen the world around us begin to grow again.

"Speaking of magic . . ."

"Is it time already?" Rani says. She flips my hand over, revealing my palm. The snake burn has since faded, but I still see the outline of it. Honestly, I don't think it'll ever really be gone. But maybe that's not the point. I'm still connected to the Snake Master, just as he is to me.

I nod.

"Well, don't be too long this time." Rani stands. "You know how Shima likes to hear all about it. Last night, before you got back, she wouldn't even let me sleep. She kept going on and on about tasty rats. . . ."

I laugh. "I won't." I hug Rani good night, then head back downstairs. In the throne room, the Pit is already inching open, waiting for me, just like it has been these past few nights. There's a tether between this Pit and the one Rani and I made. Some nights, in dreams and in reality, I hear his voice echo through the throne room.

"*Daughter . . . ,*" he calls.

I channel my magic, calling it up from my veins. Where the cobra once rose, a new sensation fills my belly. A connection, that cord.

The Pit bends to my will, but it also fights back. It has a new resident, after all. That doesn't disturb me. My magic is mine to harness.

I learned much from the Snake Master. How to wield my impossible powers. How to open the door to the Eternal Night. But also, how to *close* my magic, concealing my mind and thoughts from his. It was the only way I could make my plan without him knowing of my betrayal.

And though I've realized I don't need the Snake Master to control my powers, he is still part of my life. But I *will* control my future—he has no say in that. Not anymore.

So every night, I've put my magic to use. I do what Raya would have wanted.

I draw my magic out, envisioning a stone instead of a door. The snakes hiss when I succeed, and a gem from the wall dislodges itself and floats into my open palm. I will the soul within it to be released, not stopping until the cold, empty gem in my hand stops glowing. I drop it back into the Pit.

Another night, another soul freed.

When I finally command the Snake Pit to shut, I wipe the sweat beaded on my brow and stand. "Good night, Sahil."

The Snake Pit rumbles.

I leave the throne room and shut the doors behind me. My magic is strong, but steady. Just like *all* magics will be someday. Stonebringers will forge mountains again. Flametalkers will craft light with just a spark. Tidesweepers will create oceans with their touch.

A new world is about to dawn before us—one full of the novelty of magic and wonder.

Acknowledgments

As this chapter closes, we would like to thank the following incredible people:

First, our literary agent, Pete Knapp, whose belief in this series never wavered. Thank you to the whole PFLM team for your help on this project!

Our editor, Kristen Pettit—you continue to push us to create exciting and vibrant stories, and your sharp editorial instincts helped us craft a beautiful finale. Clare Vaughn, working with you has been a treat! We can't wait to see where your editorial career takes you.

Jon Howard, Veronica Ambrose, and Monique Vescia on the production side, for their attention to detail on this series.

Fatima Baig, cover artist extraordinaire: once again, you have created a stunning cover we can't stop staring at. Chris Kwon: thanks so much for the beauty that is the dust jacket and interior design. We're so grateful to be able to flip through these gorgeously designed pages!

The HCC Frenzy and Epic Reads teams respectively—thank you for your help in launching *Sisters of the Snake*. Maeve, Tammy, and Marisol, thank you all for your excitement and dedication to help us launch this series in Canada. Abroad, it was a pleasure to have Simran at HarperCollins360YA on our team in the UK, and endless thanks to HarperCollins India for spreading the *Sisters of the Snake* love!

Team OwlCrate—holding another edition of *Sisters of the Snake* was wildly cool, and a total dream come true on our author checklist. Thank you, thank you, thank you!

Hearing the audiobook edition of our book was also very surreal, and Soneela Nankani's vivid narration was so special to hear.

The Forest of Reading and Red Maple committee: hearing about our nomination was one of the highlights of our author career so far! Seeing and chatting with students reading our book has been so gratifying. And, as always, thank you to the teachers and librarians who have been supporting us on our author journey.

Thanks again to those who have blurbed our books, including Sona, Dhonielle, and Tanaz. Sarah Raughley, thank you for your Quill & Quire and CBC features, and your incredible generosity. And to our wonderful street team, the Snake Squad: your help and dedication is something we'll continue to cherish. Maeeda Khan and Sarah Gregory, thanks for being excellent moderators and friends.

Our writing community and friends: you're all doing exciting things, and we can't wait to see your work shine!

And, finally, a special thanks to our family, friends, past teachers and librarians, booksellers, and readers for your encouragement and support.